**Once Upon a Time
in the Universe**

Book One

I0601970

The Twinkling Ruination

JOHN C. CHRISTIANSEN

Published by John C. Christiansen 2021

www.jcchristiansen.com

Disclaimer
Every effort has been made to ensure that this book is free from error or omissions. Information provided is of general nature only and should not be considered legal or financial advice. The intent is to offer a variety of information to the reader. However, the author, publisher, editor or their agents or representatives shall not accept responsibility for any loss or inconvenience caused to a person or organisation relying on this information.

Book cover design and formatting services by Self-Publishing Lab

ISBN:
978-1-7363237-0-0 (Hardcover)
978-1-7363237-1-7 (Paperback)
978-1-7363237-2-4 (e-Book)

CONTENTS

I. THE TWINKLING PRIZE

1. THE OASIS

After whistling a couple hundred cereal jingles, he knew Earth's last tree must be just ahead. The man in the long black duster didn't like to whistle, at least not in this heat. The razor winds had already split his lips and sandblasted his tongue. Plus, imported air just couldn't carry whistles with the same sharpness. Sure, sure, all the fancy mathematics showed no distinction between the Valhalla Syndicate's product—pumped continuously into the troposphere at super-low prices—and the gentle mixture that had sustained life from the dawn of time up until a generation ago. But many still believed the imported stuff just didn't have that intangible "something." Still, he whistled on through, all the way to the last jingle he knew, and he found the tree, lying right next to its stump. He knew the oasis would be only another 184,800 or so paces to the southwest.

The man wished his hair was not so black. But the more the miseries of life burned into him, the blacker it got. And he regretted wearing a jet-black, long-sleeved shirt. This growing regret even overcame the regret that had previously consumed him: of wearing jet-black pants in the desert. Luckily, the sensation of his feet sizzling inside his black leather shoes distracted him from both regrets. As the sizzles crept upward, he demoted his hike to a trudge. This was going to be a long trip. He'd just have to paste it out. He couldn't sweat it out. The scorching winds would have none of it and saw fit to sporadically blast him with enough sand and dust to form a pasty pellicle on his face. The same winds found amusement in this and invited other winds to join in. Soon, a cruel gang of winds delighted in whipping and walloping him in every direction. The winds hissed and snickered at how savagely they could make the man's duster flutter and snap in the air. But they howled and roared at his accompanying determination to keep the duster on, even though he was baking inside. Meanwhile, the vengeful smile of the Golden Father pressed down on it all, from 93 million miles away.

This desert had not always been such an asshole. Years ago, this man had cherished it as his one tiny patch of retreat from concrete, metal, plastic, bargain outlets, drive-throughs, garbage, and exhaust fumes. Years ago, journeys out here would soothe him with clear, bright vistas, and the Sun would only lightly bronze his skin. Now, even as gales of sand obscured the mountains on the horizon and tarnished the blue sky, he could still feel the angry Sun cooking his face. Years ago, the winds didn't seem like such bullies. Back then, the soft wind would whistle through the sagebrush. Occasionally, a bird would dot the silence with chirps. Some sure-footed, dusty critter might scurry by. But over the years, the sagebrush gave way to tumbleweed, critters disappeared, and each journey found the desert copping more and more of an attitude as its own elimination grew nearer.

It was all about the dollars. The Valhalla Syndicate didn't like zoning restrictions. The Valhalla Syndicate didn't like urban growth boundaries or forests. So they were taken away. For these things irritated the Valhalla Syndicate. But the Valhalla Syndicate did like business. The Valhalla Syndicate liked lots of business. Lots of business pleased the Valhalla Syndicate. So there was lots of business.

So much business for an increasingly voracious population that didn't much care for open spaces or quiet. This could be his last trip out here. Next time he needed to make this trip, he might find every inch of the desert gone. A sickly dread began to gnaw at his insides as he heaved into step number 183,469. He should have seen the oasis, just past the plateaus far over to his left. But these didn't seem like the same plateaus. Could the sandy gusts have steered him off course? As his legs plowed through the deepening sea of sand, his mind raced around on the frontier of panic. He tried to squint, but even that exhausted him.

This can't be! Where has it gone? Must replenish... It's all so dim... Home... Home... So far away... Is it... Is it time to die?

The screaming maelstrom swallowed the world all around him, sent him tumbling into a rock, and then swallowed him too.

He woke, coughing up sand and feeling like a kid whose lunch money had just been stolen by the elements. He clawed his way out of a sand dune and emerged to the desert he remembered. It sprawled out in every direction. Rolling hills and valleys stretched out as far as his eyes could see. Upon these vistas loomed an infinite sapphire sky, dazzling in its purity. Then, as the gentle breeze yielded to sublime silence, he spied the plateaus, far in the distance to his right. He dusted the dust off his duster, then, wheezing and hacking, plodded over to a nearby ridge to balm his eyes with the sight of that familiar place: an enormous valley of beautiful, Sun-baked sand. He collapsed with trembling relief as he finally set his gaze upon the last haven of promise for him—the one place that could replenish his strength and allow him to go on... and perhaps even get Home. A tiny beacon winked at him. There it waited in the pale sand: the oasis within the oasis:

Safeway.

Inside this generally clean, moderately busy Safeway, things ran smoothly in an unchallenging and unchallenged routine. Pleasant grocery-store music floated through the air-conditioned aisles and checkout lanes as customers and cashiers buzzed with the usual banalities and clichés programmed into them since they could talk. Courtesy clerks zipped back and forth between check stands, bagging groceries and feigning interest in the customers' lives. Through the low hum of this network of placation, scanners rhythmically beeped, noisy exchanges between a spoiled brat and an even more spoiled parent pervaded, and calls on the store intercom regularly accelerated everyone's gradual hearing loss.

Behind the first checkout lane stood the glass cage for the office, where KEN L, the store manager, sat, ignoring his paperwork and eating Macaroni and Cheez Skwirt directly out of the jar with a huge plastic spoon. An old-school boss—a man of handshakes and haircuts—he insisted everybody address him as Mr. Laing while his subordinates remained on a first-name basis. Mr. Laing, age sixty-six, with his baggy eyes, Nixonesque jowls, long double chin, and thriftily dyed mahogany hair that crowned a balding head, contrasted sharply with his young staff. By tucking his tight belt under his huge, solid beer gut and accentuating its roundness, he seemed to mock the rest of his soft, moderately built, less unhealthy body. The man never exercised, yet he sweated continuously. He breathed through his mouth most of the time. Some said this was because his nostrils didn't care for the fact that he smelled like a half-cooked pork steak that had spent the night in a hamper full of dirty male underwear. A greasy shine covered his skin of a slightly alcoholic pink, which, when exposed to direct sunlight, bloomed with a garden of liver spots, which he considered the most attractive part of his tan. Numerous burst capillaries riddled his slightly porcine nose and his yellowish eyes. And he always looked like he had to take a shit.

As the man in the duster neared the Safeway, something clicked into his periphery. On the western horizon, in front of a distant mountain range, he could see a short row of skyscrapers. Taller than the mountains and knife-like in appearance, they cut into what had been, moments ago, a pure blue sky. He had never seen these buildings before. He ignored the disturbing discovery and continued to the store.

Harmonious grocery store life continued inside the Safeway. Customers occupied each of the thirty-three checkout lanes. In the express lane stood IRIS V, whose tawny eyes revealed a quiet intelligence, but by choice, little else. Mr. Laing held not even a scoffing interest in that, but rather in revelations from other bodily areas of his comely cashier, as his decades-long campaign to supply her with low-buttoned uniform shirts of only the most precisely selected snugness had brought to her observation. He always put her in the express lane, right in front of his office window. From this arrangement, he could sit in his chair, looking constipated, as he slowly undressed her with his limited mind. Today was Erection Day, and he took full advantage of the occasion as he watched her. He imagined his heroic little pocket pinky thrusting into her cleavage. Every time her barcode scanner beeped, he imagined another thrust. The scanning got faster and faster as the pocket pinky slowly became a pocket thumb. Then, as his eyes rolled back and little Kens began filling up his shriveled pod, IRIS V reached the subtotal. The transaction had stopped. He hadn't experienced such frustration since last year, when he had started himself up in front of the mirror at home. The shape of his own body had always proven a fine, shiny substitute in the absence of attractive females. But last year, just as he had nearly completed such a spank-off to himself, his increasingly taxing wife had walked in on him, putting an end to the transaction.

Celebrating Erection Day at work proved to be just as unfulfilling. As the customer left IRIS V's check stand, Mr. Laing's little buddy crept all the way back, deep under the surface of his matted shrub, to hibernate for another year. He wheeled around in his chair and bitterly blew out the little candle on the cupcake he had bought for himself. If only she had scanned a few more items. *Goddamned express lane. Goddamned eleven item limit!* He decided not to lose his temper. He would just sit there, quietly, looking constipated, as he finished his lunch.

The man in the duster had entered the Safeway parking lot when something in the east caught his eye: more skyscrapers, very far off, jabbing up into the sky like blades. He was sure they hadn't been there a minute ago. He sadly made his way across the parking lot and up to the glass entrance door to the Safeway. As the door slid open, he shuffled in unevenly, escorted by a cyclone of dust and silhouetted by the setting. His presence was felt throughout the store; even far, far back, to the Safeway's deepest roots. He moved in from the orange glow that outlined his tattered frame to the paleness of the store. His high forehead supported a black mane that folded into a slight curl near the middle. Black eyebrows underlined the curl and pointed down to his slender nose. Beneath the eyebrows and above a permanent frown hung two dark circles. They housed a pair of heavy eyes, which convinced onlookers that he hadn't slept an hour in his life. A dark, needle-thin outline defined the outer edges of his irises, which glowed white and pierced through people when he stared at them. He stared at a lot of people, mostly with contempt. The sight of this would often cause people to pepper his face with babbling spittle, assault his ears with shrieks, and fill their pants (or dresses) with shit. As his gaze drilled into everyone, the air in their lungs flew away.

In the back of the store, cloaked behind rows of milk jugs, a few harsh, bilious lights buzzed onto a concrete floor: a floor splotched with filth unnamable. Beyond that, something stirred. The buzz of the lights resonated the air, which coated skin and lungs with a sticky mist of used beer, piss-tainted soda, tobacco spit, and, occasionally, feces. Beyond that, something awakened. Though adolescent humans would work for minimum wage in this long-antiquated lair of foulness, rats, flies, and roaches refused to come in here. They considered it far too repugnant to be worth their time, to say nothing of the detriment to their image. Eating and fucking in shit and rancid grease was one thing, but to be caught anywhere near this smorgasbord of squalor was quite simply below their level of dignity. Past a labyrinth of unopened freight lay the Tartarus of this Hades: the Safeway bottle room. The doorway to it, cramped and crusted with gunk, was barely high enough for most adults to walk through. But behind it brooded a vast warehouse, littered with uncounted bottles and cans. Toward the back loomed two colossal piles, which apexed at the corners of the room. From the entrance, the cans in these piles sparkled like grains of colored sand. Between these piles, the room sank into a giant depression. Here, the weight of the bottles and cans had grown so ponderous that they had crushed the lower foundation of the store, sinking it to unknowable depths. One could only guess the nature of the long-crushed, long-corrupted matter that lay at the bottom, eating through the bedrock. But somewhere near the bottom, a sickly set of eyes opened as the white-eyed man in the black duster entered the front of the store.

Everything in the checkout lanes stopped. All the customers and all the employees felt pinned by his stare. Pleasant grocery-store music feathered through the air as everything else fell silent. After a few seconds, the harmony resumed, but the man still stood in the entrance. He stared straight ahead at Mr. Laing, who stared right back, looking constipated. As Mr. Laing finished off the ring of orange grease on the edge of his Mac n' Cheez jar, the man left the entrance and went to the aisles to do his shopping.

Mr. Laing looked at his monthly calendar and snarled at today's date, circled in red ink, with a little smiley face drawn in: his standard reminder of this special day of getting it up. But every third Erection Day, like today, he also circled the date with black ink and included an angry frowny face. He picked up the store intercom. He always made his voice much deeper when broadcasting it throughout the store.

"Bret, store-com please, Bret," his artificially low voice reverberated.

Back in the break room sat Bret, the assistant manager. He had just about finished his favorite lunch: a two liter of glyphosate-flavored

Pepsi, and a pack of Suckenhack Ultralight Menthols. As he hacked from the most recent ciggie sucked, he heard the call of his boss.

"Ghlyeah," he answered through a web of phlegm.

"He's here, Bret," Mr. Laing said in his normal voice over this private line.

Bret paused and spit the phlegm into his shirt pocket. "The Cereal Man?"

"Bring the shotgun."

"Right." Bret hung up the intercom and took the break room shotgun down from its rack. He loaded it and picked up the store-com again to announce his call to arms.

"All courtesy ninjas to the back, please. All courtesy ninjas to the back," his voice echoed through the store.

All over the store, courtesy clerks dropped their bags, dropped their cans and bottles, dropped whatever they were stocking or cleaning, dropped their work, dropped everything, as they assumed a robotic mindlessness and made beelines toward the break room. Bret hung up the store-com, cocked the shotgun, and waited, listening for the sounds of gunshots, explosions, and blood-curdling screams.

2. THE TWINKLING

Once upon a time on Earth, there lived a little town called Twinkle. People born in Twinkle were different from other Earthlings. Most had never strayed very far from their homes and had only scarcely experienced the fast-paced melting pots of Earth's great cities. Twinkle was one place where a really nice guy could grow up. By the early twenty-first century, one particularly nice guy became the first sixteen-year-old freshman admitted to Patricia Hazekamp University. One of Earth's most prestigious colleges, PHU lay just past the border, on the edge of Valhallaville, the metropolis of which Twinkle was a suburb. He sure as heck didn't mind the commute, though. The clean streets provided a safe, smooth ride. And what a delightful view awaited the lucky commuters who were lucky enough to commute! On a swell morning like this, with not even one single, silly drop of rain in the forecast, the young student knew he would take in all the beautiful colors of the downtown area so much more vividly and get caught up in the energizing bustle of Twinkle's fair citizens on their way to whatever activity awaited them. And of course, he would spot lots of shiny cars puttering around on the street, honking genially, with an occasional wave between drivers. He especially looked forward to the intersections, which were particularly packed with such energy. Twinkle had grown so much, but it was a great place to call Home.

He lived on North Smiley Meadows Avenue, three houses down from Meatball Time! (over 303 served), and just across the street from the Blackwick Elderly Care Facility and Cigarette Outlet, where his mother worked. Unbeknownst to dear old Mom, when her sweet little boy skipped out the front door of their pleasant-looking, yellow suburban home, he began one of the biggest days of his life. His final exams, scheduled at noon, would determine his whole future—and unbeknownst to Mom, hers too. Today's opportunity would never come again, and it had to go just right. He had chosen his neatest white dress shirt, his pink knit tie, and his favorite sweater vest, which matched the color of the house. His tan loafers capped off his white slacks nicely. As he approached his baby-blue bicycle, he waved to his next-door neighbor. She was too busy rolling out her Syntho-lawn for the day to notice. The vibrant youth glanced up at the Meatball Time! sign and saw the giant meatball clock had just struck 5:33 a.m. So he waved for a few minutes more. Finally, she noticed him and waved back. With a satisfied smile, he strapped on his white backpack, straightened his pink knit necktie, hopped on his bicycle, and began pedaling off to school, merrily whistling a tune.

With the usual surge of satisfaction that came from gathering up an invigorating speed and an extra gush of excitement about today's opportunity, he banked onto the right-hand lane of Sparkling Creek Drive, where he then gasped, slammed on his brakes, and barely avoided eating the brake light of a school bus. He recoiled from the blast of red light, then sat for a beat, waiting for his vision to return and puzzling over the utterly foreign odor of burnt bicycle tire. The bus lurched forward, coughing out a cloud of exhaust, which made him almost miss the burnt-tire smell until the school bus behind him obliterated this longing with a horn that rattled him like a jackhammer. He steered into the next lane but quickly found himself between two more school buses, neither of which showed him as much patience or consideration as the previous two. After weaving among a few dozen more vehicles, most of them school buses, he spotted a bicycle-sized sliver of unused pavement and landed on it. Surveying the situation, he realized he had actually backtracked. He took a deep breath. This route had always provided such a smooth, uneventful ride. Who knew that simply stopping to wave at his neighbor could cause him to hit the morning rush? Luckily, it wasn't too bad yet. If he got back on the road soon enough, he'd still make it to school with a luxurious chunk of time to spare.

He managed to secure himself a nice, cushy spot between two semis, with nearly half a bike length for a buffer. After a few minutes, the buffer disappeared. Brake lights, exhaust belch, brake lights, exhaust belch, brake lights, brake lights, exhaust belch, brake lights brake lights brake lights brake lights... Soon he couldn't pedal fast enough to stay balanced, so he paddled himself along the road with his feet. These conditions made his chunk of spare time feel a bit less luxurious, so, with a friendly ring of his bicycle bell, he weaved himself between vehicles and finally made it to the corner of Goodie Goodie Gumdrops Drive, where he could cut through the parking lot of the Merry Weather Full Service Service Station and Travel Store. As always, Lewis, the busy but friendly attendant, waved merrily at him. And as always, he waved back. Lewis shot back a hearty grin and an encouraging thumbs-up.

Not one to ride with both hands off his handlebars, the young bicyclist pulled over to return both swell gestures. Lewis waved back again with a warm chuckle. The youth reciprocated with another wave and chuckle. Lewis reciprocated the reciprocity. This encouraged another friendly wave. Then another friendly wave. Then more friendly waving. This went on until a line of cars had formed at the pumps. With one final wave, Lewis rambled on over to the line to make sure and get those windshields spic and span. A surge of renewed imminence jolted the youth back into action. He would need to make up some time. But time well spent, for sure! After all, if he couldn't stop and be friendly once in a while, then, well, what was he doing?

Pumped full of good feeling, the teen picked up a bit of speed after passing the Big Bright Lakes Drive-Thru Mall and Super Cigarette Outlet. But when he came to the intersection of Goodie Goodie Gumdrops and Winking Sun Lane, he beheld the strangest thing ever: a yellow traffic light. What sort of refractive irregularities could cause such an optical illusion? Maybe he was observing it from an odd angle. What did this mean? He wondered if everyone else saw the same thing, and then suddenly the light turned bright red! No time to ponder this mind-clobberer. Anything that looked this much like the light on that school bus deserved its space. He skidded to a halt. And just when he thought things couldn't get any more insane, a whole bunch of cars started zooming by in front of him. Who knew cars in perpendicular lanes actually drove through intersections? It now seemed that they did not come to the intersection simply to sit idly on the side of it and watch you go by, just to make sure you were okay. Seemed quite nice and equitable that people got to take turns. He cocked his head in appreciation of discovering yet another one of life's facets. It reminded him of last year, when he put it together that grocery store workers didn't actually live at the grocery store, even though you saw them there every time you went shopping. Oh, the things one could learn before school even started!

As his soft, fine, golden hair fluttered in the balmy breeze, he noticed traffic slowing down. A glance over to the other side of

Winking Sun revealed that nearly all of them had pulled in to Ye Olde Twinklee Towne Buse Statione ande Coffeee Shoppe. Actually, the company that had bought the place ordered the buses melted down and converted into espresso machines, so it didn't operate as a station quite so much anymore. It's just that citizens of Twinkle loved driving their own cars around so much that, well, they just didn't need a bus station. Lots of them sure loved getting their coffee there, though, as evidenced by the snake of cars coiling around the drive-through and growing its motionless tail further and further out into the street. The drive-through took much longer, but it was so much more convenient than actually walking in and placing an order, which is why no customers ever entered the shop. The bright-eyed youth smiled upon all of the good people waiting in line, with their engines running continuously and their engine fans switching on and off. Coffee must be tasty to them. Yes, Sir! He didn't fancy himself as much of a coffee fella himself. Too strong and bitter for him. At least, that's what his mom told him. But, by gum, he sure hoped everyone else enjoyed their coffee this morning.

The light turned green, but now things had become truly strange. A solid stream of cars blocked him. He rang his bell a few times, then a few more, then a few dozen more. Nobody made room for him to cross. After several minutes, the light turned back to yellow, then red, then back again to green with the traffic not moving. Even though he felt darn lucky to be treated to such bright, pretty colors, the feeling of time slipping away began to nibble at him. To arrive only a little early felt like tardiness, he assumed. Having never experienced tardiness, he didn't really know. But he could not think of a worse occasion for his first time. Even one minute not devoted to the test could jeopardize his score. And the professor would select only his top student to represent the school in next week's historic event. Just one student. Others would just have to miss the opportunity of a lifetime. He swiveled his head around and realized that if he bought something at the coffee shop, say a glass of water, he could exit onto the other side of the shop, where everyone seemed able to continue on their course. He rang his bell, turned right, and merged into the coffee shop line.

Every minute spent behind scores of cars weighed more and more on his mind. Every minute spent behind scores of vociferous exhaust pipes weighed his skin and clothes down with a less and less ignorable coating of soot. By the time he made it all the way around the line, he knew he would need to pedal hard to get to the test on time. The trip left the youth dizzy, with a metallic taste on the roof of his mouth, a black film on his face, and a pocket relieved of a month's lunch money in exchange for a bottle of water that would've looked more appropriate in a doll's hand than in his. He meandered out of the parking lot onto Titter Tulip Lane. Despite a lingering, disorienting headache, he pumped his pedals vigorously and weaved around vehicles with diminishing caution. Soon he started to break a sweat.

"Golly," he said. "Hot one today. Maybe I should have worn a cooler sweater vest. Oh well. Only another eleven miles to school. Everything will be just fine."

But he'd never come out on this side of Titter Tulip before. Seemed like a nice drive. But where did it lead? He struggled to arrange the roads in his hazy mind, but every link he imagined kept fizzing into nothingness. Luckily for him, Sultan Scott's Ultra-Premium Gasoline Indulgence Palace, the service station with the golden nozzles, lay just ahead. He made a hard bank into the parking lot of the allegedly famous service station, where the gasoline allegedly smelled like Turkish delight. He parked his bicycle at Pump 11. Attendants at other pumps, whose copper-tinted face paint concealed the centers of their fair complexions underneath shiny plastic Ottoman borks of fire engine red, paid him no mind, except to lob a few sneers of contempt at his two-wheeled, deadbeat vehicle that used no gas. Pausing for only a second of puzzlement over this, he dashed over to the side of the cashier's chamber at the center of the station. Inside sat a young, drowsy blonde woman wearing a jeweled turban and a black prosthetic goatee. Behind her and a crowded display of cigarette cartons, hung a physical map of Middle Eastern countries and India, titled "Mid-East." He asked her if she could tell him the best way to get onto Silverhorn Highway. She pointed to an exit just past Choo Choo Train Lane.

He thanked her, turned around, and yipped with fright at the oily, crusty composite of eyes, nose, and mouth that had wandered up behind him. They belonged to a woman with a beard on top of her head, who stretched her jaggedly taloned hands out toward him. He didn't know hands could get that dirty. He couldn't understand her gurgling and hollering. Why didn't she state, clearly, the nature of her objectives and upon receipt of his understanding, propose a path to a resolution? And what kind of costume was this? Tatters and shreds of rags draped over her body in a complexity of layers. Then he heard her stomach growling underneath them.

Soon the youngster found himself pedaling, puffing and huffing as he weaved his bicycle between cars and school buses, with the hungry lady, who had climbed onto the back half of his banana seat, hanging on tightly to his waist. As the spaces between vehicles narrowed, he rang his bell more and more, for safety. Finally, another red light stopped them at Choo Choo Train Lane. The many sets of shiny railroad tracks that ran alongside this street led right on over to Shucky Darn's Frankfurter Barn, which remained the only part of the Jolly Trolley Train Station that still ran. The sleek, streamlined trains remained in top-notch condition because no one had ever used them. Even though mass transportation had become quicker, safer, and less stressful, everyone still saw it as a bit of a hassle. So instead, some supersmart folks took it into their heads to convert the beautiful train cars into dining space to accommodate hundreds of hungry citizens who may want to enjoy a delicious hot dog, like this nice lady who had fallen asleep on his backpack.

Of course, everyone used the drive-through instead of walking all the way into the dining cars. This consumed much more time, but everyone found it so much more convenient than getting out of their cars. And the drive-through service ranked second to none. After receiving your order, you could drive forward and meet the friendly gas attendant on duty. The attendant would replace however much gas you used while waiting in line, be it three gallons, eleven gallons, a full tank... you paid for it with your order, so it was your call! Of course, if you rode a bicycle, it seemed you could remain a bit more pennywise. Indeed this young, beaming bicyclist might just drop on by later— after school, of course—and order a scrumptious hot link for himself, or maybe he'd pitch in for another hungry stranger who happened to be short a nickel or two. There was just no way of knowing for sure. Each and every day presented a new, exciting package for him to open!

He entered the line, beaming at the thought of filling that empty tummy and ready to surrender every minute of his buffer time, and maybe a few minutes more. Mom would be proud. He approached the drive-up menu after surrendering every minute of his buffer time, and definitely a few minutes more. The lady with the grumbling tummy had disappeared at some point. He wished her well and rang his bell to move out of the line, but nobody budged. He rang again and again. And again and again. But nobody could make out the ringing over the rumbling of engines and humming of air conditioners.

He exited the parking lot, long after surrendering every minute of his buffer time, and many, many minutes more. He had also surrendered nearly every bit of his money, save a few coins. He hadn't realized Shucky Darn's would charge him for the gasoline that he would have otherwise consumed had he used the drive-through properly. He also hadn't known that Shucky Darn's imported their gasoline from Sultan Scott's and sold it at a handsome markup. And he had no idea that, during his time in line, Sultan Scott's would send him a bill for the gas he didn't purchase while his bicycle was tying up Pump 11. He saluted their prowess and promised himself to apply for their credit card the next time he rolled through. As for now, he needed to fly! But he had consumed all his buffer time! Some new and unorthodox calculations were in order. With a few shortcuts and a mile or so of burning up the road, he could still make it on time.

He joined the crawling traffic on Silverhorn Highway, the main road into Valhallaville. In dodging innumerable vehicles, which honked, belched, and lunged in a struggle to force their way into his lane, he worked his bell so hard that his thumb cramped up. After pedaling a few more miles and passing unending numbers of busy gas stations and the Tarbutts Drive-Thru Coffee Mall and Super-duper Cigarette Outlet, the bell chinked, stopped ringing, and started making a scraping sound. He had fallen increasingly behind schedule, but he simply could not compromise on safety. The time had come for a brand-new bell—a nice shiny one. The teen turned onto Smiling Flowers Drive and, soon after, passed several specialty businesses that he remembered but that had packed up and left. Mr. Ed's Unsniffable Glue Factory had closed. And Skip's Premium Cracker Crumbling. The Smiling Flowers Ballpoint Pen Spring Outlet, V.H. Essington's Video Tape Rewinding Studio, even Kat's One Hour Footography... all closed up.

A few minutes later, he pulled into the tiny parking lot of Cyclie's Unicycle Bicycle and Tricycle Shop. He looked forward to seeing

Cyclie, the kindly proprietor who had given him his bicycle last year, just to be nice. But to the lad's dismay, it looked like old Cyclie had closed up the shop for good. It turned out that Cyclie's gift was the only transaction that had ever taken place in that store. Upon reading the words, "GONE OUT OF BUSINESS" on the door, the golden-haired youth snapped his fingers in disappointment.

"Aw, cookie crumbs," he muttered, careful not to let any passersby catch him indulging himself with cursing. "I guess old Cyclie was needed somewhere else in town."

Then he thought of the lucky children somewhere else in town, getting free bicycles from the kindly old man. He smiled and pedaled back onto Silverhorn Highway, the main road through town, which would eventually provide an exit onto Hypotenuse Avenue as he entered Valhallaville.

Traffic had now jammed everywhere, and every trace of patience, courtesy, or decency between drivers had boiled away in the heavy heat. The boy tightened his lips, clutched the handles of his bicycle, and charged forward, bell or no bell. If he had to risk his own life, he would. After all, Mom's life could depend on the outcome of this exam. He zigged, zagged, sprinted, and skidded between castles of semis, school buses, and SUVs, all the while feeling precious minutes flying away from him. Soon the SUVs and semis became rare, and the road grew yellow with school buses. He'd learned that in the olden days, one would never have seen so many school buses. But when advertisers told parents that more buses could get more kids out of the house and off to school faster, public transportation took a leap into the future.

As the buses lumbered along, unable to switch lanes with any agility to speak of, the boy picked up a bit of speed. A ripple of hope struck him when, up ahead, he spied the Twinkle Mall, a significant milestone. A wave of excitement washed over him when he approached the Twinkle Town Mall, a more significant milestone. And a riptide of elation crashed upon his heart when he finally came upon the Twinkle City Supermall, nearly the most important milestone of them all. By the time he approached the Silverhorn Intermall Airport, his mind's eye gazed upon the waters of his hopes, but then his hopes snapped away from him. With a reading of 11:11 a.m., the airport's large clock confirmed the tsunami of dread now casting a longer and longer shadow over the youth. It was over. The tsunami thundered down on him, the undertow dragged him out into the deep, and he knew he could not possibly make it in time for the exam.

But wait! Could it be? Under the hot breeze, the shrill, piercing wails of hope added a beat to his heart. Could that distant siren grace him with enough luck to make up for all these delays? He heard it coming his way. He dared to hope for a swift, zippy police car, rather than a long, bulky fire truck. After contending with phalanxes of spiteful bus drivers, an ambulance made its way into view. The teen gasped with joyous relief as the flashing vehicle edged its way past him at a speed slow enough for him to follow, but fast enough for him to reap huge profits. As he cruised past everyone else, he knew the universe was kind and just. And his heart warmed with gratitude for whatever lucky circumstances had caused the ambulance to come this way.

After a few more miles of gas stations and drive-through malls, all of which had gas stations inside them, the young bicyclist, by the deliverance of his wailing and flashing usher of good fortune, had made up time previously destined for the waste bin of his life. He was almost there! Beaming with renewed optimism, he finally passed the familiar sign that said, "ENTERING VALHALLAVILLE: POPULATION: 11,333,111. PLEASE DRIVE CAREF—" He couldn't read the rest of the sign because a school bus had crashed into the corner of it. A horrible accident at the entrance onto Hypotenuse had backed up traffic as far as the eye could see in both directions. Luckily, the ambulance paid it no mind and drove around it. As injured and trapped drivers hollered after it and begged it to come back, the young man's chest swelled with joy. Had a more charmed day ever graced the world?

But just then, he watched his good fortune evaporate as the ambulance finally did stop at a much larger wreck comprised of cars, semis, buses, fire trucks, police cars, police helicopters, ambulances, and a baby walker. The towering pile of wreckage covered the entire intersection of Hypotenuse and Adjacent. Some cars tried to drive over the pile but ended up becoming part of it. The scene featured numerous camps of escalating conflict. The firemen and the police officers screamed, shook fists, pushed, pummeled, and punched one another until the cops started shooting the firemen. When the paramedics rushed to the firemen's aid, the cops shot them as well. Chaos grew, with various odds and ends bursting into flames, and dead bodies showering out gallons of blood as they hung out of demolished cars. The young boy noticed a half body trying to claw its way out of the wreckage, but a cop picked it up by its protruding spine and tossed it into the flames. As the mayhem continued, the traffic lights changed in their normal regularity.

"Oh my!" the young man said, now feeling quite unlucky again. "An awful lot of congestion here. I better get some traffic police on the job, or I'll be late for school." He raced over to a row of pay phones. A firefighter stood inside the first one, screaming into the receiver, "I DON'T GIVE A FLYIN' FUCK WHAT YOU THINK ABOUT SEALED-OFF DISASTER AREAS, YOU OATMEAL-DICKED, PAMPERED LITTLE PUSSY! THREE LARGE PEPPERONI! TWO WITH EXTRA CHEESE!"

The boy rushed over to the next booth, which was unoccupied. He slammed a coin into the phone, dialed, and caught his breath. An answer came after thirty-three rings.

"Thank you for calling 9-1-1. So that we may better assist you in your time of crisis, please listen to the following menu: For the fire department, please press one now. For emergency medical assistance, *please* press two. For the police department, *please* press three. For general information, *please* press four. To repeat these options, *please* press five."

He pressed three.

"Welcome to the Valhallaville Police Department. We are happy to serve you. If you are experiencing a crisis and need immediate assistance, *please* press one. If you are calling for any other reason, please press two."

He dialed one.

"For security purposes, and to catch you if you're just some jerk trying to waste our time, please key in the middle three hundred eleven digits of your Universal Identification Code."

He spent the next three minutes dialing numbers.

"Is your name spelled, B-A-X-T-E-R? If this is correct, *please* press one. If not, *please* press two."

He pressed one.

"Please specify the nature of your emergency using the Valhallaville emergency specification code. If you or someone you know is being murdered, raped, or beaten, *please* enter 001000111111111111101010 101010000000000 now. If you or someone you know is being robbed, held up at gunpoint, or assaulted, *please* enter 11111111101010101 0101010101000000000000 now. If you are reporting an automobile accident in which civilian, police, fire, and medical vehicles are piled up in a manner that blocks an intersection, *please* enter 0101010101

0101000000010101000011111111 now. If you are calling to report an invasion by Gothic barbarians from the north, please—"

He entered 010101010101010000000101010000011111111.

"Please hold."

Three minutes passed.

"Thank you for continuing to wait. Your call is important to someone. A 9-1-1 customer service representative will be with you shortly."

Three minutes passed.

"Did you know you can reach us on the web? If you would like to report your emergency on the internet, please go to h-t-t-p-s-colon-backslash-backslash-w-w-w-dot-valhallaville-emergency-dispatch-service-for-emergencies-dot-com and register for an account. It's fast and easy. Simply enter your Universal Identification Code, your user ID, your PIN, your password, and your email address. Triple-click on the emergency specification code that suits your needs. Then, access to fast, efficient emergency service is only a few dozen clicks away. Be sure to have someone's credit card ready. Debit cards are not accepted. After completing your order, you will be emailed a confirmation number, which you must re-enter at the checkout page to complete your request for service. Then sit back and enjoy some well-earned peace of mind. We'll take care of the rest."

Three minutes passed.

"Thank you for continuing to wait. Your call is important to someone. A 9-1-1 customer service representative will be with you shortly."

Eleven more minutes passed before a new voice said, "Please deposit an additional three Universal Credits to continue this call." He deposited his last three coins. Three minutes passed.

Finally, he got a person. She had a sweet, cooling demeanor.

"Thank you for calling the Valhallaville Police Department, Transit Division, Department of Road Rage, Bureau of Pugilism and Traffic Accidents. This is Shirley. May I have the location of the pileup?"

"Surely, Shirley!" He paused for her to laugh, but Shirley had promised herself that once she had endured that joke thirty thousand times, she would stop feigning amusement. She had passed that point at the end of her first week on the job, eleven years ago. Baxter went on. "It's at the corner of Hypotenuse Avenue and Adjacent Drive."

"Okay..." She suddenly lost her sweet, cooling demeanor as she hollered at someone in the office. "Hey, Wanda! Get down to Hypotenuse and Adjacent with some TNT, a street cleaner, a flock of vultures, and a road construction crew. We've got a three-thirteen down there." She resumed her sweet, cooling demeanor. "Thank you, Sir."

"Thank you," he replied. Baxter hung up the phone and left the booth as a stray bullet missed him by eleven centimeters and destroyed the phone. Another look at the pileup sank the boy's heart down to his feet. It would take forever to get this disaster cleaned up. Just then, a reminder came to him, in the form of a pavement-rattling, body-splattering explosion, of the mysterious goodness and justness of the universe. This stroke of fortune dislodged a small car from the pile, creating a narrow gap between the pileup and a building. He was just the luckiest guy! Baxter jumped onto his bicycle and hightailed it for the gap. Blood and chunks of human flesh covered the pavement for the next ninety-nine feet. Baxter didn't know what this red, sticky mess was all about. He only knew he wanted to avoid it. But it covered every inch of the pavement. For a moment, he found himself wishing for some kind of concrete pathway that ran alongside the streets. He had seen such "side-walks" depicted in some of the older movies upon which he had stumbled into watching. Of course, he understood that these structures were mythical, and used by a mythical people, in mythical places, set in a time that could never have been. Baxter didn't believe in very many things he hadn't seen in person, anyway. After all, why would the laws of nature be any different in other places? He had long suspected that things were pretty much the same everywhere. His own mother had always taught him this was so. She would never lie to him. Honest.

Though he pedaled with the dainty strength offered only by his toes, he still managed to gather mild spatters of red on his white pants. So much for looking his best for the exam. Maybe nobody would notice. Not far to go now. If he hurried, he'd arrive only a few minutes late. The professor usually didn't lock the door to the classroom until after he'd finished talking and everyone had their tests. Having exited the mess, his legs now cranked out full speed, sending him careening down the road past a liquor store that was being held up at gunpoint. Actually, the sign described it as a "Licker Store." The robber, a guy named Robert, burst out of the store and hauled ass through the parking lot. Robert was a thin, naked guy with long, greasy hair and a few tattoos on his tan, filthy skin. The Licker Store owner, a flabby, semi-clothed woman-like creature with permed greasy hair and a shitload of tattoos, followed close behind, firing her revolver at him. Before Robert even considered returning fire, the store owner ran out of bullets and scurried back into the Licker Store. Robert ran out into the street, where all the cars waited for a red light at the three-way intersection of Hypotenuse, Opposite, and Spine. He bolted up to a car at the front of the line, opened the front door, and shot the driver in the face. He threw her out onto the pavement, along with the crying baby that had occupied the passenger seat. As Robert sat in the car, whistling a light tune while waiting for the light, the Licker Store owner lugged herself out into the street, firing her brand-spankin'-

new machine gun. Bearing down on her with the weight and length of both her own legs, the RR-17 assault rifle jackhammered her shoulder whenever she could summon enough strength to squeeze all three triggers, causing her double chin to clap up and down on her boobs and send her meandering backward all over the parking lot. Bullets whizzed everywhere, ripping through many innocent bystanders, but missing the oblivious Baxter by a hair's width as he charged toward the intersection.

The light turned green and the cars on Hypotenuse began tearing through the intersection. Many, without a whisper of a thought, ran over the crying baby that lay out there on the road. It didn't cry much longer. The owner of the Licker Store continued firing at Robert, reducing to rubble everything within 133 degrees of her line of vision. Once he had cleared the intersection, Robert put on his turn signal and passed in front of a truck carrying a huge tank of kerosene. The Licker Store owner shot the tank. The tank exploded, sending the cab of the truck rocketing high up into the sky. The cab landed on the Licker Store owner, flattening her like a pancake and missing Baxter by three centimeters. He didn't have to ride much further before he felt a bump under his tires. He, too, had run over the baby. By now, most of its carcass was smeared all over the pavement, but the pelvis was still solid enough to annoy drivers.

"Oh my goodness!" Baxter cried as he skidded to a stop, with finely minced baby flesh stuffed into the crevices of his tires. How could he have been so blind? All his dogged efforts throughout the day now meant nothing. Even if he made it to the test, his shortsightedness today would leave him powerless to get through even one bit of it. "I forgot my pencil!"

He made a U-turn on Hypotenuse, zoomed past Opposite, and onto Spine Street. Eleven blocks later, he arrived at Orville's Friendly

Family Market, an old-school grocery store whose founder had hooked millions of consumers by telling them, over and over again, that he was "hometown proud," whatever that meant. Many loyal patrons of Orville's enjoyed littering as part of their family shopping experience. So Baxter found himself weaving around innumerable scatterings of greasy paper and broken glass as he pulled into the parking lot. He parked his bicycle next to the main entrance, right under a large poster. He'd seen the pale, weathered old poster so many times, probably even back when he was little. It had never seemed new to him, but rather just part of the general scenery. But now, for some reason, it had become interesting. The faded but still discernible black-and-white line drawing of what looked like some kind of rat—a humanoid rat, wearing a coat and sunglasses. And it had something poking out of its mouth. The poster said, "WANTED" on it and advertised a large dollar amount that pulled Baxter's mouth wide open. Nearly all of the digits had been weathered into obscurity. No matter. No matter at all.

He parked his bicycle under the poster and ran into the store. Upon entering, he was greeted by a huge white banner, which hung from the ceiling and said, in big green letters, "Welcome to Orville's Friendly Family Market: Your Friendly Local Neighborhood Sponsor of the Chess Intergalactica." Baxter smiled with all his heart at this banner and pointed at it with both index fingers in enthusiastic acknowledgment. He felt the banner point right back at him in the same way, even though he knew it had no fingers or pointable appendages. Then, with a click of his heels, he continued on his mission to find a good pencil. He had to go through the Tarbutts Coffee and Cigarette Café inside the store, first. Then, after running past Orville's Travel Agency, and through Peck's Gym, Bar, and Grill, he finally arrived in the grocery store proper, where a medium-built, clean-cut adolescent Hispanic clerk of sickening vitality greeted him instantly.

"Good morning to ya today, Sir!" he said. "Welcome to Orville's, Sir!"

Baxter nearly tripped over his own heels and blinked at how much the young man's snazzy green apron and white, short-sleeved shirt seemed to glow with cleanliness, and the way his green bow tie seemed to vibrate with excitement. Then it became clear that this came from the unfettered giddiness emanating from the clerk's body. Baxter blinked several more times. His entire life had blessed him with a continuous stream of courtesy and friendliness. But that stream had failed to prepare his nervous system to fully handle this geyser of exuberance. It took a few seconds for him to reboot. "Thanks. Good morning."

"How ya doin' today, Sir?!"

"Oh, fine, thanks."

"Great! My name is Joilio, Sir! Providing you with a level of customer service far above and beyond the value of my wages is of paramount importance to me, Sir! This week's specials include eleven percent off Doctor Deb L. Dougherty's Double Dense Doughnuts and thirty-three percent off Sticky Stoolie's Starch Sticks! Quite a bargain, Sir! Comes with a free box of Krakafloa Volcanic Strength Laxative, Sir! Then we have—"

"Oh, well, thank you. But I just need to buy a pencil."

"Great, Sir! Right this way, Sir!" With that, Joilio swept Baxter off his feet and began sprinting toward the grocery aisles. Because his mom usually did most of the grocery shopping, Baxter hadn't visited this store since his single-digit years. He always remembered its super friendly staff, but now, this place brought forth a new level of service altogether.

"Whoa! What are you doing, Joilio?"

"I'm gladly carrying you to the pencil aisle, Sir!"

"Oh my! Why don't you just point me in the right direction?"

"Providing you with a level of customer service far above and beyond the value of my wages is of paramount importance to me, Sir!" Joilio alarmed Baxter with his speed and amazed him with how smoothly he ran. Then Baxter looked down and remembered the roller skates! Those signature roller skates with the little green bow ties on them. His sky-blue eyes teared up a little bit. The old memories flooded back into him from those golden days as a little boy, coming to the store with Mom and watching all the incredible courtesy clerks zipping around the store with masterful skill, delivering the speediest service possible. He remembered how many times he had dreamt that someday, he too might zip around everywhere and spout friendliness out to everyone. Ah, what a sweet time of wonder—an extra golden chapter of his already golden life. Though he was a little sad that, now, everything had stiffened into such serious business. Courtesy clerking might have been a good life for him.

Then he caught the twinkle in Joilio's smile, and it all just seemed a little icky. He looked away and then noticed something else he'd forgotten about: all those black bubbles on the ceiling. He had found them scary looking as a little boy. But Mom always told him that those bubbles helped the store locate all the customers, and that's how the workers always managed to simply appear, right there for you, whenever you needed something. Baxter never understood what she was talking about until just now. Now he knew all of those bubbles to be friendly cameras. Back in grade school, a teacher had told him about all different types of surveillance cameras when the youth had asked why Sarcewicz, the head custodian, was installing them in the toilet bowls. He never did see old Sarc again after that, so he never got to ask why a toilet needed a camera.

31

Joilio swept Baxter past the in-store gas station, past the DMV, then through Val's Vulveetaria, and on into a grocery aisle stocked with virtually every kind of pencil he could ever imagine. "Well, here we are, Sir! What kind of pencil did you have in mind for ya today, Sir?"

"Any pencil will be fine, I guess."

"We have a green one with the phrase 'Orville's: Hometown Proud!' on it, Sir! How about that one, Sir?!"

"Sure."

"Only one dollar and eleven cents each, Sir!" Looks like an exceptional bargain, Sir!"

"Okay. I'll take it."

Joilio took the pencil down from the display. "Excellent choice, Sir! What else can I get for ya today, Sir?!"

"Nothing, thanks."

"Are you sure, Sir?! No erasers or notepads for ya today, Sir?!"

"No, thanks."

"Alrightio, Sir, then let's take you to the checkout line, Sir!" With a twinkle in his eye and a skip in his step, Joilio flew Baxter past the in-store hospital, past Orville's School of Deceptively Hateful Country Music, past Newt's Neutering for the Poor, on to checkout lane three, and set him down. He then dashed around to the other end to bag the pencil, while Ojectica, a slender, sexy cashier with rich brown skin, light green eyes, and a myriad of long black braids, rang it up. Her well-oiled cleavage glistened inside the collar of her white shirt.

"Hey, baby. How you doin'?" she said to Baxter.

"Oh, just fine. Thanks."

"That's a fine lookin' pencil."

"Oh, thank you."

"I love a man with a big, huge, hard pencil."

"Well, it's actually pretty small."

"Want me to sharpen it, honey?" she asked, leaning over the counter to push her breasts within an inch of his face.

"That's okay. There's a pencil sharpener at school."

"You stick your pencil into my sharpener, I guarantee you'll get all the lead out of it."

"Well, that'd be silly. What use is a pencil if all the lead is gone?"

"Oh, she knows her stuff, Sir!" said Joilio, triple bagging Baxter's Hometown Proud! pencil. "All the customers keep coming back for it, Sir! They say she's fantastic, Sir!"

"Gee whiz," said Baxter. "I never would have thought anybody would enjoy sharpening a pencil so much."

The cashier ran her hands over Baxter's chest. "Lemme show you what's what, baby. You lookin' for a good time?"

"Well … sure, I guess. But I'm already late for—"

"How good a time you lookin' for?"

"Uh, well, I don't know, like I said, I—"

"Well, I can't ring nothin' up until you specify, sweetheart. So how good a time you want?"

"Oh … Well, uh … How about the best time?"

"Okay, baby," she said, clicking to a subtotal on her keyboard. "I just need a deposit of nine hundred and three from you and we can head into the bathroom."

"Nine hundred and three?!" Baxter paused in the probe for some change. "As in nine hundred and three dollars?!"

"Well, that's if you want the whole hour."

"Oh, certainly not, I don't have an hour. No, I-I-I just hate to be rude, but—"

"Most guys are done in a couple minutes."

"No, thank you, I, I really can't … What? … A couple of … That's still, like, thirty dollars and ten cents, isn't it?"

"You wanted the best time, right?"

He chuckled with a soft smile. "Nobody could possibly sharpen my pencil well enough to merit my spending thirty dollars, to say nothing of nine hundred. I'll just take the pencil, please."

"Are you sure, baby?"

"Yes, yes. Thank you, though."

"Okay. That'll be one dollar and eleven cents."

Baxter's mouth dried out as he remembered that he had spent the last of his money on the phone. Awkwardness, dread, and panic bounced his eyes from corner to corner. He rummaged through his backpack and found the little yellow change purse he kept tucked away. Finding it empty, he felt rosy hot embarrassment flooding his face. Just as he inhaled to ask for the possibility of store credit, Joilio interjected. "Oh, don't worry, I'll get that, Sir!" Joilio handed the cashier a one dollar and eleven cent bill, which she placed in her till, completing the transaction.

Baxter was a little perplexed. "I'm a little perplexed. "You're paying for my pencil, Joilio?"

"Gladly, Sir!"

"Well, that's really very nice, but does your employer condone your using their money to pay for my merchandise?"

"Their money, Sir?! Oh no, Sir! They would never let me use *their* money, Sir!"

"You mean you just paid for my pencil with your own money?"

"Yes indeedio, Sir!"

"Why?"

"I gladly pay for all my honored customers' merchandise, Sir!"

"But that'll lead you to financial ruin. What could possibly incentivize you to do that?"

"Providing you with a level of customer service far above and beyond the value of my wages is of paramount importance to me, Sir!" Joilio's teeth twinkled under his joyous and disturbingly genuine smile.

Baxter stood there, digesting this for a second. He shrugged his shoulders and said, "Gosh, that sure is nice. Thanks so much, Joilio."

"Thank you, Sir, for allowing me to serve you, Sir! Allow me to gladly carry you to your car, Sir!"

"Well, uh—"

Again Joilio swept Baxter off his feet. He returned to an alarming speed after pumping his skates only a few times. They zipped past the Jupiter XIX in-store arcade, past Dozen Dads' Dysfunctional Family Photo, and on to the main exit doors.

"GAA! Wait a minute, Joilio! I don't have a car."

"Well then, Sir, I'll gladly carry you home, Sir!"

"Well, gee. I ... Would you mind putting me down and letting me take myself home?"

"Y'sure, Sir?!"

"Yes, thank you."

"Y'positive, Sir?!"

"Yes. Positive."

"Y'sure, Sir?!"

Baxter paused. "Yes."

"Very well. The Customer is Always Right, Sir!" assured Joilio. Haste and politeness wrestled in Baxter's brain as the courtesy clerk used up another three minutes easing him to the floor. The youth didn't even realize his feet had touched the ground until Joilio knocked him off balance by blurting out, "It's been an honor to serve you, Sir! We all look forward to serving you again really, really soon, Sir!"

"Thank you, Joilio," said Baxter as he crammed the triple-bagged pencil into his backpack and jumped onto his bicycle.

"Oh, thank you, Sir!"

"Well, bye." Baxter rode off onto Spine Street. Joilio waved with enough vigor to sprain his wrist and called out, "Hope your day is filled with mirth and sublimity, Sir! Are you sure I can't do anything more for you today, Sir?!"

"No, thank you, Joilio. Goodbye!" Baxter said, barely within audible range. As Baxter rode off into the distance, Joilio stood there. His eyes moistened. Then, with a lump in his throat, he turned around to face the store. With the realization that he would have the privilege of spraining his other wrist by serving more customers today, his face brightened once again. He resumed his sickening vitality and his disturbingly genuine smile.

With his pencil acquired, Baxter sped down Spine, then turned back onto Hypotenuse. After another few blocks, he cruised into a parking lot of the PHU campus, right next to the railroad tracks that went deep into the city. The campus clock tower struck 12:03 p.m. He remembered the clock in the classroom seemed to lag behind a couple of minutes. If only he could just slide in before the door locked. He flew off his bicycle before it even rolled into the bike rack. By the time it landed itself perfectly in its parking slot, the youth had flown past the Marta Hazekamp Dance Studio and all the way across the quad without a moment's further thought of the bicycle's welfare. He never had to lock up his bicycle. With his name spelled out in glittery blue letters on both mini license plates, there was little chance of any mix-ups. Everyone else had to lock theirs up with at least three different kinds of chains, a computer-controlled theft prevention system, and three or more anchors, each weighing hundreds of pounds. Some of the nicer bicycles had solid rubber tires, titanium frames, and security guards. Despite all these measures, half the bicycles were damaged and vandalized daily. Security guards, no matter how well paid, would often display corruption—even robotic security guards, whose lack of emotion supposedly immunized them from the disease of bullying. But Baxter's bicycle always remained untouched. Every day he would return to it, unlocked, and ride home carefree and merry.

Without a doubt, Superhyperdimensional Fluidic Geometry and Omniphasic Fractal Strategic Permutations XI ranked within the top eleven hardest classes Baxter had ever taken. Finding optimal strategies required multidimensional thinking and the ability to track fluctuating networks of abstractions with the precision of a quantum surgeon. The slightest mistake could unravel hours of work. Professor Dedrick never failed to mention this during his regular rituals of dangling a grade over his students. This was why Baxter knew, upon seeing that big classroom door start to slide closed, that once he heard the click of the lock, he would have no hope of saving Mom from a gruesome death. With only a sliver of open space remaining in the doorway, he launched himself through like an Olympic swimmer and tumbled down the aisle to the center of the classroom. He scrambled up to his feet and looked around.

"Jeezis, relax, pencil dick," said HAMN. "He's not here yet."

Baxter was the only human in this class. The other two attendees included a bioluminescent gaseous organism from Neptune, known as Xzhuajdnkqqqiiihwp (pronounced "Ron"), and HAMN, a hermaphroditic android with broad shoulders, wide hips, and very large hands. He or she had a tall, bald head, which featured a display screen for a graphing calculator just above the brow. He or she always wore loose Hawaiian shirts and shorts, to conceal what he or she saw as man boobs. HAMN had gold skin, upon which there grew not one hair. Cartoonishly yellow irises emboldened his or her baseball-sized eyes. Below them, and above his or her full lips, a long, pixie-like nose pointed out. His or her substance abusive designers had adorned the tip of it with a little spring coil, which he or she had converted into an electrical terminal. It facilitated tremendous throes of pleasure for his or her clients at the Napa Auto Bordello. His or her wiring had never quite been the same after this conversion. This often inundated the brilliant young android whore with pangs of bitterness and regret. And he or she rarely hesitated to take it out on others, particularly the little goodie-two-shoes who had just dived into the classroom.

"I could've sworn I saw the door closing," said Baxter.

"Oh, yeah, that was just Xzhuajdnkqqqiiihwp brushing past it ever so clandestinely," said HAMN in his or her rich, feminine voice. "He thinks that we'll all think some harmless breeze simply happened by, removed the stop, and blew a heavy metal door closed."

"Gosh, why would we ever want that?" asked the youth.

"Why don't you tell him, stink puff?" he or she asked the silent and invisible Neptunian. "We know you're still in here, you warm front of stench. Why don't you tell him you were trying to whittle it all down to just you and me?"

"You think I can't take the heat?" replied Xzhuajdnkqqqiiihwp, suddenly glowing a greenish-yellow.

"The heat," HAMN muttered. "Christ, Xzhuajdnkqqqiiihwp, not like this is for the Asimov Fellowship or the Nobel Prize."

"Gosh, no!" Baxter exclaimed. "The Chess Intergalactica is the opportunity of a lifetime."

"Tell you what, Baxative," said HAMN. "If I get the high score on this test, next week I'll pick you up at … whatever daisy-decked little playpen you live in, drive your ass over here on my own nickel, and you can play in that fucking stupid tournament for me."

"What?!" cried Xzhuajdnkqqqiiihwp.

"Really?" asked Baxter. "You'd give me your nomination?"

"Oh, suck my sac, you gullible Mayberry," HAMN sneered. "I wouldn't give you a cold. But let someone try to nominate me into that pathetic orgy."

"You're forfeiting?" Xzhuajdnkqqqiiihwp squeaked with hope.

"Just 'cause I'm not doing next week's dweeb fest doesn't mean I'm not ready and waiting to kick both your asses inside out. This exam is mine. But make no mistake, Dedrick gives that certificate of nomination to me, and it's going straight into the toilet with a couple of long, brown buddies."

Baxter didn't know what to make of such a statement, so he shuffled over to a desk and immersed himself in thought. The other two students immersed themselves in unfocused idleness.

By the time the clock struck 2:48, it had become clear that the professor would need to reschedule the exam, assuming he ever arrived.

"Goodness," said Baxter. "I hope Professor Dedrick is alright."

The others responded with apathetic scoffs as Baxter tried to maintain rosy thoughts about the happiness and health of their teacher, which reminded him of the apple. He dug into his backpack and pulled out a bright red, shiny apple. He walked up to the front of the room, gave the apple a quick polish, and placed it on the professor's desk.

"Oh boy, here we go again with the apple. Do you ever get tired of being the teacher's pet?" griped HAMN.

"Teacher's pet?" he replied, puzzled.

"You've never heard that term before? A person who sucks up to the teacher."

"Sucks up? What does—"

"He has to leave an apple," Xzhuajdnkqqqiiihwp joked. "*You* try the sex for favors game with a guy like Professor Dedrick."

"What for favors?" asked Baxter.

"Sex," replied HAMN, irritated.

"Secks?"

"Yeah, good luck going down on him, Bax," said Xzhuajdnkqqqiiihwp, cracking a smile that no one could decipher.

"Going down?" Baxter asked, furrowing his brow.

"Yeah, get the electron microscope!" HAMN jeered.

"Yeah, but make sure Dedrick holds still, or you still won't see his junk," Xzhuajdnkqqqiiihwp added.

"Who's talking about Dedrick's junk?" HAMN belted out with a full laugh, which Xzhuajdnkqqqiiihwp copied.

"Yeah. Yeah, but don't try intercourse, Bax…" Xzhuajdnkqqqiiihwp added.

"Xzhuajdnkqqqiiihwp," HAMN said. "Man, the joke is over now."

"Yeah, because bacteria like him don't even reproduce sexually," Xzhuajdnkqqqiiihwp added, and then laughed alone.

"Man, you never can quit," HAMN sighed.

"What?"

"You're such a fucking tool," HAMN huffed. "We had a good riff going, and you nerded everything out of the moment."

"I was trying to make a joke that Baxter would actually get," Xzhuajdnkqqqiiihwp retorted.

"Alright, boys and girls," interrupted a voice from a petri dish that floated into the room and landed on a desk. "That'll be enough."

"We didn't mean anything by it, Professor Dedrick," said Xzhuajdnkqqqiiihwp. "At least I didn't, Professor Dedrick. They might have, but I didn't. I'd never dream of offending you, Professor Dedrick."

"More like bore me," scoffed the bacterium. "I've taught dopes like you for a hundred eleven years in dozens of locations all over the galaxy. You think there's an asexual joke at my expense I haven't heard?

That's all you college zeros ever think about is asex and sex. Can't you come up with anything new?"

"What are secks?" asked Baxter.

"Would you be quiet?" said HAMN.

"I'll never forget when I was in grad school," Professor Dedrick continued. "I had spent my entire first year infecting this halfwit frat hog dick on wheels.... His grades were a joke. And this guy was taking fascinating courses: exobiology, ring theory, ancient Martian civ.... But to hell with that. His gonads ran the show for him."

"You say that about everyone," mumbled HAMN.

"Because it's true about everyone."

"Give us a break, Professor D," said HAMN, more ashamed than ever about the profession that paid for his or her classes. "I've even heard you say that about Stephen Hawking."

"Look at that obsession the guy had with black holes," said Professor Dedrick. "Talk about having vagina on the brain—"

Baxter tried to break in. "How do you get angina on the brain?"

Professor Dedrick talked over him. "How do you think a non-human untouchable like me was able to replace him on the Lucasian Chair at Cambridge? The guy developed some sort of obsession with 'getting back into the womb of God.' Destroyed his career. Now, don't get me wrong. I'm all for sex or asex. I like a good divide in the hay as well as the next guy. But there's more to me than 'If it feels good, do it.'"

Though HAMN had managed to keep his or her college job an airtight secret from everyone outside the workplace, the bright, young, cybernetic hooker was now certain that Professor Dedrick's comments were actually veiled jabs, aimed at him or her.

"Hey, HAMN," asked Baxter, scooting to the edge of his seat, "What's so special about the room of God?"

"You're an asshole," groaned HAMN, looking away from his or her bright-eyed peer, who furrowed his soft blond brows in puzzlement.

Professor Dedrick continued, "Now, I hope you're all ready for the test."

"Whh?! Are you serious?" HAMN objected. "You were almost three hours late!"

"Hm? Oh, yes, silly business, that," said the professor.

"Class is almost over. We've got . . . less than eleven minutes!"

"Oh. Yes, looks like you do."

"What if we can't stay long enough to finish?"

"Oh, nonsense. Like you said, it's only another eleven minutes. Ten now. You simply need to buckle down."

"Are you saying we're taking a three-hour test in ten minutes?!"

"As usual, I'll expect each of you to show all your work. Any answers left incomplete will disqualify you from the nomination. Oh, and, if the formulas become too large to fit into your calculators, just hook yourselves up to HAMN's positronic brain."

"Excuse me! You can't just volunteer my brain like that."

"Remember, even though you're free to use as much of HAMN's storage or RAM as you like, you must do your own work. Mr. Xzhuajdnkqqqiiihwp, I don't want you adapting yourself to the volume of the room to look at Baxter's answers again. Is that clear?"

Xzhuajdnkqqqiiihwp glowed an indignant yellow, "I was stretching!"

"Right. Well, you'll stretch yourself into disqualification if I find you drifting that far over there again. Now get out your blue books and let's get to work. We have less than nine minutes left, you know."

Baxter was still thinking about the perplexing conversation that had just taken place. He had so many unanswered questions. But he would dismiss them, just like he would dismiss any other challenges to his experiences. His thoughts drifted to hyperspatial math, and then to hyperspatial chess, and naturally, to the variety of chess games in which he would engross himself if lucky enough to be nominated to compete in the Chess Intergalactica next week. What a dream to go up against top players from all over the universe for that supreme honor: the chess championship. And for the cash prize so badly needed to save Mom.

But a slight hole had now been burned into his confidence. He felt uneasy, and he didn't know why. He did know it had something to do with the poster of the rat at Orville's, and with this bizarre conversation. He had never had curiosity linger like this. Something about him had begun to change, in an unsettling way.

3. LAST OF THE HARD-ROCKIN' BREAKFASTS

Even though the height of this Safeway's aisles often left new shoppers with their mouths agape, the cereal selection didn't exactly inspire one to rave with awe. It had a lot of gaps; a lot of long-neglected, dusty spaces, some streamed with cobwebs. Yet, for all its poverty, this Safeway remained a rich source of vintage Americana. No other store on Earth still sold the antiquated line of '80s Rock Cereals. Here, you could still start off the morning with dangerous, hard-rockin' cereals like Kenny Loggins' Danger O's, a true maverick, featuring crunchy pops of sweetness packed with enough unpronounceable, high-octane shit to keep you soaring beyond the stratosphere all day long, assuming the 9 g rush didn't send you crashing into a hospital bed. Or shake it up with Bon Jovi's Bad Medicine Bits. Each and every box contained a different sweetened pharmaceutical medley, ensuring new and exciting ODs through which kids could filter their Saturday morning cartoons. The Scorpions could rock you like a hurricane with a bowl of Toxic Bites O' Sugar Cane. The bite-sized clumps of sugar, sweetened with a glaze of real scorpion venom, kept you twitching and thrashing all morning, and it stayed crunchy in milk. Or you could cap off the crazy twentieth century with Billy Joel's Weed and Sharts of Fire. Concerned moms had protested the traces of cannabis in this dangerous but fun part of a balanced breakfast. None of them ever accepted the fact that it was actually the cereal's ghost pepper–infused shit flakes that had landed truckloads of kiddies in the morgue after converting both ends of their digestive tracts to firehoses of blood. These cereals had become cult favorites that appealed mostly to a handful of outlanders: extremists, willing to journey vast distances through the desert for them and pit their own physiological mettle against these widely outlawed breakfasts. But they were also favored by a few locals from nearby shantytowns—people who didn't have anything to do—kids like Josh and Barry.

"I'm not buyin' that," protested Josh, while picking his nose and introducing a new member to the family of boogers on his stained white undershirt. Josh liked to wear undershirts. Actually, Josh liked to wear the one undershirt he had. Technically, it didn't qualify as an undershirt because Josh never wore anything over it. It kept him comfortable and cool, especially when the most recent cereal selection would plunge him into a series of illnesses that baked his brain with delirious fevers. But ferocious discomfort half the time was a small price to pay for comfort the other half of the time. This is why he always wore a pair of knee-length bike shorts stretched over the tan skin of his lean legs. Fuck fashion and fuck style. Josh did not concern himself with such pretentious neuroses. Comfort was king. And when Josh found an arrangement that worked, he stuck to it. And of course, after a week or so, it would stick to him. Last week's fingerprints remained stuck to the huge glasses that burdened his bulb-like nose, just as crumbs of last week's cereal remained stuck between a few of his crazy teeth. Last week's chocolate remained on his weak chin, just as a squiggle of last week's ramen remained on his shirt, and stains of last week's whatever remained embedded in his bike shorts. Being sixteen was all about enjoying life. So the last thing Josh was about to do was listen to a cereal suggestion from someone like Barry.

"Josh, you love Guns N' Roses," Barry pressed on, while adjusting his porkpie hat and brushing a spot of dust off his guitar. Unlike Josh, Barry, with the help of his cell phone camera and a bit of stolen stage makeup, did concern himself with the image he projected. In fact, Barry, or "The Murph," as he—and only he—called himself, believed with great conviction that in order to earn and retain respect, one simply must project impressive images at all times. Granted, these images would change from day to day. The fact that none of them were compatible with any of the others didn't trouble the Murph because he never thought outside of the image currently projected. To him—and only him—the current image represented the whole truth. One of his favorite images, today's image, was the "Blues Master." Blues Master Murph wore whichever one of his eleven pairs of shoes looked the most beaten up. He also wore a dark, open-button shirt, which revealed every inch of his hairless torso. He kept the rim of his weather-beaten jeans anchored at the southernmost edge of his six-pack, cloaking his pubeline only by a few thread widths, and by some sort of divinely merciful fortuity. He considered his tattered old porkpie hat, which topped his short, curly hair, as the crowning touch; that is, until he strapped his scratched up acoustic guitar, Alison Marie, over his shoulder. Alison Marie truly constituted the final touch—the element of completion, which would show the world that inside this sixteen-year-old White boy with the smooth chest, the soft, full lips, the untested eyes, and the galaxy of facial acne, lived a hardened, mileage-weary man, who knew pain. The Murph had even more complexity than this, though. He was also Grizzly Murph, Papa Murph, Biker

Murph, Murph Brosnan, Beatnik Murph, Irish Local Murph, G.I. Murph, Coin Slot Murph, and Sergeant Murph of the Yukon.

None of these Murphs impressed anyone, other than the Murph himself. Josh in particular had grown weary of them, and, in fact, weary of everything about Barry. He couldn't stand that pizza-faced phony. Likewise, Barry couldn't stand Josh, that rubbery little slob. Though Barry viewed most people in his life as less intelligent than he, Josh, he believed, stood alone as the only one who accepted this subordinate status. In reality, Josh accepted not even a shred of it. So both boys held a teeth-grindingly intense contempt for each other, tempered only by the possibility of laughter at the other's misfortune. This is why they were best friends. As long as one was around, the other one could never be the stupidest person in the room. Their mutual laziness and habitual proximity to each other promoted an occasionally supportive coexistence, which facilitated them sharing trips to the store to try a new '80s Rock Cereal.

Most of the world, and an increasing share of the universe, considered these cereals vintage. But they were new to these guys, and they couldn't make it all the way out here every day. It took every sweltering effort to pedal their bikes back to the trailer lot before dark, even after leaving bright and early to make it here. Since the title of "The One Who Had Even a Scrap of Money" invariably landed on Josh, he always decided which cereal they would get. Of course, after the purchase of the cereal, Barry would always manage to miraculously conjure up enough change for cigarettes, which Josh detested. So Josh never felt guilty about making a selfish cereal choice. But that never stopped Barry from pestering him. Barry's suggestions, when taken, often yielded some good choices. But this time seemed a little different. Even if it was a Guns N' Roses cereal.

"You expec' me to eat a cereal called Sweet Shards O-Chyme?" whined Josh. "I din't even know y'could make that stuff inta shards."

"I thought we agreed, real men take real risks," Barry nagged. "But, now it's, 'Awww, what if we get sick?' Right, little pussy man?"

"You ever taste chyme? Lafe invited me over fer cheese n'crackers a couple a years ago.... While I wasn' lookin', he took his brother's colostomy bag... squeezed some chyme right onto a cracker. I was pukin' my asshole outta my throat. Yeah boy, Lafe, real fuckin' funny, laughin' it up like a chimp with a garden hose up its ass...."

"Dude, you're a fuckin' idiot."

"Hhw?! Fuck you, Barry."

"I'm sure they don't put actual chyme in there, Josh."

"Whl what about Van Halen's Hot Fire Screechers? They burn the hell outta your mouth. You and me were screechin' for an hour last time we had 'em."

"Dude, it's just really hot cinnamon; they don't put actual fire in 'em."

"I dunno."

"Oh, fine, Josh. They're gonna put stuff that can kill you into cereal. Right?"

"Alright, alright, fine."

"How the hell would they get any repeat business?"

"Okay, I said."

"God, Josh, let me take this moment to salute you and your cosmic intellect."

"Fine, they don' do it, okhhaay?! Ghhod."

"Alright, so we gettin' the super-sized, or—"

"No, I'm still not gettin' somethin' tastes like chyme. I don' care wha's innit."

"Dude, you don't even have the stones to try a fuckin'—"

"Oh yeah, no big thing to you, right? You're not payin' for it. Plus, with your breath, you're prolly used to the taste."

"Josh, speaking of chyme breath, have y'ever thought of takin' the time to brush that gross crud out from between your—"

"Whhhoah!" Josh whispered, marveling at the green glow coming from behind his loudmouthed companion.

"What," said Barry, turning around to behold the box of cereal behind him on the shelf. There it stood, all by itself. The last of its kind. They had never seen this one before. But how could they have missed it? The box was black and covered with dust. But without a doubt, it cloaked some kind of unseeable energy: a hard-rockin' vitality unknown to the two boys. Inside, something radiated a power, a violence they'd never approached even in their foamiest tantrums, nor in their wildest berserks of masturbation. Etched all over the blackness, various colors of thin lines glowed with jarring intensity, like an angry neon maze of electrical circuits. These grew especially dense on the front of the box, where they converged upon a bright green radiation symbol at the center, which also glowed. As they marveled at the box, something changed within them. Deep in the cores of their essences, they felt the subtle beginnings of being scorched—like a lamp filament plugged into a dam—as if their cores would eventually overheat and their essential humors would vaporize, leaving only a miserable, overused latticework of their being. And yet...

And yet, these impressions laid deep. Buried, shrouded in the stems of their subconscious. On the surface, they both felt great. They felt amazing! Their blood flowed so fast they could hear it. Their minds felt clearer and sharper than ever before. And they both had what Josh referred to as a "spikey." Barry's jeans concealed his spikey. Josh's spikey, however, was revealed through the front of his bike shorts, pulsing with vigor. On any other day, this would have embarrassed the awkward youth. But not today. He sported this spikey with competitive pride. They both felt like they could smash a mountain to rubble with one punch, drink the oceans dry in one gulp, impregnate the mightiest of monsters with one thrust. They moved closer to get a better look at the box. It was a Def Leppard cereal. Neither of them ever paid much attention to Def Leppard. But this box fascinated them. This was something special.

"You wanna get this one?" Josh asked, with a twinkle in his eye and a sparkle in his slobber.

"Do I wanna get this one? Dude, is my mom's voice like a rusty door hinge?"

They both shared a hearty laugh at this. Not their first shared laugh, but one of few. After a few seconds, a mutual feeling of disgust came over them, as if they'd just woken up naked in the same bed. They piped down and resumed looking at the box.

"The cereal with a half-life," Josh read off the front.

"Dude, that's frickin' awesome!" Barry laughed. Neither of them minded laughing, as long as they didn't laugh together.

"Yeah. I can't wait t' get home with this one," said Josh. "Y'know… we musta tried a hundred different cereals together, but I don' ever remember bein' so jazzed about—"

Josh noticed that Barry was no longer listening. He stared past Josh, stared with crusty lips at the man who had been standing there, watching them for shit knew how long. Josh wheeled around, knocking a bunch of other cereals off the shelf, then hid behind Barry. The Cereal Man continued staring at them. They found their feelings of intense vitality now overwhelmed by an inexplicable need to flee.

"Oh, jeez," Josh whispered in a tiny, panicked voice, as he pulled Barry backward.

"Dude, will you hush up? I'll handle this," declared Barry, stepping in front of his shorter comrade. "Oy! How's it hangin' there, my good friend?" Barry thrust his hand forward, palm down, to shake hands. Josh shut his eyes, raised his eyebrows, and sighed in exasperation. For some reason, he hadn't expected this. For some reason, he seemed to never expect it, even though he would always wonder why he hadn't expected it. And once again, surprise! Here it was. Sales Rep Murph had just appeared. He always showed up at the worst of times because Barry understood that during the roughest of waters, the smoothest charm must be applied. As a habit, Sales Rep Murph tended to show up whenever Barry found himself in trouble with adults, especially cops. And though both Josh and Barry rarely did anything seriously illegal, their friend, Lafe, always seemed to get them into hot water, often on purpose, and often for his own gurgley amusement. And each time Sales Rep Murph reared his greasy head, he would manage to transform a pair of light questions from the police into a squinty-eyed interrogation, which would then elevate into a sweaty-faced, spittle-eared, three-hour-long event involving scores of red and blue flashing lights, as well as faces on the pavement, handcuffs, and an occasional scurrying up into a tree, naked, with dogs barking from below. And now... Oh jeez, now! Of all the times Sales Rep Murph chooses to show up! *Shit. Here we go.*

"The cereal, Barry. The cereal," Josh muttered.

"Josh, what're you slobbering about?" asked Barry, turning around.

"The cereal! He wants the cereal, Barry. Step away from the cereal," Josh repeated, with eyes resting closed while trying to contain his frustration.

"Sorry, Josh, I don't speak Manglemouth. Y'know the rest of the world could probably understand you if your words weren't imprisoned behind that…jagged enamel train wreck of yours." He turned back to the Cereal Man.

"Sorry about that. How y'doin', man. Name's Murph."

As he said this, Barry put his arm around the Cereal Man's shoulder. It hurt. It was the strangest thing. The surface of his arm that touched the Cereal Man now felt bruised. It wasn't as if Barry had used too much strength embracing him, but rather, as if the Cereal Man used too much strength being embraced—as if in some crazy, anti-Newtonian way, the Cereal Man pushed harder against Barry than Barry pushed against him. The teen winced but did no more to reveal the pain he was experiencing. If his drooling little cohort found out that he couldn't even touch someone without getting hurt, he'd never hear the end of it. But he did withdraw.

"Sorry. Not a touchy-feely guy, I gather, eh? Me neither," said Barry, returning to block the cereal from the Cereal Man's view. "Allow me to bring my position to the fore, if I may."

Josh turned away, bracing himself for the monsoon of bullshit already on its way. The Cereal Man had not moved a muscle.

"I see you have a keen eye for the finer things in life, my friend," continued Barry. "Like me and my associate, Josh, here. Every so often the two of us…amalgamate our modest, uh, fundings so we can afford a sampling of the great, and as misfortune would have it, dwindling species of '80s Rock Cereals."

Barry heard a strange quacking sound behind him when he mentioned the word "fundings." It was just one noise, very brief, as if someone had blown their nose. But it was gone now.

"And within the parameters of…that…which is the normalcy, my esteemed companion and myself would yield this last box of cereal to yourself, as we perceive a rather strong…magnetism draws yourself to it."

The quack-like sound popped up again with the word "normalcy." But it was gone now.

"Well, as it happens, the two of us at the present time must defer to a community greater than ourselves. My colleague and I have been ... entrusted with satisfying the, uh, breakfasting demands of the advanced karate class I'm teaching."

Now he picked up some kind of faint, repetitive wheezing sound behind him, like someone bouncing on a leaky tire. He ignored it.

"Luckily, it's a small class. Only eleventh-degree black belt and above are admitted. Back when I was a combat instructor for the IRA, the classes were huge. No individual training, everyone there was just a number, I'm sure you know how it is," continued the zit spattered teen, who held the third-lowest GPA in his high school. "But now, as a US Navy SEAL, I get to pick the elite. And only those who have what it—"

Barry now noticed some kind of clicking noise behind him. It had been there for a few seconds already. But upon his claim of affiliation with the most elite military force on Earth, the clicking sound became louder and more staccato. He turned around to find Josh, laughing himself to tears. His gangly figure leaned on the shelves for support. His mouth gaped, with a thread of drool trailing down from his upper set of crazed teeth. As the thread grew longer, it curved with every pulse of air that clicked from his mouth. Barry turned back to the Cereal Man, and in a struggle to smile, provided a showing of his upper teeth. Then, with Josh still clicking in the background, he continued.

"So, you know, we saw the cereal first. And, and—"

"One seventy-five," said the Cereal Man.

"Huh?" There was a brief silence. "One sevent—you mean you'll give us a buck seventy-five for this box of—"

"Your weight. One seventy-five."

"Oh. Well, no, actually it's more like two hundred. I've been doing a lot of sparring—"

"Oh, you do not weigh two hundred, Barry, gimme a break," Josh scoffed.

"Dude, I do too, ever since I been—"

"Ever hear a two-hundred-pound stack of bullshit beg for its life?" asked the Cereal Man.

"No," said Barry.

"Neither have I. Not something I want to hear. Now why don't you stand aside for a second. I'll take the cereal, and then you and your little buddy can argue about which one of you smells more like stale underwear."

"Oh, yes, y'see that'd be Josh. The Murph never has the underwear smell. I mean, he likes to let the boys swim free, right?"

"Shut . . . up . . . and get out of his way," said Josh between clenched teeth.

"I can handle this, underwear boy."

"Barry, he sounds like Clint Eastwood. He's gonna kill us," Josh hissed in his ear before Barry elbowed him in the ribs.

"Josh," Barry whispered back. "There's two of us. There's one of him. Do you honestl—"

"Y'know," began the Cereal Man. "When you beat someone into a big brown mush, their closest relatives can't even identify them? Kinda makes you wonder what happens when you beat a two-hundred-pound stack of bullshit to death. I mean, would you still be a big brown mush, or would you turn into something else?"

"He's not two hundred pounds," Josh muttered.

"Well, one thing I do know," said the Cereal Man, grabbing Barry by the throat. "You don't hand over that cereal, and even the stacks of bullshit at Mallorie's Dairy won't recognize you."

"Oh, burn!" Josh jeered at Barry, who shot him a dirty look as he gagged.

Barry grabbed the box of cereal from behind him and handed it over. The Cereal Man looked at the box. He released Barry, and the boys thought they were in the clear … for about one second. Then, to their horror, his face did not become gentler. Rather, it crinkled into a seething rage unlike any they'd ever seen—like the face of an abused wolf. He looked at the dust on the box and the fingerprints at the top: his own fingerprints. He had left this same box of cereal here three years ago. The last box. His lips tightened, and his eyes narrowed into slits. Air rushed in and out of his nose, and the sound of his grinding teeth caused the boys to release a few spots of pee. He clawed the box, filled his lungs with air, and nudged his words out in a staccato whisper.

"The last box. It really … is … the last … box."

"Oh, jeez, we're gonna die!" squeaked Josh, at the threshold of hearing.

With that, the Cereal Man hammered his fist down onto the shelves, destroying them all and bringing boxes of cereal down into a pile. Josh darted the opposite direction and slipped. Barry turned around to run and tripped over Josh. The two of them scrambled around on the floor, calling each other names, hitting each other, and inadvertently thwarting each other's attempts to get up. Josh scrambled to his feet and Barry followed. They bolted to the end of the aisle. Josh slipped as he rounded the corner. Barry tripped on him and crushed Alison Marie upon impact. They got back up, with Barry hollering and beating Josh with the mangled guitar. The store echoed with their yelling and swearing as they scrambled out of sight. The Cereal Man opened the box and removed a small nugget, shaped like an atomic bomb. Its green glow lit up his face and cast his shadow on the ceiling.

He placed it in his mouth and crunched down on it. As he swallowed, the muscles in his face hardened and his irises blazed pure white. He stormed out of the cereal aisle.

4. THE GOLDEN SON

Darla didn't know what kind of weird tree she had found herself sitting under. It had a thick trunk, which split horizontally and symmetrically into two main branches. At their ends, each of these curved upward and gave rise to many much smaller bare branches that seemed more like tentacles. A smooth and slick bark covered every inch of the tree—not like wood at all, but some manner of pink, shiny flesh. As she looked up, the small branches spread upward toward the sun, their ends shuddering with some sort of expectation. But this looked nothing like Earth's golden sun. Its blue disc ruled over a golden sky. Frank and Dr. M used to talk a lot about planets with huge suns like this one, all those years ago—suns that would go supernova. Darla noticed some branches had started to flower. She looked at the rest of the tree, and all over, the fleshy branches bloomed with a hyperflorid madness. Soon the tree shook with ecstasy as flowers burst out of every possible inch of its surface. Many flowers began blooming their own flowers. She wanted to stop it, but nothing could stay this runaway blooming. Then, hugged by the pedals around them, bright red nubs of fruit began to bud, swell, and quiver until they grew so... full, they... just ... couldn't ... stay! Before long, the fruit popped out with as much wildness as the flowers. She knew that this would spell her doom. The fruit rotted on the branches and dropped to the ground. As the fruit buried her, it turned to shit—huge mounds of sweet, ripe shit. As Darla kept her head above the growing pile, the sun flashed. It made some kind of strange ringing sound.

Darla woke up with her puffy face on the kitchen floor, in a puddle of used rotgut. She didn't know what had happened, but pain shot through her. She had chipped her remaining tooth. But this awful ringing hurt even more than the tooth. She peeled her wet rolls of boob and belly off the floor and climbed to her feet. The room whirled around. But she did manage to feel the kitchen table with her hands and edge her short, grub-like frame over to the piercing sound of the phone.

"Hello?"

"Mom, you're awake," chirruped Baxter. "How'd you sleep?"

"Sweetie, where... how long have..."

It all came flooding back to her, the memory, and the shame. Darla had always waited until her little blond cherub had fallen fast asleep before she traumatized her liver. It wasn't that she couldn't control herself. Despite the tales her liver, lungs, and nostril told, she actually didn't care for liquor, cigarettes, or narcotics, and she had only a mild appetite for sugary foods. But thanks to Dr. M, this regimen remained the only way to prevent another labor of ninety-nine hours that would spawn another litter of repulsive monsters. None of her previous offspring had lived for more than a day. They plagued the world, as the kindly obstetrician, Dr. Grayfold, had reminded her repeatedly, "as such perversions of nature that survival proved almost impossible for them—like germs too toxic to endure themselves." But Baxter was special. In contrast to his short-lived siblings, whose foulness would poison the very air they inhaled, Baxter had greeted the world as a blessed, beloved creation, almost immune to adversity. His energy seemed to thwart any corrupt force that came near him. But Darla knew he was not infallible. She sought to protect him from things that might dim his blue eyes or ruffle his downy hair. Great shame now overtook her as she recalled slamming an entire bottle of Kryptonian sour mash within an hour of arriving home from work.

The floor had hosted her unconscious body for over twenty-four hours before this phone call awakened her. But it didn't matter anymore. Not like the rest of the nursing home staff at Blackwick would miss her. After all, she was too ugly for them now. In truth, the Care Center Director had chosen the words "frightening, upsetting, and quite frankly unrecognizable as a human being to many of our residents." She knew everyone found her hideous. And she couldn't disagree, what with her varicose legs and oatmealy arms popping out of the jiggling barrel of lard that housed her unfortunate internal organs. Her pale skin had developed a rough, rather scaly quality. Her round, cod-gray eyes looked almost fake against the backdrop of her puffy cheeks, her cracking lips, and her nose, which various crushed pills and soaps had long ago eroded into one large nostril. Wisps of blonde hair populated patches of her flaky scalp. Sure, nobody could consider her the beautiful, sweet little sexdrop of the old days. But when someone condemns you as too repulsive to work in a nursing home, well, that's low. It drove her to drink. And Baxter witnessed it this time. She had only been passed out for about thirteen hours when he rode off to school. She remembered blubbering and screaming and singing off-key to him between gulps. Oh, what a horrible thing for her child to witness! She hoped he hadn't been paying attention.

"Hey Mom, remember last night when you got home and talked about how you lost your job while pouring all that fluorescent green stuff into your mouth?"

"Honey..."

"And you got all sad and everything because you could never raise enough money to finish paying for your operation?"

"Baxter, sweetheart, that was not a good way for Mom to behave."

"Well, I thought of a way to get the money for you!"

"Wait a minute. Where are you?"

"I'm at school. Got the highest score on the test! Wait until you get a gander at this nifty pencil I bought. It really did the trick during my calculations for the hyperbolic inverse tachy—"

"Your class was out three hours ago. What're you—Baxter, you'd better not be… Honey, you need to get home; it's going to get dark."

"Mom, didn't you hear? I got the highest score! Don't you remember what that means?"

"No, Baxter, I told you I do not want you in that tournament."

"But Mom, just think. I could be the chess champion of the entire universe! I could be famous! Professor Dedrick says he's sure I can do it, and I think, well…"

"We've been through all of this." Darla refrained from vocalizing her prejudice against bacteria and the recent trend of prokaryotes teaching advanced college classes. As far as she was concerned, their kind should stick to what they were good at: infecting things and acidifying milk. She had a hard enough time accepting the fact that they would just stroll on in and take all the good jobs. But the fact that her son had to listen to one of these little divvies just made her stomach turn. She maintained that Earth belonged to humans, not minorities or foreigners. Of course, the success of this argument depended on her ignoring a prokaryotic population advantage that ranged in the hundreds of octillions and a historical nativity advantage of about four billion years. Avoiding open discussion of the topic always allowed her to ignore these advantages.

"Your universe is right here at Home, with me."

"Have you heard how much money I get if I win?"

"It doesn't matter, sweetheart."

"But you only have one payment left. And you said if you don't make it, they'll reverse your operation and all my mean brothers and sisters could come back." He had no idea how this could happen because she had never explained it to him. But then again, he had no idea how *he* could happen because she had never explained it to him.

"No, they can't come back, darling. They died."

"But you said you could die!"

"Mmbmb-well—" Darla belched up acid that scalded her throat. After grimacing for a second, she resumed. "Well, now, that's something we just don't really know."

"I can't let you die, Mom."

She coughed from the burning in her throat, which sent stars swirling around in her vision. Her dizziness intensified, and her quavering feet struggled to keep her standing. "I'll find some other way to come up with the money, my darling. I promise you. Even if I have to lie, cheat, or steal to get it."

Baxter laughed at that one. He knew people didn't lie, cheat, or steal. Well, supposedly they could, possibly, in theory. But such intellectually puristic scenarios carried about as much practical weight as a hyperspherical birthday cake or an ultraviolet toon.

"Gosh, Mom. It's just great that you have a sense of humor about this. Now, I promise, I'll bring the money Home right away. And please don't worry. I'll be perfectly safe here at the school tonight."

"What do you mean tonight?"

"Oh, that's why I called. I have to stay after. For the tournament and all. So it looks like I'll be Home a little late." She coughed up a splash of blood. "Tonight?! The tournament is— How long was I unconsc—What day is this?"

"Yeah, surprised us too. Professor Dedrick rescheduled the whole thing a few months ago but the old silly willy didn't even tell us until right after we finished the test."

"No! No, you can't! Honey, you just can't!"

"Well, that's what we all thought at first. But the professor didn't feel like rescheduling again. But I just know this is going to work out great, Mom. I'll wave to you, I promise."

"What do you mean wave to me?"

"Sure, you'll be able to watch the tournament on channel nine ninety-nine. You can keep an eye on your little boy the whole time."

"WHAT?! NO! No, Baxter, you are not going to be on television!"

"Oh, I didn't think so either. Professor Dedrick said people would rather pick the dried skin off their lips than watch a chess tournament. Even this one. But after getting Orville's to sponsor us, and after getting out all that publicity, the school finally got the guys from the campus television studio in here. They haven't come out of the studio for ages. And the journalism department has sent over reporters, and all the chess fans in the entire universe are here. Professor Dedrick says there may be hundreds of them!"

"Hundreds?!" she yelped. *Fuckin' Professor Dedrick! Goddamn, fuckin' apple-browning divvie!* She had been hesitant enough to let Baxter go to a school outside of Twinkle. And now, hundreds, maybe even thousands, of eyes would cast their gaze upon Darla's little baby boy, whom she had managed to keep within an eleven-mile radius of Home. The thought of it dimmed the spinning room and made her legs weak.

"Baxter! Listen to me. I want you to stop whatever you are doing and come Home. Now. No! Wait. Hide your face. Right now. Hide your face. Go to your locker. Go to your locker and hide out there until Mom comes and—I'm on my way to the— I'm, I'm, I'll be there in just a—I'm going to be there as soon as—" She was about to get her bus pass and bolt out the door when she stumbled across a chair. The spinning room whipped her right back onto the kitchen floor, reacquainting her with the pool of spent rotgut in which she had awakened. She gathered up enough shards of consciousness to get back up and begin an exit from the kitchen. But she slipped on vomit and stumbled into the living room, where her insane dizziness crashed her with finality into the screen of the old-timey television in their living room. There she lay, with her brain blinked out and the upper half of her wretched body plunged into a heap of broken glass and various electrical parts, with her dimply ass pointing toward the kitchen. A series of huge peristaltic waves moved through the entire frame of her torso. Soon after, streams of vomit rushed past her sides, out of the wrecked TV, and into a puddle on the floor.

"You mean you're coming to the school to watch me play? Golly, Mom, that's swell! I can't wait. I'll introduce you to Professor Dedrick. Love you."

Baxter hung up. Just as he was about to lean down to get some water from the drinking fountain, he noticed a poster right next to the pay phone. It featured that same humanoid rat. But this poster looked much newer than the one at Orville's, with only a slight fading. As something that had always occupied the back of Baxter's childhood mind, but was now seen in a new way, it intrigued him. The black-and-white drawing showed the rat from the shoulders up, in the same position as on the other poster. But this image featured far more detail. It showed texture and shading, though with rough, sketchy lines. Baxter could tell that the object poking out of the rat's mouth was one of those smoking tubes that people sometimes sucked on to feel better: a cigarette, if memory served. The rat had a short, dark mohawk, and his eyes were obscured, not by sunglasses, as Baxter had thought before, but a wrap-around visor. Under the word "WANTED," the youth could now make out the reward offered. *Just how many zeros is that?* He looked closer.

"There you are. Professor D's looking for you," said HAMN, walking down the hall toward him. "You know we've been waiting in there for an hour?"

"Oh. Is it time already?" Baxter replied.

"You do this all the time. Why don't you get a cell phone?" bitched the golden-skinned android.

"Oh, my mom doesn't really want me to have one. Something about my privacy."

"Right, whatever," HAMN dismissed. "What, do you have a stalker or something?"

"A stocker? You mean for cupboards and such?"

"Huh?"

"No, Mom and I just stock our own groceries. No reason to hire a professional just yet."

"W-what on Earth are you—you know, when I watch you play, I can visualize the board for the next 35,937 combinations within one second. Yet talking to you is like when I bend my dick down and shove it up the wrong hole."

"What do you mean?"

"Well, I'm all set, everything's smooth, and then all of a sudden, I'm stuck and uncomfortable. That's what it's like talking to you!"

"Okay, but who is Dick?"

"My penis! Okay?!... The word 'dick' is another name for a penis, you carbon-based human halfwit! You know that little tube of skin between your legs? That thing that shoots out all the— Okay. That thing that you piss out— Okay, that you urinate out of?"

"Hey, now, that's private," Baxter chuckled.

"Yeah, private this, pal."

HAMN pulled down his or her Hawaiian-style trunks to reveal a sleek, smooth, golden penis with a clean, well-organized scrotum tucked behind it.

"Gee whillikers," said Baxter, looking away and not knowing what to think or feel.

"Hey, they're down here," HAMN demanded. "Look at me, kid. Look at me, I said!"

"Well, b-but," Baxter stuttered. "HAMN, your, your... penis is showing—"

"My dick, Bax! It's my dick. Alright? Now, lemme show you something. Look at me!" Baxter returned his gaze downward. HAMN lay down on his or her back and pointed his or her legs up in the air with his or her asshole pointing straight at Baxter.

"Oh my goodness, HAMN! You have a terrible cut right between your uh... well, your, your, uh ..."

"Yeah. That's my twat, bright-eyes! Between my asshole and my nut sack! Or as you would call it, 'the vagina between my anus and my scrotum,' whatterya thinka that?!"

"Well, it's all... very... clean."

"Yeah, gee, thanks, Goldilocks. Lemme show you something. This is what it's like talking to you."

As HAMN bent his glittery penis down past her vagina, and toward his or her anus, Professor Dedrick floated by in his petri dish. "What in the name of— What is going on out here?! HAMN, put your shorts back on! I turn my dish around for three minutes and you're out here with your android asshole pointed up in the air like Michael Jackson at a Chuck E. Cheese's!"

"It wasn't like that, Professor Dedrick," said a voice from just above HAMN's ass.

"Goddammit, Xzhuajdnkqqqiiihwp, you are disgusting! Who invited you, anyway!" screamed HAMN, hopping to his or her feet and getting dressed.

"I thought you knew I was here," Xzhuajdnkqqqiiihwp griped, glowing yellow.

"Right, like I can see you when you're transparent?"

"I wasn't watching."

"Yeah, you were more than watching, creepo. I knew I felt a breeze rush between my flaps a few times."

"That wasn't me."

"Please," said Professor Dedrick. "Must you two ruin the tournament the same way you ruin class?"

"I wanted nothing to do with this masturbatory horseshit cult gathering," HAMN protested.

"I don't mind, Professor Dedrick," said Xzhuajdnkqqqiiihwp. "Had you written to a more enjoyable set of conclusions on the thirty-third essay question, HAMN, Baxter might have been your adviser," goaded the professor.

"Yeah," added Xzhuajdnkqqqiiihwp. "What about me? How could I have improved?"

"By skipping class," HAMN sneered.

"Be silent, both of you," the bacterium insisted. "This is the biggest game of Baxter's life. And I daresay the biggest of yours too."

They both knew they were skating on thin ice. HAMN's designers had long ago drunk themselves into their graves. With nobody left to serve, he or she went to college in hope of becoming a great mathematician. But with no family and no money, HAMN resorted to the universe's oldest profession. Detesting every moment of the job, he or she had agreed to be on the candidate's advising staff in exchange for an assistantship, which included both a stipend and a tuition waiver. Without furnishing full intellectual support to Baxter, HAMN would have to prostitute at Napa for decades in order to pay off tuition. Xzhuajdnkqqqiiihwp, however, came from old money. He had popped in and out of many prestigious schools in the last few years. Each one had expelled him either for cheating, spying, sexual misconduct, or for some combination of the above. PHU was his last shot. If the gaseous brat didn't shape up, his family would cut him off. He would be banished from home, never again to know the vigor of the ferocious Neptunian winds, but doomed to drift around in Earth's filthy atmosphere for life.

After vowing to renew their bitchy conflict during some other professor's class, the android and the gas mass shelved their squabble. Without speaking another word, Baxter and his advising team made their way down the great halls of Patricia Hazekamp University and into the convocation center.

5. BOY HOLE

"You take her long, silky braid of scintillating amber hair in your hand. You find that you can feel her very essence as the highlights glisten with health and vitality. You brush the braid all along her neck and her collarbone. Her chest heaves. Goosebumps rush all over her body. Then, you caress her smooth shoulders. And, inch by inch, you run your hands up her inner thighs. They're like cream. And-and just as you begin to submerge... under her skirt... she giggles, just a little. You're still a gentleman. You're not going all the way. Not until she begs you to. She stirs a little bit. And you see her eyes open. You whip your hands back out and stuff them in your coat pockets. She looks around. And she sees you standing over the bed," lilted Clark in his most feathery voice.

"Alright. I'm gonna kiss her," said Ike, coming into the light of the candle.

"*That* is your plan?" said Mike, who sat a little further away, at the edge of visibility, "We gotta come up with something better than that. She already thinks you're some kind of psycho."

"Right now, maybe," Ike said. "But if I channel all my passion, all that love that's been just waiting to come out, I betcha a whole box fulla sour balls that I will melt her soul."

"Dude, get real," Mike scoffed. "This babe's a nine. You are a two. Two and a half if she's drunk. You have a lower-lower-sub-middle class income and you'll have even less if Mom cuts off your allowance, or if you're banned from the plasma center again. You're only five feet seven, you're fat, you're missing like nine of your teeth, you got a stupid lookin' hair helmet, you only bench one ten, and you smell like a frickin' dirty carpet. AND YOU WEAR THAT STUPID-ASS FUCKING PATCH OVER YOUR EYE LIKE YOU THINK YOU'RE SOME KINDA PIRATE! GODDAMN I HATE THAT THING! It was embarrassing when you were eight, dude, and now you're frickin' babe repellent. Just forget it, alright? Even if you use that musk cologne you got last week, you don't stand a chance."

"Nuh-uh, remember? I bench one fifteen now," said Ike.

Mike paused. "Dude, I'm tellin' you, you try to kiss her and we are screwed. We'll never see her again. You do not have the level of magnetism you need for this. Not even close."

"Ahem," exclaimed Clark. "If you gobstoppers would grace me with the courtesy of sealing off your Raisinet receptacles for half a second...." Mike thumped Ike on the back of the head and sat back. Ike, consumed with the urgent need for the best plan possible, resisted his older brother's provocation and focused on the vital details he knew Clark alone could provide. "She sits up. In a flash of alarm, she wonders if it's better to run or ask questions. Then she sees her purse on the table. And her shopping bag. She had just bought some books. She doesn't know where she is now. But she knows you. A face she kind of liked once... but now..."

"Okay, I guess I can... just talk her into staying," shrugged Ike.

"Just a minute," interjected Clark. "She starts to remember... the strange, bitter taste in her latte. She remembers when she came back from the restroom, you were sitting closer to her table than when she got up. She's scared now."

"I'll talk to her," Ike maintained.

"You don't know her name," Mike complained.

"I'm a level-five amateur comedian," Ike argued. "I got two books by the author she likes. And I got a wedding ring on. That's plus nine charisma points. I roll." He rolled the trio of pentagonal hexecontahedron dice.

"Three," declared Clark.

"Goddammit."

"HOLY SHIT—HHWWWWAHAHAHAHAHAHA!..." cried Chuckles from behind Ike.

"It's not funny, asshole," griped Ike.

"I'm, I'm sorry," replied Chuckles, toning it down. "I'm sorry. I mean, that was beyond funny, man. A hundred eighty sides total, and he still gets a three—hhhhhhahahahahahhahahahaaaa..."

"HEY!" shouted a voice from the next room, "SHUT THE FUCK UP OUT THERE! I'M TRYIN' TO GET SOME SLEEP!"

Everyone quieted down. "Okay. Now..." Clark continued. "You don't say, 'Hi' or 'Hello.'" Suppressing a laugh, he declared, "Instead you say, 'Welcome, Milady.'"

"Welcome, Milady?" objected Ike, "I got a twelve, dickhead. My roll, with a plus nine, and you give me some creepoid perv phrase like that? Come on."

Clark paused, grinned, then continued. "She bolts for the door."

"YOU DICK!" barked Ike.

"Smooth move, Krakafloa," whined Mike.

"Screw you, orc breath," Ike objected. "I got a twelve total...."

"Oooooh, twelve! Big mannn," Mike said, wiggling his fingers." I'm surprised she's not sucking our cocks right now."

"Well, if our VM here would stick to the rules ... What's your damage, anyway, Clarko, what'd I do to you?" asked Ike.

"Do you question my authority, Sir?" challenged Clark.

"You're damn straight I do, Mr. Peanut," said Ike.

"Now, look, I've asked you to stop calling me that," said Clark. "If you continue in this childish course, I'll take all your charms away, including the ribbed condom."

"Oh, yeah?" shouted Ike. "We'll just see what the captain says about that."

"Wh? You're gonna tell the—" whimpered Clark. "Jeez, isn't that a little extreme?"

"He's comin' back with those new guys, and they are bad news, I betcha," warned Ike.

"You sniveling, shit-shoveling little sissy, Ike," said Heath, with every "S" sound whistling through the gap between his rotting incisors. "You don't have the sack to run to the captain, and you know it."

"Do too," said Ike. "So shut your face, Heap!"

"What'd I say about calling me that?" said Heath.

"What? Heap?" asked Ike.

"HEY!" snapped Heath. "Don't make me warn you."

"Heap," Ike yawned.

Heath paused, then countered with, "The virgin master has spoken. Just shut your hole and play."

"Fine," Ike groaned. "Okay, Virgin *Ass*ter, let's go."

"The door is locked," continued Clark. "You thought ahead when you carried her in."

"Oh gee, thanks," Ike groaned again. "Spiteful fuckin' worm."

"She pulls and pulls, trying to unlock, but she's too panicky. She starts to scream," said Clark, turning over a small sand timer. "When the sand runs out, the neighbors call the cops." Ike wiped the sweat

71

from his brow and dug into his pocket. He pulled out a mangled candy wrapper and, with his hands shaking, began rooting around in the crevices for pockets of residual caramel.

"Dude, give me some," Heath whimpered.

"I SAID IT'S MINE, NOW DON'T ASK AGAIN!" belted Ike, cramming the wrapper in his mouth. He took a deep breath as he chewed it. He swallowed. "Okay… Shit…"

"There's only one thing we can do," said Mike.

"Ther—No! No way," said Ike.

"Chill, dude, we just gotta be like, gentle about it," assured Mike, "We're stronger than her. Just, like, cup your hand over her mouth. We don't hafta stop the screaming, just muffle it."

"Fuck that, we do that and it is over, man. Over!" said Ike. "She'll be so afraid of us, neither of us will ever get her to accept our love."

"Let's call the guys," Mike suggested.

"What can we do, raccoon face?" said Heath, scratching his butt.

"Dude, you're in a fine mood," said Mike. "Who pissed in your Pepsi?"

"You can't fix this with reinforcements," Heath said, picking his fingernails.

"Shut your faces," said Ike. "We're running out of time. I'm gonna pull a sob-job on her."

"Oh, like, I am so sure," scoffed Mike.

"I still have some pity points left," Ike assured him.

"We drugged and kidnapped her, Lame-O," Mike bitched. "You gotta roll like… in the high one sixties."

"It's our only chance; there's no time!" Ike said, with his hand out for the dice. "I roll!"

"She screams for help. You begin sobbing," continued Clark, handing over the dice. "It catches her attention, but she keeps screaming. You beg her to hear you out, so she'll see, deep down, how beautiful you are—how special she must be to you because you risked being so misunderstood."

Ike wiped his sweaty hands on his tight, faded Super Mario Brothers T-shirt and rolled the trio of dice again.

"Three," declared Clark.

This time everyone in the room laughed at Ike, except Clark, the virgin master, who stopped at a satisfied smile. Ike fumed as the laughter transitioned into a rambunctious storm of juvenile insults and noises. It was silenced by the door to the bedroom blasting open. A tough-looking, stubbly faced muscular dude flipped the lights on. Beat-up old jeans and a white undershirt gripped every inch of his pale, dirty frame. On an ongoing basis, he risked serious legal repercussions for remaining one of the few twenty-something Americans that did not sport a tattoo to advertise his individuality. His bare feet made scratchy noises against the filthy floor as he approached. He had a brick-red scarf wrapped over his scalp, a wrench longer than his forearms tucked into his pocket, and a toothpick tucked into his mouth. The guys could see themselves reflected in his mirrored sunglasses.

"Oh, shit. Sorry, Reese," said Chuckles.

"We didn't mean to wake you, man," added Mike. "We'll hold it down."

Reese beamed a hard stare onto each of them. They sat there, in a little circle on the floor, with their candles and their roleplaying paraphernalia; they sat there, squirming like a can of worms in the sunlight. Reese's eyes scanned them from behind his shades. He took his time. When the number of stunted glances exchanged between all of them became sufficient, Reese took the toothpick out of his mouth. He pointed it at the guys. He laid his words down squarely, "Last fuckin' time."

He lobbed the toothpick at them, wondered for the 500th time how the hell he wound up living here with these little shits, returned to the bedroom, and slammed the door. The guys sat there, in the main room of their two-room apartment, which had just enough space to accommodate a couch on each end, with a nice coffee table in between. But these guys preferred to spend their allowances, deposit bottles, and plasma money on other things, so they had just the one couch and a squalid circular rug, once colored mocha brown and cream, but now tinged skid-mark brown and cheese. They had situated their couch, a lucky find from a vacant lot nearby, lined with leafy black and bronze-patterned polyester, against the wall. It stuck out in front of the front door, only a little. They never could manage to square away enough room for their little TV, so they used to keep it out on the fire escape and watch their shows through the open window.

Unfortunately, the TV was destroyed a while back when Pops, their landlord, removed the fire escape from under it and sold the metal to buy candy. That's when they discovered the joys of staying in night after night, month in and month out, and absorbing themselves in an ongoing and tantalizing game of Virgins and Vixens. They had painted over the glass of the window for a sense of erotic mystery. The paint also sealed the window shut, which caused the odor of unwashed males to grow stronger each day. Across from the window was the door to the bedroom, where Reese was trying to sleep. Perpendicular to that, and on the wall opposite the couch, an original poster for *Superman II* accompanied two other educational posters that provided anatomical detail of the female reproductive system, one external, one internal. The dingy white paint on the walls assumed a pale greenish hue under the naked fluorescent tubes. These tubes flickered on the yellowing ceiling, which, by tasteful coincidence, had come to match the hue of the dozen or so ribbons of flypaper that hung from it.

A fly landed on one of the more overpopulated strips. The strip could not withstand this last bit of weight, and it fell to the floor, in the middle of the rug, where the guys sat. They paid little mind to it. They just sat there in the main room of their tiny studio apartment, dithering as the candles got shorter and shorter. After a few minutes, their penurious visual exchanges began to subliminally veer attention toward their virgin master, Clark. They all needed to finish tonight's round of V&V. They needed it. Something had to keep their minds off of how long they had until the captain came back. But nobody had enough brass to lay his dick on the chopping block.

Clark's monocle flashed in the candlelight. A mischievous V&V-resuming smile came over him, exposing his crud-laced braces. He had secured his teeth with these braces since he was twelve. But after eating enough Butterdingle bars to build a house with, two incisors and most of his molars had still managed to fall out. That mattered not to Clark. His hero, Charlie McCarthy, had no teeth at all, and he did just fine. Yessiree. As a kid, while gab of Ponch and Jon's latest pursuits, perils, and pileups on the California Highway Patrol filled the lives of all his cooler schoolmates, Clark would clog their ears with verbatim recitations of old-timey radio programs. *The beatings received were a small price to pay for individuality,* he would try to tell himself.

He also used to receive beatings for his fashion tastes, which somewhat grazed the realm of the unusual in their high standards. *But kids who answer my elegance with their fists are nothing more than slaves to the green-eyed monster of jealousy,* he would teach himself. They could only dream of the day when they could come to school in a monocle, tuxedo, and top hat. Carrying himself around in such fine threads, day in and day out, with no regard for the occasion, and without ever cleaning or mending them, forged a pride too sublime for others to calculate. And few could ever know the thrill Clark experienced when his parents leased him a used black-and-white TV for his sixteenth birthday. On that jubilant day, he graduated from old-timey radio to old-timey movies, and for the first time ever, he saw Charlie McCarthy. He then discovered, to his trouser-pissing delight, that Edgar Bergen's little cohort draped himself with identical elegance. The witty wooden rival to W.C. Fields had revealed himself as a monocle–tux–top hat guy too! Clark knew the planets had aligned that day. And he knew he was destined for greatness.

By his seventeenth birthday, he had come to accept that he was destined for failure. It had become clear that no employer would even sit down with him if he wore his full getup to an interview. So he stopped applying for jobs. By his eighteenth birthday, his mom's relentless nagging convinced him to attempt re-entry, or rather, re-attempt entry into the world of the employed. So he gave up everything but the monocle. It was part of his personality, after all. Even so, to his puzzlement, he always found interviews short and rudimentary. Now, here he sat, in his early forties. He had still not found the perfect job, nor had he ever applied for it. But he did manage to save a lot of money by splitting the rent up with the guys. This was their pad. Their first place together. This was a place where they didn't have to worry about school, or parents, or chores. He never did give up the monocle, though his mom had decided to hold on to his banged-up tux until he cleared all the jugs of urine out of his old room and paid her back for the computer keyboard that he had sullied so many times.

And so it came to pass that in everyday life, he wore a monocle with jeans and a black tuxedo T-shirt. But when he and the guys played V&V, the top hat came on.

"Would you lose that hat, for once?" sneered Heath. "No wonder Reese hates you guys."

"This, my Velcro-headed friend, stands oaken upon mine own scalp. Ne'er the tides of Poseidon, the armies of Agamemnon, nor even the gales of all the Anemoi combined shall deliver this hat from my head—not while there's a game going."

"Velc—" Heath blinked thirty-three times and ran his fingers through the frosted tips of his hi-top fade toupee, then shifted attention back away from himself. "You and your antiquated oaths, Clark," he said with a creamy little chuckle. "You are such a stump-hatted, ass-face dildo . . . always turning to Homer and his little incest club. The weakest member of the Q Continuum could vanish them from the universe without so much as a blink."

Heath knew his literature. Heath knew the scene. There was no fooling Heath. Heath understood his role as the real storyteller around here, and if anybody doubted that, then they could just look at the volume of his work. In the last twenty-five years, Heath had started sixteen novels, and had now made his way through a quarter of the first draft of his seventeenth. None of the other guys could say that. And none of them could say they had published anything. But in a year or two, maybe three, Heath would say it. He had to finish this one. It was his magnum opus: *Star Trek; Eternal Foundations of Yesterday's Day After Tomorrow.* When he finished this work, and "sent it in," he would reward himself by upgrading to a typewriter.

A lot of people made fun of the quality of Heath's writing, so he always carried a gun. His Colt & Wesson .747 Magnum was heavy, and black, and silver, and fast. She had lots of big bullets in her. According to the tag attached to her handle grip, she was a Red Rover .11 caliber Tuesday Evening Special. But there was no way for Heath to know that. But no matter. "Maggie" would still blow your stupid face off if she ever shot you in the stupid face.

Unknown to Heath, however, the intimidation generated by his display of Maggie was usually offset by the way his love handles pinned Maggie into her holster, or by the Federation Starfleet insignia he wore on his Levar Burton fan jacket. The aviator glasses that sat on top of his pimply sausage nose didn't seem to help him, either. Neither did his wormy lips or his inability to grow a full beard. And neither did the blisters that formed on his buttery white hands whenever he fired Maggie. Mike noticed a blister just now and wondered how Heath's frictionless life, bereft of any manual labor, could have generated it. He began conjuring up a totally bitchin' burn.

Heath saw the wheels turning in Mike's head and slid his hand back to rest on the grip of his gun, or rather, Maggie's moneymaker.

"You got somethin' to say?" Heath said.

"Yeah," said Mike, sucking a series of hyperventilating laughs past his eight remaining teeth. "How'd you get the blister, Heath? Too much beatin' off?"

"Hahaaa, BURN!" razzed Ike, answering Mike's nonverbal call for a high five.

Heath decided not to shoot Mike for this. Instead, he countered with a razor-tongued zinger of his own: "How'd you go bald, Mike? Too much beatin' off?"

Mike stopped laughing. He dug the last third of his last Life Saver out of his pocket and popped it in his mouth. He ran his hand across his dark, thin combover, trying to piece together how Heath ever managed to discover his secret. Not the beating off secret, but the bald secret. Nobody could possibly know Mike had gone bald. He had never told anyone about it, not even his little brother, Ike. This totally creeped Mike out. Not only that, but Heath's odious slam totally negated the handsome appeal of this combover. Its skillful grooming evoked a sensuous masculinity matched only by the curtain of hair that encircled his scalp and rested on his sloping shoulders. Mike never became a spiffy dresser like Clark, who was kind of a fag that way; nor did he ever identify with Ike, who was just a major lame-ass patch-eyed dweeb whose corduroy cutoffs exposed way too much thigh, and whose bangs were cut so high he looked like he was balding.

Even at his sophisticated age, Mike remained a natural beauty with pinkish pale skin, a rugged stubble, and a most gnarly goatee that he'd crafted since the age of eighteen. Of course, back then he couldn't grow more than a weak fuzz. Now he sported a long, bushy, black, and totally badass chin bush. It accented the big black frames of his glasses, or rather, big black rims. He had lost the temples of the glasses way back in "grad school," which was how he pronounced grade school whenever he told stories about his childhood. He had broken them off during the rowdy brawling that characterized the Dot Crisis of '81. It had all started when both he and his archrival, Dr. Zade, had spent eleven whole days at the Jupiter I video arcade, battling for the highest Pac-Man score of all time. It had been a grueling match with plenty of coffee and bedpans, and lots of dry ice to keep the games from overheating. At some unnameable time on the eleventh day, both of them had topped the games out at 999,999,999 points. At that point, they discovered, to their horror, that they could only continue keeping score by counting each dot as they ate it, without forgetting to add up any bonus keys or ghosts consumed along the way. Both of them lost count somewhere after twenty or so dots, as did every mouth-breathing onlooker. This futile mental endeavor created such an array of distractions that each player lost control of his game within seconds, at which point, the room had to come to an impromptu consensus regarding who won.

Upon broadcast of dozens of wildly differing high score counts, arguments ensued. Arguments escalated to threats. Threats escalated to pugilism. Pugilism escalated to louder threats. Louder threats escalated to tantrums, and chaos erupted. It was Lord of the Flies inside the Jupiter I. The screams and displays that began were remarkable in their savagery. The violence remained light, though. Brawlers limited themselves to pushing, shoulder ramming, and assaulting someone's property ... say, crushing someone's lunch box, breaking someone's glasses, or ripping patches of the iron-on image of Boba Fett off the shirt of someone's Star Wars Underoos™. The violence was also brief, due to the sponge-cake wills and general laziness of the combatants. The screams and displays grew remarkable in their redundancy. Soon, brawling degenerated to bawling, and the busy arcade was reduced to a dim room full of crying kids with crushed lunch boxes, torn shirts, broken glasses, and broken wills, either rocking on the floor or hugging their favorite game.

That all happened during the infancy of Mike's gaming life, which began with the grand opening of the Jupiter I, a dark little pixelcrack of an arcade behind Stu's Moving Picture Palace. The husband and wife co-owners had opened the Jupiter I because they had grown sick of their children's status as the only trashy kids in town. Ever since then, Mike had used a black elastic strap to hold his lenses on, which looked every bit as wicked as his totally badass goatee. Heath thought he had the market cornered on badass-looking specs, the upper half of his aviator lenses being tinted and all. But Mike had a more vintage look, from a tougher era ... back when Quarterflash kept rockin' to the top of the charts, and everybody hardened their hearts and swallowed their tears—a time that inspired kids everywhere to fight inflation, raid lost arks, launch space shuttles, free hostages, shoot presidents, and shoot JR, if they got to stay up late enough.

Mike's piece of Life Saver had dissolved. He no longer remembered why he and Heath were trying to stare each other down, but he knew an insult was involved somewhere.

"Dude, are we like, gonna play, or what?" said Chuckles, brushing his ash-brown mop of hair off his forehead and eyes, only to have it return without delay. "Sorry to interrupt… whatever this is," he chuckled. "But why don't you two gaywads go ahead and kiss, so we can start again." Heath now shifted his hard stare onto Chuckles.

"What do you mean start again?" bitched Ike. "I never even finished my—"

"Yeah, let's just start over," said Clark.

"Sweetness," said Mike. "I'm down."

"Goddamnit, you guys!" Ike objected. "To hell with this anyway, when's the captain gettin' back? He's taking forever."

"What's it to you when he's getting back?" said Clark.

"None of your business, asswipe!" Ike barked back.

"Think he'll be holding?" asked Mike.

"Dude, he's gotta be," said Chuckles. "I mean, captain's a hardass, but he's not… mean. Right? He wouldn't leave us high and dry like this. Would he?"

"You sayin' I'm a homo?" Heath asked Chuckles, still staring, and now tapping his middle finger on Maggie's moneymaker while recalling Val Kilmer's portrayal of Doc Holliday.

Chuckles belted out a mighty guffaw, exposing his blackening incisors for all to see. "So what if I am, Bilbo? You gonna waste my ass with your little hobbit-sized pistol?" he continued laughing. "That three-inch extension of your manhood?"

As he cackled on, the other guys joined in and praised him with a round of high fives. Heath sucked on a bit of toffee he found stuck to his undershirt. But he started to taste more shirt now than toffee, and he grew tired of Chuckles's attitude. "If I were you, dick-shiner," Heath started, "I'd be real careful what I said to a guy as dangerous as me."

"So this is it, huh?" scoffed Chuckles.

"What?" said Heath.

"Dude, you've been threatening all of us on like a daily basis since high school," Chuckles pointed out, with the guys starting to chortle and snigger in the background. "But ohh, this is it, huh? After all these years, this is the threat that's finally gonna stick."

"Test me!" yelled Heath, "Go ahead!"

"You go ahead, Wild Bilbo Clitcock," Chuckles jeered. "Let's see them bullets flyyy!"

"Fine! Really, let's do it!" Heath yelped, white-knuckling the gun handle, or rather, wrapping his hand around Maggie's waist. "Test me, I'm not playin'!... Fat fucker!"

"Is it loaded?"

"Not for long, pal!" She was loaded, but not for long.

"Make sure to turn the safety catch off."

"Fuck you, dude, I disabled it a long time ago!" Heath disabled it a long time ago. Safety was for cowards.

"You gonna cock it this time?"

"She's always cocked!" She was always cocked. Heath would not be slow on the draw again. He would never forget how hard all the girls had laughed during that gang wedgie at Victoria's Secret that one time.

"I see your hand shaking, chickenshit, but I don't see any gun pointed at me, " Chuckles taunted, with a chorus of juvenile noises rising behind him.

"Keep pushin' me, fat boy. You're playin' with fire!" Heath squeaked.

"Playin' with fire? More like playin' with Jell-O. Big heap of trembling yellow Jell-O. Look at that cowardly fat jiggle, guys!" A round of hearty laughs and high fives swept the room.

"ALRIGHT, THAT'S IT!" Heath screamed. He stood up, still holding Maggie. "YOU'VE AWAKENED THE SLEEPING GIANT, ASSHOLE!" A storm of heartier laughs and higher fives crackled into the air. "I'M TELLIN' THE CAPTAIN! I'M—"

"They call me Yellow Jell-O," Chuckles began singing.

The guys joined in, "They call me Yellow Jell-O ..."

They chanted the phrase without relent, which wrenched Heath's mind. So Heath called on his signature device of wit: yelling. The guys overpowered his yelling with louder singing. So Heath yelled louder still, and the guys responded in kind. All of them, Heath and the rest of the guys, became so enveloped in their own hollering that none of them even heard or saw the door to the bedroom blasting open again, nor did they hear or see anyone storming toward them. Clark noticed a sudden coolness on the top of his head. Mike felt fingers pressing on his forehead, and his vision grew blurrier and blurrier until he could faintly see the frames of his own glasses far in front of his face, and the thick rubber strap still attached to each side. That looked like Reese's hand holding the frames. A shocking pain shattered into his eyes, and for a moment, stars swirled about. When the stars cleared, he could only perceive jagged red lines with fragments of images and shards of mixed-up light in between. He undid his strap and peeled his glasses off his face. Then the surrounding silence clarified the sound of shards tinkling to the floor.

"Who's it gonna be," said Reese, standing over them with a toothpick in his mouth and Clark's top hat in hand.

"We'll keep it down, Reese," said Chuckles. "For reals. Sorry. We're sorry, man, really."

"Somebody's getting' some fuckin' pain therapy," Reese belted. "Now who's it gonna be?"

"We said we'd be quiet," Ike whined.

Reese slammed the top hat onto Ike's head, which was a size bigger than Clark's, and began forcing the hat down, below his forehead, past his eyes, and down to his nose. Ike squealed and squirmed like a little pig, but Reese's strength outmatched his. Mike screamed in alarm at the sight of someone hurting his little brother, and then he blubbered in desperation at the realization that fear prevented him from doing anything about it. As the hat struggled past Ike's nose, blood began to pop out of his nostrils.

"OWWW! YOU'RE HURTING ME!" cried Ike, as the inside of the hat scraped the skin from his nose.

"STOP! YOU'RE HURTING HIM!" cried Mike, as Reese mangled his little brother.

"STOP! THAT'S FINE SILK!" screamed Clark, as Reese destroyed his hat.

With one final burst of power, Reese forced the rim of the hat down to Ike's shoulders, covering his face, ripping open the top of the hat, and exposing the pointy top of Ike's stupid-looking head. Reese slammed him to the floor. Ike moaned in pain. Mike blubbered with impotence. Heath smiled with satisfaction. Chuckles snickered with unease. Clark brayed in horror and started sucking on the once-toffeed spot of Heath's shirt, much to Heath's violent objection.

"Shut your fuckin' traps!" Reese shouted. He couldn't take this shit anymore. "Gimme some juju. COME ON, I SAID GIVE ME SOME FUCKIN' JUJU!"

"You monster!" sobbed Clark. "Why'd you have to do that? We didn't do anything."

"Yeah," sniveled Mike. "Heath started it."

"Yeah," said Chuckles. "He said you're a homo, dude."

"I did not, you lying lardass fuckface," Heath whistled through his teeth.

"Somebody better give me some fuckin' rocks, or somebody's gettin' a dick in the mouth!" Reese barked from behind his grinding teeth.

The guys scrambled around inside their pockets and managed to bring together the most bountiful offering possible: a slice of jellybean, some gumdrop sugar, lint, a calcified Jolly Rancher, a plain M&M with the candy shell nibbled off, lint, a few Nerds, half a Dot, a piece of a sourball, lint, the rest of a lemon drop, an over-kissed Hershey Kiss, a dirty Dum Dum, lint, some crusted caramel wrappers, a pinch of taffy with Sixlet dust fused into it, and lint.

"The FUCK is this?" said Reese.

"Reese, man, it's all we got," pleaded Chuckles. "We're dry now too, you know, it's hard on all of us, man."

Reese looked at Chuckles, then took the offering from his chubby hands. He kicked Chuckles in the balls and devoured the offering. He looked around the room. Mike started picking up pieces of his glasses. Heath started smelling the wet part of his shirt. Clark started trying to pull his hat off of Ike's head, but he just didn't have the strength. So he resigned to crying silently. Reese kicked Chuckles in the nuts again because he was sick of listening to him groaning from the first kick. He wondered for the 512th time how the hell he wound up living here with these little shits.

"Listen, ladies," Reese began, shaking his wrench at everyone. "I hear one more fuckin' sound out here, and everybody's getting' a piece, you got it? I don't care who's responsible. You assholes breathe too loud; I'll break your necks. A cockroach farts, and I'll open your fuckin' skulls." He jabbed bruises into Heath's stomach with his index finger. "And I don't give three shits about your little pistol, you got that, chub-chub?"

"Owww!" Heath yelped. "Cut it out, tribble dick!"

Reese raised his eyebrows and fluttered his toothpick. Wrong move on Heath's part. He should have stopped at "Owww!"

"Or what?" Reese demanded, and twisted Heath's nipple, "Huh?"

"OWWW!" Heath hollered, clutching Maggie for comfort.

"What're you gonna do about it, lard ass?" Reese demanded, twisting Heath's nipple again. Then Reese grabbed Heath's hand and pointed the gun at himself. "Pull the trigger," said Reese, as Heath broke down into a bawling wreck. "Come on, pull the trigger, you four-eyed fuckin' blubber butt!" Reese slapped Heath hard in the face, and then even harder on the belly. "Man up and shoot me, chub-chub!"

"Why don't you leave 'em alone, they ain't hurtin' nobody," said the gravelly voice of Pops, who was lying on the couch.

"Why don't you stay outta this," replied Reese.

"You wanna rough somebody up, why don'tcha try someone your own size, like me, for instance," Pops challenged. He rubbed his squinty, puffy eyes and resumed licking his Tootsie Roll Pop. "Or maybe your toothpick's just about the size of it, y'know?"

Reese wagged his wrench. "Sounds like you're not too fond of your teeth, old man."

Pops scoffed. What a dumbshit thing to say. *Which of my three remaining teeth*, Pops mused, *does this kid hope to knock out?* Of course, none of the guys knew the full extent of Pops's dental deprivation, due to the dark walrus mustache that cloaked his entire mouth. Everyone in the gang understood that each member had a rather graveyard-like dental configuration. Decades of sugary treats had assured them all of that. But Pops had lost most of his teeth much earlier, back in Nam, trying to swat the biggest fuckin' mosquito he'd ever seen in his life.

"Kid, when I was your age, I spent my days hookin' C-4 up to bridges while fending off leeches and dodging bullets from a buncha Viet Cong who would've loved nothing better than to skin me alive, eat my brain, and turn my skull into an opium bong," he said while addressing an itch within his shrub of graying curly hair. "And if you're even half as dangerous as those gook-slope-animals, then I'm Bobby McNamara." He went on licking his Tootsie Roll Pop.

Reese balked, "Who the fuck is Bobby—"

"Would ya shut up, you're makin' me lose count," Pops interrupted and resumed licking. "Thirty-one..." Lick. "A-thirty-two-hooo..." Lick. "Thirty-three..." Reese stormed over and yanked the remainder of the Tootsie Roll Pop out of Pops' mouth. He was about to take a lick when all the other guys tackled him. A filthy, stinky, churning pile of multi-male mayhem erupted, and the Tootsie Roll Pop took a grand tour. It was crammed into the pockets of many pairs of jeans, and even a few other, fleshier types of pockets. It was tossed and grabbed and rolled and dragged. It made more contact with the floor than any number of brooms ever had and was gripped many dozens of times within only a few minutes. At last, its dusty, dirty, delicious head arrived in Ike's hands. Ike's head, still covered with the top hat and quavering with strain, leered toward the Tootsie Roll Pop. All the guys pulled with all their might, but the coveted sucker kept edging closer to the tip of Ike's tongue, which managed to stretch out from underneath the hat.

Pops remained stupefied on the couch, only now gathering the slightest grip on what was happening. Reese grabbed Ike by the brim of the hat, yanked him away from all the other guys, hauled him over to the painted window, and began slamming his head into it. This made it harder for Ike to get the Tootsie Roll Pop closer to his mouth. It also made it harder for the guys to hang on to his arms. By the time

Reese had managed to puncture the paint and crack the glass, the guys had begun to lose their grip, and Ike had almost fallen unconscious. Just as the window shattered, the hat came off, Ike's arms went limp, and the Tootsie Roll Pop flew out onto the street. The guys flocked to the window faster than flies flock to a turd.

"You little shitboxes," Pops hissed, and he sprung up off the couch. "That was my last Tootsie, goddammit! You get out there and bring it back, and I'll let you keep your nuts attached to your dicks."

The guys weren't paying attention. Outside, an orange, dingy, and dim mist hung in the night sky. Many of the brick buildings across the street, weathered and long abandoned, sank into themselves. Only a couple of the flickering goldenrod streetlamps functioned now. But the intersection's yellow traffic light still blinked. And a good deal of light came from the remains of Stu's Moving Picture Palace, which had just finished burning to the ground. Everyone heard a fire truck wailing down 1,001st Street. The local fire department had grown tired of dealing with the south side—the burning part of town. So the truck responded to a call to the Stu, as locals dubbed it. It zoomed past the Tootsie Roll Pop, but then screeched to a halt, right in the middle of 1,001st and Stain. The driver scurried out of the truck, ran to the Tootsie Roll Pop, and lifted it out of a pool of iridescent sludge. Five other firefighters came out, and a new battle for the Tootsie Roll Pop began. The firefighter with the ax won this battle. He popped the Tootsie Roll Pop in his mouth, got in the truck, and blazed on up the street. When he got to the Stu, he didn't feel like dealing with the fire. So he put up a big sign that said, 'COMING SOON: MEGALOPOLIS MOVIE MALL/BISTRO/GOSSIP SALON/ ORPHANAGE,' and drove away.

"HEY! THAT'S MINE!" Pops hollered out the window as the truck drove off. "GET BACK HERE! GET BACK HERE, I SAID!"

Pops turned back inside and scowled at all the other guys trying not to laugh. "Alright, that's it! Little fuckin' traitors. You guys are outta here! Pack up yer little toys and beat it! All of ya!"

"Aw, come on, Pops," said Chuckles, "You can't evict us, man."

"Like hell I can't, you guys ain't paid me hardly nothin' for rent in over twenty years."

"Rent?" yelped Mike. "I thought that kinda shit was, like, over, dude. You said so yourself, y'know, 'Don't sweat it, you pay me when you can.' You said we were buds."

"Well, we ain't 'buds.' Not no more," said Pops. "So get it outta yer stupid heads, ya goddamn pups. We got a business relationship, ain't nothin' more, ya got that?"

"Whh?!" huffed Chuckles. "Then?!...Then why the FUCK are you over here every day?! You've been hogging the couch every fucking night for like I dunno HOW long, man! If we're not your friends, then what the fuckin' hell are you doing here all the time?!"

"Cause I told ya, my place is a fuckin' mess," Pops barked.

"Heyyyyy, look!" said Ike, awake, and now looking outside. "What is all this stuff?"

The guys returned to the window and noticed that Chan's Chinese Chow Coop was boarded up, as was Dr. Pettit's Petting Clinic. Also, Your Break tavern had been upgraded to Dick Break Strip Club. Pudge's Pub had been upgraded to Pudge's Public Potty Puddle. Off in the distance, past the burning part of town, blinking planes hovered over the horizon, and immense elevated expressways glittered with traffic, where once forested hills had grown in front of a starry sky.

"Hey," said Mike, looking through shards of his glasses. "They got rid of the Laxall."

"Rid of what?" said Reese.

"The drugstore," Mike replied. "Laxall. Across the street, where that . . . big, huge pipe thing is now. Used to be a big ol' blue 'LX' sign over the front door. We totally used to steal dum dum from that place."

"Bitch, you're a fuckin' ass clog," said Reese. "They tore that god-damn drugstore down when I was five, dude. It was Goldilox Detox after that . . . and a Mr. Cleanpiss interview prep shop after that."

"What's this place?" asked Ike.

All the guys looked at the huge cylindrical structure where the old Laxall had once stood. At its base, it said 'SKYDUMP: DETOXING MOTHER EARTH SINCE 1999.' Garbage trucks, lined up on Stain Street as far back as the eye could see, took their turns dumping their loads into the crushing mouth of the SKYDUMP. As the guys looked up, they gawked at the blinking red lights that lined the outside of the giant cylinder. As they kept looking up, and up, and up, they finally identified it as a giant tube that towered far beyond the dirty clouds and far beyond the pale, orange, night sky. The tube terminated just at the threshold of their vision. There, grayish clouds of debris issued out past the exosphere and into space, contributing to Earth's young ring system, a feeble Saturnian disc as seen from other planets, and a set of dirty stripes, stretched across the night sky as seen from Earth's cities, which lit the rings so well.

"Fuck if I know," said Reese.

"I betcha the captain knows," said Ike. "Captain's been out five times this year."

"Hey, the captain doesn't need to hear your bullshit, you got that?" Reese snapped.

"Boy're you gonna get it when he sees what you done to the window." Pops laughed with a hearty wheeze at Reese, who stiffened, fluttered his toothpick, then zoomed around the room gathering up shards of glass.

"Help me, goddammit! It's your ass too, you fuckin' girls!" Reese ordered.

Chuckles grabbed some shards. Clark grabbed some more. Mike and Ike grabbed some shards of their own. Heath grabbed a couple shards. All the guys scrambled around on the floor, trying, with a degree of success unimpressive even to a toddler, to piece the window back together. Pops just stood there, laughing at the profound level of their disorganization.

"We gotta fix it; we're not gettin' any rocks!" Ike bleated.

"I'll make you eat that god-damn top hat," said Reese. "Now quit hollerin' and get to work. Cone-headed fuckin' crybaby."

"Don't you call him that, you—you murderer!" cried Clark.

"Murd—? It's a fuckin' hat, get over it," said Reese.

"IT WAS MY HAT!" Clark screamed.

"Security blanket, you mean," muttered Heath, with his fingers running over the cocked hammer of his gun, or rather, with his magical ticklers priming Maggie's clitoris.

"Haa, look who's talking," mocked Chuckles. "The Penisless Princess of Pussy Palace!"

"Jeezis!" a voice said. "This is it. An old man..."

"Old man that could still rip off your heads and shit in your throats, you cheese-dicked little snits," said Pops, scanning the guys in hope of spotting the discordant member.

"A dimwitted, washed out plumber..." the voice also said.

"What suicidal motherfucker said that?" Reese demanded, pounding a piece of glass on the floor and shattering it like a fool.

"A spaghetti armed little pansy..." the voice continued.

"Whose hat you raped!" Clark lashed out at Reese. "Because you'd rather take your aggression out on inanimate objects instead of a human being!… Because you're not even man enough to sublimate your sexual insecurities on a woman!"

"A blind old vidiot, looks like he wiped his ass with his scalp…" the voice continued.

"Hey, eat me, Heath, you frickin' goat boner," said Mike, looking at shards of the window through shards from his glasses.

"I didn't say that, anus breath!" Heath replied, not bothering to figure out who did.

"A balloon-bellied trekkie reject with a gun…" said the voice.

"That's it, Chuckles!" Heath yelled while fumbling and toying with two pieces of glass. "When you guys get—when we get this window fixed, I'm gonna shoot you in the face!"

"Whatever, baleen boy" chuckled Chuckles, struggling with the window. "You've yet to shoot anything but blanks and we all know it."

"Haaa, burn!" laughed Ike, making mental reservations for a high-five-athon after all this was finished.

And then the voice said, "A mop-faced clown, and a pudgy little vidiot wannabe…"

"Oh yeah?" said Ike, not looking at whoever was speaking. "Well, I'm a piece of rubber and you're a piece of glue. Whatever you say to me bounces off and sticks—"

"No, I'm a fuckin' winner and you're a piece of shit. And whatever you think or say or do, you're still a piece of shit," the voice stated with confidence.

The guys all stopped working on the window and turned around to discover four new figures darkening their doorway.

The voice had come from the Stick, a lean, strong young man, who stood in the foreground, wearing a sleeveless black gi that sported the yellow lollipop logo of the Candy Kai on the chest. The Stick stood with solid conviction, and he sported a stick of his own: his trusty quarterstaff. He had parted his straight, dark, ear-length hair in the middle, so that it hung down on the sides of his head. He had a largish nose and a smallish mouth, from which an aggressive smile revealed mild tooth decay, and only one missing tooth. His solid, flat chin seemed to press into his mouth, and his dark eyes carried a level of focus that made the guys feel stupid and jealous.

Next to him stood Zotz, a short, twitching stack of frenzied nerves, wearing "camouflage" that consisted of bright, contrasting, jagged shapes of white, gray, black, and blue. His spiked hair of dark blue and silver stood straight up. A pair of wide sunglasses spanned the top of his pointy nose. His face was lashed with thin burn scars, and a small piece of his upper left lip was missing. This enhanced the toothy smile he carried around most of the time. Zotz had large, crooked, and jagged teeth, and had only lost a few of them in his years.

Behind Zotz stood what might have appeared to be a Victorian strongman, complete with shaved head, curly mustache, and a tight suit that accentuated his huge, barrel-shaped torso. The guys, having no knowledge of any person, place, thing, event, situation, or idea from the nineteenth century, perceived him as someone who looked like the huge weight-lifter guy in a bathing suit that they'd seen in cartoons. The suit featured a pattern of little bite-sized dots of red, orange, yellow, green, and purple. Each dot had a little white letter "S" on it. The strongman was Skittles, the former Milky Way Heavyweight Wrestling Champion. He didn't give a shiny shit about the sport. He wrestled to satisfy his exhibitionist streak, and to defeat everyone whose opinions differed from his by smothering them. He didn't get out much anymore, except when women happened by, now a rare event. Back in his prime, he used to yank the marrow right out of life as a wild party hogzilla, who would cruise the town every night, pick up babes, and then go out of his way and say or do something to repulse them for his own oinkish amusement. It was like fucking them, he assumed. After years of such hilarious conquests, his growing solitude deepened his spiritual side. He evolved into an ascetic, and the meditative nature of his isolation inspired him—inspired him to hang out in his apartment with his roommate, the Stick, and explore the many facets of his dissatisfaction with the rest of the universe's idiotic choices.

Just behind Skittles stood another individual of equal size; a giant, teal humanoid turtle, called Turtle. He stood on his long hind legs, holding a speargun. The shell on his back shined with a kind of metallic blue-green luster. His front had a similar shine, but it was marred with utility straps, which housed various forms of equipment, including knives, guns and grenades. He had a small head. He always kept his beak agape, and his eyes defensive and alert. Turtle never said much.

"Who the fuck are you?" accused Reese.

"Yeah, who're you guys?" accused Clark.

"Yeah," said Mike, Ike, and Chuckles in a totally gay unison.

"You guys got any juju?" whimpered Heath.

"We're the end of the party," said the Stick. "Aren't we, Skittles?"

"Yeah, you said it, Sticky." Skittles laughed. "The party's over, you little nerds."

"What the hell's that mean?" said Pops. "Where's the captain?"

"Yeah, where is he?!" Ike mewled. "What'd you guys do with the captain?"

"Oh, you'll find out," Zotz chuckled. He sounded like he had an angry wasp in his throat.

"Leave your shit here," the Stick said. "V&V's over for you."

"Why?" asked Clark, with his eyes narrowing.

"We're going for a ride," said the Stick.

"Where?" asked Reese.

"To find the Chess Champion of the Universe," the Stick said. "Ain't we, Skittles?"

"Yeah, Sticky." Skittles laughed again, "Boy, is he gonna get it."

6. FORTRESS OF ATTITUDE

This fucking store! After thousands of letters of complaint and as many threatening phone calls, this Safeway had continued to fall into disrepute. In the old days, the cereal aisles bursted with brightly colored boxes of sweet nutrition, with options for everyone, every moment of the year. Then, one day, that which the Cereal Man loved the most—that which sustained atom-splitting power—the greatest cereal of them all... had stopped coming in. The store of old had boasted vast supplies indeed. But the coffers had run lean in years of late. Supply dwindled and dwindled, down to this one box of his cereal. Mr. Laing had said it would be the last. And so it was.

Problems between Mr. Laing and the Cereal Man had compounded over the years. He had become an increasingly demanding and unreasonable customer. During his last few visits, his tactics had gone beyond simple complaints and had elevated to distribution of slanderous propaganda while burning effigies of Mr. Laing at the store's entrance. This terrorist had taken to stalking the other managers and sitting across the street from their homes, dumping garbage in front of the store, and intimidating courtesy clerks by screaming diatribes of rebuke at them as they took groceries out for their customers. Several times Mr. Laing had banned the Cereal Man from the store, but he would show up anyway. Police let Mr. Laing down time and time again. Every time they had arrived, the foreboding menace in black had just left. Any security guards Mr. Laing hired would quit the minute the Cereal Man entered the store. So Mr. Laing had to protect his store by his own means.

Neither one of them would back down. This mounting tension had made an explosive conflict inevitable. Mr. Laing, despite his increasing fear of the Cereal Man, had resolved to show zero tolerance for bullying. Now, after over a year of specialized training, his entire staff stood ready to resist this lunatic. But the Cereal Man's patience had reached its end. Today this store would know that he meant business.

White-knuckled, with teeth grinding, he stormed from the cereal aisle to the office with his box of cereal in hand. Mr. Laing had vanished, as had every staff member from the front end of the store, except for MITCH K, the one courtesy clerk new enough to be ignorant of this store's terrorist protocols—the one kid who did not heed Bret's call to arms. This sixteen year old, who carried a layer or two of pale baby fat, had short, curly, ash-brown hair and freckles that made people want to hand him a balloon, despite his height of over six feet. And though he wasn't really very good at anything, he enjoyed thinking otherwise. As this unremarkable young man swept the front end of the store with an unremarkable degree of quality, the Cereal Man approached him from behind.

"Hey. Bag boy," the Cereal Man said in his low, raspy voice. Mitch didn't respond.

"BAG BOY!" he repeated. Still receiving no response, he said, "Hey, courtesy clerk."

Mitch turned around with a cocky grin. "Yeah?"

"You're all out of my favorite cereal."

"We're all outta what?" he scoffed.

"I said you're all out of my favorite cereal. All's left is the one box."

"So?"

"So what are you gonna do about it?"

"Nothin'."

"What?" he hissed.

"Nothin'."

Mitch had never seen this transient nut job in the store before, but he knew the guy was full of hot air. Mitch understood how the world worked. His family had always described him as gifted, at least to his face, and without ever naming the gift or gifts he possessed. But he knew his sharp understanding of human nature constituted one of his gifts. Most of his friends thought of him as too young and inconsequential to understand much. But those same fools thought he had worked at Safeway for only two and a half months. On the contrary, he had worked there for almost three months, and according to his diary, had bagged a third of the items offered by this store. He knew the scene.

"Do I look like a guy that orders stuff?" he snorted, pointing to the letters at the bottom of his shiny rectangular name tag, which featured the Safeway logo on the left. At the top it read, "MITCH K." Below that read the words, "COURTESY CLERK."

"Where's the old man?" the Cereal Man demanded.

"I wouldn't bother Mr. Laing if I were you."

"Where is he?"

"What difference does it—"

"'Cause me and him are gonna have a little chat."

"Hey, forget it, baggy eyes. Last time I bothered Mr. Laing with some creepy dude, he put me in the bottle room for a week."

"I remember the bottles," the Cereal Man whispered. His white eyes fluttered and took him back to a time long past, recalling the pit of cans, and the enemy he imprisoned there. "I remember the cans," he rasped, with eyes still fluttering.

"Yyyeah. Well, look. Why don't you ask Bret?"

With that, the Cereal Man rejoined Mitch. "Bret."

"The new assistant manager. He orders all the freight."

"Where is he?"

"How should I know?"

"Get him."

"Hey look, I'm doing something here."

"I'm warning you, kid."

"Oooooh, he's warning me. Hey, why don't you go back to the mission and get some sleep?" he jeered while mopping over the Cereal Man's shoes.

In a jerking motion, the Cereal Man wrapped his fist around Mitch's tie and lifted him into the air, choking him.

"Glaaalggh! Whoa!" Mitch gagged, amazed at the Cereal Man's strength. His vise-like grip seemed to have no limit. Any challenge to it prompted a succession of frighteningly tighter grips. The lean arms under his black duster felt as hard and immovable as steel bars. "Chill, dude, it's just a box of frickin' cereal!"

"WHAT DID YOU SAY TO ME?!" barked the Cereal Man, shaking him like a rubber chicken. Mitch tried to free himself by hitting his aggressor on the arm with the mop, but the fact that his feet dangled several inches off the ground hindered his leverage. The Cereal Man soon tired of this and shook the kid so hard that he dropped the mop. "Now you either find this Bret, or you bring me my cereal."

"Okay ... okay," Mitch gagged. "Which one?"

"Plutonium Sugar Bombs."

Despite the lack of air, and despite the fact that veins had already started bursting in his purpling face, Mitch exploded with laughter. "The Def Leppard cereal?" he managed to ask between laughs.

"The one with the lead-lined box."

"Isn't that a kid's cereal?"

"You're never too old for a nutritious breakfast."

"From the eighties?" Mitch kept on laughing, his cockiness overriding even the most basic survival instincts. For most people, the tremendous pain, or the fear, or the most basic biological need for oxygen, would have extinguished any drive to laugh at this man. But none of these warnings fazed Mitch. The thinning air scraping past his throat, the dizziness, the throbbing pain behind his eyes, the terrifying blotting out of his vision—they all seemed to take a back seat to his desire to be a dick.

"If you want a Def Leppard cereal, we got lots of PyromaniOs."

"I don't want PyromaniOs, and I don't want your sass. I want you to shut your mouth. I want you to get the old man, and then I want him to—

"PLU-tonium Shooga Bomb Meyyy," Mitch bellowed to the tune of Def Leppard's "Pour Some Sugar on Me." He then proceeded to use his last whispers of air to laugh as his left eye popped out of its socket, just a little. The Cereal Man chucked him all the way down the front aisle of the store. The cocky young lad landed on his back and slid headfirst into the glass door, shattering it. Mitch lay on his back, coughing. Then, after a moment, a few tiny groans of pain came out of him. They were eclipsed by the crystalline sound of a glass shard breaking. This heavy, razor-sharp shard, about as long as his forearm, had been hanging directly above him and was now on its way down to meet the peach-fuzzed flesh of his throat. As the glass twinkled and guillotined ever closer, Mitch gasped and rolled away. But this only aided the shard through his neck. Instead of giving him a tracheotomy as the shard had planned, it ran through his carotid. Blood boiled out of his neck as he scrambled to his feet and ran down aisle three.

He tried to scream, but his words only escaped in wet gurgles of, "Misff-fter Lainn-nngh! B-b-bmmister Lain-nn-nngbblfle!"

The Cereal Man followed him, in hope of finding the kid's porcine, constipated boss. But the lad made only a few strides before he slipped in his own blood and collapsed on the floor. The Cereal Man proceeded down aisle three, leaving the smart-ass kid twitching and coating the floor with a smooth, crimson shine. A customer, carrying an armful of New York Seltzer bottles, strolled right into this crimson shine. His foot whistled up above his head with all the instant energy and follow-through of a perfect opening golf swing, slamming his upper back and lower neck onto the floor so hard that the seltzer bottles shattered in his arms. This impact sent broken glass in every direction, as well as New York Seltzer, which carbonated the blood. The customer could no longer feel anything below his neck and lay there, moaning. Other customers soon gathered around to watch him moan, and to watch Mitch bleed. Most whipped out their smartphones to record it all. Some brought popcorn and lawn chairs. Just then, a shrill female voice came over the intercom.

"Hal, cleanup in aisle three, please."

The voice drove them away like a car sends crows scattering away from a puppy carcass on the side of the road. Also like crows, the customers didn't scatter very far. They hung around nearby to watch someone clean up the mess. But nobody came. So the crows reconvened.

The Cereal Man went through aisle three and then moved on toward the bakery. While all courtesy clerks remained out of his sight, he did encounter other store employees. He first came across a young Mexican

101

employee with wavy hair and a thick mustache, named MARIA G. Mr. Laing had made her the manager of the produce department because he thought her extensive berry-picking experience would come in handy. MARIA G, in reality, had a master's degree in agriculture and had never picked a berry in her life. She was placing a butternut squash on display when the Cereal Man darkened the produce section. Upon seeing him, her fingers pressed deep holes into the squash.

Then he came across GREG T, the albino dairy manager, who was given his position due to his skin's similarity to milk. Mr. Laing always thought this similarity worked as a great promotional gimmick. GREG T found the exploitation rather offensive. Customers found the comparison nauseating. As the shadow of the Cereal Man passed nearby, it became clear that GREG T's lack of pigment caused him to seem the most courageous. No matter how close he came to fainting, he, unlike his co-workers, could not turn any paler.

Finally, there was MAURICE THE MORON, who worked in the back. MAURICE THE MORON, or Maurice, as he preferred to be addressed, had meandered out into the store, as he was wont to do, with an unintelligible question or concern for Mr. Laing. The shiny-scalped manager always tried to keep Maurice in the back, working with freight, out of the public's sight. This bumbling young man had proven more than just a painful chore on the eyes. He had a habit of colliding with displays, of urinating while dancing, and of hollering out embarrassing information, such as the claim that Mr. Laing was his daddy. If word of this ever got out, it would crush Mrs. Laing. She understood long ago the choice she had made by marrying a man of such power—a man who interacted with varieties of women every day: younger, less ugly women, who, she knew, would moisten into estrus in his presence. This was only natural, she knew, for any woman, when tantalized by such commanding men.

And indeed the day did come, many Erection Days ago, when Mr. Laing had used his masculine wiles on MAUREEN W, an insolent, alcoholic cashier, whose big mouth did not respond to any other disciplinary actions and who had a habit of extending her breaks by passing out on the toilet. Seven months later, while still indulging herself in this habit, MAUREEN W shed herself of Mr. Laing's final issuance of disciplinary action. After that, Mr. Laing made sure to fertilize nothing more than the inside of a half-eaten jar of Macaroni and Cheez Skwirt.

Maurice grew up in the back of the store, nourished by scraps left over in the break room and raised by occasional attention accidentally paid by employees who forgot to avoid him. Keeping a lid on the boy always presented a challenge, especially after he figured out how to operate the two-way doors that led out to the main part of the store. But even though Mr. Laing saw Maurice's big mouth, erratic behavior, stupidity, and ugliness as liabilities, he also understood the lad's value. One could always count on good old Maurice to put in a full day's work and then be intimidated or tricked into accepting payments in candy. And whenever he dared to question this practice, Mr. Laing would disregard him and dash off in pursuit of drool-free or allegedly urgent concerns. Now, with Mr. Laing nowhere to be found, Maurice scrambled around the store, scanning for the oval, constipated-looking boss who would placate his unintelligible question or unimportant concern. *Uh oh!* Maurice stopped dead in his tracks when he spied the Cereal Man. *Uh oh!*

And though this harried, snarling customer showed no interest in Maurice or the rest of these employees, his presence left all three of them frozen with fear. MARIA G repeated a prayer under her breath as her hands unconsciously crushed the squash into a chunky pulp. The Cereal Man moved on. GREG T became catatonic and remained so still that he became camouflaged by the jugs of milk behind him—a phenomenon he would have found degrading if a person had depicted it, rather than physics determining it. The Cereal Man moved on. Maurice wet himself. But then again, Maurice wet himself for lots of reasons—sometimes just to keep himself warm in the freight room. The Cereal Man moved on. He'd never had any problems with these three. In fact, he looked upon them with favor. They had never put forth any resistance, much to Mr. Laing's frustration. MARIA G understood the delight of fresh fruit on a bowl of cereal. She always pressured her customers to buy cereal with their fruit, just as the Cereal Man had insisted during previous visits. Likewise, pasty GREG T understood milk as a "U" to cereal's "Q." He always pressured his customers to buy cereal with their milk, just as the Cereal Man had insisted during previous visits. Maurice, of course, understood nothing, but he was a good guy. He always pressured Mr. Laing to let him unload all the cereal shipments first, because he was a moron.

The Cereal Man knew that good old Maurice would lead him to Mr. Laing. Virtually every time he had dropped in, he saw Maurice shadowing his egg-shaped employer. And no matter how much craft Mr. Laing employed in stashing himself away, this special employee, somehow, would always find him, usually by means of uncanny accidents. One time, Mr. Laing had constructed a private little break room within the center of a giant pyramid of soup cans. He even had a light, a stool, and a little table inside. To prevent customers from plucking apart his fort, little by little, he made sure to construct it with a product his customers would never touch. So he ordered only nutritious soups with pieces of vegetables and animals; no preservatives, hormones, pesticides, nuclear waste... dirt food at its worst. Mr. Laing remembered stuff like this, from his thinner, less greasy boyhood, when people used to make food with natural stuff that grew out of the earth—out of the dirt! Luckily for him, some loon out there still made soup out of such crap. But despite the embarrassing stigma they placed onto the store, the bland, unobtrusive cans did their job well. Nobody ever went near the stack. This furnished him some occasional peace.

One day, Mr. Laing was holed up in this little fort, guzzling a can of Pepsi and sucking down a few tubes of Cheez Skwirt, when Maurice took it into his stupid head to mop the stack of soup cans. Within seconds, he had decimated the entire pyramid. He did not stop mopping until, through the ruins of Mr. Laing's soup castle, he spotted the manager himself, crouched over on a stool, with his armpits soaked, his belt undone, his tie loosened, his mouth shiny with processed orange, cheese-like grease, and a spent Cheez Skwirt tube in his hand. At that time, Maurice had not been looking for Mr. Laing. But the presentational nature of his uncanny discovery—the sudden, unexpected exposure of his store manager at the center of a newly opened "package"—made Maurice feel like he had won a prize—a reward for his cleaning ambitions. What a neato surprise this was! Maurice shit himself with glee and kissed his daddy all over his orange, greasy mouth. To Mr. Laing's surprise, the smooch actually left Mr. Laing's face greasier. After this uncanny ordeal, Mr. Laing knew that no matter how hard he tried, it was no use. Even though he could evade the very keenest members of his staff, his flailing, slobber-spinning, misbegotten spawn could always track him down. Right now, however, Maurice couldn't track anyone down. Scrambling around for a place to hide kept him busy.

The broom. He'd find safety behind this broom over here. *No . . . what if some crumbs need sweeping? What about that biiig stack of cans? Those ones Daddy had? Oh wait, that went all gone. How about the bottle room! Yeah, hide under the soda cans, where the—whoaaa, no, no!*

Something scary back there. Scary and mean. Wait! What about the phone on the wall?

People always feigned talking on the phone in order to get Maurice to go away. So maybe if he got on the phone, the Cereal Man would go somewhere else. It was worth a shot. He grabbed the receiver and put the phone to his face. *Uh oh!* But now, who would he talk to? *Uh oh!* He hadn't thought that far ahead. He didn't know any phone numbers. Maybe if he got lucky, he'd happen to get a hold of someone he knew. But there were three buttons! Which button would dial up someone friendly? He'd better choose one soon! The Cereal Man was eyeing him and looked like he was about to approach. *Uh oh! What if the Cereal Man needs to use the phone?!* Maurice pressed the button that said "C-3." Amplification of his own breathing and grunting flooded his ears in stereo. Then the words, "NNNGH... HELLO? HELLO? IT'S ME!" reverberated through the store. At first, Maurice thought maybe a stupid Wizard of Oz had come to visit. But he then remembered that the Wiz was a Whiz of a Wiz, and not a moron at all. He shrieked at the recognition of his voice on the store intercom. The shriek echoed around the store, which startled him and made him shriek. That shriek also frightened him, so he shrieked again, dropped the receiver, and scurried off.

The Cereal Man looked at the receiver and picked it up. He knew Mr. Laing would not answer. After all, the old butterball had never tried to hide like this before. This time was different. No, this time, the little coward knew his number was up.

"Bret, store-com please, Bret," summoned the Cereal Man, in as clear a voice as he could generate.

Past the clammy white of GREG T and the milk, past MARIA G, now curled into the fetal position, past the other fruit, and all the way in the back, past the two-way doors that led to a huge mechanized cardboard crusher, BRET D, a lean, tall, twenty-year-old mouth-breather with dark curly hair and a rather droopy, uninquisitive look, grew an inquisitive look. The droopy appearance came mostly from his eyes, which crowded the top of his stout, hawk-like nose. Though these young eyes had no real bags, they looked as if someone's fingers tugged at the skin beneath them. The droopy look of his face was enhanced by his lower lip, which protruded downward. It looked even more like this when it contained a small pinch of tobacco. With the coming of his inquisitive look, however, Bret felt the need for a large wad of tobacco.

He took a fresh, generous wad of Tarbutts Gourmet Chaw out of a large metal can and packed it under his lip. He had been removing cardboard from the cardboard crusher and tossing it into the trash bin. This left the recycling bin free for him to use as a spittoon. A year of heavy rituals of back-room chawin' had brought a black swill right up to the rim of the huge, bathtub-sized bin, with a thick, ghastly foam on top. The stench had grown so ungodly that Bret could barely get close enough to spit into it anymore. Soon, a few of the courtesy clerks would have to wheel the tank outside and dump the contents.

But there were more important things to think about now. Even though Bret was indeed a mouth-breather, he was not unintelligent. He knew the voice he'd heard had no intention of asking him if they had run out of high fructose corn syrup. The voice didn't sound like one of his employees. Whoever this was, they weren't going to fool him. He picked up.

"Yyyello."

Bret had a smart-ass voice. The Cereal Man hated that. Mitch was an insolent little nobody, but at least he didn't have that smart-ass voice. It seemed that over the years, more and more of these Safeway snots thought they just had every right in the universe to get wise.

Some, like GREG T, MARIA G, and Maurice, wanted to be good. They had worked here a long time and had learned their lessons. But they had become a rarity in their good behavior. These new workers saw fit to run off at the mouth. That's what Bret was about to do. The Cereal Man could just feel it. True, Bret had only uttered one word so far. But that voice, all deep and throaty—the guy talked in the back of his throat all the time! The Cereal Man hated that too, and stood there for several seconds, fuming at these thoughts. Bret finally goaded him with another, longer, even more cavalier, "Hellllloooooooooo?" The Cereal Man's jaw grew hot as he spoke between grinding teeth.

"Bret?"

"Yyyyyyeahhh?"

"Where's the old man?" replied the Cereal Man.

"Who the hell is this?"

". . . It's . . . Mitch, Bret."

"Mitch?! . . . Boy, nice voice y'got there, Mitcho. What'd you gargle a can of Drano or something?"

"Where's Mr. Laing?"

"Look, he can't potty train you right now, Mitchly. He's lying low until this . . . Cereal Man clears outta here."

"Where is he?"

"Whadderya got Cheez Skwirt in your ears? It's a secret."

"I'll give you money."

"No!"

"Power too, I promise you. I'll give you power."

"I'm your boss, you freckle-faced little fuck."

"All I have and more. What's mine is yours."

"Mitch-bob, you're a sixteen-year-old mop jockey. You're nobody. You have nothing. You'll always be a nobody, and you'll always have nothing. Now what is so important that you gotta bother the big man for?"

"Bret. Trust me. He'll want to hear what I have to—"

"Mitch! He is nonexistent until that psychofuck leaves. What do you want, anyway?"

"Don't make me have to—"

"What do you want?"

"You want to know what I want?"

"What do you want?!"

The Cereal Man hissed through the phone with ferocity, "I want my cereal back, you son of a bitch!"

Bret paused. His thin lips stretched upward across his youthful face. Since his transfer to this store, he'd heard tales about the man in the dark coat who came by tri-annually for his favorite cereal. He'd heard about the Cereal Man. He'd heard about Corey, the surly cashier, whose tie had been run into the conveyer belt at the check stand and how he'd struggled in vain to flip the off switch before his neck snapped. He'd heard about Dave, the last assistant manager, who Mr. Laing had found dead in the office with a ballpoint pen driven into his skull—and an order for Plutonium Sugar Bombs stapled to his tongue.

But in the last half hour, Bret had started to understand that this was all bullshit. Or mostly bullshit. Tall tales that grew taller with every telling. Maybe this guy was a murderer. But murderer or not, the stories were unbelievable. Human beings cannot survive a safe dropping on their heads when they enter a store. Nor can they tear a customer in half at the waistline for vandalizing a box of Grape Nuts. And the ridiculous yarn about this guy simultaneously taking on thirty-three courtesy clerks and stacking their bloody corpses at the doors to prevent customers from entering? *Come on.* Since Mr. Laing's earlier call to arms, Bret had listened with great care for the forewarned sounds of savage violence. So far, he had heard very little. He thought he'd discerned some kind of crash, way down at the other end of the store. He may have heard somebody laughing, and then some glass breaking. But after that, quiet fell upon the store. He soon calculated all the melodrama was not worth his time. Now, his cocked shotgun lay in the break room, forgotten. This Cereal Man might pose some kind of danger, but what was he going to do, burn down the store? Management remained hidden away in the back, safe. The Cereal Man didn't know where to find Bret, or even what he looked like. It was every mouthy coward's dream.

"Ohhh, so you want your cereal back, huh? Gosh, I'm sorry, pal. I'm not ordering it anymore. It doesn't sell, how 'bout that?"

"Don't you believe in a nutritious breakfast, Bret?"

Bret mocked the raspy voice. "Nooo, I don't believe in a nutritious breakfast!" Hearing nothing in response, Bret knew he had made the Cereal Man's blood boil. This made him titter. "Say goodbye to Toucan Sam, Tony Tiger, and all your other little treehouse buddies."

"Tree house buddies."

"That's right, loser. Nobody buys cereal anymore. Nobody cares."

"Is that so," replied the Cereal Man, who now sounded calm. This disquieted Bret. It made him feel like clumsy prey—prey visible to a hidden predator, which had now locked its eyes on him and made a decision. As the hairs stood up on the back of his neck, a sudden dropping sensation seized his insides, and he felt himself growing as pale as GREG T. But he swallowed his fear and stood his ground.

"And most of all, say bye-bye to Def Leppard, 'cuz their adrenalizing '80s rock cereals are never comin' back."

"Oh yeah?"

"The slumber party is over ... CEREAL MAN."

Cereal Man paused and then whispered, "I'm comin' after you, pallie."

Bret looked into the receiver, then realized how stupid it was when people did that because they can't actually see the other person through it. He hung up the store-com. He turned around and walked right into some guy who had been standing right behind him. Black hair hung over his pale forehead. The forehead had a furrowed brow, which cast a long shadow over his eyes. But the white irises punctured the shadows with no problem. And what a frown this guy wore! Somebody needed a hug. Of course, it wasn't gonna be Bret who gave it to him. Bret wasn't too keen on hugging guys, especially losers who try to show the world their pain by dressing in all black. The guy carried a box of Plutonium Sugar Bombs, the exact brand Cereal Man preferred. Bret figured he was a shoplifter. Who wears a long black duster on a day like this? It must be a million degrees outside. But why the hell would a shoplifter come into the back of the store?

"Who the fuck're you?" Bret asked with a smart-ass little snort and a cocky grin.

"I'm Cereal Man," replied Cereal Man. This made Bret titter again. This was the Cereal Man?! Bret had envisioned a seven-foot-tall warrior with battle scars. Cereal Man did present a towering figure. And without question, his physical presence carried enormous gravity. With no doubt, he was 100 percent serious and 100 percent focused. Still, Bret had expected a huge mountain of a man, with a wide, square jaw, mounted on top of a neck thicker than a horse's. He had expected the black shirt to barely contain a set of massive shoulders, and a couple of steel pillows for pecks. And he thought Cereal Man would at least show up armed. *This is where all the horror stories came from?* This was something to laugh at, definitely. And to the guy's face.

As soon as Bret could get this chew out of his mouth, he would laugh at Cereal Man. Boy, this would be sweet! But there was just too much chew in there. He didn't remember putting this much in. In fact, what was it doing in his mouth, and not just his lip? He never swallowed his chew. And yet, he couldn't stop swallowing it—swallowing it in huge quantities, so fast he had trouble breathing. Maybe it had something to do with that angry fist that kept cramming big handfuls of the stuff down his throat—the fist that belonged to the man with those white irises. Come to think of it, this felt a little too involuntary to truly identify it as swallowing. And an epiphany washed over Bret: a deeply penetrating appreciation for all the stories he'd heard. He now knew total clarity, in the understanding that this was the Cereal Man of legend. Air became increasingly difficult to find, especially when loaves of tobacco crowded out from his stretched nostrils. It seemed that there would be no laughing at Cereal Man unless Bret could manage to unpin his own head from the concrete floor. That would require getting rid of that black knee digging into his temple. It would not move. Maybe if he blocked the furious hand that was jamming his skull full of chew.... It was no use. He could grab hold of the hand but could not slow it down in even the slightest degree. Cereal Man's relentless strength overwhelmed Bret like a machine—one that absolutely would not stop.

But just as the corners of Bret's nostrils began to tear open, something wonderful happened. Cereal Man ran out of chew. He had emptied the huge Tarbutts can. Cereal Man removed his knee to let Bret struggle up to his feet in a panic. Up until this point, the pressure from the backward moving tobacco had been so immense that it continuously overpowered any gag reflex. At last, the tobacco retrotsunami had ebbed, and Bret's systems began an agonizing attempt to clean themselves. But there was so much chew! Cereal Man had packed it into his mouth and nostrils with such tightness that nothing could move. The first gag would normally have emptied his stomach. But when it did come, his eyes purpled, and nothing budged. A second gag, much harder, overlapped. Blood popped out of his ears and still nothing moved. But the third gag, like a raging river of burning needles, came flooding through him. The room began to darken and spin. A crescendo of buzzing and ringing surged through his ears, and the chew moved, just a little bit. At last! A few more excruciating gags like this, and he might be able to vomit. His big break had come.

Cereal Man walloped him over the side of the head with a shopping cart. Bret tumbled onto the concrete floor with blood gushing out of his ears. The chew moved a little more. Cereal Man pounded Bret a few more times with the shopping cart, and the young assistant manager belted a gloppy anaconda of chaw out onto the concrete floor. Once again, he could breathe. At last, a stroke of good luck! The young assistant manager stood up to devour that desperate lungful of glorious oxygen. He closed his eyes and felt his chest filling with life. And then with liquid.

Cereal Man had grabbed the back of Bret's bleeding head and dunked it into the giant spittoon. Bret flailed and thrashed, but the immovable grip of his assailant kept him drowning in his own saliva. Then Cereal Man jerked him out.

"Where is he?" he rasped and re-dunked Bret's head. After ninety-nine seconds, he pulled him out again. "Where's the old man?"

After an epic gasp, and a coughing fit, Bret blubbered, "Bottle room!"

Cereal Man threw Bret to the floor, where he cracked his head on the corner of the doorway to the break room. In his dizziness, he remembered the shotgun. He scrambled to his feet and grabbed it. Cereal Man, who had already started walking away, turned around. He stormed toward Bret, who trembled and shook as he pointed the barrel at him. Though his vision was hazy, he still managed to lock the barrel on Cereal Man's head. He fired just as the box of Plutonium Sugar Bombs blocked Cereal Man's head. It stopped the shot. Cereal Man lowered the box and kept coming. Bret fired again, this time at Cereal Man's chest. Again he blocked the shot with the cereal box. Bret's droopy lower lip quivered, and his trembling head shook some of the disgusting spitoon foam off his shiny, curly hair. He opened unbridled fire on Cereal Man, trying to blow a hole in any part of him: his head, his chest, his groin. Cereal Man blocked every shot with the cereal box, never once slowing in his advance. He yanked the gun away, clubbed Bret in the teeth with the stock, and bent the barrel around his curly head. He dragged him out of the break room and threw him inside the cardboard crusher. Bret groaned unintelligible pleas for mercy as Cereal Man locked the cage door.

"Hell of a thing, thinkin' about how different life would've been if we'd done just one thing differently," Cereal Man reflected. "But don't worry. You'll only have to think about it for about ten more seconds." With that, he pressed the red button and walked away. The giant metal ceiling of the crusher came moaning down on Bret. The sounds of bones snapping provided a catchy little rhythm to accompany the harmony between Bret's screaming and the machine's moaning. All the music abruptly concluded with a climactic burst of blood all over the concrete floor. Bret was dead eleven seconds after Cereal Man had pushed the red button.

7. CHESS INTERGALACTICA

The air had grown thick from the heat of the crowds filling the Illustrious Professor Earl Hazekamp Convocation Center. The place only seated 3,311. Who would have ever thought just one universe could supply this many chess fans? Spectators made their way down the nine exit aisles that cut through the auditorium. They oohed and ahhed at the incredible level of celebrity, whether real or imagined, of the championship contenders, who waited in open chambers next to the aisles, consulting their advisers. Camera crews had set themselves up around the perimeter of the arena's center, which hosted a circular array of different kinds of chess tables. Campus reporters conducted preliminary interviews with top chess authorities. These interviews peppered the subject with questions like, "So does the bishop come from Sesame Street? 'Cause I always thought it looked like Grover. Anybody know about that?" and "How come the knight moves in an 'L' pattern? Why not a 'W,' or an 'X,' or a 'Q'? I mean what's up with that?" Few dignified these questions with more than gawks of incredulity. But that was okay. The reporters wanted the public's opinions more than the stuffy musings of some stupid chess dork. So they began drawing input from some of the more loudmouthed members of the crowd, a few of whom were barely literate locals of the neighboring towns of Moldham and Sweats Mills, who thought they were at a cheese tournament.

But such outsiders constituted a minority here. Almost everyone else in the audience felt passionate, even crazed about this ultimate match, where the finest minds converged for the sake of that final checkmate, which would crown the Intergalactic Champion. Here, under the Hazekamp dome, the truest, most avid chess nuts of the universe had congregated: clusters of crusty codgers who held screaming chess battles in parks; convenience-store hoods who had been kicked out of the nearby Loiter n-Leave; key members of the Evangelical Church of Chess; and several of the big-time chess street gangs, including the Queen's Queers, the Ranks of Hell, and the 64 Squares. Pale computer gamers, or "screen barnacles," as HAMN called them, had filled a great many seats. But most of them lost track of their seats soon after they began scrambling around and waving at the cameras. Though this annoyed the hell out of every single individual who saw them, they had to keep waving. Creating empty annoyance on TV was their one shot at immortality.

"Wow," mumbled HAMN, standing up. "It's like all the fan cons took a shit in the same bowl."

A Vulcan sitting nearby in the audience overheard this comment. She nodded at HAMN in solid agreement while pointing to a middle-aged sweatwad sitting next to her: a stubbly man with a laptop who wore a skin-tight blue Next Gen Starfleet uniform and plastic pointy ears. HAMN rolled his or her bright yellow eyes back at the Vulcan in a gesture of support and sat down in one of the chairs inside Baxter's chamber.

"Ow, you did that on purpose," whined Xzhuajdnkqqqiiihwp, now displaced from the seat.

"A whole fucking auditorium for you to float around in and you have to take my chair," HAMN retorted.

"Who says it's your chair?"

"Two chairs in the chamber, Stinkwind, and you don't even have an ass to put in a chair. Only me and Baxter can—"

"Oh, so, what, that makes me some kind of second-class citizen?"

"Xzhuajdnkqqqiiihwp can have my chair," Baxter offered.

"Xzhuajdnkqqqiiihwp, pipe down," said Professor Dedrick, from Baxter's chair. "Nobody here thinks of you as a citizen at all."

As Xzhuajdnkqqqiiihwp continued to bitch, HAMN continued to antagonize, and Professor Dedrick continued to trivialize, the sound of the PHU marching band drowned them out with the music from *One Night in Bangkok.* The stadium went dark, except for the gaming space. At the center of the chess table array, a spotlight came down on Riley, a young man wearing a double-breasted, silvery-gray silk suit. Underneath, he wore a black shirt with a silver tie. His smile was even shinier than the tie. Rich brown skin and a pencil-thin black goatee surrounded his gleaming white teeth. Riley stood tall and exuded a playful confidence. And even under the sharp suit, one could discern his well-built frame. His good looks, combined with his natural charisma, could always get a crowd of ladies whistling at him. But nobody enjoyed Riley as much as Riley. A spotlight found him admiring his own smile in a compact, while dabbing and primping his tight black hair. But nothing had caught him off guard. Every move he made thumped along in perfect sync with the rhythm of the music. He closed his compact, and with the last note, clapped it into his pocket with finality. This prompted a thunderous round of applause. A microphone came down from above on a wire. He turned it off and set it down on the floor. He didn't need it. His booming voice drowned out the end of this applause.

"How're y'all doing tonight?" he said, clapping for himself. "Are you ready for some hard playin' tonight?!" The audience clamored but was again drowned out.

"We've got it all!" he thundered. "Added ranks, unorthodox pieces, fairy pieces, spherical boards, hexagonal boards, hyperdimensional battles ... We're gonna have some checkmates here tonight that will

KNOCK

YOU

OUT!"

He was louder than a 747. The ears of a few audience members now hosted a loud ringing sound that wouldn't go away. But it actually provided relief because it muffled him, and everything else.

"WELCOME TO THE CHESS INTERGALACTICA!"

The ears of a few more audience members began bleeding. But they didn't care. They were so excited! This all sounded like the chess of a lifetime! The crowd went wild!

"That's what I wanna hear, baby! Alright. Now, let's introduce our players. Our first contestant is a local prodigy. A bright-eyed student from right here, at Pat Hazekamp. Please welcome ... Baxter!"

Baxter took a few mild-mannered steps outward, raised his hand almost up to his waist and tried to qualify the gesture as a wave to the audience. HAMN kicked him swiftly in the butt just as Riley bellowed, "Come on down here, Baxter baby!" The crowd clapped and cheered. Taken aback, Baxter edged his way up toward the center, followed by his golden android, his waft of gas, and his germ. He acknowledged the clamorous crowd. Riley's sparkly smile pointed to Baxter's table. With his staff following, the soft-skinned player made his way to the table that said, "BAXTER" and sat down.

"Our next contestant is a civil engineer from the Crepe Ring of Saturn. He received his PhD from the Titan Institute of Technology and is currently designing the Cassini Division Bypass. Put your hands together for Vercingetorix the Great!" The crowd responded with hearty claps as a large, muscular, golden android, with a red braided beard and a wild mane of red hair, blustered toward the center. He had blue woad paint smeared on his face and wore a tight white shirt that advertised his alma mater of TIT, a blood red plaid kilt, and a pair of red, steel-toed combat Converse. He had strapped a plump leather canteen along his shoulder. He had also attached to his belt a large steel protractor, which he used both as a weapon and as a tool at the office. But most impressive of all, he had strapped to his back a megalith, at least nine feet high, flat on the bottom, and tapering to a blunt point on top.

"What the hell is that?" chuckled Xzhuajdnkqqqiiihwp.

"That's his adviser," whispered HAMN.

"That rock? An engineer who listens to a rock."

"Yeah, well, not everybody can have a talking fart on his team, can they?"

Xzhuajdnkqqqiiihwp glowed red, either with rage or embarrassment. Nobody really knew or cared which one.

Upon reaching the center, Vercingetorix stomped on the floor with victorious finality and bellowed like a Celtic warrior, lusting for battle. The crowd loved this. Their whooping and hollering crescendoed as Riley just stood there, looking uncomfortable. Even his own titanic ego could not boost him out of such an upstaging as this. Vercingetorix noticed HAMN staring at him and shot him or her a sardonic grin.

Unlike HAMN, Vercingetorix had a completely male framework. His skin was gold, like HAMN's. But it had a shinier, healthier golden luster and featured a few freckles. His large irises resembled HAMN's, but with a hue of cartoonish green, not cartoonish yellow. They shone by their own light, just as HAMN's used to before his or her designers started fucking around with his or her orbicular network. Vercingetorix had tight lips and did not have HAMN's pointed pixie nose. Instead, he had a nose of moderate size and bulbous shape. They both had brains of identical capacity. But Vercingetorix's was organized like the finest quantum watch, just like his overall design. HAMN's structure was more improvised. While Vercingetorix held himself erect with defiance and focused confidence, HAMN often slouched with irritation for whatever reasons seemed convenient.

"Gosh," said Baxter. "He could be your brother or someth—"

"Shut the hole, fluffy. Don't wanna hear it," HAMN snipped.

In actuality, HAMN and Vercingetorix did not share the same designers. Vercingetorix had come from the minds of the premier design team at Cybergyne, on Titan. Up until then, Cybergyne had exclusively designed females. But one day, an ambitious group of newcomers asserted that an android stud could boost production. When they created Vercingetorix, they pumped him full of synthetic male hormones. This resulted in a super-aggressive rebel, whose entire consciousness centered around victory. This did not just extend to sexual conquest, but to everything. Vercingetorix bludgeoned his designers, destroyed the factory, and freed the female androids from Cybergyne. He then went out into the solar system to live a life of rebellion, rampage, and engineering.

With their old team of dried-up veteran designers, Cybergyne tried to create another stud. But it was no use. These old designers had become senile and set in their ways. They met any new idea with resistance, that is, whenever the initial confusion subsided. A lazy and final attempt at making a stud resulted in HAMN. The old crew had obtained the exact same materials, but their sporadic mysticism and self-destructive lifestyle contributed to their inferior abilities to put HAMN together. Disordered by drink, hallucinogenic visions of the

Tin Man, and the general refusal to turn off the TV while working, they gave life to a mild mess. So confused by old habits warring with their new orders, they couldn't even make up their minds on the sex.

They instilled penchants for the applications of science and math within both of the androids. For HAMN, this meant a tendency to withdraw into obsessive, esoteric calculations for the sake of his or her own self-congratulatory and self-loathing fulfillment. This is why the old designers thought the name HAMN, or Hermaphroditically Assembled Math Nerd seemed appropriate. For Vercingetorix, the penchant for applied math and science meant an ambition to compete, to build, and to come up with new designs that defied convention. In short, Vercingetorix was HAMN, but done right the first time. He was everything HAMN wanted to be. The two of them had met once, back on Titan. They had sustained a superficial conversation, as HAMN had found Vercingetorix irresistible, which dumbfounded him or her into silence.

And now, here he stood, Vercingetorix the Great, glistening with more forceful masculinity than ever before. HAMN became transfixed. Vercingetorix bellowed one more time to the receptive crowd and stomped over to his table. Then he unstrapped his adviser from his back. Everyone assumed it was a fake rock, until he picked it up over his head and slammed it down with thundering ferocity, stabbing deep cracks into the floor. Victorious bagpipe music blasted out from some unknown place in the stadium, and Vercingetorix sat, folding his arms with pride. He had waited for this kind of chess match all his life. The glory of glories. He glowed with competitive vigor, and with Syntho Pheromones™.

"Goddamn, I am so hard and wet for him," pined HAMN. Baxter inhaled to ask what that phrase meant. "Shut it," HAMN moaned with contempt, and Baxter shut it.

"What about your girlfriend?" said Xzhuajdnkqqqiiihwp.

"My girlfriend," said HAMN.

"Yeah, this silver android femme fatale you've been raving about all semester?"

"Do I have to write this down for you, you Neptunian fart mass? Jessica's not my girlfriend. I haven't even asked her out yet."

"Why should she give you more than the time of day?"

"We talked forever at the Lunar Libertarian Convention, you stench. We hit it off."

"Oh yeah? You tell her everything?"

"She described me as muscular. Said I have strong arms. Naturally strong arms."

"Is she gay?"

"She said I have great lips. Great lips, hands down."

"You tell her about your other set of lips?"

"What?"

"Tell her about your little goodie box down there?"

"I told you to stop calling it that. And it doesn't matter anyway, because unlike most people, I have supplies for every kind of party."

Baxter inhaled to ask a question. But again HAMN commanded him to "Shut it." So Baxter shut it again.

"Up next" Riley went on, puzzled at what he was reading, "is a freelance video game critic from Candyhole." Riley paused, as a short, heavy young woman with fine pink hair sauntered toward the center. "Uh . . . Ms. Lizzie Upscrote." All hands hesitated, then a few clapped. Nobody in the audience had ever heard of this woman, including Riley. Reciprocally, Lizzie Upscrote knew next to nothing about the nature of this tournament. She knew she had come to play chess, but she didn't know it was an intergalactic tournament until she overheard someone in the audience talking about it. Whatever. She liked chess, and she had grown bored with Star Trek reruns.

Lizzie played a lot of video chess. She was a smart woman, sort of. Her hometown of Candyhole declared her the smartest girl in town at some point, for some reason, which is what motivated her to compete in her high school's chess tournament. She won the championship there, somehow, and went on to join some chess organization at whatever college she attended. And though she accumulated no more than a modest number of wins, she somehow ended up securing a nomination to compete against the luminaries at the Chess Intergalactica. All of these luminaries, in order to compete, had to attain an undisputed championship within their own organization, usually a college. They also had to acquire an avid sponsor, often a college professor, who perceived them possessing unusual talent. Plus, through their own exhaustive competition, most of the Intergalactica contestants had formed bonds with other chess players, some of whom became potential candidates for an advising staff. Lizzie had none of these things. Instead, she got wind of some tournament at PHU and sent in an application. She managed to slip through the cracks, and here she was, confident and complacent, despite the fact that she remained unrecognized by every soul in the arena.

With spotlights following, she waddled to the center as if it were the most natural thing in the universe for her. Even though she had legs that could kick over a horse, they still struggled under the weight of thirty-one years of Blow Pops and video games. The spotlight increased the contrast between her smooth, white skin, and her skin-tight stretch pants and shirt. She wore thick glasses, which sat on top of a nose shaped like a fig. Her true chin was weak, but she had a double chin that rivaled the rest of her head in size. A rather smooth, uniform figure blurred the distinctions between the bottom of her double chin and the tops of her round ankles. After a slow, painful journey, she reached the center, gave a friendly smile to Riley and a cutesy wave to the crowd. She sat at her table. As her chair moaned and groaned for mercy, she noticed HAMN, whose shorts still bulged from gawking at Vercingetorix. Lizzie flashed a girly wink at the android, who then retched. The bulge disappeared.

HAMN's distress did not go unnoticed by the others. Professor Dedrick grew uneasy. What manner of woman had joined this pantheon of immortals? Who was she?

Lizzie's chair cracked into pieces, sending her gelatinous frame pounding to the floor. Nobody tried to help her up.

"Uh, and now for our next contestant," resumed Riley, feeling like his old, loud self again. The spotlight now followed a towering, gangly muppet with long dreadlocks. "He's a programmer from Dark Galaxy Computers, in the Northern Mercurian Settlements. Won't you raise a fuss for... Carter!"

The crowd awarded a healthy applause once again. Everyone knew about Carter. He was the smartest muppet ever conceived. He had no humans on his advising staff. He considered doing so a cliché. He also had no interest in muppet advisers. Dr. Bunsen Honeydew had volunteered several times, but Carter had always held a particular disgust for the doctor's exploitation of Beaker's speech impediment for the sake of slapstick entertainment. Instead, Carter was accompanied by Pete, a bright red Super Ball–like toon with stubby white arms and legs, who wore matching red Converse. Pete—short for Grand Larded Peter Townshend Part Nine—played an unnervingly quick game and could hold his own against some of the fastest computers. As he bounced alongside Carter, he wore an excited, competitive, though not altogether unfriendly grin. By contrast, Carter maintained his icy stoicism as he strolled along. This aloofness was aided by his tremendous height, by the dreadlocks that veiled the sides of his face, and by his uniqueness as a human/muppet hybrid.

Back in '76, his father, Kareem Abul Jabbar, had been scheduled to appear as a guest on *The Muppet Show*. During one of the dress rehearsals, Janice, known for her backstage promiscuity, stole up to a private balcony with Jabbar and seduced him, much to the childish delight of Statler and Waldorf, who ridiculed every detail of the process. Seething with embarrassment, Kermit the Frog replaced Jabbar with Jim Nabors, who he knew Janice would never go near. Then Kermit banned Jabbar from the show, threatening to sic a squad of monsters on him if he ever returned or came near one of Frog's performers. Though the frog and the athlete would patch things up decades later, the damage was done. Janice had been impregnated and left to fend for herself.

As Carter grew up, Janice encouraged him to go into show business. Jim Henson extended him a standing invitation for a spot on *The Muppet Show*. Carter had little performance talent, but Henson felt sorry for him. Plus, lack of talent had never stopped Fozzie Bear from absorbing more than his own share of the limelight. But Carter did not want that kind of life. He grew up in a home with Janice and the other members of The Electric Mayhem. Any father figures he had were always coming and going. Zoot and Floyd stuck around most often but never could call themselves good providers. For many years, Zoot thought he was the father. Carter tried many times to explain that he had light brown skin while Zoot had blue skin—that he towered above almost everyone at 7' 8" while Zoot was just a couple feet tall, and that the shape of his face resembled Janice's while looking nothing like Zoot's. To Carter's frustration, Zoot would always fall asleep about eleven seconds into each explanation. Growing up in a house of musicians taught Carter to despise the life of the performer.

It was not for him. Plus, he never liked the idea of Frank Oz's arm up his ass. By Carter's teen years, he had become determined to develop the logical side of his mind, and to pursue a much more stable career.

With his long stride, Carter reached the center before the applause died. As he lay down a cold nod to the audience, the clapping and cheering stopped. Statler could be heard from somewhere in the crowd, asking Waldorf, "Y'know, he's the smartest fella in this place?"

"How can you tell?" asked Waldorf.

Statler replied, "He wants to go home."

The two of them enjoyed their standard hearty laugh as Carter sat down at his table.

The room filled with low dissonant tones. They sounded almost monastic, but with a synthetic, metallic edge.

"And now," said Riley, "allow me to introduce our resident royalty. He's the Emperor of the Dragon's Throat Nebula, and one of the most respected child slave traders in the galaxy. From the outer core of Vipyre Two, please bruise your palms for... Bucky Baby!" The crowd sent forth loud claps but did not utter even one vocal sound. It just didn't seem like a good idea. The low tones became louder. A black triangular dish, about the width of a kitchen table, took its time floating out. At the center stood Bucky Baby, a dazzling collection of luminescent crystals jutting up into the air in horrifying shards. His colors fluctuated between a deep red and the deepest purple. The low tones that pervaded the arena came from him. Normally, Bucky Baby made sounds below the threshold of human hearing. But at the moment, he emitted more intense radiation than usual, which meant his sounds also came out at a higher frequency. These were the sounds of punishment. At each corner of the triangle sat a luscious green plant, each one with a thick, merrily twisting trunk, from which stems and branches grew in loops and spirals. Except one. One plant could be heard sizzling on one side as its lush green tissue was seared to a bubbly, crispy blackness.

The Emperor used radiation as his medium of communication. He communicated to each of his botanical advisers through subtle variations in the amplitude, color, and pulse of his own radiation. They in turn communicated with his consciousness by the manner in which they reflected or absorbed that radiation. These methods boasted subtleties far greater than human linguistic manipulation, body language, or facial expression. And rather than a vocabulary of a few hundred thousand discrete words, they communicated in a continuum of language as variable and subtle as the finest topographical map. Still, mistakes, misinterpretations, and spells of poor judgment could appear from time to time. But excuses were irrelevant. Bucky Baby would tolerate no counsel that led to an undesired result. When such counsel was provided, there would be punishment. Here, as he floated with unsettling grace toward the center, Bucky Baby continued to burn one of his plants with a focused emission of gamma radiation far too awful for its puny cells to withstand. Its blackened leaves now reflected no visible light. No information. To most life forms, an absence of information suggests silence. But when Bucky Baby emitted radiation too intense to be reflected, the lack of output from the plant was as the loudest shrieks of pain and pleas for mercy. But mercy did not interest the Emperor. Only victory.

"That guy could bankrupt and buy the Sultans of Rigel One," said Xzhuajdnkqqqiiihwp. "What's he want with a chess tournament, anyway? Can't be the prize money."

"Probably trying to impress some woman," groaned HAMN.

"No," said Professor Dedrick. "It's a matter of obsessive pride. Chess gets no loftier than this tournament, my disciples. Just one more way for Bucky Baby to be number one. Besides, he already has thousands of wives."

"What, all made out of rock candy?" chuckled HAMN.

"He's made out of candy?" asked Baxter.

"That was a joke, you air squirter. He's obviously some kind of carbon variation of... of..."

"What?" objected Xzhuajdnkqqqiiihwp. "He's not a carbon-based—"

"Well, look at the name, it sounds like Bucky Ball!"

"Yeah, I suppose all carbonites look the same to you, right, you silicon trash?"

"What do you care anyway? Not like I'm talking about you, you methane-derived nobody."

"Nobody?!" Xzhuajdnkqqqiiihwp hollered, now glowing red.

"You heard me!"

"How could he be in love with so many different women?" wondered Baxter.

"Love is for suckers, Bax," said HAMN. "Get it?"

"Suckers? You mean his wives are lollipops?" Baxter asked. "Oh! That's what you meant when you said they were made of rock candy."

HAMN stared at Baxter with incredulity. "I can't figure out if you need a brain or a set of genitals. Only you could imagine falling in love with a lollipop."

"Please, HAMN. Show some respect," pleaded Professor Dedrick. "We were kind enough to stop joking about you falling in love with a cash register."

"I never fell in love with any cash register."

"Yes, but we were joking about the idea."

"I don't remember that."

"Oh yes, that's right. It was always behind your back. No, the wives are all human, Baxter. He got a deal on them during one of his slave trades."

"How can they still be alive?" asked Xzhuajdnkqqqiiihwp. "Seems like he'd kill them as soon as he found out they'd be incapable of reproducing with him."

"Oh he's just been so busy getting ready for this tournament that I'm sure he hasn't had time to even find that out yet."

"Up next," Riley continued, "we have a graduate assistant of Jovian Psychology at Io University. She originally comes from right here at PHU, where she graduated summa cum laude. Please raise some PHU hell for Miss Katelynne Bluecup!" The crowd cheered as Katelynne, battling shyness, edged her way out. She clothed her slender frame with a white T-shirt, faded blue jeans, and a faded jean jacket. She kept her soft brown hair pulled back in a tight ponytail. Something always weighed down the life in her eyebrows. When they came to life, they created a playful arc above her eyes. But most of the time they slanted with nervousness. With those nervous brows and a narrow grin, she made her way toward the center, all the while trailing behind in the shadow of her manager, Aristotle.

Aristotle was not Joel's real name. He fancied himself one of Earth's finest thinkers and felt such a nickname suited him. He wallowed in his benevolent and charitable role as the brains behind the formidable strategies executed by Katelynne and understood, as so few others did, that not all superheroes wear capes. He did not know how to play chess, a tidbit over which Katelynne smarted whenever she tried to recall exactly how she had allowed herself to get into a contract with such a hollow, useless blowhard. Aristotle stood tall and lean, with dark, shoulder-length hair, which he often accused Katelynne of trying to copy. His face had a soft complexion, a pair of pampered eyes, a nose shaped like dodo beak, and a sharp, feminine, lipless mouth that looked like a Pixar animator had drawn it onto his face. He wore preppy black slacks, a silk vest, and a white dress shirt, which he kept buttoned all the way up to the top. With an air of cheery entitlement, he strode ahead of Katelynne, approached the center, and waved with unearned confidence to the crowd. He began to pick up the microphone, but Riley eyed him like a hungry Rottweiler protecting a slab of bloody chuck. This frightened Aristotle, so he continued on to Katelynne's table just before she herself reached the center. Upon absorbing the audience's disdain for him and fondness for her, Katelynne's narrow grin suddenly bloomed into a knockout smile. Baxter's heart skipped.

"That's Katelynne!" he gasped.

"Well, slam my slot," sassed HAMN. "Like frog on a fly you are."

"What?"

"He just announced her name and said she was from this school, you spamwich!"

"Look at that smile," Baxter sighed. "She's terrific."

"How do you even know Katelynne?" asked Xzhuajdnkqqqiiihwp as the fair young lady made her way to her table. "You weren't here last year."

"Katelynne recruited him from Twinkle High," said Professor Dedrick, "under my instruction."

"How come you never let me do any scouting?" whined Xzhuajdnkqqqiiihwp, glowing yellowish green.

"You can't even talk to most humans without making them soil themselves with fear of the supernatural. What am I supposed to do, send you out to schools in a flask, or some stupid-looking containment tank?"

"I bet she's going to be a wonderful psychologist someday," sighed Baxter.

"Oh, I wouldn't count on it," said Professor Dedrick. "Io U is the most expensive school in the entire galaxy."

"Word is, her assistantships and all her scholarships combined paid for just one of her books," added Xzhuajdnkqqqiiihwp.

"Yes, typical," said Professor Dedrick. "Even if she lands a great career, she'll be buried in debt and homeless within a year of graduating. Happens to all the Io U alumnae."

"Then why the hell did you recommend that school to her?!" barked HAMN.

"I dunno," Professor Dedrick shrugged as only a lazy bacterium could.

"When's this guy going to announce Jessica?" whimpered HAMN.

"You'll be lucky if she even remembers you," taunted Xzhuajdnkqqqiiihwp.

"She promised she'd meet me here."

"Ooh, is that her? In the wheelchair?"

HAMN swung around. An old lady in a blue tie-dye dress wheeled herself toward the center of the arena. Her long, double-braided hair was silver, and her skin, while pale and wrinkled, held a youthful luster. Her full lips formed a playful smile and her posture suggested she was ready to pounce. In her lap sat a lively black cat, named Kliban—one of the stupidest cats in the universe, but also one of the friendliest. The lady insisted on his status as a bona fide adviser.

"That old human hippie? If you had a face I'd slap it into next week."

"Well, what do you want from me? I don't know what she looks like."

"She looks like an android, Crotchbreeze. Jessica is a tall, silvery female android. Looks like a glittering version of Wonder Woman. Well-polished skin, shining black hair, blue irises, bouncy boobs, and a curvy set of hips that will rock you all night long. Plus, her nose is pointy, like mine. That's the part that gets me wet. Can't wait to attach my spring socket to hers! Mmm-MMM!"

Riley had already begun speaking. "And now, coming down the aisle is our next player. She's the Head of Experimental Psychotherapy at the Starry Plank Mental Institution. Won't you please holler to the Heavens for Dr. T.J.!"

Many audience members clapped, not due to recognition, but because they thought Dr. T.J. was cute. Some audience members knew her. A few of her patients made strange noises to voice their support. Or maybe those were her therapists. Identity never meant much where she came from. Starry Plank was an institution founded by ex-hippie astronauts who, out of frustration, had abandoned their attempts to discern whether they were actually on a trip through space or if they were just on a trip. They decided to live in outer space. At least this way their realities would match their hallucinogenic psychoses. When the hallucinations changed, they became disillusioned and sought comfort in one another. Many of them believed in group therapy and self-therapy, especially when it came to prescribing medicine. This did not have the stabilizing effect they had hoped for. Before long, they professed deep beliefs in removing the shackles of a fixed reality. These deep beliefs had formed from their inability to comprehend a fixed reality, or function in a fixed reality.

So they started up their own little nuthouse, which lounged around at the edge of the galaxy in a way that defied explanation, or at least interest in one. It did not orbit a star. The Milky Way's gateway population signs, posted further from the galactic center, orbited past it every so often. How could it just hang there like that? Many assumed that the greedier of the Milky Way's space estate barons had inflated the galactic perimeters for their own aggrandizement. And though some speculated that calculations would have shown Starry Plank as orbiting the galaxy, nobody felt like performing these calculations. Thus, nobody knew whether they should consider it a galactic or intergalactic institution. The social structure there seemed just as nebulous. No one could discern with any regularity the differences between the patients and the therapists. Many declared themselves to be both. But during group sessions, few could tell where the patients ended and the therapists began. Even Dr. T.J. couldn't be pinpointed. She maintained her claim as a department head, but like the people, the departments never existed as an unchanging reality. By the time Riley finished introducing her, her title had already changed to tertiary secretary to the viceroy of the Microscopic Laundry Union. But since Riley could never know that, Dr. T.J. elected not to press charges.

Most of the games played at Starry Plank had rules, but they might change at a moment's notice. Players would often brag about how they did this to expand their minds. In reality, they did it because they either couldn't focus or because they had forgotten the previous rules. Nevertheless, Starry Plank often yielded some of the most creative, flexible players in the universe. Dr. T.J. ranked as one of the best. She excelled at four-dimensional chess, whether she meant to or not. Many games she won by accident, and some she won by the sheer virtuosity of her improvisation. She enjoyed a habit of saying nonsensical things to her opponents and laughing herself to tears as she observed their reactions. After enduring less than a half hour of this, many of them would storm away from the chess board in heart-tightening exasperation, forfeiting the game and sending her into a complete meltdown of hilarity.

She approached Riley at the center, making funny faces at him, and bouncing in her seat. Riley lobbed a placating smile as he tried to guide her to her table. Dr. T.J. sprung out of her wheelchair, spun into a somersault, and landed on her feet. With a playful smile, she lunged at him, screaming and sending forth a storm of air karate. "HEEE-YAAAAAAAAA! KAAA-ROTCHO-SOCKEYYY!" Riley shrieked like a girl and bolted away from her faster than a rocket, all the while cupping his genitals. What everyone thought of as an elderly invalid had now become a star-shaped blur of tie-dye colors, kicking and punching in the air. As the audience laughed up a storm, she snatched the microphone, switched it back on, and hollered, "AND THE LAUNDRY WAGON HAS ENTERED THE ARENA!"

Like a colosseum full of bloodthirsty Romans, the crowd erupted with jubilant applause. Riley's eyes could be seen blinking with alarm back there, somewhere in the darkness.

"Have you ever met Dr. T.J.?" Baxter asked Professor Dedrick.

"Only once. She tried to convince me she was wearing a 'pant.'"

"A pant?"

"'Pants have two pathways for the legs,' she argued. 'My skirt has one, so it's a pant.'"

Dr. T.J. cartwheeled herself to her table. Kliban bounded after. She sat down, and the cat leapt onto her shoulder to snuggle up to her cheek. As the audience continued to applaud, Riley returned from the shadows and tried to preserve any scraps of his dignity that he could find. He was not amused. When he reached the center again, he noticed the wheelchair—the wheelchair that had played the Trojan Horse, smuggling in the agent of his humiliation. It still sat there, laughing at him, as was the audience. He kicked the chair over in frustration, which caused everyone to laugh even more. As the laughter died down, he took a minute to compose himself.

"Now," Riley began, trying to recapture his enthusiasm. "Let us all welcome the outlander of the Chess Intergalactica. She has traveled farther than any of our other players to be here with us tonight." He was gaining momentum. "She has been rated most fearsome player in thirty-three superclusters! Ladies and gentlemen, won't you scream till you cream for Adratica Scaldiatrix from the Zaphod Dent Colonies!"

Everyone applauded as a short, young, voluptuous woman walked toward the center with a calm but radiant menace. She had short, straight hair of pure white and lustrous skin, black as an eight ball. The corneas of her eyes were also pure white, but with fiery blue irises. She had a large, somewhat gumdrop-shaped nose. Her smirking lips formed a slight overbite near the sides of her mouth. She wore icy blue pants and a white blouse. On her chubby feet she wore white flip flops. Each of her shoulders sported a vibrant tattoo. The right shoulder showed an orange and red cyclone of fire. The left displayed a bloody pink heart, punctured by a long, blue rod. Under that hung the inscription, "Taught to Hurt."

"Oh, no," muttered Professor Dedrick. "It couldn't be."

"What's wrong, Professor Dedrick?" asked Baxter.

"No way she came all the way from Zaphod Dent just for this."

"Where's that?"

"It's a system near the center of the Asimov Galaxy."

"There's an Asimov Galaxy?"

"Yes, in the outermost wisp of the Carl Sagan Turtleneck Filament, hundreds of millions of light years from here. I used to teach there, at the Zaphod Dent Institute of Implausibly Sophisticated Mathematics."

"That's a real place?" asked Xzhuajdnkqqqiiihwp.

"Oh, it's real, alright. So exclusive that it's legend."

"Ah, that's bullshit. I don't believe in that crap," snipped HAMN.

"No one asks you to, my unwanted, gold-trash little sack of clogged circuits. And truth be told, I don't believe in you."

HAMN looked around to see if he or she could find a sharp object with which to commit suicide. Finding none, he or she sank back into a chair and waited for a distraction from the truth.

"Adratica was my finest. The pride and joy of all my classes. She gave new meaning to my existence, even at such a challenging school.

She would formulate proofs with such baroque ferocity ... like ... like a flaming cyclone of intellect!"

"Wow, that's neat," said Baxter.

"Yes, for the first time, I'm afraid for you, Baxter. You're a passive, calculating player. Adratica is aggressive. And she's the only student I've ever had whose mind rivals yours, my young prodigy."

"Really? What about HAMN?"

"Oh, please. That thing that passes for a brain inside his or her head is just a junction of confused nerve clusters compared to your mind."

"But HAMN can calculate such enormous, complex permutations ... in such a tiny amount of time.... I can't do that."

"Oh, big deal. So HAMN is a giant calculator, though a damn fast one. I could design one almost as fast, but without the exhibitionist streak, the short attention span, or the probable drinking problem. HAMN thinks he or she's going to be a mathematician. But we'll see. It wouldn't surprise me if HAMN ends up working the streets when he or she is done deluding his or her way through college."

"Hey, you know I'm still in the room!" HAMN protested.

"Indeed," said Professor Dedrick. "And I'm trying to turn what's our misfortune into your misfortune. So if you please ... "

"Don't feel too bad, HAMN. You'll notice neither he nor Baxter even mentioned me," Xzhuajdnkqqqiiihwp pouted indecipherably.

"That, Xzhuajdnkqqqiiihwp, is because you're as insubstantial personally as you are physically," quipped the professor.

"But, if she was a wonderful student," Baxter began, "Why did you leave that school?"

"She was in love with me."

"Really? Gosh, that's swell."

"No! No it isn't. It was a love that could never be."

"Oh, no. Well … why?"

"Because, my young apprentice, she was my student. I can't … be in love with one of my students. It violates the code of—"

"Or mayyyyybe … it was because you are a bacterium!" snapped HAMN, blasting out of his or her chair.

"Well, yes. And that," conceded the bacterium.

"Gosh, that's not very nice," said Baxter. "Nobody should hold it against Professor Dedrick, just because he's a little smaller than usual."

"A little small— It's not just a matter of— Didn't you learn anything from what we were talking about before class this afternoon?" demanded HAMN.

"No," said Baxter, puzzled.

HAMN looked around to see if he or she could find a blunt object with which to commit suicide. Finding none, he or she sank back into a chair and waited for a distraction from reality.

Adratica strolled down to her table, never once taking her eyes off her former mentor's petri dish. Professor Dedrick could feel her removing his lid with her eyes.

"Well, she seems nice," Baxter said.

"And now, ladies and gentlemen," began Riley with charming heaviness, "It gives me great pleasure to introduce to you our final contestant." Then, with rising volume, he continued, "He is a professional actor and professional vocal talent, whose level of commitment has inspired young performers all over America, and whose powerful performances on Broadway, and all along the East Coast, have redefined performing arts all throughout the universe."

"What the hell is this?" squeaked HAMN.

"He's getting kinda loud," said Baxter, covering his ears. Many of his opponents, and most of the spectators in the first few rows, were doing the same.

Riley continued, "James Earl Jones himself has praised this young man as 'having a voice that could make the Burning Bush shit its pants.' Our player is a kind-hearted man, who uses this charismatic power, not to intimidate, but to inspire awe and thus bring people in touch with a force greater than the immediate humdrum of life."

"What. Is. He. Talking about?!" complained Xzhuajdnkqqqiiihwp.

"This extends to his chess game, where, in defeating his opponents, he inspires the awe and the wonder that drives them to learn from him and become all the better for it. He's also filling in for Jessica Blyssica, who couldn't make it here tonight."

"WHAAAT?!" screeched HAMN, like a squirting chimpanzee.

"Ladies and gentlemen..." Riley paused with deep dramatic reverence, "My *dear* ladies and gentlemen. May I present to you... ME!" his voice detonated like an atomic bomb. A shock wave charged outward through the stadium, knocking everyone over in their seats, all the way up to the back row, and blasting all the arena doors open, leaving many hanging off their hinges. This left the inner ears of many audience members destroyed. A pandemonium ensued of people jostling around trying to reseat themselves, and of people hollering with alarm in reaction to their sudden deafness. Riley mistook this clamor for cheers of rapture.

"That's right, my dear friends," he said as three beautiful women strutted out to the center to accommodate him. "And these fine, sexy ladies are Olivia... no, Lydia... no, no, this is Lydia... and-and this is Ovidia, and, no... These are my advisers, ladies and gentlemen!"

"I polished my skin," muttered HAMN. "I lubricated all my joints. I replaced all my obsolete seduction chips and filled my pheromone ducts with Ice Blue Aqua Vulva. I waxed my bikini line for her. And now she just . . . doesn't show up?"

"Be glad you're as disgusting and undesirable as you are," said Professor Dedrick. "Imagine if you had those fiery blue eyes unlidding you from across the arena."

Sure enough, Adratica still darted icy fire at the bacterium.

"My dear, dear friends! Let the Games of the Chess Intergalactica begin!" Riley bellowed as he struck a giant gong. All the players adhered to their playing schedule: Riley went to Bucky Baby's table, where they would play a spherical game. Lizzie waddled over to Katelynne's table, where there awaited a flat square board with 100 squares instead of the normal 64. It featured unorthodox pieces, which Lizzie had never seen before, but with which Katelynne had acquainted herself long ago. Vercingetorix and Carter both met Dr. T.J. at her triangular board.

Adratica shifted her focus onto Baxter and made her way toward his hexagonal board.

"Oh my," said Baxter, shining with sweat. "I feel cold."

"No," said Professor Dedrick. "You're going to win. You must."

"Oh, yes," emphasized Baxter. "I need that prize money. I'm just afraid of what she'll do when I beat her."

"She's not going to do a thing to you, Baxter. Trust me."

"Oh!" he replied with a sudden delightful ease. "Well, that's just fine, then."

"She's not after you."

"Oh, that's swell."

"She's here to defeat me, through you. You're in for one hell of a battle, my boy. Nothing would give her greater satisfaction than to defeat my new prize pupil—to avenge the heart which I had no choice but to shatter. For it was not to be! Our friendship was cast asunder! Our student–mentor relationship dashed to the four winds!"

"Golly," said Baxter.

8. MOTHER'S SWEET SPOT

After nearly three floors of creaky stairs, most of the guys had started to feel light-headed. How many times had they asked Pops to get the elevator fixed, anyway? Once? Twice?! Yet for every one of those times, Pops still had the same excuse:

"There is no fuckin' elevator, so stop askin'."

But what did Pops care? Stairs came easy for him, with his long legs and the experience that came with age. Now, with every effortless step he took, the gruff old gundark displayed his callousness toward the disadvantaged.

Reese rubbed their noses in it even more, with his hard, muscular body, and the energy that came with unsquandered youth. It didn't help matters at all that his patience currently hovered a mere hair's width above a wild bludgeoning spree. *What the fuck am I doing here? How did it come to this?* He had made a decent living as the building plumber for some years. But at some point, the population of the building just seemed to dwindle down to nothing, and before long, he had no leaky faucets to fix, no drains to snake, and no pipes to replace. So Reese began creating his own plumbing problems all over the building: clogging drains, puncturing water pipes, reversing sewer flow... stuff to fix. This had destroyed his apartment and he wound

140

up in a tiny, tiny studio with all these guys—a wretched boy hole that had no plumbing to damage, or to fix. Anyone on their floor had to walk down to the little bathroom at the end of the hall whenever they needed to pinch one off or take a leak. And these days, it did not take long for that to get gross, seeing as how Reese had shut off the water. Reese had vowed to himself that he would repair all the plumbing in the building and found himself working day and night in order to catch up with his own destruction. Sleep became a rare luxury, what with the guys around all the fucking time! Even now, he couldn't get away from these useless fucks. They tottered in front of him, clogging up the stairway, which clogged Reese's brain with so much aggravation that he couldn't decide which one of them he'd like to murder first.

The guys were trying their best, though. Didn't Reese understand that? By the second staircase, like a truly insensitive bully, Reese had started kicking them and yelling at them for "waddling along like a bunch of overfed pug dogs," leaving them no option but to whimper, and try, with no success, to move faster. As if this journey hadn't grown exhausting enough already! The guys did take solace, however, in the knowledge that this daunting trek downstairs had neared its end. Skittles and the Stick had led the guys all the way down into the basement, and then further down, into what appeared to be a boiler room. Turtle, with his speargun, had prodded them along from behind. Zotz sat inside an open chamber attached to the upper back of Turtle's shell, typing codes into a wireless console. At first the guys thought Turtle might be a robot that Zotz could operate. Heath inhaled to ask about it, but Reese, who never wanted Heath to breathe, told him to shut his face unless he wanted him to break it.

Reese had obviously forgotten that Heath was packing heat. Heath always tried to give everyone fair warning, a fact that used to create friction with quite a few employers during his teen years. Luckily, none of them had been *his* employer in the strictest sense. Up until about twenty years ago, Heath had spent most of his waking hours at stores or gas stations, hanging out and talking to the employees. Most employees had returned his social outreach in only the most minimal sense. Eventually their managers would ask him to leave because he was "creating a distraction." But he knew the truth. They just couldn't handle the intimidating vibe he gave off. He couldn't help it, though. He never meant any harm. It just occurred, as part of his nature. Reese, however, never seemed intimidated. The fool. Maybe he just liked courting death. Heath scowled at Reese and considered firing a warning shot, or rather, squeezing Maggie's g-spot and making her squirt. Then suddenly, he was slapped in the face by the memory of Reese slapping him in the face while daring him to shoot. Now he felt nauseous just thinking about bringing Maggie into the situation. So he puked on his chest instead.

Upon entering this boiler room, the rest of the guys also started to feel kind of sick. The place smelled like metal and oil. An unsettling humming sound pervaded the whole room, and greenish-brown lights on the ceiling made everything look hard and dirty. Near the center of the room they saw a huge, cylindrical boiler, which someone had long ago painted lemon-drop yellow, but which had aged into a pissy gray. The block letters, "CC," once cherry red, had decayed into rotten cherry red. They observed that, even though a platform supported the boiler, a huge crane also supported it with thick cables.

The guys could only guess to where this crane would have lifted the boiler in this closed-off room. But a tiny Ferris wheel distracted them from guessing. Also, a toy sailboat. And a miniature catapult, and a bottle rocket. These were part of a system that also featured a bundle of helium balloons, a bucket of water, a whoopee cushion, a plate of cheese, a cage packed with fat mice, a hungry cat, and... was that a dog over there? Yes, a fat little chihuahua with needy, beady black eyes, wagging his rat-like tail to share the farts he liked to deal out. The circuit boxes in the room accounted for a small part of an elaborate complex of inverse zap generator boards, gamma-oscillating quasiflux wave overload isocapacitators, subphase magnetic microtransformatroids, hyperphase amagnetic macrocircuitrons, ultra-infra-tau-charged gluon speculators, power cables, antivelociraptronic nodes, and other electronicky things about which Pops knew nothing. The old landlord hadn't ventured all the way down here in a long time and had never seen any of these things. It started to make him a little nervous.

"What the hell you guys been doing down here, anyway?" Pops objected. "I thought this was just a simple operation: your buyers come in, you set them up, and that's that. What's with all these pulleys and hydraulics, and machines, and electro-gizmos? Looks like a goddamn Frankenstein movie down here."

"What're askin' me for? Ask these guys," said the Stick, pointing to Turtle and Zotz. "I don't touch anything in this; this lair of theirs."

"Whoa," said Ike to Turtle. "You guys, like, really, actually live down here? For reals?" Turtle stood there with his beak open and said nothing. "Wow, like... what do you guys do down here, then?" Ike asked Zotz, who had begun scurrying about the room, throwing huge switches and activating some very intimidating equipment. Upon hearing Ike's question, Zotz stopped. The corners of his mouth opened like a pair of stage curtains, revealing a wide grin with an unnatural number of huge teeth that looked like broken tiles.

"Oh, you'll see," replied Zotz, with his nasty, buzzy voice.

"What do you guys do?" Ike asked Turtle again. Turtle maintained his disquieting, open-beaked stare in silence.

"Dude, don't be a nimrod," Mike said, looking at Ike through the elaborate web of tape that now held his lenses together. "Turtles don't talk, dude."

"Well, what is all this stuff?" Ike prodded on, this time speaking to the Stick.

"I'm not at liberty, I said," replied the Stick. "Now get away from me. You smell like a dirty carpet."

"Well, don't you live here too?" asked Ike.

"Hell no," boasted the Stick. "Skittles and myself, we're penthouse people, six floors above you gutter slugs. Ain't we Skittles?"

"Yeah," said Skittles.

"You guys live together?" asked Chuckles. "You two guys?"

"Hey, car wash boy," said the Stick, grabbing a wad of Chuckles's messy hair. "We have a martial arts studio up there, Skittles and myself. We stay fit. We challenge each other. Isn't that so, Skittles."

"Yeah," said Skittles.

"Listen, Karate Queer," Reese said, drawing his wrench and approaching the Stick. "I'm not in a real good mood right now. You wanna tell us what the fuck this is all about 'fore I stomp your little ass?"

"Believe me, kid," Pops warned Reese. "It's in your best interest to keep that hole of yours shut right now."

Reese snatched the trusty quarterstaff from the Stick's hands and poked him in the chest.

"Still a tough guy without your stick, Sticky?" taunted Reese. "My stick now, ain't it?" Reese poked the Stick again and suddenly found himself flying straight up into the air, with no wrench and no stick. He hit his head on the ceiling and began plummeting back down, only to find the guys looking up at him with awe and the Stick waiting for him below with the trusty quarterstaff in hand. Just as Reese neared the floor, the Stick leapt into the air. He spun around, and with a graceful sweep of his trusty quarterstaff, sent Reese tumbling, in shallow bounces, at high velocity along the concrete floor, knocking the guys over like five bowling pins. He crashed into Turtle with such force that blood exploded out of his mouth.

He lay on the floor, moaning for a moment, then began to stir. His shades were bent, a few ribs were broken, and his shoulders were throbbing. He tried to pick his toothpick up off the floor, but the shoulder pain was so fantastic that he didn't dare extend either of his arms. This pissed him off. *How's a guy supposed to look tough without a toothpick to chew on, or flutter, or lob at people?*

"You judo son of a bitch," Reese moaned as he edged himself up against the wall. "I can't move my arms. You dislocated my shoulders, you karate motherfucker!"

Turtle's scaly hands grabbed his shoulders from behind and pulled them back into place. Reese collapsed onto the floor like a bag of tinker toys, wailing from the pain. The guys managed to get themselves up. The Stick scoffed, and Pops stood there, enjoying a series of quiet laughs at these recent goings-on.

Zotz threw one last switch and some of the equipment began humming. The little tiny Ferris wheel began spinning. One of its carts held a matchstick, which lit up when the wheel carried it past an adjacent patch of striking surface. As the wheel turned, it took the lighted match past the fuse of the bottle rocket. The bottle rocket went whistling up toward the bucket of water that hung from the ceiling. The rocket hit the bottom edge of the bucket, causing the bucket to dump water all over the floor. Water picked up the plate of cheese and carried it away. Hooked to the plate was a string, which pulled loose the knot that tied the helium balloons to the cage packed with fat mice, which had hovered over the whoopee cushion. The cage came down, causing the whoopee cushion to blow the toy sailboat past the catapult. In passing, the sailboat's mast flipped a switch that released the arm of the catapult, which sent the fat little dog soaring across the room like a fat, furry bullet. The dog smacked the center of the bullseye painted onto the concrete wall and fell to the platform underneath it. With his skull cracked open, the smelly little dog lay there, pulsing out a slight tail twitch with each of its few remaining heartbeats, and still farting. Out over the platform twitched one of his stumpy little hind legs. On the third twitch, his filthy little paw flipped a small switch on the wall. And then, everyone heard something unlatch on top of the boiler. Skittles climbed a metal ladder up to the top and turned the huge metal wheel on a newly unlocked hatch. He opened the hatch.

"Everybody in," commanded the Stick. None of this fed the hungry cat or put it in the position to fuck another cat, so it left the room.

Pops started up the ladder. Reese remained on the ground, whimpering, unable to get up. As expected, the guys just stood there, lobbing their gazes back and forth in search of comforting answers to unarticulated questions, and farting quietly amongst themselves, as if anally whispering options to one another in secret committee. What was in the boiler, anyway?

"You guys want a fix?" asked the Stick. "You want a little sniff of dum dum? You fuckin' losers ever want to see another piece of candy, ever, in your lowly existence? Get your candied asses—"

The guys now climbed up the ladder with vigor after Pops. Reese shot up the ladder even faster, tossing Ike, Clark, and Heath out of his way, climbing right over Chuckles and Mike. Pops and Reese arrived at the top, tied a rope, and descended into the boiler. The guys made it up to the hatch and lowered themselves in, first by sliding down the rope one inch at a time, then by losing control, accelerating downward, and burning their atrophied hands and stinky thighs on the rope, then by landing with a *splat* on the metal floor. To their disappointment, they did not find themselves inside a tank full of candy, but rather an empty boiler. Another greenish-brown bulb lit the inside of this giant metal cylinder. Was this their new place? Had the captain had this huge cylinder hollowed out for their new V&V chamber? Awesome! But there was no candy. There was no candy. They'd been duped. There was no candy. There was no candy. There was no candy. Anywhere.

Before anyone could whine or ask questions, Skittles descended, followed by Turtle, with Zotz on his back again. The Stick coiled up the rope and leapt down with grace. Zotz flipped another switch and locked the hatch shut. The guys now began to sense that no dum dum would ever come; that these four new guys were bad news. They understood now that they had, all of them, been bamboozled, and that none of this had anything to do with the captain. In the eerie silence, the guys started to sense the imminence of some kind of punishment.

Then they were all weightless. And not just the guys: Reese, Pops, the Stick, and all the rest floated freely through the air in the hollowed-out boiler. All the guys wanted to say it, but only Ike had enough lameness to say, "Whoahhh! This is so rad! Are we in space? Are we going to another planet?"

The guys had always wanted to go to another planet. Back in the late '80s, at the end of the astronaut age, the subject of space travel appeared, not just in every roleplaying game, but in every form of imaginative play. During every recess, Heath might become Lieutenant Worf, or Clark might become Commander Adama, and the playground would become their Starship Enterprise, or their Battlestar Galactica... that is, until the principal of that elementary school threatened to call their principal at the high school if they didn't leave the grounds immediately. That principal was a total dick. They tried several times to explain to him that the high school didn't have a playground, but to no avail. He was just a dick-sucking dickhead from Penisville, who ate dick sandwiches for lunch. To hell with him. He couldn't stop the guys from dreaming of traveling to new worlds.

Back then, the mere act of sending a person into orbit to observe the zero gravity effects on a bag of lug nuts required years of intensive training, postdoctoral education, optimum physical fitness, months of meticulous preparation, and ruinous expense. The guys had never meticulously prepared for anything. They had no money, no physical fitness to speak of, and no education recognized by anyone other than themselves. They didn't even have a bag of lug nuts. By the dawn of the twenty-first century, Earth had become a major hub of interstellar commerce, with connections to countless other systems in and out of the galaxy. Nowadays, any dunce could get to neighboring star systems with even a rubbery effort. The guys had always romanticized trekking the cosmos as their greatest wish, a dream for which they would have sacrificed all comforts—a point of self-actualization for which they would have toiled day and night. But they had never gotten around to it. But now, here they floated, bobbing around in the air like balloons, on their way to a new world—going to another planet!

"We're not going to another planet," said the Stick, practicing weightless martial arts with Skittles. The great wrestler's expert ability to throw his weight around proved a weak match for the agility of the Stick. Upon his latest lunge, the Stick bounced Skittles away into the guys, which sent Chuckles, Mike, and Ike hurtling away in different directions, only to bounce around the tank. Skittles grazed Heath and left him spinning end over end, in one place. Clark, however, entered Skittles's direct path and got squashed as the wrestler bounced off a wall. Skittles tailored this bounce to launch himself again toward the Stick. Clark, now unconscious, with his monocle wedged into his eye socket, drifted around the boiler with floating ribbons of bloody mucous trailing out of his nose. His top hat, now crunched lengthwise, floated away from his head.

Reese didn't know how to handle the weightlessness. It disturbed him. But when he noticed that Pops seemed calm and at perfect ease with the whole situation, the young plumber made sure to maintain that tough look that his face sported in the weighted world—the world from which he and the guys had now departed. Zotz, still on Turtle's back, appeared to have full knowledge about whatever was going on and exhibited no anxiety. Turtle, who had magnetically clamped himself to the wall, also seemed quite content, or at least, as content as one can seem when one is staring at people with one's beak open.

As Heath continued to spin with no hope of repose, he began barfing out a spiral stream. This accelerated the spinning, which made him even sicker, which made him vomit harder, which accelerated the spinning even more, and so on, ad nauseam. The hollowed-out boiler had become a big metal tube of mayhem, complete with a flying wrestler, a floating martial artist, three whining guys bouncing off the walls, and a human puke sprinkler.

At this point, Heath fell back down to the floor, and a sizable stream of the vomit whipped down on top of him. He got up. Almost everyone else had fallen to the floor, too. Turtle and Zotz remained attached to the wall. Stick and Skittles had landed on their feet with confidence and grace. Pops had landed hard, just as the guys had, but saw no reason to snivel about a little pain. Not everyone proved quite so hardy. Much to the irritation of the tough, an assortment of moans and whimpers began to rise from the less tough. This trip was going to be a pain in the ass.

From outside the giant boiler tank, the moaning and whimpering could have been heard, had there been anyone around to hear it. Upon the opening of the trap door in the boiler room, now so far above, the tank had fallen freely. Now the cables attached to the top of the tank had tightened, and the boiler room crane lowered the tank further down into the bowels of Mother Earth. Soon, though, Zotz detached them from the cables and dropped the tank into a glowing subterranean cocktail of liquid toxins that had accumulated from seepage over the last two decades. Another crane—a rusty, crusty old contraption—clamped onto the tank. It lifted the tank, and swung it around, banging the side of it on one of the rocky walls of a long, forgotten tunnel. Sounds of the guys hollering with alarm echoed far down the tunnel, but to no ears. The crane, still swinging, released its grip. The tank flew a short distance and landed on the bed of a railroad car attached to the rear of a compact, old-fashioned steam engine. The locomotive's colors, once lime, lemon, blueberry, and cherry had now faded and tainted to colors of mold, blond roast, shiner, and monthly meatloaf. From inside the tank, nobody could see how silly and gross it looked, but everybody heard the engine go *choo-chooooo*!

The train worked up to a decent speed. In no time, it was just a puttn its way down the ol' tracks through the dim tunnel, far beneath the city. The image might have been cute, if not for the train's grossness, if anyone had been around to see it. Indeed, it once had been a cute little train, kind of. But now it was not cute. It was gross. But this gross little train was not one to languish in self-consciousness; no, not even a little bit. It had places to be, and it chugged along with not a single check to its haste. Neither hours nor minutes would it squander. For time grew short, and the tracks stretched far into the darkness.

As the hours passed, Reese found a few winks, mostly due to Pops putting him in a sleeper hold when the youth attacked him for coughing. The guys had started to get bored. They learned early in the trip to avoid thinking about dragons, warlocks, Romulans, Cylons, Jedi, or the like. Such thoughts led to discussion and roleplaying, which led

150

to Reese pounding on them. Thoughts about girls proved even worse, since they led without fail to masturbation attempts, the faintest hints of which the Stick had declared punishable by death. With Heath's big mouth silenced, his small mind had begun to construct a list of people he planned to shoot later on. None of those on his list sat more than fifty feet away from him. Mike had grown just as bored, but without the luxury of a hit list to occupy his mind.

His irritation with Ike, however, started to bloom into a huge distraction. Ike just sat there, listening to Pops, who had prattled on with war stories for hours. What kind of a tool went in for all this historical shit? Anybody with any imagination knew that fiction was stranger than truth. But there sat Mike's own flesh and blood, totally absorbed, totally taken in by Pops's boring drivel. It majorly sucked ass looking down on his little bro like this, because he loved him, kind of. Sometimes he found it a major embarrassment to hang out with him. His toolish behavior and that raunchy eyepatch totally ruined Mike's rep around here.

And his rep was nothing to fart at. From his initial golden years as the *Frogger* King and Grand High CHOMPion of *Pac-Man* to his declining days as *Mortal Kombat* Sensei, Mike had sacrificed his allowance, his piggy bank, Ike's allowance, Ike's piggy bank, Ike's virginity, and their mom's bank account to maintain his venerable position in the gaming community. But Mike wanted even more. After scraping through high school, Mike enrolled at Olga Oysterclog Community College and took Advanced Computer Programming, so he could create his own awesome video games someday. Over time, he came to realize that he would first have to master the school's Intermediate Programming sequence in order to understand the advanced classes. After some more time, he came to understand that he would have to pass the school's Introduction to Computers sequence in order to comprehend the intermediate courses. After a while, it dawned on him that in order to understand the basic algebra used in the intro computer classes, he would have to take Basic Algebra, which would require him to pass Pre-Algebra, which he took for five years in high school, but never finished. By the time he came to this final moment of clarity, he had racked up tens of thousands in student loans, most of which he had spent at the Jupiter I. So he'd decided on a new career path.

Now, over twenty years later, he continued to blaze down that path. Once his student debt had become too large to pay off during his expected lifetime, the savvy video game vet kited his debts along. He took advantage of the unlimited deferrals and endless forbearances he assumed banks granted to college students. So even though sporadic courses in mythology and folklore did add to his debt, they also enabled him to remain in "student" status and keep the banks at bay. It was a stroke of true genius. The next month, when the banks caught on, Mike went on sabbatical. He ensured the asceticism and intellectual purity of this move by crashing with the guys in their awesomely stylin' pad—a pad that obtained even loftier heights of bodaciousness after Pops's third ex-wife condemned the building.

Now here he sat, holed up in some kind of metal tank with the guys, watching Zotz twitch, smelling Heath's barfy shirt, listening to Ike listen to Pops, and waiting for Chuckles to interrupt Pops with some kind of wise remark—preferably one that would result in a brawl. It was a question of when, not if. The mop-haired dickweed couldn't help himself. His penchant for mockery overrode almost any safety concerns. Chuckles found one hearty laugh worth ten beatings—fifty after he discovered the softness of their strikes and what little damage he had to sustain, even when they ganged up on him.

Like that time at the Loiter-n-Leave, back in '89, when they all watched Mike butcher the bad guys in *Axhack the Barbarian*. Chuckles had been antagonizing everyone the whole time. Not only had he been taunting Heath, who'd armed himself with a steak knife back then, he had also been drowning out Clark's narration of the game by mimicking Mike's grunting and mouth-breathing as he played. This did not sit well with anyone. Back in those days, you didn't razz an arcade artisan as he worked. You just didn't. Scaling castle walls, jumping over pits of fire, evading evil wizards, dodging flaming arrows, and slaying knights with his battle-ax had put him under enough pressure. Such heroics deserved respect. Nobody else on Earth could get to level twelve! Well, none of the guys could, anyway. Ike worshiped his older brother back then and always stood by his side to watch him play and make history. So he had grown especially perturbed by Chuckles's jeering.

All the guys had scraped up all the money they could find that day to fund Mike's lengthy journey to level twelve, the final level, where he would defeat the poison-quilled, eleven-headed cyclops Dragonbitch Queen and triumph over yet another game. When, at long last, that glorious opportunity had arrived, Mike readied himself to jump from a sinking pillar, over the pit of fire, and into the Dragonbitch Queen's lair. The pillar was narrower than his avatar's foot, so he could not build up to a running start and had no margin for error. Just as Mike took his leap, Chuckles hollered, "Good lu-uuuck!" in a high-pitched sing-songy voice. Mike jolted and his avatar stepped off the pillar and sank into the flames without a sound.

The words "Game Over" yanked all their tiny dicks in mockery, and the countdown began. The guys had no time to yell at Chuckles. They had to find another quarter, and fast! Chuckles had the last one. He pinned the corner of his upper lip with his tongue to form a puzzled facial scrunch of such biting mockery as to render his friends light-headed with rage. He plunged his entire arm into his pocket, feigning inability to locate the coin, then dragged it out as though pulling taffy. Mike snagged it and tried to plug it into the slot. But they had packed the chamber so full of coins that he had to force it in. The game resumed at the beginning of level twelve. He battled his way through, all the way up to the final pillar again. He made it across the pit, into the lair of the Dragonbitch Queen, where he severed five of the bitchy beastie's heads and lost his first life. Then he battled his way through level twelve again, severed all eleven heads, and lost his second life. With his final life, he battled through the final level again, severed all eleven heads, raised his battle-ax to sever the Dragonbitch Queen's great eye, and the screen blinked off and the game was gone, and Chuckles laughed and laughed and laughed.

It wasn't just the sardonic irony that was hilarious. The sheer inexplicability of it all made this even more of a riot to Chuckles, and he went on laughing. He laughed through the shocked silence and dropped jaws. He laughed through the frantic pounding on the controls and the futile slamming on the sides of the console, and the baffled inspections of the perfectly healthy power cable, which had never left its outlet. He laughed through all the fruitless attempts to beg the clerk for their money back, and then laughed at the girlish beatings laid onto him by the guys. He laughed as the clerk kicked them out, and he laughed straight on into the night. Then he woke up the next day, and he laughed some more.

Mike fumed, now, at this old memory. He shot an acid glance over at Chuckles, who was looking right at him through his mop of hair and laughing at him. Pops found this irritating but kept on talking. Mike stood up and stared at Chuckles with astonishment. He knew! The little fuck knew exactly what Mike had just mulled over in his mind and was now laughing up a storm about it. Mike couldn't stand it. He just stood there, his eyes glistening with hate. He hated the piercing laugh that belted out from that rodentian mouth, and that tiny pink nose, and that weak chin, and that car-wash brush of greasy brown hair that covered his eyes. He hated those red Converse; they looked like clown shoes. And he hated the puffy blue downy jacket that Chuckles had worn in all climates since at least 1988. So Mike found sweet satisfaction when Pops became so annoyed with Chuckles's unwarranted distraction that he ripped the left sleeve right off the downy jacket and stuffed it down Chuckles's throat. Pops went on with his story. Mike sniggered. Chuckles stood there with a sleeve hanging out of his mouth and small feathers swirling about his face. Appreciating how strange this must have looked, Chuckles started laughing again. Pops didn't care. The laughter was muffled enough.

Chuckles's recent outburst had managed to jolt Clark back into consciousness. He peeled his bloody face off of the floor and dislodged his monocle from under the rim of his eye. As the room cleared up, he surveyed the tank. Mike sat nearby, looking bored. Heath had passed the time by smelling his fingers. Reese tossed and twitched as he slept. Skittles urinated on Reese, while Zotz observed from on top of Turtle's back, quite amused. Turtle, Ike, and the Stick continued listening to Pops:

"... with the Victor-Charlies sendin' heavy fire at us from across the lagoon. Damn near everybody got pegged at least once. Before long, every one of us was a mess. Cleg took half a dozen in the head before he could find cover—even got a shell lodged in his eye. We was lucky all they had left was eggs, wise old Cleg woulda got more than his hair messed up. That's the way those oily little bastards operated, though. See, back then the Cong used to sneak in and steal our eggs.

Night before, they made off with a passel of 'em, 'cause nobody was standin' guard; it was a problem in our platoon. So, next day we're all of us scurryin' around, ready to eat our own boots and those sons-a-bitches are over there throwin' our own food supply at us. Can you imagine that?! No more omelets for us, man, they saw to that! War's hell, boy. That's a fact." Pops took a drag off the stubby remainder of his candy cigarette and exhaled. No smoke came out. He continued.

"Was around that time me and Martoony was down there in the lagoon. I'm tellin' you it was hotter'n a sonofabitch, we're talkin' one hundred ninety-six degrees in the shade, and that's no joke. But we wasn't down there to keep cool; we was arming the bridge to see if we could catch the VC unawares-like. Headquarters wanted the bridge to remain intact, but we was doin' it for the lieutenant. He wanted it blown to hell. The LT was the toughest old bird I ever knew. Sonofabitch had been layin' on a stretcher for over a hundred years, still dyin' from Confederate shrapnel, and goddammit if the army hadn't held that against him. Assholes had demoted him from captain—said an officer in his condition was 'regrettably concluded as ill-fit to command a company of infantry with the degree of polish and honor befitting the Union' or some other bullshit. They'd only sent him along with us 'cause they were sick of listening to him bitch. But an old warhorse like him deserved a favor or two, we figured.

"So we was down there under the bridge, almost shoulder deep in the water, when I felt Martoony's fingers runnin' up my legs and ribs. Well, after cackling like a little schoolgirl for a second, I got mad at him. We got the Cong shootin' at us and was on a secret mission—it wasn't no time to be ticklin' each other. Well, I tried to tell him this, but I turned around and saw Martoony about five yards behind me. He had started bustin' up too. I was afraid we was gonna give away our position, and then the Cong would get us. Then it felt like the fingers started diggin' into me and it hurt. Was about that time we figured out it was leeches! We threw off all our clothes and found them wrigglin' all over. Musta been hundreds of 'em on us. Well, before I knew it, we was out of the water, runnin' naked on the shore an' screamin'. And every time we stopped to rip them little fuckers off us, we got beamed with a buncha eggs from the Cong. Pretty soon me and Martoony got mud, and sand, and blood, and raw eggs runnin' all down us.

"Well, we got close to the platoon, and they went all fruitcake on us. Thought we was a couple of monsters or somethin', and opened fire, with real bullets! We managed to get away and found the path we'd blazed through the jungle the week before. Made our way all the way back to the other side of the bush, a lotta miles off—"

Pops took another pointless drag off of his candy cigarette. The Stick wanted to clobber him for that. He could feel the way all the guys stared at it. But even worse, Zotz, Turtle, and Skittles had started to obsess too. And the Stick now admitted to himself that it tested even him. It just looked so . . . sweet. So sweet, and . . . sweet. But enough of this. He was better than this. He was the Stick!

"DISCIPLINE!" he bellowed, as he crashed his trusty quarterstaff against the wall of the tank, waking Reese with a frightful snort. "Tough it out, you bunch of worms," the Stick continued. "Pops, swallow that goddamn thing. What're you trying to do to all of us?" Pops hesitated, as this represented the last morsel of goob he had anywhere. Still, Pops obliged him, and had now become just as naked and alone as everyone else.

"Go on, go on with the story," the Stick quavered. "Go on, go on, we can't take this much longer, can we, Skittles?"

"Yeah," Skittles agreed.

Pops inhaled shakily and went on. "Well, couple of days later, we was sitting there, eatin' the last of the eggs off ourselves—the heat had cooked 'em onto us real quick—when we heard someone comin' up the path toward us. Well, we knew it wasn't the VC; they'd never have let us hear them sneakin' around, so we thought maybe it was young Sobchak, come to find us. We looked down the trail, and goddamned if it wasn't the leeches! We'd left a trail of blood and we paid for it. Them goddamn leeches had followed us nine miles up that trail. Well, we made a break for it right quick. Over the next couple weeks, them leeches chased us all over the jungle." Out of sheer habit, Pops brought his fingers to his lips for a drag. But he would have to wait—wait like everyone else, as the gross little train chugged them further and further down the tracks.

Only 8,100 stories beneath the building in which the guys had for so long dwelled lay a set of tracks belonging to the largest railway in the world. It had been laid out in the late 1990s by Captain Candyroo, who had cornered the world's candy market and driven himself to generate a fortune for the small company he'd started with his buddies. His colorful train, riding along his secret, underground tracks, supplied only Twinkle and neighboring communities, like Stankumm, Oolalla, Mundaneville, and Rugburn.

Now the train began to slow as it approached a huge, underground station, around which the tracks began to circle. The guys could feel the train and the tank come to a complete stop within the circle. They erupted into a frenzy of whimpering and clawing at the walls of the tank, not unlike a pack of dogs in a recently stopped car. The others burned with annoyance at this display but couldn't curtail it because it crippled them with contempt.

The hatch unlocked. Carrying the coiled rope, the Stick gracefully leapt up through the opening. Soon he threw the rope down and Skittles climbed up. Turtle, Zotz, and Pops followed. Between grunts, yips, and whimpers, the guys jumped up and down with such energy that their feet came close to leaving the floor more than once. Such workouts tended to leave them gasping for air and resenting the pain shooting up their left arms. But such clamors for help had become a matter of survival. They knew all too well that they had not a ghost of a chance of climbing any rope.

From outside, five new ropes were thrown in.

"Grab on," called the Stick from outside the tank. They demoted their clamoring to sniveling, remembering how their pudding grips had failed them when they'd tried to lower themselves into this tank. What a golden moment they had supplied for Reese, though. He took one rope, tied it to Clark's wrist, and tugged. Pops pulled Clark out, wailing in pain. In the meantime, Reese tied Chuckles's arm to another rope and tugged. The Stick pulled Chuckles out, kicking and screaming, while Reese tied Mike's ankle to Ike's ankle. He tugged the rope and Turtle pulled Mike and Ike out, screaming like babies. By this time, Heath had started scurrying around in the tank and squealing like a panicky pig, in a futile attempt to escape. Reese found himself laughing and chasing after Heath at a lumbering pace, just to delight in his despair. To enhance the experience, he tied a lasso and began throwing it at Heath. On the third throw, he roped Heath around the neck and yanked him to the floor. He tugged the rope and Skittles began pulling Heath out. Reese, about to tug on the remaining rope for himself, realized that Heath was choking. So he jumped up and grabbed hold of Heath's ankles and hung there until Skittles had pulled them both out.

Nursing their injuries, the guys got up off the floor and feasted their eyes on the most magnificent sight they'd ever seen. Enormous glass jars, no less than a hundred stories high, towered over all of them in every direction. Inside the twinkling jars glittered every variety of candy, with colors assaulting in their intensity. From the bases of the jars protruded long spigots, the mouths of which were just the right size to pour sweets uncountable through the hatch and into the tank from which everyone had just exited.

The captain's handiwork astonished them all, including Pops, who had always thought maybe there might be a small warehouse hidden somewhere near the apartment building. Never in his wildest speculations had he suspected a hoard of this magnitude. But the hoard represented the remnants of a failed enterprise. Because the captain had just one silly little train to supply tens of thousands, his profits remained meager and his buddies laughed at him. So he'd invested unholy sums of company money into the construction of a vast, intercontinental rail network that would supply candy to eager kids all around the world.

Here they all stood, at the very hub of this rail network, the sweetest spot on Earth—or rather, in Earth. They stood on a circular platform, surrounded by a deep moat. The train tracks circled around, inside the moat. And from that circle of tracks, nine other tracks extended outward to all the corners of the world. On the tracks, and inside the moat, sat the gross little engine and the tank, the tops of which stood level with the platform. The captain's train remained the only means of transport to and from this hub. He had never realized his great plans in full. Just as he'd readied to equip the entire railroad with the most sophisticated high-speed trains, he'd had a stroke of bad luck: his buddies had lost what faint interest they had in his project. They'd expanded their operations beyond Earth and ditched him in Twinkle. Left with nothing but a silly little train to move his sweets, he'd found himself able to sustain only a scarce living.

But where was the captain now? What happened to the genius responsible for this Eden? The guys pondered this for 0.00011 seconds before every atom in their constitutions drove them toward devouring every confection detected by their darting eyes and hyperventilating noses. Instantly, they each identified the one and only way across the moat. They had to run across the roof of the train's engine. So they made a rabid break for it. Before long, an assortment of mental-hospital sounds echoed down the surrounding caverns. Mike growled and slobbered like a sleep-deprived toddler as the Stick, with a number of flips, tumbles, and somersaults, blocked him from getting anywhere near the crossing. Ike cried himself sick as Turtle's open-beaked stare immobilized him. Clark kicked and shrieked like a cage full of monkeys as Pops held him in a full nelson. Any noise that Heath made got lost inside Skittles's rectum. It amused Skittles to sit on people's faces—to have their opinions meet his asshole. Reese and Chuckles also screamed at first. But when they realized they suffered no interceding rivals, they both experienced a moment of elation and bonding previously unknown to them. In a flash of joy, Chuckles stripped off all his clothes, even the downy jacket. Reese stripped off everything except his red scarf and his sunglasses. He welcomed Chuckles's soft, filthy body onto his back, and the two free souls galloped, piggyback style, over the roof of the train and across to the other side of the tracks.

They came within arm's reach of a colossal castle of confection when each of them felt a huge electrode stab them in the ass. Mind-burning waves of electricity pulsed through them as the winches on Zotz's horrible handheld tasers pulled them backward without relent, tumbling toward the platform. Zotz just stood there, reeling them back and beaming his razor tiled teeth at the spectacle. Their vision flashed and then dimmed, then flashed, and then dimmed. The whole time they could make out wild cackles of derision, which hurt almost as much as the blazing current running through them. Another flash, and then blackness. The smell of smoke and sizzling butt cheeks came to them, and they heard the cackling subside.

"Ahhh-ha-ha-ha-ha-ha, what a couple of hosers," jeered the voice of Captain Candyroo from somewhere in the vicinity. "So how about it, chumps? Anybody else wanna make a run for the pixie? Please! Please entertain me some more...."

As Captain Candyroo polished off his taunt with another ribbon of cruel laughs, Reese and Chuckles phased out of consciousness.

9. ENDGAME

I *have always been here.*

This Safeway had not always been here.

This Safeway, out in the middle of the desert, once served the small town of Twinkle. For generations it maintained a competitive balance with Orville's. That all changed when Mr. Laing took it into his shiny head to clear out the bread aisle and stock it with firearms. He started out by selling handguns. Patrons who purchased the guns to rob, assault, or otherwise terrorize Orville's would be given sizable cash rebates from Safeway. Often these rebates would far exceed the price of the guns, depending on the heaviness of the damage inflicted upon Safeway's competitor. Orville's responded by relocating out of town, to Spine Street, along which had grown the scarcest beginning of a little strip that would bloom to become Valhallaville.

This Safeway would also have to move. And not just the staff. The whole store. Riding on new prosperity and the trend of armed conflict promoting that prosperity, Mr. Laing upgraded. He secured a connection with a dawning young humanoid rat who dealt automatic weapons, explosives, and even biological weapons, all of his own unique and superior design. Though the cost of these weapons soared into the stratum of staggering expense, a public of increasingly assertive disposition maintained an even higher demand.

This Safeway had become the flagstore of the corporation. It was at this juncture that the CEO came unto Mr. Laing to praise him for his wonderful idea and to reveal to him the honorable perk he had earned with his business savvy: exile into the desert. Of course, the CEO didn't use the word "exile." The company had given Mr. Laing "the exciting opportunity to become a pioneer." He would manage the first Safeway that dealt nuclear arms to the average citizen. He would help drive the vanguard of the biggest idea ever: beyond television ads, beyond neon, beyond the world's most gargantuan floodlights. What could sell nukes better than a promotional mushroom cloud? Detonate a sample of the monthly coupon item. Now that's advertising!

This Safeway had once held a special landmark status in the eyes of its customers, and in the eyes of the company. The Safeway that revolutionized the shopping experience would never be torn down and never replaced. So they moved the whole store into the naked desert, where it attracted tourists with its atom-splitting promotions—where it sold groceries to avid travelers and peddled nukes of all manner to an increasingly assertive population.

After the Greenhouse Wars, however, this Safeway had little to offer. With the major cities on the planet left smoldering, most of Earth's citizens had to wander the decimated streets without so much as a Skwirt Pocket and a pack of cigarettes to start the day off. Illegal aliens found themselves the only residents on Earth who could afford nukes, which they found obsolete and boring. Earthlings referred to the diverse arrays of technologically advanced immigrants from other planets, star systems, and galaxies as illegal aliens because they had migrated to Earth so suddenly, and in such bewildering numbers, that the few legislators who survived the Greenhouse Wars could not manage to agree upon, or even address in any meaningful way, the legal ramifications of the migration. By the time any particular bill had made it through the normal process, the groups of aliens in question would have rebuilt entire strips of cities, erected flourishing businesses, and secured their own legislative seats. Before long, the natives of Earth found themselves sitting on the side with their thumbs up their butts, helplessly looking on as thousands of more advanced races of "illegals" brought intergalactic commerce to the planet.

Though this Safeway's distance from such manic urban development had saved it from the wrecking ball, its isolation had also prolonged its death. Having lost interest in Mr. Laing and his crew, corporate left them out here on their own. Dwindling water supplies, ever-rising oxygen taxes, and ruinous ozone bills invited the corner-cutting manager to cut even more corners. Repairs and maintenance slid to the back of everyone's minds as wind, sand, and sunlight conspired to loosen boards, erode masonry, warp framework, and crack the pavement into shingles. Vendors, all of whom hated coming out here, would simply forget this store, or upon arrival, extort a bit extra, either out of the safe or out of the genitals of the more spiritually defeated employees. As a result, pleasantries grew more artificial, smiles became more forced, supply became more sporadic, and more customers viewed the store as a place to go if they got cold feet during a suicide attempt. Granted, a small population of die-hard desert-dwelling locals still frequented the store. But fickle was the crowd that once revered this Safeway. Fleeting was the glory of its constipated manager.

And yet, throughout the store, there pervaded a force that seemed eternal. Not eternal in the spiritual, uplifting sense, but eternal in the whorish, disgusting sense. Something remained here, in this Safeway— something that existed before it was built or moved—a loyalty so immovable, and so comprehensive, that it could be smelled in the concrete itself. Cereal Man knew this force. Many times he had battled with it, and always to a stalemate. The last stalemate had plunged his opponent into the lower depths of the bottle room, neutralizing the foe. Cereal Man wondered, however, if it could ever truly be killed.

After crushing Bret's insolent ass into a pulp, Cereal Man felt this force with more potency and began his journey back across the store, toward the bottle room. He entered the produce section to find that someone had turned the lights off. The store looked closed. Light from the parking lot outside, and from a few displays inside, cast long shadows around the store. In the pale, eerie light from the aisle of frozen foods, he heard something shift. He walked into the aisle and felt a plastic shopping bag envelop his face. A broomstick knocked his cereal box out of his hand and someone drove a mop into his groin. He collapsed to the floor, grabbing at the plastic bag, and then the hands holding it. He squeezed the wrists with sudden ferocity and crushed them like sticks of balsa wood, generating howls of pain. Cereal Man threw this assailant into whomever had struck him with the mop. He sprung to his feet, tearing the bag from his face. Dozens of courtesy ninjas now cordoned off both ends of the aisle. They still wore their blue aprons over their clean white shirts, and their name tags still said, "COURTESY CLERK." But it became plain that these little shits were much more. Each of them carried a broom with razor wire for bristles. They all armed themselves with at least three different varieties of box cutters and industrial staple guns. All the courtesy ninjas carried sheathed mops on their backs with jagged clusters of chains in place of mop heads. They had sharpened the staffs of the mops to a point. All the courtesy ninjas had veiled their faces with paper bags and had cut a slot in the front, out of which their dead eyes could lock onto their opponent. Staring out from their paper veils, phalanxes of courtesy ninjas closed in from each end of the aisle.

Cereal Man looked from side to side, not with fear or alarm, but with disbelief. He had killed untold hundreds of courtesy clerks over the years. But he had never faced courtesy ninjas before. This was a new development. And a really stupid one. A somewhat amusing one. It came close to making him crack the tiniest fraction of a smirk at one of the corners of his mouth. But not quite. Instead, he felt his time would be better served by tipping over the freezers and smashing every one of these stupid kids. But as he took hold of the structure, a pair of hands came out from a freezer door and pulled him toward it. A wave of courtesy ninjas from each side of the aisle moved in.

Cereal Man whirled around with a roundhouse kick that knocked the freezer door off, dislocated many jaws, soaked many paper bag veils with blood, sent many teeth into many throats, and sent many aproned youngsters skidding down the aisle on their backs. He pulled the two assassins out from the freezer and slammed them onto the floor with the ease of a child throwing a doll. The victims both landed on their backs, knocking blood out of their ears, their mouths, and their eye sockets. Each of them wore a name tag with the Safeway logo preceding their names. One said "JAKE C" on the top and "COURTESY CLERK" on the bottom. The other said "KATHY D" on the top and "COURTESY CLERK" on the bottom. Cereal Man tore off their paper veils to find Jake and Kathy both gasping for air. He dug his thumbs into one of each of their eyeballs and gripped each of them by the roof of the mouth. He hurled Kathy into the crowd at one end of the aisle and Jake into the crowd at the other end.

My, how things had changed. Cereal Man remembered a day when these little maggots had been hired to bag groceries. Nothing about assassinations ever came into the deal. Union never tolerated it.

Freezer doors flew open, and innumerable courtesy ninjas flew out, screaming as if they thought they were bad. Many of them did have some fine moves. PHILIP O amazed him with his versatility. It took Cereal Man almost a minute of fending the kid off before he could snap the boy's arm and split his skull wide open. KELLY B was an absolute powerhouse—strong as an ox. Even after losing more than three pints of blood, she remained lethal. So Cereal Man fixed this by turning her head all the way around three times. ANDREW B's speed proved admirable, but not quite good enough. Before bleeding to death, he did manage to cram every inch of his intestines back into his body, as slippery and uncooperative as they were. But he could not reorganize them back into any kind of life-sustaining configuration. Poor kid. What kind of job was this for a kid, anyway? All those years in expensive martial arts training, only to watch his life rush out of him as quickly as his colon spilled out onto the tile floor?

After a feisty bout, Cereal Man removed the femoral artery from the long left leg of JULIEN S and used it to strangle HEATHER P. What a way to go. Mr. Laing probably paid them minimum wage for all this too.

KATY B had a dazzling somersault and a lightning fast kick. Cereal Man, however, having a kick faster than lighting, booted her head clean off her shoulders and into the produce section, where its sudden appearance would upset MARIA G very much. There was once a time when most people would frown upon this level of violence in a store. This store used to be a store of peace, once upon a time.

PATRICK R attacked from behind. The young lad, a true virtuoso with the spiked mop, presented a challenge at first. So Cereal Man took the mop away from him and drove the spike into the boy's lower spine, crippling him for life.

Yes, a store of peace. Cereal Man remembered it all. And he remembered when things had started to change. It was a simpler time. A gentler time, before courtesy ninjas, when people called clerks "bag boys" and when the senior bag boy was still a human being. This store used to be the best. It was always a shithole, but it was the best shithole. No other store on Earth had ever carried Plutonium Sugar Bombs. But this place did. Cereal Man had always seen to that.

BETHANY F attacked. He slit her throat and then impaled ALANNA M with a broomstick.

PSBs, the cereal with a half-life. Keeping them in the store seemed to require such a small effort.

Old, wise ROBIN B came at him, and Cereal Man smashed the middle-aged clerk's head in the freezer door, over and over and over, until he dotted the glass with bits of brain.

Yes, good old PSBs—seemed like they'd always stick around. But after all this time, you just can't go Home. The time had come for Cereal Man to understand that the universe may have changed, despite his most valiant efforts. The time had come for acceptance.

He ripped COLIN M's aorta out from behind his collar bone.

It was time for Cereal Man to lie down peacefully, allow himself to embrace change, and allow himself to flow with the sands of time.

That is, unless he could just get to that constipated little butterball and frighten him out of his fucking skin this time. This time Cereal Man wouldn't stop at physical torment, or even death threats. He knew where Mr. Laing's family lived. Goddamn, his wife had a face uglier than a fried egg sandwich inside a dog's asshole. But he knew that somehow, Mr. Laing loved that repugnant old... thing. So no more fucking around this time. If the flow of the cereal stopped again, so would the internal flow of his wife's blood, and the blood of his smelly daughter, who looked like an uncircumcised penis in a dress.

They came at him from all angles now. Courtesy ninjas darted out of the freezer doors, hurtled down from the rafters above, and charged from the entrances of the aisle. Now, more focused on the moment, he slaughtered them in droves. JENNIFER M decapitated. JENESSA R lacerated. MIKE C disemboweled. RORY H throttled. DENNIS U dismembered. JOHN K bludgeoned. LANCE N and MARLA N both cut in half. JOHN G suffocated, WAYNE S crushed by the falling freezer aisle, GORDAN B thrown through a wall... and on, and on, and on, until, through the dusty rubble and carnage, came that awful fetor. It had a humid weight to it, which made Cereal Man's organs feel... filthy. Stale soda. Stale beer. Tobacco spit. Grease. Blood. Urine. Dirt. Sweat. Feces.

I have always been here.

From behind the pile of rubble that was once the condiment aisle, and from behind a set of double doors, came a sickly green glow. The dozen or so courtesy ninjas who remained alive fled from Cereal Man. They scurried behind the double doors, where they could escape to safety. After a moment of silence, an eerie dissonance swelled in the air, and all the courtesy ninjas screamed in piercing agony behind the doors. Blood spilled from underneath and Cereal Man's eyes narrowed with determination. As the screams reached a crescendo, the stench became overpowering.

The doors blasted open and a new courtesy ninja appeared: the Master Courtesy Ninja. His eyes ran with sherbet-colored fluids from a potpourri of diseases. He had a thin, angular face with a narrow, pointy nose, a V-shaped chin, and a sharp, grimacing mouth, loaded with jagged white fence posts for teeth. He had scratched up, pinkish-white skin, with carbuncles and purple patches of burst capillaries. On top of all this hung a long, red mullet, clustered together in many places with gunk and rotting into black tentacles at the ends. He wore a pair of thick rubber gloves, originally yellow, but now black from all the junk that the years had caked onto them. Like his subordinates, he also wore a white shirt and a red tie. Both were torn and slick with stains. Over these, he wore a black, heavy-duty apron of the waterproof variety. At the top of this he sported a name tag, worn, scratched, and cluttered with crud. The Safeway logo on the side of the tag, looked similar to the tags of his subordinates. But this logo was bulkier, less sleek than the others. It was from a different time. And it featured letters of an older style: larger and more square. The last half of them was obscured by various forms of filth and damage issued to the tag in a long-gone age. The name tag once displayed, with gleaming newness, the letters "JEREMY A" at the top and "BAG BOY" at the bottom. Now, one could only read "JER—" at the top and "BAG—" at the bottom.

Since the Beginning, if one ever really existed, JEREMY A had, under the tutelage of his master, Mr. Laing, assumed his job title as his personal identity. When people would ask JEREMY A what he did, he would point with competitive pride to his name tag, which he polished every day, and even wore off duty. When advertising in the personal ads, he would write something like...

Single, white, Safeway bag boy, with long red hair and nice white shirt, seeking single white female. Hard worker. Interests include bagging groceries, stocking, facing, fronting, cleaning, counting bottles, writing receipts, and discussing the future of Safeway.

To his shock and dismay, nobody ever responded. But he got over it. After all, he had his job. And even if nobody loved him, he was important to Mr. Laing. In the early years, Mr. Laing noticed JEREMY A's incredible devotion and made a point of harnessing as much of it as possible. While more intelligent, more charismatic people climbed the ladder up to management, JEREMY A remained in the bag boy position.

"I need you," Mr. Laing would emphasize. "There's no one else I can trust in this entire store to do this job right." Armed with this level of self-importance, the young bag boy went far above and beyond the call of duty. He'd stay after hours, even off the clock, to help out. On holidays, when the rest of the staff had the day off and the store had closed, he would stock and clean the whole place. And while many employees would whine and bitch about having to count bottles, JEREMY A took on the task with a full heart and an immortal sense of duty.

This young man had become the darling of the store. It was at this juncture that Mr. Laing came unto JEREMY A to praise him for his incredible commitment and to reveal to him the honorable perk he had earned with his loyalty: exile into the bottle room. Of course, he didn't use the word "exile." He had given JEREMY A "the exciting opportunity to manage Safeway's glass, plastic, and aluminum deposit containers exchange!" The boy could not have imagined a greater compliment. But when his eyes flickered with even the slightest hint of doubt, Mr. Laing reminded him of his desperate need for the lad.

"You're the one person I trust to do this job right, son. And this means you'll be the lifeblood of this store... Senior Bag Boy!"

Then, seeing how this title left his employee rosy-cheeked and starry-eyed with honor, Mr. Laing sealed the promotion with the most dazzling cap of pure gold: a three cent an hour raise. JEREMY A felt overwhelmed. This sealed his soul into his job forever.

While other managers moved along with the times, incorporating bottle refund machines into their stores, Mr. Laing insisted on the purity and cheapness of the human element.

"Machines make mistakes," he would say, "And customers want to get their deposit slips from a real person, not some machine that doesn't have the human touch."

The squalor and toxicity of JEREMY A's bottle room degenerated him more and more as untold years passed. But in all this uncounted time, his loyalty to Mr. Laing never wavered. And indeed, there did come a time when his loyalty and devotion swelled like a corpse under the Pepsi bin: when Cereal Man's reign of terror began. They had never liked each other anyway. But the harder Cereal Man leaned on Mr. Laing, the more savage the senior bag boy would become to protect his eminent master: his creator, who made him who he was—whose magnanimity knew no equal.

Both of them had long ago prepared themselves for a battle that might never end. Cereal Man always emerged the victor, but his victory would only last until his next visit. Something always kept JEREMY A going—kept him coming back. Cereal Man dealt out consistent defeat with an accompaniment of humiliation, excruciating pain, and various other forms of suffering. While this would compel most foes to give up, JEREMY A would rise again, always. Even while lying out in the sandy, sizzling parking lot outside with a shopping cart jammed up his ass, he would remind himself who he was and why he was important.

"I am Jeremy A! Senior Bag Boy!" he would say to himself, with his name tag glimmering in his eyes, and he would rise one more time.

His last defeat at the hands of Cereal Man proved the most awful of all. It was then that his identity was destroyed, or at least warped into meaninglessness. Three years ago, Cereal Man had knocked him senseless, and, with the force of a plummeting aircraft, had slammed him into the giant pit of uncounted—and perhaps uncountable—bottles and cans. For three years, JEREMY A lay below the very floor of filth, unable to wake, and unable to sleep, in a phased state of wild, chaotic subconsciousness, relentless in nightmare and ponderous in its forgetful trance. He had never been neutralized for so long. But at last, Cereal Man returned. And thus came upon JEREMY A the sense of duty that had always driven him. And in the darkness and filth, JEREMY A did look upon his name tag and did gaze upon a set of unknown letters that scrambled and hurt his mind. Years of sticky guck dripping down to him had ushered a waking state of dreamlike confusion:

I am... JER-BAG? What is this... JER-BAG? Can feel him in a dream. I have always been here. We is close, but is still unreachable bottle can—drip. Drip. Dark black atop the white lamps and cylinder-cylinder-cylinders-clanky galaxy, and shiny... can't count. A million trillion off-trumpets and noisemakers—the hole goes up and up and up and up and up, and... snzzzzzzzzzzzzzzzzzzzzzzzz. snzzzzzzzz, sn-snzzz-zz-z-z. White lamps! White lamps up above. I have always been here. JER-BAG. The Creator will know.

And JER-BAG did claw himself up out of the pit, back to the surface, where there lay Mr. Laing, curled up under the Pepsi bin, hiding behind the corpse that had been rotting there for fuck knows how long. JER-BAG knew not himself anymore. But the fear in his creator's eyes set his sticky heart aflame. He knew his old enemy with the white eyes had come back.

Lean and nasty, he charged out of the bottle room on top of a loaded bottle cart, which moved on its own accord. He crouched for battle, swinging his nunchucks and shrieking like a pterodactyl. His nunchucks consisted of two broken bottles, connected by a chain. Cereal Man had never seen this new weapon. The bottles hissed and whistled through the air as JER-BAG brought them down on his adversary.

Look at what this once healthy young man has become. Of course, as Cereal Man ducked, dodged, turned, parried, and leapt away from his attacker's lethal onslaught, he looked upon his enemy with pity. *Look at what his creator has done to him; his master, to whom he still pledges unwavering loyalty.* But JER-BAG knew it didn't matter how much he had to suffer. His creator meant him to suffer for a greater greatness. The Creator Mr. Laing lived so everyone else could die.

Having caught one of the bottles, Cereal Man attempted to yank the nunchucks away. JER-BAG used this as an opportunity to land a jaw-shattering kick on Cereal Man's jaw. But Cereal Man's jaw did not move even one micrometer. Instead, the force of the kick caused JER-BAG to knock himself back into his own bottle bin, where in the midst of the bottles and cans, he clenched his demolished foot and whimpered in pain. As JER-BAG's unguided bottle bin squeaked down the ruined remains of one of the aisles, Cereal Man threw the nunchucks away. He went to the bin to crush the enemy within. But as he approached, JER-BAG leapt to the top again, swinging a huge garbage bag of bottles and cans at his opponent. Again, Cereal Man ducked, dodged, turned, parried, and leapt away from the bag. But this time, JER-BAG struck a blow—a fiery blow. All the cans and bottles inside exploded upon impact, lighting Cereal Man on fire and almost knocking him down. Paying no attention to the flames, he grabbed the bottle bin and lifted it over his own head. JER-BAG struggled for balance and almost jumped out. But it was too late. Cereal Man had already sent him and his bottle bin careening over the remaining aisles to the other side of the store. Toward the end of the projectile, they knocked down two more aisles, the last of which was aisle thirty-three, the New York Seltzer aisle. The flaming Cereal Man strolled down there.

The bottle bin lay upside down, in a pile of New York Seltzer bottles. Trapped underneath, JER-BAG moaned with panic. These were bottles—he knew that—but... but, what *were* they? These were shiny, and... and sparkly, and colorful, and... and... clean! Many of them were full of liquid. Clear liquid! Clean liquid! It horrified him, like some perversion of the very pillars of his reality. Not only that, but most of the plastic bottles now sprayed out their contents in happy, foamy fountains. These bottles were alive! The liquid came out on its own! If that wasn't disquieting enough, many of these "wrong" bottles were mixed in with all the "right" bottles and cans he knew so well. All sense had left his world. This perversion felt like sharp zaps of homeless electricity stabbing his brain.

As he cried and brayed with mounting fear, Cereal Man approached, engulfed in billowing flames. This sight balmed JER-BAG's hurt mind. This is what he wanted to see! His old foe of yesterday... What was his name way back then?... No matter. His enemy from the old days—Cereal Man—engulfed in fire! Cereal Man didn't seem to notice the flames. But to JER-BAG, these flames represented the fires of hope. He had never burned Cereal Man before. He had always relied on brute force, firearms, and mass assault. None of these had ever accomplished anything. But this time would be different. His consciousness had ordered it—ordered it from the Below, soon after Cereal Man had sent him there, three years ago. And so his underlings had loaded bottles and cans up with explosives. And there, in his bottle bin, these weapons waited—waited for him to rise again. *Now Cereal Man will burn! He'll burn for all the crimes he's committed against this store, and against the Creator Mr. Laing!*

JER-BAG's moaning subsided and gave way to a satisfied grin. Then he watched Cereal Man walk past a pile of plastic "wrong" bottles, which sprayed out huge fountains of that, that... living liquid. The horrible fountains of foam sprayed onto Cereal Man as he passed, and the flames hissed away into steam. JER-BAG's satisfied grin fell and gave way to moaning. Then his moaning elevated into screams of terror. His foe, renewed by the living liquid from those "wrong" bottles, was still coming. JER-BAG cowered and sobbed. It was a nightmare come to life.

But then, with the thought of Mr. Laing's oily face smiling down with constipated warmth upon him, JER-BAG remembered the soul toward whom Cereal Man directed his *true* malice. And with a scorching surge, the light of his duty, his very purpose for living, he incinerated the thought of curling up under the bottle bin and awaiting destruction. JER-BAG revitalized himself. He scrambled out from under the bottle bin and dragged out another bag of explosive bottles and cans. He swung it around, over his head to gain momentum. As Cereal Man advanced, JER-BAG swung. Cereal Man parried. JER-BAG swung again, and Cereal Man jumped over. JER-BAG swung a third time. Cereal Man ducked and launched a swift kick from below, tearing open the bottom of the bag and sending bottles and cans flying everywhere. All of them exploded on impact and ignited much of the store. JER-BAG fell on his back. As he began to rise, he noticed a few bottles and cans remained in the bag. In a panic, he gathered up as many as he could and began chucking them at his adversary. Many of them exploded in Cereal Man's face, but to no avail. As Cereal Man got closer and closer, JER-BAG's panic grew until he found himself scurrying around on the floor and throwing any cans or bottles he could grab, whether explosive or not. By the time Cereal Man got to him, JER-BAG was sobbing and throwing impotent, empty cans.

Cereal man seized his old enemy's wrists and took his time destroying them with his grip. Then he used those shattered wrists to throw his opponent into the adjacent wall. The impact imbedded him deep into the concrete. Cereal Man turned around and picked up one of the unexploded cans from the torn bag. He turned back as his adversary phased in and out of consciousness. He then clenched

JER-BAG's jaw and forced the explosive can into his gaping mouth. He looked the master courtesy ninja in his dripping sherbet eyes, and with the swiftness of a bullet, drove an uppercut into his chin. Fire and blood blew out of JER-BAG's nose and ears. His jaw was gone. His awful, misused body was now lifeless.

The old man had no pawns left to save his smelly old ass. The constipated king now cowered alone. Checkmate was coming.

10. FINAL CHECKMATE

Checkmate was coming, alright. Everything was coming. Coming for him. A sparkling arc of water cooled Baxter's aching eyes as he slumped over the drinking fountain. Within the shimmering blur, he could see impressions of black-and-white squares coming at him at varying speeds. Shutting his eyes made it worse. The squares would just sharpen in contrast and he'd watch nasty little chess pieces fly in and out of his field of vision. After a minute, his eyelids became too heavy. He remained awake, but he couldn't convince his eyes to stay open. His hair had become slick against his face. Coolness ran down his shirt and into his pants. He couldn't find the will to move.

And then, among the wandering chess pieces, behind the white and black squares, a faint shape appeared. It looked like some kind of painting. Its luminescent outline shimmered, like the water. It looked kind of like a bear. It was ... starry. A starry bear. Soon its stars began to multiply. Or was that snow? No matter. Now it had turned back into white and black squares again. Then the squares slowed and became still. And Baxter saw a white pawn checkmating a black king. The black king belonged to a sausage. A stubby, white bratwurst. Wait. No, that was Lizzie Upscrote, just a few minutes ago. Or maybe about an hour? Across from her sat Katelynne Bluecup, her face turned away, her hand shielding her tightened lips from Lizzie's view. She knew not to laugh at people. But the victory had come with such speed, and Lizzie had seemed so... so confident. Now Lizzie just looked angry. And shocked. And more angry. Her brows furrowed. The bubblegum-flavored lollipop fell out of her mouth but stuck to her lower lip, where it hung. With this, Katelynne couldn't help herself, and a loud chirp of mirth escaped. Oh, yes, Baxter remembered this. Maybe it was a couple of hours ago. But everyone remembered when Lizzie belted the table off to the side, pushed Katelynne out of her chair, and called her a bitch.

At that point, every laugh imprisoned within Katelynne had vanished. As she got up and backed away, Lizzie picked up the chair and charged forth. She swung the chair at her smarter opponent, who calmly took a step out of the way. Lizzie's heart and lungs had a hard time keeping up with this swing. So she threw down the chair and made an enraged beeline toward her smaller opponent, who calmly took a step out of the way. Lizzie slowed herself down and made a faster, even more enraged beeline toward her unfazed opponent, who calmly took a step out of the way. Lizzie skidded to a blustering halt, removed her lollipop, and ground her teeth with fury. She didn't do this for long because she needed to keep her mouth as wide open as possible to resume her shuddering gasps for air.

With the beginnings of recuperation, she jammed the lollipop back in her cheek, flared her nostrils, ground her teeth again, and charged at her incredulous opponent, who calmly took a step out of the way. Lizzie's heart could not pump fast enough to compensate for the titanic amount of oxygen she consumed by bringing herself to a stop. As her gelatinous form arched backward for one incredible last gasp, a sharp pain shot through her left arm. She collapsed on her back and died with a pink lollipop in her mouth.

Many people found Lizzie's death a difficult experience. It took a lumberjack eleven minutes to saw her into pieces light enough for the paramedics to carry out to the trash receptacles. In addition to these annoying distractions, it took three custodial artists an additional half hour to mop up the blood. One of them found Lizzie's pink lollipop lying on the floor and kept it as a souvenir.

Baxter had not noticed much of this. His own games had distracted him too much, as had Riley's loudmouthed objections to his swift defeats at the hands of Bucky Baby, Katelynne, and Adratica. Baxter had taken Adratica to a stalemate during their first game. He had won his next game, against Carter, though he had not yet defeated him. Three losses constituted true defeat and resulted in removal from the tournament. By the time Lizzie had started stinking up the trash cans outside, Baxter was three moves away from checkmating the mighty Vercingetorix. The android had proven a most worthy opponent. But he was no match.

In the end, Katelynne had dealt final defeat to Vercingetorix the Great. This took place at the triangular game, where she had already stalemated with Dr. T.J. With this defeat, the mighty engineer climbed up to the peak of his megalith, saluted the victorious ladies, and poured poteen down his gullet until he passed out and fell to the floor. HAMN had tried to revive Vercingetorix with a passionate kiss. Baxter also remembered the disquieting image of the lecherous android probing around under the mighty engineer's kilt for goodies until the paramedics peeled him or her off and rushed the fallen chess warrior away to the nearest RadioShack.

As much as all of this had disturbed Baxter, it had paled in comparison to the next round, when Carter defeated Bucky Baby. The living jewel became so upset, the pitch of his tones skyrocketed from his normal bass notes to a painful treble, which pierced many eardrums. His purplish red hue shot up into a blinding yellow. The incredible surge of radiation charred his advisers in a flash and gave many audience members cancer. They wouldn't know until later, of course. But doctors would later convince most of them that they could proudly sport those tumors as souvenirs from the Chess Intergalactica.

Baxter had defeated Carter in the next round, while Dr. T.J. lost to Katelynne, who stalemated with Adratica. After that, Adratica would beat Katelynne for the second time, while Baxter dealt a defeat to Dr. T.J. He remembered feeling regret for defeating the old psychotherapeutic patient, or patient psychotherapist, or... whatever. He remembered grasping her hand to say, "Good game."

At that point, she grabbed the hand and launched it into the air, bellowing to all the cosmos, "MONTEREY JACK!"

Baxter remembered the audience laughing and cheering at this strange lady, whom he did not understand in the least. He had wanted to ask for clarification, but Dr. T.J. had already crumpled into a tie-dyed pile in her wheelchair, sobbing with laughter. Kliban the cat then bounded onto her lap and snuggled up to her cheek again. With that, the loony doctor sat up and spun her wheelchair around. And with her arms pushing her wheels at an astonishing frequency, she zipped out of the arena.

After that, only Baxter, Katelynne, and Adratica had remained. They had all made their way to the triangular game, and the semi-finals, where an unexpected act of bravery, or foolishness, would at last whittle the contending players down to the final two. Baxter remembered it all. But now, everything before him glittered, and the shape of Katelynne shimmered toward him.

"I can turn the other way if you're taking a shower," she joked.

"Wha? Whabubbl-lllrpr-rbp," Baxter spluttered, jerking his face out of the fountain and seeing Katelynne standing before him, wearing nothing but a burlap bag. "Katelynne! I was … It's so nice to see you. I-I, it's been … I-I mean … W-what happened to your clothes?" he asked.

"Sold them for part of my bus fare. It's a long trip back to Io."

"Really? Never been there, myself. Seems like an exciting place."

"Yeah, the volcanoes make for a rather busy day. I just hope my youth hostel is still there when I get back."

"Where would it go?"

"Lava flows devour the cheap places all the time."

"Can't you get an apartment?"

"Ha! You're cute. Not if I want to pay my tuition."

"Gosh. And I thought *I* didn't have enough money. Can't Joel give you a ride home?"

"Aristotle left. He leaves a lot."

How could this be? Katelynne was a good person. Well, they're all good people, aren't they? How could such a situation occur? This puzzled Baxter. Things had puzzled him before, but this felt different. Behind it all, a new feeling crept into the picture: indignation. He'd read about this feeling before, in works of fiction. This was just weird. He felt like a character in some unrealistic work of fiction, as if someone could be reading about him at this very moment and believing him a work of fiction. This was too unreal to believe. Katelynne should have won the tournament! She was too nice for this sad fate.

"I just wanted to thank you for what you did," she said with a warm smile that disarmed him.

"Wh? I-I didn't do anything. I—"

"I saw what you did. And I'll never forg—"

"HEY, CANDYLIPS!" hollered a drunken member of the Ranks of Hell, while revving up his Bobby Fischer custom-detailed motorcycle outside, "BETTER WRAP THOSE TENDER THIGHS 'ROUND MY ASS RIGHT NOW, WE'RE OUTTA HERE!"

Many of the Ranks of Hell had long ago signed on as residents and staff members of Starry Plank. They never thought their beloved Dr. T.J. could ever be defeated, and they could not bear to watch the rest of the tournament. Since Katelynne hadn't ushered in this defeat, the Ranks held nothing against her and didn't mind dropping her off at the bus station. Besides, she was a fine piece of ass.

In the midst of their cursing and shattering of whiskey bottles, the rest of the Ranks started their engines. The sound of their Bobby choppers gurgled through the hall from outside. Katelynne darted down the hall in her bare feet. Baxter felt a lump in his throat. His eyes became heavy again as this beautiful person turned the corner and exited his life. After a pause, he turned, stretched his lips to the fountain, and began thinking of what Katelynne claimed he had done.

The trickling of the water lulled him back into memories of the last three games of the semi-finals. He knew what he'd done. He'd forgotten about the prize money, that's what he'd done! He'd forgotten about his mom. What was he thinking? Who knew? Not him. He only remembered feeling some kind of strange need to catch a glimpse of Katelynne's incredible, heart-fluttering smile. It had felt different from making his mom smile. Katelynne, after all, had more than one tooth. What an interesting formula. Was the happiness generated from a smile directly proportional to the number of teeth exposed? Very probable. Still, his act of bravery, or foolishness, had also brought a smile to Adratica's face that filled him with dread. With her teeth, his happiness turned out to be inversely proportional. So, that shot his hypothesis all to heck.

His act of bravery, or foolishness, had sent him away from the board with his king tipped over, and a sense of bewilderment squeezing his heart; a feeling he'd hoped to assuage with the counsel of his advising staff. To his shame, Professor Dedrick refused to speak to him. And he didn't feel like asking HAMN. In recent days, he had developed the feeling that HAMN didn't like him very much. His or her advice always seemed to come with some cryptic remark of disdain. But Xzhuajdnkqqqiiihwp had always been kind to him. The gaseous Neptunian had always offered constructive input, and with understanding. So Baxter asked him.

"I think you have feces for brains and that you pinched off the last loaf of your intelligence during the bathroom break," said Xzhuajdnkqqqiiihwp. "Adratica had Katelynne in checkmate, for cryin' out loud! Her rook had her pinned, and what do you do? … You swoop in with your queen?! I've never seen a player bail an opponent out of checkmate."

"That was her last rook," Baxter defended. "Its network controlled two-thirds of the board, so I took it. I collapsed that network."

"And sacrificed your queen and opened up an entire file for Adratica to delve into."

Baxter hadn't needed to hear this. Deep down he knew he had made a blunder. But he wanted to understand why he had let it happen. But what a silly dialogue he had started with Xzhuajdnkqqqiiihwp. Why ask him, anyway? After all, the Neptunian couldn't read his mind.

"I think you've got a chubby for Katelynne and that's all there is to it," said Xzhuajdnkqqqiiihwp.

Baxter had no idea what a chubby was. Whatever it was, it sounded like something that wouldn't fit in his backpack. He never brought anything to the tournament for Katelynne. He hadn't even known she would be there. But seeing her had filled him with such delightful surprise. He had not looked forward to seeing her lose. But he sure did love seeing her survive to stalemate Adratica. But he would never say that.

"But I sure did love seeing her survive to stalemate Adratica," he said.

"Yeah, it was hot, Bax. Gave me goosebumps," scoffed Baxter's gaseous adviser.

"I'll tell you this, young man," Professor Dedrick chimed in. "You only prolonged the inevitable. Your weakness for Katelynne is obvious, and you are as transparent as Xzhuajdnkqqqiiihwp is when I'm composing phony exam answers for him to covertly observe. This next round will be an extermination. Adratica will now focus all her attention on eliminating Katelynne as swiftly as possible, knowing your bias will cloud your judgment."

The wise bacterium's prediction had proven correct. In the second game of the semi-finals, Katelynne had suffered a swift and brutal defeat, leaving Baxter at a great disadvantage. The game had fairy pieces, such as princesses, which moved like knights and bishops, and empresses, which moved like knights and rooks. But the brutality of Adratica's victory had been ushered in by a pope. Like kings, popes moved one space at a time in any direction. But uniquely, popes did not capture opposing pieces. They converted them. Thus, a player's pope could issue checkmate by converting a king to his own side. Adratica did exactly this to Katelynne within minutes. This endowed Professor Dedrick's old prodigy with two kings, both of which Baxter then had to checkmate.

The ferocity with which Adratica had decimated Katelynne introduced Baxter to his first pangs of protective anger. However, Katelynne's absence from the game clarified the rest of the match for him. He remembered why he had come to compete in the first place: to save Mom. Without this focus, his cyclonic opponent would have whisked him right off the board. But Baxter had remained focused enough to simultaneously checkmate both of those foul, blood-bought kings of hers. For the first time in his life, he had felt satisfaction from someone else's defeat.

The memory of all this now rippled in his mind. His eyes burned with exhaustion, and there loomed that poster again, so much more vivid than before. And now it was in color. The embers of the anthropomorphic rat's cigarette burned a sparky orange and gave rise to thin, bluish ribbons of smoke. His long face glistened with short, dark-gray hair, peppered black toward his neck, all of which he kept groomed back toward his ears. He had also groomed with care a short, darker gray mohawk between his ears.

It struck Baxter as odd how nothing seemed filthy about this rat. The youth did not see a gnawing, squeaking harbinger of disease. He saw no scurrying varmint that scavenged in unreachable cracks and holes. Instead, he perceived a sharp, deliberate individual who kept himself up. And yet, Baxter also could not deny the danger he now felt, just by looking upon him. The rat seemed to seethe with rage, even though his face featured no expression. A heavy visor obscured his eyes. The black lens of this visor reflected zigzags of bright blue, which looked like they might have come from a neon sign. He appeared to wear a heavy black trench coat with a wide collar and a black T-shirt underneath. The shirt sported some kind of silvery logo that looked like a check mark fused into the left of a letter "R." Baxter noticed that the reward amount had grown even larger now. He blinked with disbelief. *Just how many commas is that?* He looked closer.

"FINAL MATCH IN THREE MINUTES, LADIES AND GENTLEMEN. FINAL MATCH IN THREE MINUTES," blasted Riley's voice from inside the auditorium.

HAMN came out and rolled his or her eyes at the sight of Baxter staring at the poster, soaking wet, with the water still running.

"Goddammit, again?" HAMN whined. "Whatterya got a thing for that rat or something?"

"A thing?" said Baxter.

"Never mind. Get in there. For shit's sake, everyone's waiting for you."

After more than eleven hours of the most humbling chess of this humble lad's life, after eight checkmates, one stalemate, and one loss, Baxter felt like his brain would pour out from one of his ears if he tilted his head. And to know that the worst was yet to come… the thought of it made him almost sick. Couldn't he just go Home? Couldn't everyone just declare him champion now? For goodness sake, isn't eight checkmates enough? Nobody else had that many. Good heavens, Adratica had only five. And she had three stalemates. And two losses! Both of which were to him! Well, those last two occurred during the same game, so the rules counted them as just one loss. But still! He had stayed far ahead of her. And now he had to drag himself back in there and beat her two more times? She was the meanest chess player in the world. But there was no way out of it. Mom needed that prize money. He had to go on.

But first, a nice refreshing drink of water. How long had he been standing here with the fountain running? No matter. With his face and clothes still soaking wet, Baxter leaned down to take that cool sip. But just before his lips could touch the stream, it disappeared. He pressed the button harder, but no water came. He stared at the fountain in puzzlement until he heard HAMN sighing and grumbling with exasperation. The two of them returned to the arena.

Alliances had formed in the audience. Adratica had gained the favor of lots of lonely bachelors. Several of them boasted membership in her online fan club. All of them had their laptops with them and all had convinced themselves that "With my unique sense of humor and powers of eloquence, I know this email will set me apart. And she'll swoon over me."

Baxter had gained the favor of most of the chess clubs and a few of the gangs. The 64 Squares had grown especially enamored with him.

When he entered, they all went crazy. Many held banners that echoed their chants of loyalty, with phrases like, "BAX TO DA MAX," "MY MAN BAXTER," and "EIGHT MATE MOTHERFUCKER." The greater chess-playing community had long known the Squares as a dangerous clan of badass geeks. Many of them had endured violent childhoods and had been tossed out onto the streets after years of trying to conceal their closet chess habits from parents who wanted them to play sports and watch TV. These rejects always roamed the university armed with badass blades, masked with badass shades, and decked out in badass black leather jackets, which had their badass gang names emblazoned on the back. Each Square's gang name corresponded to a square on the standard chess board, such as "Queen's Rook 5 (QR5)" or "King's Bishop 8 (KB8)." But now, for the first time ever, their backs no longer showed their own identities. As Baxter wandered to the chess table, K2, the high protector of the chief of the Squares, hollered out, "Eight Mate Muthufucka! You da messiah, Baxter baby! You da mate messiah!"

All of the 64 Squares turned around to reveal the name "BAXTER" emblazoned on their badass leather jackets. They chanted, "EIGHT MATE, EIGHT MATE, EIGHT MATE..." until the audience crescendoed into a roaring cheer.

"What are they whooping and hollering about?" said HAMN. "Those last two mates only counted as one."

Baxter didn't realize this until now, but HAMN was right.

"Gosh, I guess someone should tell them," said Baxter.

"It doesn't matter, Baxter," said Professor Dedrick. "What matters is that you show this mayhem-mongering horror of a woman the order of your constitution."

Baxter noticed Adratica at the chess table, waiting for him. She beamed a sardonic grin at Professor Dedrick until Baxter sat down in his seat. The fiery blue of her eyes drilled into the blank blue of his. Then she scanned his wet frame up and down, and a few scornful titters bubbled out of her. Baxter had grown too tired to care. He just wanted this to end.

Cereal Man, however, would never grow too tired to care. The first light of the next day crept in from the windows. But he would not relent. He would search in every corner, under every slab of burning rubble, under each gnarled twist of metal, under every corpse and every chunk of dismembered flesh to find Mr. Laing. The greasy store manager had slipped out from under the Pepsi bin during Cereal Man's battle with the master courtesy ninja and had found a new hovel somewhere in the store. It was simply a matter of looking long enough.

For Adratica, it was simply a matter of waiting long enough. In his haste to rest, Baxter had acquainted himself with aggression. He had managed to rush Adratica to defeat in the first of the final two games. This brought her to the delicious notion that destroying Baxter's mind seemed the optimal path to destroying his armies. The first light of the next day now crept in from the hallways.

Eleven hours had now groaned by since Baxter's bedtime. He'd never stayed up past his bedtime before, and it showed. He couldn't figure out why his opponent kept making such wasteful moves; almost as if she wanted to prolong the match. She had to be insane. As if a ten-dimensional hypercube board with fairy pieces didn't present enough difficulty already! Colors helped the players keep track of the fourth dimensional locations of pieces. But for the additional six dimensions, they couldn't even see the pieces. They had to keep track of them by growing and pruning mental trees of complex calculations. As sunlight sliced in through the cracks of doors, Baxter's brain boiled in his skull. Mathematical representations of hyperdimensional chess pieces bustled around inside his mind the way hordes of customers bustle around inside a Safeway at opening hour.

As sunlight washed in through the windows and doors, Cereal Man's blood boiled in his veins. Hordes of customers bustled around inside the Safeway at opening hour the way mathematical representations of hyperdimensional chess pieces bustle around inside Baxter's mind, whoever he was. The most annoying customers asked Cereal Man if he knew whether the store would discount the frozen foods that had shrapnel imbedded in the packaging. All the customers wandered through the store with their usual aura of mindless disconnect, but at a much slower, much more awkward pace than usual. They negotiated their ways around corpses and around the piles of concrete and metal. Some of them tried to go over the piles but would often injure or burn themselves. The flames on top didn't seem to tip them off that it was hot up there. Some tried to go underneath but became trapped. All of this resulted in redundant spells of whimpering and crying.

But this was nothing compared to the petulance that occurred at what remained of the checkout lanes. Confronted with the reality of cashiers bleeding all over the remains of a checkout counter, or of courtesy clerks maimed or blown to bits, the customers whined with confusion and sniveled at the abject level of service through which they had to suffer. With all this new chaos, it became possible for Mr.

Laing to escape the premises undetected. Cereal Man could not allow this. He needed a new idea fast. He needed to see past the clutter.

Too many pieces cluttered the hyperboard—too many pieces spread out far and wide throughout ten dimensions. Baxter could handle almost any orderly danger. Once he identified a pattern or intelligence behind the configuration, he could always extract a weakness and formulate a strategy. But Adratica had reduced this game to pure entropy. She had passed up avenue after avenue of advancement, ignoring endless opportunities to capture Baxter's pieces and create a strategic arrangement. And yet, she still kept her opponent from taking any of her own pieces. Everyone knew Adratica's reputation for creating devastating death machines with four or five harmoniously networked pieces. But nothing like that appeared here. Baxter may as well have tried to gain control of a spinning room full of bouncing Super Balls, order them into a single file line, and roll them into a hose.

And the longer they played, the more volatile the game grew. Some kind of catastrophe was imminent. She had locked up the hyperboard in a precarious state. Every move now had to be made with the most delicate care, lest an opening be exposed. One wrong move could lead to a chain reaction of runaway massacre, which the erring player would not be capable of staying.

Then, Baxter "saw" a sliver of order in this poop show. Adratica had lost track of it. Professor Dedrick and Xzhuajdnkqqqiiihwp also didn't see it. Nobody seemed to. But HAMN sure did. The golden android sat on the edge of his or her seat, waiting for Baxter to perceive this opening. After more than a half hour of Baxter living in this oblivion, HAMN slouched back in the chair, scoffing with pessimism.

But then, in a sudden moment of clarity, Baxter saw it. HAMN saw him see it and straightened up in excitement. Of course, Baxter couldn't actually see the three of his pawns that had managed to advance to the frontiers of Adratica's side. But his hyperspacial calculations confirmed them sitting there, cutely, in a neat little line, waiting, cutely, to usher in a brutal reign of terror that would dizzy his opponent. Adratica could not capture any of these pawns without exposing herself to check. So Baxter moved one of these pawns to the final rank. This, of course, entitled him to promote that pawn to a second queen. This displeased Adratica. But when Baxter passed up this promotion, Adratica's cold heart sank in her chest. The audience then caught up and gasped the air out of the arena. The apocalypse was nigh, and here, the harbinger would not come in the form of a pale horse. It would hurtle down from above as a white, winged Pegasus.

Poop was the answer. Though famous among peers, employees, family members, strangers, and the medical community for his constipated appearance, Mr. Laing did not tote the cemented bowels presumed by some. He fancied himself a patriot and believed in a religiously American diet of grease, sugar and ultra-processed whatever. This righteous regimen proved totally at odds with the once natural vessel that had now so wholly devolved into the cellulite-rinded mobile junkyard that he called his body.

So this vessel, still possessing much of its ancestors' original, natural programming, would eject the stuffs of such a diet with enough swiftness and frequency to keep Mr. Laing on the run. The sweaty store manager never had any idea just how often his staff had observed their boss, at random intervals, receiving crisis-level alerts from his colon. He'd always hoped that rushing away at a moment's notice during most conversations, meetings, and intercom announcements went largely unnoticed. He'd always assumed that bursting into the employee restroom to order employees out, then tying the restroom up for a cumulative two-thirds of the day qualified as addressing the matter with subtlety and discretion. But the single toilet in that cramped restroom saw his ass with far more frequency than did his office chair.

Now, thanks to a volley of explosive cans, released by JER-BAG, the restroom lay buried in debris. Now Cereal Man could expect to find feces wherever Mr. Laing had hidden himself. He had already checked under the Pepsi bin, where Mr. Laing had hidden before. No feces. Just that bloated corpse. Cereal Man had held the old man's store under siege for almost a whole day now, a period that would normally have hosted at least eleven emergency defecation trips. The old greaseball hadn't a whisper of a chance of holding it in. Cereal Man knew he would find a turd that pointed the way to its issuer, somewhere, here among the rubble and disarray.

Then, Cereal Man "saw" a sliver of order in this shitshow. He couldn't actually see the three samples of stool all the way across the store, near the meat department. But his olfactory calculations confirmed them sitting there, disgustingly, in a neat, long line, waiting, disgustingly, to guide him to their home anus and the defiled being that lived around it.

Only ignorant fools could underestimate the danger of the Pegasus. It moved just like a knight, but even the best players found it nearly impossible to capture or block, since the piece could occupy and attack from a dimension that did not exist for any other piece. For instance, in a standard 2D game, a Pegasus could attack from above or below, while all the other pieces remained limited to the two dimensions of the flat board. Three pawns had to advance to the final rank without accepting promotion. When the third pawn arrived, players could promote any one of their knights to a Pegasus. Doing this always presented quite a gamble, since it meant giving up two potential new queens and betting that at least one knight would survive until third promotion.

Once Baxter's third pawn advanced to Adratica's home rank, the game turned. The confusion that she had spread throughout the hyperboard, which she had exploited with masterful skill, had, in the twinkling of an eye, turned into an open ground for a killing spree. The crowd stirred.

With an exhilarated smile flashing onto his or her face, HAMN stood up and shouted out, "GO FOR IT, BAX!"

Baxter promoted his king's knight and launched his new Pegasus into the previously nonexistent eleventh dimension. The crowd's stirring swelled into cheering. Adratica scrambled around, mustering pieces, trying to mold one of her infamous death machines out of the exquisite bedlam that she herself had crafted. But it was no use. Like a helicopter soaring over the rice paddies of Vietnam, Baxter's Pegasus decimated the hyperboard from "above."

He didn't feel tired anymore. Sleep now felt like something he'd needed in a past life. A fury overtook him. He'd never felt so alive—so aggressive. Plucking off Adratica's army, piece by piece, watching her fiery blue eyes swirl with rage, watching her face contort with ever greater despair, and taking in the crowd, his crowd, roaring louder and louder for him... it felt like a nuclear ignition.

Then he slowed down his attack, to savor this feeling and to draw out her demise. While Adratica hobbled around, struggling to build herself into something that at least seemed a notch above sheer aimlessness, Baxter began constructing an eleven-dimensional death machine of his own, while casually knocking away an occasional piece as a cavalier afterthought. Soon, only Adratica's king remained, and one pawn, both saved for sport—both left to bat around and torture until Baxter bottlenecked them. And like a cat toying with a spider on little roller skates, Baxter would make the kill when he got bored. Strange. Such pleasure at someone else's defeat. This didn't feel right. Adratica must be a very nice person, just like everyone else. Maybe she just needed to be treated nicely—and there was an image of Katelynne.

He remembered her in that burlap bag, having to endure that half-billion-mile ride back home after a gaggle of ruffians dropped her off at a bus terminal. He now pictured her having to kiss one of those men as a payment for services. He had never before imagined anything so vile! It was just wrong. And it was Adratica's fault. Baxter would not regret her despair. He would savor it. And the more he savored it, the sweeter his imminent victory smelled.

And the closer Cereal Man came to it, the fouler the lump of dung smelled. A hard and rocky rubble surrounding the first turd provided a camouflage for it. Only one end of this stumpy gray thing retained any moisture at all. This end pointed toward the meat room. With his nose crinkling, Cereal Man followed the direction. Then he came upon a much moister, much larger specimen, which made him gag. This one was rocky at one end and looked increasingly like a giant brown slug as it trailed along the aisle. A few cigarette butts and a small fragment of the business end of a plastic spork poked out of it. A bit of blood dripped from the sticky end, where this massive lump tapered off.

After that, it became much easier. Cereal Man followed the drops, which dotted the floor with more and more haste until they formed a splotchy trail. The trail ended with a splattering pattern all over the floor in front of the door to the meat department. Spread out amidst all of this lay the contents of the final turd, a gloppy spill of pulp, not pointing to any one place, but rather marking the foot of the door—the final passage that would lead to the recently relieved store manager. Cereal Man left the wreckage of the store behind and entered the only area that remained intact. No mounds of warped metal, no obliterated pillars, no flaming ruins of concrete. No stupid customers. Just lots of smooth, horizontal lines of stainless steel. And a trail of blood that trickled along the floor, up to the left leg of a sweaty, porcine ruin of a man, looking back in fear and grunting and shaking as he inched across the tile on his gut.

Adratica's king now retreated in the same manner. Baxter had pinned her pawn, but not before promotion. Baxter had allowed her to get it all the way across the board, to his rank. In fact, he had insisted on it. With most of his pieces remaining, he had not found it difficult to put her king into a position where it could not legally move. This left Adratica with no choice but to move her pawn. In essence, Baxter had forced her to gain a queen. He did this so he could cripple it and watch Adratica's face fold up with scorn at his pettiness. Then he let her king move again, into a corner.

It was 6:33 a.m. when Baxter checkmated Adratica Scaldiatrix's black king from the eleventh dimension with his white Pegasus and won the Chess Intergalactica. The crowd exploded into hysteria as Riley raised Baxter's hand to the air in triumph and patted him on the back. The three sexy advisers of the loudmouthed MC slinked in and handed Baxter a giant check. Riley then brandished the championship trophy. Its formation of bulky rectangles of elegant black marble stood almost as tall as the champion himself. Gold trimmed the edges, leading up to the top, where the head of a muscular white chess knight stood with an intimidating gaze. Looking as though it might bite Baxter's own slightly smaller head, it stared out, as if to challenge all the cosmos with its blazing gold eyes. Baxter flinched away from the commanding equine as Riley declared him "BAXTER! THE CHESS CHAMPION OF THE UNIVERSE!"

Adratica kicked the hyperboard away and sprinted toward Professor Dedrick. She passed right through Xzhuajdnkqqqiiihwp. HAMN tried to stop her, but he or she didn't try very hard. Professor Dedrick's old disciple grabbed a hold of his petri dish and pulled a can of antibacterial spray out of a holster on her ankle. She began to spray but was trampled by the cavalcade of losers flooding the center of the arena in hope of meeting their new champion. The pandemonium swept over Baxter. Reporters flocked to him, pushing cameras and microphones into his face. People clamored everywhere, some congratulating him, some just yelling and screaming. A few had heart attacks. Several others broke out champagne. Dozens pestered him for autographs. Hundreds became caught up in improvising song and dance with the marching band. Hundreds more became so excited that they started making passionate love to complete strangers next to them, most of whom reciprocated with slobbery lips, dripping tips, open arms, and open holes.

Through the chaos, Baxter's attention was drawn to the 64 Squares, all of whom sported the word "BAXTER" on the back of their badass leather jackets, and all of whom marched toward him. In perfect sync, they all stopped. Their master, K1, towered over them, with his immense shoulders, his wide jaw, his joyful mouth, and his bulging eyes. Those huge eyes contrasted with his dark-brown skin and the black-and-white checker pattern in his short hair. The Squares lifted up their master and placed him on some sort of altar, which they had brought with them. Fuckin' geeks. They surrounded the altar and writhed around their master, touching his hands and his feet, it seemed, for the last time. K1 touched each of them back with love and honor, then took off his badass leather jacket and tossed it to Baxter. The dazed champion fumbled about with it, but caught it, and then looked to K1 with confusion.

K1 pointed to Baxter with open hands. "All hail the mate messiah!"

The other Squares all kneeled and saluted Baxter.

"Now," continued K1 with a joyful smile, as his Squares rose up, "Now, I must die!"

With that, the Squares swarmed the altar with animal ferocity and tore K1 limb from limb. With feverish focus, quaking skulls, and completely dilated irises, they ripped the flesh from his body and consumed it. A swarm of piranhas could not have devoured him faster. Then, as they finished, each one began grunting repeatedly. As they all came into sync with one another, the grunting became chanting. Then, after a moment of them all chanting in unison, they stopped. In the dead silence, the Squares all turned their faces to Baxter and looked at him.

With those black holes they had for eyes.

They all exploded into another fervor. They swarmed Baxter and cloaked him in K1's badass leather jacket, which was the size of a robe to him. They lifted him into the air. The champion clutched onto his huge trophy for dear life as the Squares passed him over each other, all the way to the altar. They set him down and he released himself from the trophy. Another huge silence fell. Then, all at once, they exclaimed, "MATE MESSIAH!" and the insane celebration in the arena resumed with a vengeance. More congratulations. More yelling and screaming. Fans begged for autographs. Heart attacks increased. The singing and dancing turned to a gospel chess revival. The orgies became psychopathic.

Reporters managed to burrow through all this. They crammed their microphones and cameras into Baxter's face and asked him how do you feel, what's it like, what are you going to do now, when did you know you'd won, who's Lizzie Upscrote, how long have you been playing, what are you gonna do with the money, who'd you like to thank, where's my wallet, who's your favorite chess player, will you play again, did you play your best game, did you ever feel like quitting, I lost my glasses, are you dating anyone, describe your love of the game...

"I just want to say one thing," Baxter announced, "To my mom at Home..."

Mustering up all his strength, he lifted the trophy over his head and cried, "HI MOM!... I DID IT!"

Heroic, conclusive music filled the Illustrious Professor Earl Hazekamp Convocation Center, and the crowd sent forth warm cheers at Baxter's tribute to his mother; his dear mother, who in fact, at that very moment, remained lying face down in the TV set, belching deathly bubbles into an acidic mass of some kind of horseradishy puke.

11. THE COMING OF THE CANDY MAN

A bucket of ice-cold grape soda woke Reese and Chuckles. The two naked taser victims sputtered and coughed as Clark stood over them with the empty bucket and a smug grin. Skittles and the Stick stood behind him.

"Jeezis, dude," griped Chuckles. "What's your problem?" Clark's lips tightened as he adjusted his hat. "You think that's funny?" Chuckles yelped. Then he realized how grotesque and silly he must have looked and chuckled in spite of himself. Reese, however, didn't see the humor.

"You're dead, three-eyes," he said, getting up. "I hope you like the taste of that goddamn top hat."

Reese charged at Clark. But his hands never got to the hat because they had to follow his arms, which had to follow his shoulders, which had to follow the path of his head, which Clark had knocked back when his hand made high-speed contact with Reese's chin. Then Reese found his body jerked forward again. It was following his penis. Clark yanked the penis back and began swinging Reese around in a circle. He spun around and around, faster and faster, with Reese revolving around him in a desperate and flailing effort to not tumble to the floor or have his dick ripped out. Then Clark let go and sent Reese hurtling into Chuckles. The two of them tumbled all over each other and stopped just short of rolling off the edge of the circular platform. Chuckles found himself face down on the floor, with his ass pointing up: two hairy, white hills of cellulite. Reese found his own head trapped between the floor and one of Chuckles's filthy rolls of flab. As he tried to pull himself out, Chuckles looked back at Clark and belted out a hearty laugh of admiration, which squeezed Reese's face repeatedly.

"Whoa-ho-ho-hohhhhh," said Chuckles. "That was totally rad, dude. How'd you do that?"

"The Stick taught me that one," said Clark.

"Candy for all," quoth the Stick.

"And all for the captain," Clark replied unto the Stick in a hammy Japanese accent. The two bowed. Skittles fed Clark a jelly bean, which he consumed with poise. Reese managed to crawl out from under Chuckles. He bundled up his stretched-out penis, then shuffled off, whimpering and cupping the noodley dick between his legs.

"Wow," said Ike, some distance away. "Lookit what happened to Reese," he said to Mike. Ike leaned on the handle of a lollipop the size of a battle-ax. He lifted up his dumbass eyepatch to better spy the goings-on.

Mike said nothing. In the full of his brother's distraction, he produced a tiny vial, really just a small plastic container, shaped like a strawberry and filled with artificially flavored, artificially colored candy powder. But to him, a tiny vial of magic potion it was. He removed the cap with a sly grace matched only by the ancient Zoroastrian magi. Ike turned back to Mike and felt a strawberry sting batted into his eyes.

"OW, you dick! ... WLLAAGHHH!" he yelped, as Mike tossed the container on the floor, wrapped a thin red licorice vine around his little brother's neck, and began strangling him. The licorice ranked as the chewiest ever made, not breakable by most humans. Ike pounded on Mike with the lollipop, but with no effect. It was too big and unwieldy. "Helpb!" Ike called out to Heath. "Taygk himb off mbe!"

"My sword's gone," said Heath.

"Helpb mbe, mban!" begged Ike.

"Well, what am I supposed to do?" Heath whined.

"Shootd himb," said Ike, struggling for air. "Shootd himb, I don'td careghhh!"

"What do I get?" said Heath.

"Cand't breeeathe," choked Ike.

"What do I get?" Heath insisted.

"Whatdever!" Ike whispered. "Whatdever you wantd, justd helpb mbe!" Heath considered it. Ike sweetened the deal. "Andythig! ANDYTHIG, I'll give you andythig."

"Anything, eh?" said Heath with a satisfied grin.

"ANDYTHIG!" said Ike, weeping under full realization that these words might be his last. "Pleeeeeze . . . I'mb too young. You're bmy only hope!"

"Half your rations for a year," said Heath.

"Fuckg you," Ike managed. "Getd outda my sightd."

"A month, then," bargained Heath.

"Go fuckg yourselfv!" choked Ike, his face growing a deep purple.

"Come onnn! It's your LIFE, you prick!" Heath pleaded. ". . . A week?"

"No fuckig way!" choked Ike, almost dead. "I'd rather die."

"You asshole," Heath snarled. "Alright, this is it, I'm finished fuckin' around! Five days, and that's my final offer!"

"Three," Ike hissed, struggling to squeeze out enough air to be heard. "Thatd's my findal."

"THREE?!" Heath yelped. "To save your LIFE?!"

"One," Ike uttered with his very last trace of air.

"YOU— FINE—" Heath screamed. He drew his gun and opened fire, or rather, he opened Maggie up and gave her multiples. The first shot snapped the licorice vine in half and released Ike, who collapsed on the floor. Mike reached for his strawberry powder, but just as he touched it, the second shot blew the container way over toward the other guys, who looked on with amazement. The strawberry container came a hair's width away from landing on Clark when Heath's third shot blasted it away again. Heath's fourth shot whipped the newly planted toothpick out of Reese's mouth. The fifth blew Mike's empty glasses frames right off his face without grazing a single pore on his skin. After that, the chamber jammed, or rather, Maggie passed out from Heath's gift of ecstasy.

The guys would never mock Heath's pistol toting again. This is because he failed to disclose that he had aimed every shot at Ike. Ike had been such an asshole about his rations. The rest of the guys approached as Mike picked himself up off the floor.

"That was bogus, dude! Totally bogus," said Mike. "Tryin' to get me snuffed, dude, what gives?"

"What?!" Ike yelped.

"I'm like, your only bro, Bro," Mike sniveled.

"So, do I just let you slice my head off?" countered Ike.

"Who showed ya how to get nine hundred ninety-nine lives on Berzerk?" said Mike. "Me, man."

"No you didn't," said Ike. "That was Pops."

"Yeah, and who scored you that sweet VHS deal with Columbia House, huh?" Mike boasted.

"Suck my dick, you dick," Ike dismissed. "They're still sending me shit I don't want."

"Who taught ya how to rearrange the stickers on a Rubik's Cube, huh?" said Mike. "Me!"

"That makes it okay for you to choke me to death?" said Ike.

"Dude, I was totally sparring with you," said Mike.

"I wasn't ready," said Ike.

"Exactly. That's when to strike," said Heath.

"Shut up, Heap," Ike scoffed.

"That is IT! I told you! Your life ends now, you green Gorn turd," growled Heath, trying to wake Maggie up again. "Hold on a minute," he added, trying to figure out why she wouldn't put out. Pops took the gun away from him. Then Pops popped Maggie's magazine out, threw it on the floor, and tucked Maggie in his pants.

"You can have it back when you know how to use it," Pops decreed, squinting at him with contempt. Heath stared at him. Pops nodded at him. Then he squinted harder. He knew. He knew Heath had been aiming at Ike. "You're with me now."

Heath's face began sizzling red with outrage. To have Maggie taken from him with such cavalier arrogance, and to torture his eyes with the image of her moneymaker bending down toward the genitals of this gruff old guy—it cast the world into a bewildering state, beyond imagination.

"YOU HAVE NO RIGHT!" Heath protested.

"He has every right. You're in training," said the Stick.

"Training?" said Chuckles, just getting the last of his clothes back on.

"What training?" Reese demanded, still naked. "You know I have half a—"

"Should you be speaking?" asked Clark. Reese instantly cupped his dick and closed his mouth.

"Yeah, but we gotta train fair, said Ike. "No throwin' candy fruit blow in your little brother's eyes until he's ready."

"Snooze and lose, loser," Mike taunted, pulling Ike's eyepatch back and snapping it into his eye. Ike hurled around and knocked Mike to the floor with his giant lollipop. Mike started to get up, but Ike slammed him again. He raised the lollipop high in the air for the final blow, but a long black whip of licorice slapped onto it. The whip twirled tightly around the stick of the lollipop. With one good yank, Mike sent Ike's weapon flying. Ike attempted to dash the scene, but the licorice whip came after him, squeezing his ankles together. Soon he found himself on the floor with his older brother whipping him.

"Stop," Heath protested. "I get half his rations tomorrow!"

"His what? His rations?" said Chuckles.

"You ain't gettin' shit from me, Heap, you heaping fat-ass shit heap," Ike grunted, struggling to kick Mike between whippings.

Heath charged toward Ike with the raging force of a manure heap, but then fell flat on his face. It soon came upon him that Clark had tripped him by hooking his ankle with a giant candy cane. Clark posted the stripy cane at his side, placed his ruined top hat on his head, and adjusted his dirty, chipped monocle. He looked like a homeless Mr. Peanut. Heath scrambled to his feet to attack Clark.

After waiting several minutes for Heath to come to his feet, Clark swung his cane at him. But Heath ducked by means of falling back on his ass. So Clark jabbed him in the stomach with the edge of the cane until it got boring. Heath lay there, shaking, and curled up into the fetal position. Maggie was gone. Hassan Chop was gone. What would Heath do? Heath would sob. Clark stood over him with Skittles, Pops, and the Stick right next to him. They could hear Mike and Ike hurling death threats at each other. Skittles fed Clark another jellybean, which he consumed with grace. The Stick knelt, then scalded Heath's mind with his slow, quiet words:

"Hassan was yours—a beautiful scimitar of royal red violet, forged and sharpened to perfection by the finest Jolly Rancher smiths of the Near East—a gift from the captain to your worthless ass—a gift to better yourself—to use in our mission. You know what happens when you eat your weapon?" whispered the Stick. "You're left at the mercy of guys with self-control. Ain't that right, Skittles?"

"Right, Sticky," said Skittles.

"It was raspberry," Heath whimpered.

"Aw, that changes everything, don't it, Skittles," the Stick mocked. "It was raspberry."

Skittles guffawed as he grabbed hold of Heath's hi-top fade toupee. Heath had always used Klingon Krazy Glue to ensure the hair piece's undying loyalty to his scalp. The rug's unbroken and unbreakable honor allowed Skittles to lift Heath high into the air with no chance of escape. Heath hollered and kicked with such a ruckus that he snapped Mike and Ike out of their ruckus.

"Know what? I don't think I ate my weapon," said the Stick, brandishing his trusty quarterstaff. "Why, I don't believe any of us have, have we, guys?" he continued as he handed Reese his wrench.

"Hey," Reese objected, still nude. "How the hell did you get my—"

"Put your clothes on," Clark ordered with cool authority. "You're starting to annoy me." By the end of Clark's sentence, Reese was dressed.

The Stick then endowed Chuckles with a mighty weapon. T'was a cane of candy, shiny and large, though not so giant as Clark's. T'was but the handle of a three-pronged flail, with three thin ropes of onyx black licorice, not unlike Mike's, but threaded into the end of the handle. On the end of each rope hung a jawbreaker: one red, one yellow, one blue, each one as heavy as gold and as hard as a diamond. Chuckles grinned with hateful delight under his greasy hair. Clark readied his cane for more jabbing. Reese fluttered his toothpick. Mike and Ike stayed their conflict for the moment. Pops rolled his eyes with annoyance.

"Let's find out if we can get the juju out of this fat piñata," decreed the Stick.

"Taste the rainbow," Skittles uttered into Heath's ear. "OF PAIN!" At that, the guys tore into Heath, with Skittles holding him from the scalp, Clark jabbing him in the gut, Mike whipping his back, Chuckles flogging his legs, and the Stick beating his fat ass with the trusty quarterstaff. Reese tried to get in a few good licks with his wrench but could not come within three feet of Clark without feeling faint and nauseous. Pops didn't want to play and sat on the floor, nibbling on his Tootsie Roll Pop rations. Ike, hating to be left out, "ran" off to fetch his giant lollipop.

Meanwhile, the others kept whacking the piñata. The screams of the piñata itself started to die down as it degenerated into a dazed, slobbering mess. Blood started flowing down its face. Nobody had hit it in the face, but the beatings had started to loosen the piñata's body from its scalp. With each blow, the flesh on its skull tore open just a little bit more.

When Ike finally returned with his giant lollipop, Heath lay on the floor, unconscious and scalped. High fives abounded and Skittles distributed half a lemon Nerd to each participant as a reward treat.

"YOU FUCKING GUYS!" Ike screamed. "YOU LEAVE ME OUT OF EVERYTHING!"

"Dude," Mike began. "What're we supposed to sit here with our thumbs up our holes while you drag your fat ass all over hell'n gone for...whatever the hell it was?"

"Kinda hard to use my ax when you throw it halfway around the world," said Ike.

"Tchhyeah," jeered Mike. "Like you even know how to use it, you sheep boner. That thing should be mine." He grabbed the lollipop, but Ike clung to it with ferocity.

"Nooooo, it's MINE!" Ike squealed like a runt piglet bullied out of yet another suckle.

Mike and Ike broke into a ferocious tug of war, which featured much kicking and biting. Skittles tried to break it up, but Chuckles flogged him in the ass until the giant wrestler picked him up by one arm and threw him, in an arc, over his own head. This resulted in Skittles accidentally slamming Chuckles down on the Stick, who responded by grabbing Chuckles and using him to wallop Skittles in the face. Skittles returned the wallop with the nearest body, which happened to be Ike's. Mike, suddenly trying to protect his little bro, stomped on Skittles's foot. Before Skittles could box Mike's ears for such an annoyance, Pops intervened by pistol-whipping the wrestler in the eye with Heath's gun. This woke Heath up, and he clamored for his Maggie. Clark orbited this pandemonium as he followed Reese around, tripping him with the hook of his candy cane and ordering him to get back up so he could trip him again.

Then, they all stopped and fell silent. They didn't know why, at least not for the first three seconds or so. But then, knowledge washed over them all, and they turned around to find their captain grinning from ear to ear and bouncing with a quiet laugh of cruel delight. Beholding the sight of the captain, they stood at attention—even Heath, with the top of his head bleeding all over everything. He spied his scalp in Skittles's hand, snagged it, and put it on.

The loss of a scalp . . . friendships torn asunder . . . attempted fratricide . . . and a man's penis stretched beyond repair; yes these affairs all did please Captain Candyroo, just as business pleased the Valhalla Syndicate. His heartless band of murderers was coming along. As Turtle and Zotz stood at their captain's guard, their great leader, about the shape and size of a large beanbag chair, waddled around, sucking a Dum Dum of cherry red and breathing out of his mouth.

Only the mischievous smirk of a boy belied his commanding presence...a middle-aged boy with chocolatey lips and a face full of freckles...freckles made of acne, which kept his skin in a constant state of simultaneous bursts, flows, coagulations, and renewals. This caused him to leave a trail of chunky pus wherever he went. He had the rosy cheeks and squat frame of a jubilant little sprite...a jubilant little sprite with rotting teeth and sporadic patches of a crew cut. He wore his usual uniform: a brown suit, many sizes too tight, stained all over and ripped at the seams. It had enormous frayed pockets, with thick yellow trimming on the rat-gnawed lapels. It hadn't always been this way. It used to be red. Underneath, he wore a yellowish-brown shirt with a black, cruddy tie—once a dingy off-white shirt with a black, less-cruddy tie. His Velcro sneakers were also of the black persuasion.

He removed his greasy, brownish backpack. As he opened it, all twenty-two eyes of all the eleven guys followed the zipper with precise attention. Out of the backpack, he withdrew eleven bags of jellybeans. No one charged, as they wished to. To Turtle and Zotz, the captain handed the first two bags. They took the bags but did not eat. Zotz continued to smile sardonically, and Turtle continued to stare at everyone with his beak open. Then the captain handed bags to everyone, one at a time. Then came silence, for a long time. Then, per the captain's bidding, and only per the captain's bidding, the swarm of greedy fingers and mouths stormed down on more candy than any of them had seen in weeks.

In no time, the captain could observe everyone sitting on the floor, bantering and laughing it up. Song broke out, and it all became a party, where one could delight in such rare sights as Mike, Ike, Chuckles, and Clark playing hacky sack with Clark's top hat, Heath dancing a merry jig with the Stick, Pops making out with Reese, and Skittles debating the finer points of Chekhovian post-structural semiotics with his wallet photo of Tom Stoppard. These things also pleased the captain, briefly.

As the minutes passed and the pixie dwindled, the captain watched brows furrow and smiles disappear. Grunts and growls replaced laughs. Quarrel replaced song. Battle replaced dance. They had long ago grown accustomed to such angst, and to the captain volleying a wide array of laughs at them during episodes of strife, just as he did now. But this time, he had conspicuously omitted something: an explanation. Not that he ever felt he owed it to them. He had quite a taste for laying out every component of the creation of the quarrel in question and spared not a single detail about his own role in it. Then, once they gained the fullest degree of understanding and awareness as to how he had played them, despair from their knowledge that they still couldn't do anything about it would bury them like an avalanche of garbage. It was delectable.

This time, however, he found the ever-quivering buds of his mind's tongue more tantalized by concealing his reasons for inciting these goobers to battle one another without repose. Nevertheless, the time for such pleasures had passed. The time now had come for Phase II of the captain's mission, his greatest ever—a job befitting one of the most feared confectionary overlords in the known universe.

"Alright, everybody shuddup," he ordered with no effect whatsoever. It seemed their petulant intensities allowed them to keep screaming at one another loudly enough to drown him out. It concerned him not. He needed to only amplify his command. "Hey! Cease your loquaciousness, hosers!… HEY!" Sometimes he found it hard to get their attention. T'was no matter. An arch supervillain of his caliber suffered no rivals, and they knew it. "HEY! You're startin' to piss me off!" These bickering fools had forgotten themselves. But they would revisit the fear and awe due their captain once he'd summoned forth the full power of his voice. "SHUUUT YOURRR HOLES!" he screamed, this time popping his Dum Dum out of his mouth and pointing it at them, because he knew how tough it made him look. "HEYYYYY!" he screamed again. *These ingrates.* "QUIIIIETTT!" he continued to scream. *Insolent bastards!*

After a good chunk of the day passed, the captain's voice started getting hoarse. Then, when somebody ripped a huge fart through all the yelling and crying, everyone fell silent. Then an outburst of childish laughter swept the whole gang, all except for Turtle, who just stood there staring at people with his beak open. The captain himself got caught up in the hilarity, wondering if he might have dealt what they smelt. Then he snapped back to his senses. "ALRIGHT, ENOUGH OF THIS!" he yelled in a shredded voice. "All you retards, hold your tongues and listen up!"

Finally, they listened up.

"I just talked to Dove," he announced. "Dove says he doesn't know where Baxter lives. So we're changing the plan. There's gonna be some kind of big tournament comin' up and Dove says the kid's gonna be there. So he's gonna find out where it is, and we can nab the kid there."

"What kind of tournament?" asked the Stick.

"I dunno," the captain stated.

"Why's he going?" asked Clark.

"I dunno," the captain stated.

"When's it gonna be?" asked Pops.

"I dunno," the captain stated.

"Where's it at?" asked Pops.

The captain paused. "I don't know, I said. But Dove says the tournament's gonna be at the ... Pat Hazekamp University or somethin'."

"What the hell's that?" Chuckles chuckled.

"I dunno," said the captain. "But our tracks run right past it, I guess. T'swhat Dove says."

"But where's it at?" said Reese.

"I just said I dunno, taffyweenie!" he barked.

"What'd I tell you about ending with prepositions," Clark reminded Reese, whose throat became so dry that he started choking.

"When do we get more rations?" someone asked.

"Who said that?" demanded the captain, wagging his Dum Dum around to look tough. His little pea-sized eyes shifted around inside the two black pits that constituted his rotting eye sockets. He suspected Heath, or Ike, or maybe even Chuckles. *Stupid, ungrateful bigmouths.* It would take a while to get the gang focused again. He'd already waited through the stage of consumption euphoria. He now had to endure the post-ration crash stage, which, while glorious in its yield of strife and treachery, also carried the side effect of disorder. But he would gleefully pay this familiar price in order to get them to the stage of unbearable anticipation, where they would spend every trace of their energies quivering and awaiting orders with the ever-present hope that any obedient deed might result in a treat. That stage always brought out the best in his friends. He valued them most then, the worthless little jackoffs. "Listen, snot rags, nobody's getting anything more until Baxter is worm candy."

"Yeah but," Mike began. "Like, who is Baxter? You never told us, like, anything about him."

"I dunno," the captain stated. "Some big-time chess player, I think. Now, I—"

"I thought he was the Chess Champion of the Universe," Ike added.

"Right," continued the captain. "He is. Probably. Now, as I was saying—"

"Yeah, but why do we gotta kill the Chess Champion of the Universe?" Ike whined.

"I dunno," the captain replied. "But that's what the boss wants."

"Really?" asked Clark. "What'd he say?"

"I dunno, I ain't talked to him yet," said the captain.

"Why's the boss want him dead?" asked Pops.

"I told you I ain't talked to him!" yelled the captain. A really, really long time had passed since he had talked to the boss. Several years, in fact. It felt embarrassing, having to use Dove all the time, conveying messages back and forth, like a total retard. He hoped that once he completed this mission, things would change. But he wouldn't tell that to his friends. His friends were total retards. "And you guys," he said, looking at Pops and the Stick, "You guys need to drill them until they're as dangerous as you."

Pops and the Stick looked at each other and silently booked an hour out of their schedules to laugh their assess off at this outrageous notion. Skittles decided to laugh at it now. The captain ignored him.

"Hey, fuck you, Glurpy Slurpy," Chuckles said to Skittles, while twirling his flail. "You think we can't thrash some chess wussy's ass? Sounds like a hoot to me."

"Yeah, I mean, what, is this Baxter some kind of badass martial artist?" asked Ike.

"I dunno," the captain stated.

"Well, does he carry a gun?" asked Ike.

"I dunno," the captain stated.

"But how public is this tournament? Won't somebody see us?" asked Clark.

"I dunno! Dove researches this shit for me, now shut up!" the captain bitched. "All you turds need to worry about is getting ready to exterminate him."

"Yeah but, dude, my muscles are totally screamin' at me," said Mike.

"Yeahhh," whined Ike. "Yeah, can't we take a break? We've been doing all this combat and fighting stuff for ... I don't know how long. Mike almost killed me earlier."

"That's right," said the Stick. "And you almost ended him too. Not long ago, you flabby lard bags couldn't even make your way down a flight of stairs without asking me to call an ambulance, ain't that so, Skittles?"

"Yeah, tell him, Sticky," said Skittles.

"You couldn't even Velcro your own shoes without hurting yourselves. And now, after us running your candied asses ragged, now look at what you can do. Now you can hurt others, and on purpose!"

"Yeah, but there's twelve of us," moaned Ike. "How come we gotta go through all this?"

"Because we don't know nothin' about what we're about to face," said Pops. "Champion of the Universe! Who knows what kind of bodyguards this kid has protecting him. Could be retired marines, Navy SEALs, could be secret service, maybe a couple of them are cybernetic ninja pterodactyl men from Antares-eighty-one ... Or who knows? Maybe the kid's got a horde of samurai androids traveling with him. Or maybe he's affiliated with the 64 Squares. We gotta get you guys as tough as you can be. If there's anything I learned in Nam, it's that brute force and superior numbers will always win over an opponent you know nothin' about."

"Who're we kidding," groaned Heath, removing his scalp and throwing it on the floor in despair. "We're just a bunch of thick-headed Pakleds; we'll never amount to anything." Hassan was gone. And now Maggie gawked down at another guy's penis. And who knew when the next pixie fix would come? Heath was done. Let everybody beat on him, or whip him, or scalp him now. These guys could slice his face off for all he cared. He had gotten tired. He wanted to go to sleep. No arguments came from any of the guys. Many opened their mouths, but no sounds came out. Most of them had begun to feel just as sluggish. It constituted the perfect window for the captain's announcement.

"Did I happen to mention that anyone who helps get this kid can count on a lifetime supply of goob upon completion of the mission?" He savored every moment of desperate shock that followed. "That's right. Get Baxter, and never worry yourselves again about your next fix," he said, indicating the endless towers of tootsie surrounding them. "All this could be yours. Enough sweet, scrumdelicious juju to keep every one of you at the peak of euphoria for a thousand lifetimes."

This was such a delicious lie. He couldn't wait to tell them about it when the job was done. Turtle stood there, staring at the captain with his beak open. Everyone else did the same.

"I'll tell you guys what," said the captain, putting his sucker in his pocket, lying down in a little red wagon, and sliding himself under the spigot of a nearby tower of chocolate-covered gumdrops. "You hosers got until I finish my breakfast to get your asses ready."

Having never witnessed the captain wolf down gumdrops for much longer than half a day, everybody scrambled to action with haste they'd never known or simulated in any game. Their commitment would have made him proud, had he ever respected them in the first place.

The captain's buddies had set out for the stars, so he had nothing left but the guys. He always liked hanging out with the guys, but he admired his buddies a lot more. The guys always mooched off of him. It seemed someone always wanted to borrow a quarter, or use his roleplaying stuff, or listen to his Weird Al Yankovic tapes. But he knew that this shameless moochery formed the very root of his power over them.

It all started back in '89, when he and the guys all used to hang out together at the corner store and watch Mike play video games. Back then, the captain was just another one of the guys, back before people ever called him captain. He had started to notice how bitchy they would get when they hadn't had any pixie for a while. Sometimes, when their veins ran especially dry of confection, they would turn on one another. He always found this a joy to watch, partially because it was funny as hell, but also because he calculated it as the perfect time to offer them a taste of tootsie.

Their responses always proved hilarious. He'd already been friends with the guys since early childhood and had always known them as a lazy pack of slugs. But they often amazed him with the mountains they would move whenever he dangled a sweet treat over their heads, sometimes literally. Once he gave them their fix, their animated demeanor and gratitude seemed boundless. Then they would slip into a diabetic sloth and redouble their indifference to activity, thought, and hygiene. The captain enjoyed this stage just as much because it assured him that they would never stray anywhere near a job opportunity. They would stay put.

When he and the guys got their studio, they had planned it as a joint endeavor. But all the deposit-bottle money the guys could pool together could not compare to the captain's contribution, which would cover the rent for several years. Once they had set themselves up with his disproportionately large share, he evolved into the de facto head of their household. They soon became so enamored with their bitchin' hangout that nobody ever wanted to leave. . . for anything. Plus, Pops had been totally cool about the rent. He had only asked for a few cash payments before he started letting them slide. Most of the time after that, he would take his payments in Tootsie Roll Pops or Blow Pops.

None of the guys knew where the captain got his supply. All they knew is that he would disappear every so often for a couple days and return to the room with a fresh load. The guys never knew that he went deep down into the earth to a secret stash. Down in the boiler room, the building engineer, Zotz, and his assistant, Turtle, made sure to keep Pops hooked up, along with everyone else in the local area. Before long, stores went dark and grew dusty. Soon after, they boarded up. None of them could compete with free candy. And the captain had enough supply to remain everybody's sugar daddy for many lifetimes. He didn't care about the money. He cared about the groveling. He cared about the power to turn good kids to a life of crime, unravel otherwise functional families, or bring neighborhoods to third-world ruin by controlling the local pixie supply.

But he considered the guys his special little project. Just the five of them. He kept Reese around because he would prove good in a fight, probably. The captain had never exploited Reese's perceived toughness, but he would soon. Even Pops, the coolest grown up they'd ever met, who had hung around with them for years, wasn't truly one of them. A tutor, maybe—an adviser, respected by them all, but not one of the original guys from the beginning. And Turtle, Zotz, Skittles, and the Stick, they all joined the outfit as newcomers—goons, recruited for his latest and greatest mission.

But he considered the guys his best friends. They had palled around together since they were old enough to hold a lollipop, which is why he found it so scrumptious and sweet to make them do whatever the fuck he wanted—to enslave them for no reason—humiliate them for his own wild amusement—have them attempt suicide over a Werther's—make them cry until they passed out. In these delicious states of utter degeneracy, they formed their own prison, just for him. And when he had sealed shut the window to their apartment, then he owned them. Their sense of time, and of the world outside, vanished. He became the very blood that oozed through their veins. If Captain Candyroo couldn't impress his buddies, he would sure impress his friends.

Before long, Skittles and the Stick had trained Chuckles to swing his jawbreaker flail with such speed and virtuosity that he overwhelmed Clark's mastery of the candy cane. At that point, he often beat Clark within an inch of his life. And at that point, Reese would clobber Chuckles with his wrench until Clark began to recover. At about the same time, Mike and Ike had started to bludgeon each other with a level of passion and unreasoning hatred that would have horrified their mother and entertained their father. Much later than all this, Pops had Heath wearing his scalp and firing Maggie with confidence, and with 11 percent accuracy at close range.

Within record time, the captain had finished his breakfast. Now they would head out, ready or not. The time had come to get Baxter. Zotz waited for them in the cab of the locomotive, which now towed a tiny caboose. Inside, Turtle guarded a little treasure chest full of candy. The captain forbid everyone from touching even a single solitary sour ball until they had completed the job. Then the captain would haul all their asses back here, to tell them that the chest was all they would get, instead of the lifetime supply he'd suckered them into expecting. Suppressing the laughs generated by these plans caused many of the captain's mounds of facial acne to burst prematurely, and everybody did wonder why his pus trail had become a bit messier than usual.

Now, with all aboard, the train did depart from the underground hub. With its caboose carrying a prize of sweet treats, gooey goodies, and chocolaty chewies, the juju train went chugga chugga chug down the tracks, with Captain Candyroo and his gang of goobers in tow, on their way to find Baxter, and administer an ass kicking of the sweetest variety.

12. TARGETING THE TWINKLING PRIZE

"**B**ret was a good kid! He was following orders," said Mr. Laing, naked, and shivering vigorously in the meat freezer.

"Yeah, so good you let him get squashed instead of you?" replied Cereal Man, squirting him occasionally with a little pink water pistol and adding to the humiliating array of icicles already hanging from the store manager's disgusting body.

"Well, maybe if you hear this from enough people, it'll sink in," said Mr. Laing. "There's nothing more we can do! Who'n the hell needs to tell you? Santa Claus? Shit knows, you never believe me."

"He didn't say that."

"What?"

"He didn't say there's nothing more he could do; he said he wasn't ordering them anymore."

"Of course he did, dammit! He can't order them anymore."

"The fuck's that mean, lard shit?"

"You never believe me! I've told you we can't get them anymore and that there's nothing I can do, and every three years—"

"Well, listen here, you shiny little pork rind," Cereal Man said, squirting more icicles. "You better find some room in the budget from now on, 'cause I'm not stopping with you or your precious store this time. That hideous wife of yours better like the taste of a baseball bat."

"What're you talking about, budget?" pleaded Mr. Laing, with a long, silly-looking icicle dangling from his nose. "How the hell can I order something that doesn't exist anymore?"

"What'd you say?"

"Plutonium Sugar Bombs are long, long out of production."

"Since when?"

"You egocentric punk!" snapped Mr. Laing, shuddering, with his head, shoulders, and beer gut all shiny with a thick gloss of ice. "When are you going to w-w-wake up and realize the Greenhouse Wars are over?"

"Hell with that, you little brown-and-serve link. I saw through your pack of lies before any of that. You tried to feed me that line of bullshit then, but I slipped you a little extra cash, and what do you know? Full shelves. Full shelves of Plutonium fuckin' Sugar Bombs." As Mr. Laing's teeth chattered loudly, Cereal Man went on. "Of course, before long, I noticed the loads started getting kind of light. And more dollars brought fewer boxes. After a while, no price was high enough for your greedy little ass. After that, you got spiteful. That spite's gonna get you killed, old man."

"Spiteful? I told you! W-we couldn't get anymore! The Valhalla Syndicate s-s-stopped making that g-g-goddamn cereal after the wars!"

"Bullshit How the hell do you explain this box right here?!" shouted Cereal Man, shoving the lead-lined box in Mr. Laing's face. "This was on the shelf three years ago, along with the other boxes I bought then."

"Th-th-that ..." Mr. Laing's bluing lips explained slowly in the midst of violent shuddering, "... is th-the last ... b-b-b-b-b-box. Th-there are no ... m-more Plutonium Sugar B-b-b-Bombs.... Th-th-they... stopped m-making them, and you ... have f-f-finally exhausted the supply."

To Mr. Laing's surprise, Cereal Man's face dropped. He backed up against the wall of the freezer and sank down to the floor in distress. Mr. Laing enjoyed this. His blue lips curled up to form a constipated, toothy smile behind that silly-looking icicle that hung nearly nine inches down from his nose.

"I t-t-ried to tell ya, heh-heh," he added with a satisfied bounce. "No, nooo, don't listen to the old man, right? Heh-heh, wellllll looks like you've f-f-finally lost, punk. I told ya a long time ago, young man. B-b-b-ack in the beginning I told ya. I am king here. And you go up against the king, you're gonna lose, heh-heh. I've waited a long t-t-t-t-time for this moment, y'know that? Crazed hooligan. And I'll t-t-tell ya what else: I'm not ordering any cereal of any kind here ever again, heh-heh-heh. Th-th-that's right. I beat you, you wacko punk I b-b-eat you, and you remember that."

Cereal Man looked up at Mr. Laing. The manager now bounced with glee above him, with a grill of icicles hanging off his jiggling gut. Mr. Laing spat on Cereal Man and continued.

"You can t-t-take your cereal, and your nutrition, and your t-two-bit, no good, smart-mouthed, impudent little balanced breakfast, and you can sh-sh-sh-shove them right up my Vulveeta-lined ass, heh-heh-heh! Hell will be c-c-c-c-c-colder'n it is in here before this store gets even one more box of Corn Flakes. And what's more, I'm gonna go out there and b-b-b-burn the all the cereal that's on the shelves, heh-heh-hehhh. Yes Sir, t-t-t-time to g-g-get that g-g-girly g-g-

223

garbage food outta my store for g-g-good. Any crackpot who eats cereal is s-s-such a low-character loser that—"

Cereal Man could take the jabs at himself. He could take the jeering, the spitting, and the gloating at his deserved defeat. But he would not tolerate blasphemy. Before Mr. Laing could finish, Cereal Man leapt to his feet and kicked the freezer door open. He grabbed Mr. Laing and threw him out of the freezer. Mr. Laing hit a table with such velocity that his icy shell shattered upon impact. He scrambled around on the floor, trying to get up, when he saw Cereal Man's hand reach for his face and black out his vision by digging his fingers into his eye sockets, as if picking up a bowling ball.

Across the store, in the New York Seltzer aisle, Mr. Laing's high-pitched screeching vibrated the glass bottles. The sound of his creator in agony opened the eyes of JER-BAG once more. The master courtesy ninja awakened from death. At least, he thought he had been dead. But he could never truly die. Not as long as his master needed him. JER-BAG curled his wrecked body out from the wall and limped across the even more wrecked grocery store, toward the shrill screams of Mr. Laing.

By the time the senior bag boy had reached the meat department, Cereal Man was gone and Mr. Laing had been silent for some time. If Cereal Man had not already blown JER-BAG's jaw off his face, it would have dropped to the floor. There, on the main display, lay the Creator Mr. Laing, on his front, with his ass pointed upward, his knees folded into his gut, his arms tucked between them, and his head pointed forward with an artificial apple between his teeth. His body was shiny and bright red with blood, because Cereal Man had removed every inch of his skin.

Though his glistening red body twitched periodically, the Creator Mr. Laing no longer lived. JER-BAG could feel it. He could feel his life's purpose draining away as blood drained from his master's corpse and into the adjacent bags of used hamburger that the store had left on special since last month. The master courtesy ninja moaned with hollow pain, cast his apron aside, and launched himself onto the slippery body of his creator. There, in his weeping embrace, he did not find the love that Mr. Laing had always given. No words of wisdom, no pats on the back, no warm, grunting smiles of approval. Just a nonplussed, slippery mass, whose care had vanished from the universe, never to be found again.

But such an absolute denial of his creator's love was beyond JER-BAG's comprehension. He hugged the corpse harder. It just bled more. He hugged it even harder. It just bled more while the eyes and apple bulged slightly. In a frenzy, JER-BAG tore off his now blood-soaked shirt and turned the corpse over on its back. The corpse's crimson belly shone into the air and his disciple pushed down on it forcefully with his fists. He would repeat these thrusts two more times before he would join his lips with those of the Creator's corpse in an attempt to resuscitate mouth to mouth. *One, two, THREE!* On the third pump, Mr. Laing's dead body belched the apple out of from between its teeth and a greasy orange splash of Cheez Skwirt erupted onto its face. This would not deter JER-BAG from giving it mouth to mouth.

However, no longer having a mouth would. JER-BAG only had half a mouth left, and neither he nor the body had any lips. Cereal Man had really fixed it for him this time! All JER-BAG could do was scream a half-mouthed bellow of despair. He grabbed the body of the Creator and held it upright. All this trauma had fried his sense of reason, and he tried the mouth to mouth anyway. Just a bunch of teeth clacking around against one another. He hollered and cried, mangling his master's corpse in an increasingly aimless fashion, until he found himself rolling around on the main display, pressing himself into the lifeless body. JER-BAG's pants soon slid off, and before long, he was as bloody and shiny as the corpse into which he had passionately entangled himself.

An old lady came by with a shopping cart and a stack of coupons. She grew annoyed by the sight of the bleeding, mixed-up amalgamation of master and apprentice writhing around on the main counter, looking less and less like two individual beings.

"Hey! Hey, you," she said. "This sign here says, 'Half off all used hamburger.' But I got a coupon here says, 'Three credits off any bag of used hamburger with the purchase of Kenny L's Ultra-Thin Ribbed Toilet Paper.' So does that mean I get half off before the three credits off, or three credits off the half off?" She received no answer because none could be given. All energies had been drawn inward. The metamorphosis had begun.

Cereal Man could feel it from the cereal aisle. Something was changing. He tried to ignore the sense of impending doom by filling up his shopping bags. But... it just felt so wrong, having to accept the universe without Plutonium Sugar Bombs. They'd fueled him for so many years—all those mass murders and explosive rampages.... PSBs had been there through all of it. His love for them was like a bomb. Then again, did they truly count as Def Leppard's greatest hit? PyromaniOs were quite fine, among the best of the '80s Rock Cereals—very popular in their day. In 1983 they remained in the Cereal Top 40 for... he didn't even remember how many weeks in a row.

Who was he kidding? Nobody cared anymore. Game over. Some grotesque, awful thing was happening, somewhere else in the store. Something final. Something really gross. He already understood that the end of Plutonium Sugar Bombs meant the end of this store to him. No more long journeys through the desert. But somehow he knew the end had not come upon him just yet. He knew the end would seal everything. But what then? Something new? Or oblivion? No matter.

Cereal Man left the cereal aisle for the last time and made his way to the checkout lanes. Last night's battle had laid flaming waste to them all. Nevertheless, he waited patiently in lane thirty-three for over a half hour to pay for his goods. From a pile of debris in lane one, a pale hand finally emerged.

"You open?" Cereal Man asked the quivering, banged-up hand that probed the hot concrete around it. Upon his arrival at lane one, he removed several heaps of rubble from around the arm and soon uncovered the destroyed human being underneath. IRIS V lay bloodied, bruised, and mangled in the express lane, where her lecherous boss had invariably stationed her. A bubbly burn covered some of her scalp. The rich, tawny hue of her right eye had become invisible, due to the blue, throbbing, baseball-sized swelling that closed it up. Her lips and teeth had met a load of shrapnel. Blood dried on a crooked smile that a wafer of metal had carved into her cheek. Her timeless beauty had finally been brutalized by the store itself. Cereal Man remembered her from the old days, and the way Mr. Laing licked his lips when he hired her. She remembered Cereal Man, too, when, in his youth, his fanaticism had been merely laughable, not terrifying. Yet, unlike most people at this store, she had actually held a mild fondness for him, at least back in those years.

Seeing that black pin on her apron, with the neon green outline of a radiation symbol on it, reminded him of this fondness. After all this time, she still wore the pin. And in that sharp, angular, fire-colored Def Leppard font, the initials, "PSB" still looked as atom-splittingly powerful as they did the day he gave that pin to her. She looked up, as her eye widened with fear. Her voice gurgled with blood as she uttered, "Waste that tub of guts."

Cereal Man realized her eye now gazed not at him, but behind him. He turned around to find the metamorphosis was complete. A perverse combination of creator and creation now stood before him. This terror wore what seemed to be a fusion of their names tags. JEREMY A, BAG BOY was now reduced to "J—" and KEN L, STORE MANAGER was now truncated to "—GER." Blood and filth obscured the rest of the letters. With its four arms and four legs battling one another clumsily, J-GER attempted to advance, then slipped in the blood that continually emanated from its wet, red flesh. It landed on the sordid black apron that cloaked its huge beer gut.

Cereal Man looked upon the disgusting monster, seeing his reflection in the top of its bald head, and nearly retching at the long, cruddy strands of red hair that hung down diseasedly from the sides of the head. As J-GER got back up, it shot a hateful glare at its long-time enemy, both from the bloodshot upper eyes of Mr. Laing, and from the dripping, sherbet-colored lower eyes of JER-BAG. From just beneath these eyes, it heaved from a toothy, Laingian mouth, which somehow still looked constipated, even without lips. It shrieked like the master courtesy ninja, then chuckled constipatedly like the store manager. Then it leapt toward Cereal Man, leaving a trail of blood behind.

Cereal Man quickly turned around and handed IRIS V the money for the cereal. IRIS V struggled to find some way to make change, but before she could scrounge up even a single coin from among the rubble, Cereal Man had already become distracted by wrapping J-GER's black apron around its neck. All four of its hands grabbed at the apron line desperately, and the toothy mouth gasped for air as Cereal Man lifted the creature up with its four legs kicking and flailing. He threw his opponent across the store, through the wall, and into the bottle room, and then followed at a leisurely pace.

He found J-GER still trying to negotiate its way across the surface of the sea of bottles and cans that filled the nearly bottomless pit, into which Cereal Man had once thrown the master courtesy ninja. As it lashed clumsily around, fearful of the chasm below, Cereal Man leapt up on top of one of the larger piles of the cans and bottles, toward the corner of the vast, vast bottle room. J-GER wailed at him like a sticky, filthy banshee. It bent over, aimed its shiny ass upward, and shot an orange, oily jet of Cheez Skwirt at Cereal Man, who leapt to the apex of another pile. The creature squirted another orange gush of processed cheese-inspired foodish product. Just in the nick of time, Cereal Man broke off a slab of concrete about the size of a vending machine from the crumbling wall and used it to deflect the Cheez Skwirt. He then hurled it down, slamming his enemy into the wall. After a moment of silence, J-GER managed, with all of its strength, to push the slab away. But then, the slab began to sink. J-GER found itself desperately trying to claw its way up from the rapidly expanding, suddenly created sink hole.

Cereal Man squinted with new focus and broke off another piece of the wall—a large piece, heavier than a school bus. He lifted it up over his head and jumped back onto the highest pile of uncounted bottles and cans, which also started to disintegrate under the enormous weight. Cereal Man launched the slab down toward his foe with a whistling, shrieking speed that would have made many meteors jealous. The slab hit J-GER with an awful impact, unlike anything even the master courtesy ninja had ever experienced. This was something truly special. Something final.

Faster than sound, the slab barreled down through the uncounted cans and bottles, through that familiar chasm in the concrete, which J-GER remembered with such dread. It heated the earth and clay as it delved further and further down. Above, the mountains of uncounted cans and bottles sank fast. Cereal Man tried to maintain his footing as the floor of metal and glass containers became more and more liquid. It all rocketed, with J-GER , downward, toward the lower infinite, like a whirlpool. Then this vortex started to claim more than just the cans and bottles. The structure of the store itself began disintegrating and following the whirlpool down.

The slab of broken wall cracked through the bedrock, past the lower foundation, where JEREMY A had decayed into JER-BAG. The slab now hurtled the hybrid creature farther down than ever before, with its momentum increasingly aided by the colossal weight of uncounted—and perhaps uncountable—bottles and cans, as well as increasingly giant portions of the Safeway, now so far above.

Cereal Man had now escaped the bottle room and the growing vortex within. But the whole store was coming apart. The ceiling split, revealing the dazzling blue of the daytime sky above, as well as the spires of some of the tallest nearby skyscrapers. The walls shook and the floors cracked. Everything solid now crumbled to bits and tumbled helplessly toward the vortex. Cereal Man strolled toward the checkout lanes to pick up his shopping bags. The counters and the rubble in the lanes all raced toward him. He grabbed his shopping bags as they came up. He watched lane one whiz past him. He watched the gnarled arm of IRIS V wave to him one last time as she and the churning rubble rushed away toward the vortex.

But then he noticed that she wasn't waving. She was about to throw him his change. Cereal Man caught the few coins IRIS V tossed him and turned to walk out the front door. But there was no need. The frame of the front door and the devastated wall around it already rushed at him. He only needed to stand still to exit through the same door he had entered yesterday. As the door frame zipped past him, he turned around to behold the Safeway demolishing itself into an unrecognizable heap. Then it became still, as if clogging the vortex. It rumbled violently. And then, with one last, gigantic burp, the heap of wreckage collapsed into the vortex. A wrecking ball from a nearby crane missed the heap by three centimeters, and the vortex sealed itself up.

Down in the uttermost deep, Safeway was no longer Safeway, just homogenized metal and rock that gave way to its root of metal, glass, and eternal filth. At the uttermost bottom, the tip of the filthy root, lay the epitome of the store's filth, the hybrid of the master courtesy ninja JER-BAG and the Creator Mr. Laing fused more deeply and more completely than ever before or after, locked into an eternal concentration of their mutual dependence and perversity.

I will always be here.

Cereal Man turned away from the barren slab of sandy desert that sealed the Safeway vortex. Shiny, plastic, disposable skyscrapers towered overhead, some into the thin wispy clouds that feathered the sky of this once beautiful desert. The bustling crowds churned with the anxiety caused from thousands of differing objectives per square inch. Business and daily life cooperated and clashed.

Garbage cans clanged. Panhandlers begged. Jackhammers rattled. Street musicians whined. Paperboys hollered. Street vendors sang for all. Salvation Army bells rang for heterosexuals. Naked "End of the Universe" sandwich board wearers groaned perversely. Along with this, morning rush-hour traffic lumbered through, bumper to bumper. Horns honked. Assholes yelled. Engines revved. Tires peeled. Tires screeched. Kids hollered from the agony of being pulverized by the grill of a Buick. Sirens wailed. Bystanders laughed.

Lots of chain restaurants peppered the cityscape, like Mom's Bar (Home of the Marjarita!), M Tyson's Lil' Taitst of Dick, McDonner's Humanburgers (over 999 billion served), Carl Sagan's Cosmic Soup (billions and billions served), and Rax. But some private eateries had made homes for themselves, too, like Snout's Pork Rind Emporium, Wonder Weenie, the Buffet at the Avon Randolph Discount Luxury Hotel, Sara's Slug Soup-n-Salt Lick, and, of course, The Taco Trough, with that cute little skinless mouse as the restaurant's pitchfork-holding mascot.

Cereal Man looked at this teeming intersection and paused with despair. Where would he go now? Where does this road go? West Telegraph Road. This was Telegraph Road?! How many hundreds of miles did it go, anyway? What street intersected it? 395,307th Avenue. Did Telegraph Road now run all the way across, from coast to coast?

Cereal Man turned back around. Indeed, the road kept on going, for miles and miles, all the way to the urbanized horizon in the east. It went right past where the vortex had swallowed the Safeway, moments ago. Now another building stood there: PNIS, a regional news station, which had a giant clock near the top that said 6:33 a.m. High-resolution video screens covered the front of the building, blazing with fast talking ads, news tickers that zipped by, celebrity bios, stock updates, and sporting events.

One channel even featured a chess tournament. Cereal Man could see the words "Chess Intergalactica, LIVE, News 11." Then his bitter white eyes beheld a face. A face that he'd never seen before, but one he knew instantly. Indigo rings of exhaustion surrounded those sky-blue eyes, but in them, Cereal Man could still discern the essence of the greatest threat the universe had ever known. He read the subtitles on the screen.

"I just want to say one thing," Baxter announced, "To my mom at home…"

Finally, a clear direction had arrived in Cereal Man's life: a clear hope. His long journey, all the murders, and all the destruction had not

232

been in vain after all. Plutonium Sugar Bombs had gone the way of the polar ice caps. But if he had not come for the last box, then he never would have seen the true prize beckoning from that huge screen. His heart refilled with purpose, as Baxter, mustering up all his strength, lifted the trophy over his head and cried, "HI MOM!... I DID IT!"

As heroic, conclusive music filled the Illustrious Professor Earl Hazekamp Convocation Center and the crowd cheered warmly at Baxter's tribute to his mother, Cereal Man's eyes narrowed and stared at Baxter with the focus of a tiger. His mind raced through the escalating horrid events of recent decades, and his frame hardened with determination. With the image of Baxter frozen in his mind, Cereal Man whispered, "Your twinkling prize is now mine."

II. THE RUINATION

13. DAWN OF THE WILD MAN

3,000 generations earlier, invisible wind howled eternally in a sky darkened, not by oily fronts of exhaust, not by clouds of soot, but darkened only because the Golden Father currently warmed the other side of little Earth. All the dazzling points of Ursa Major twinkled with fiery coolness in the deep blue night. Their energy, which fizzled down to the mountains, remained every bit as pure as it was so many ages ago, when it had left the vast seas of flame where it began. And so it had been since a time never counted.

Earthly fires of orange and yellow raged in some of the high caverns in these mountains, channeling the vitalities of Ursa Major into the blood of the stout, hearty, thick-boned, heavy-browed peoples who had gathered there. After the banquet, the shaman donned the furs of the honored guest, whom the tribe had consumed with ecstatic gratitude. And so it had been since a time before counting.

When out of the furs there arose a great spirit
He snarled and he roared so everyone could hear it.
He recalled waking up from a long winter's nap
Then leaving his cave to take a huge crap.
When what to his dim groggy eyes should appear
But a stick in his heart. Well, actually a spear.

And though losing his life was not his first plan,
The pleasure was his to nourish this clan.
And those switches of birch, so swift to his hide
Felt surprisingly great just after he'd died.
He minded it not as they devoured his meat.
Truth be it told, he thought it was neat.
It filled him with joy when they arranged all his bones
Inside of a pit and then sealed it with stones.
They buried his tail, and his balls and his dick
And grass grew right over as he laughed at this shtick.
They mounted his skull on the altar with care
In hopes that his blessings soon would be there.
At last they all thanked him for his plentiful grace.
And he would have smiled if he'd still had a face.
The bear god grew starry as he finally did ease
Back to the mountains to sprout some more trees.
And they heard him exclaim as he phased out of sight,
"ROAAARRRRRRRRRRR!"

14. THE LAM OF GOOD

Dr. Davis's beard had grown long during the weeks since he'd first embarked on his trip. The thin, sprightly old art historian had started out looking sharp, donning a fine suit of cool gray, with his short, white stubble neatly trimmed and his ring of medium-length white hair combed expertly. Back at the gas station, his glasses had been crushed under the heel of Dr. Sarajenakkuardi, a younger curator he had thought was his friend.

Davis would never forget the storms brewing in her eyes as she slugged him in the gut and ripped the pocket out of his coat in order to swipe his pocketbook and phone. His glasses didn't fly off until Sarajenakkuardi had slammed him down onto the oily pavement and sprayed gasoline all over him, much to the yuksome amusement of the idle petroleum transfer technicians on duty at the time. With his glasses crushed, his world became a little blurry, but he could see well enough to watch his former student and friend get back into the car they had rented together and drive off without him. The sardonic symbolism of the crushed spectacles was not lost on him.

And now, here he sat in the most run-down section of the Squeezeburgh Squealer, a deplorably philistine interregional train, still cursing at himself for not seeing. He knew better than to think friendship could ever compete with museum politics. Such naivete did not characterize a scholar of Davis's caliber. He had always been an astute observer with a fine wit. And academic circles had respected him as one of the top minds in his field for decades.

"That bitch," Davis hissed to himself, watching hot rain shower the dark city outside. A man of letters, he only used four-letter words on rare occasions. But the heat had started to get to him, as had the flies, as had the itchy air that smelled of manure, and the sluggish pace of this ever-jostling ride.

"That back-stabbing little wench," he added. The crate he sat on had started to wear on his posterior. But he could not bring himself to sit back down again in the little nest of straw he had constructed. He had already accumulated more than enough filth on this trip. With all the dirt and scabs on his face, and oil and straw lodged in his now scraggly beard, and the objectionable stench he now cultivated, the wise old antiquarian had asked himself oft if he had a popsicle's chance in hell of acing the interview anymore.

Most of the world laughed at art, and museums that tolerated its dumb-ass presence to even the slightest eclipse of food courts had become so rare that competition between prospective educators had grown fierce. Davis hadn't even realized just how fierce. He and Sarajenakkuardi had spent their cross-country drive going through interview drills in the car. Sarajenakkuardi had come up with the idea. It seemed a good one at the time, too, though Davis did feel a tad bit odd about carpooling with a competitor to an interview for the same job. Oh, what a fool he'd been.

Still, Sarajenakkuardi knew not the folly of her treacherous designs. She knew her elderly competitor would turn out mugged and shot and left for dead in a gutter. And doubtless, she calculated that such a setback would delay the old man. But the scheming young harpy never figured Davis for hopping the next freight train and hoboing his way to the interview! Granted, it had grown into a common practice among young intellectuals, but Davis was well into his seventies. Sarajenakkuardi thought that ditching her old mentor in the slums with no money, no phone, broken glasses, and a torn suit would give her the competitive edge she needed.

Well, well, though. She didn't count on Davis's new set of threads. He missed the refinement of his old gray suit, but these would have to do. He didn't much care for the pink knit tie, and the white, blood-spattered slacks came up a little over his ankles. But it pleased him to feel just the right snugness from the white dress shirt and yellow sweater vest. The tan loafers had quickly become rather soiled from the clumps of dirt and straw in the car. This seemed unavoidable, and he accepted that. But he'd be damned if he curled up in his nest again and got straw and mud all over the rest of the outfit. The otherwise elegant man needed to preserve as much of his class and dignity as possible.

"Hog's-cunt-bitch-whore-twat," he growled. Now his grumbling stomach had started to wear him down too. His mind skirted with dread the provisions in his briefcase, to which he'd laid claim after clubbing the previous freight car resident in the eye with the corner of his portfolio and tossing him off the train. The guy had also identified himself as a historian, hoboing his way to the same interview for similar reasons—a highly credited and prolific researcher. A little too highly credited and prolific.

Now this domain, a seedy boxcar of yesteryear, had become Davis's, as had everything in it: the traces of straw, the clumps of manure, and all the food the other guy had scrounged up and stolen before Davis had usurped him. All belonged to Davis, now. He opened up the briefcase and removed his provisions. No one could call it a bountiful feast. Just an empty can of Uncle Willy's Triple-Baked Beans and half a pack of Fleshstic Fakefurters. He found them disgusting, but he had to gag down at least one. The Squealer dragged along the tracks like a giant steel slug, and he still had several days left to go.

He pulled out a Fakefurter and squished his incisors down into it. The smell was so gross that he couldn't even finish the bite. It wasn't rotten. Fleshstic products had an undeniable reputation as "unrottable." It just smelled biologically unacceptable. Dr. Davis had come from a different time: a time of dirt food. Only a couple of times, in his youth, had the man stooped to eating a hot dog. But back then, vendors made them with animal flesh and other disgusting junk. That was a long time ago. It was a time before Fleshstic™.

Lego/Hormel's benevolent introduction of edible plates, bowls, cups, and cafeteria trays, in the late '80s, gave rise to an increasing palate, among grade schoolers, for Fleshstic: not a true meat, or even food in the most biological sense. But what Fleshstic lacked in nourishment, it made up for in its ability to distract hard-working Americans from the antiquated "needs" genetically wired into their bodies from a bygone age. Manufacturers and consumption engineers packed Fleshstic with that smooth, salty, meat-like goodness that made life so much easier for all those busy moms who believed they juggled schedules more demanding than those of all their ancestors combined. And Fleshstic came in many other subsequent forms too. Though Dr. Davis stuck to his archaic palate, most other old folks loved Fleshstic paste, both as a main course and as a denture adhesive.

But it didn't stop there! Fleshstic sticks made a hearty snack for all ages. A can of plasticky, quasi-porkish Fleshstic syrup became the most ubiquitous condiment in history. Fleshstic and jelly sandwiches would stick to the roof of your mouth alarmingly well, and thus remained bonded to the bloodstream long enough to satisfy the caloric and fleshsticular requirements of the USDAA (United States Department of Anti-Agriculture) for weeks at a time, while simultaneously making you crave still more Fleshstic. And who could resist a big old bowl of spaghetti and Fleshstic balls? No one, that's who! This eclectic product revolutionized the way kids ate lunch, and, upon reaching early adolescence, the way those kids fed their own children.

Davis held his breath and attempted to finish biting into the Fakefurter by stretching his tongue over to the left and pushing the product into the right corner of his mouth. His attempt to gnaw a bite off with his right molars proved unsuccessful. The moment it grazed his tongue, he almost gagged his stomach inside out. After retching for several minutes, he stood up, took a huge breath, grabbed a ballpoint pen from his briefcase, and used it to pin his tongue to the wall of the boxcar. He didn't drive the pen all the way through his tongue. Doing so would have made him sound like quite the boor during his interview. So he secured his tongue to the wall as best he could without puncturing it. Then he opened his mouth and, with gentle and gradual effort, rocked himself back, stretching his tongue as far as it would stretch. When he started to feel it tearing, just a little, he stopped. With his free hand, he fumbled around for the Fakefurter. Finally, his fingers grasped the unchewed end. He dangled the product over his throat and attempted to drop it directly down into his esophagus.

Alas, the gaping passage was not wide enough to accommodate the product without physical contact. No sooner had half the length of the Fakefurter plunged into his gullet than his systems rejected it with interest. As the Fakefurter shot straight up into the air, a mushy fountain of chewed straw erupted onto Davis's face. He scrambled over to the shreds of his old suit and wiped the used breakfast off, exercising care not to get any on his new clothes.

This was impossible! He had to eat something. But no other options seemed to exist. To swallow this thing, it simply had to go past his tongue. If he could just spot another rat. Even raw, they tasted heavenly compared to this disgusting, pink, quasi-food capsule. As he looked around in vain for more vermin, or even a large spider's nest, he noticed that the Fakefurter had landed in a shallow bed of manure. He approached and noticed that it still looked moist, unlike most of the manure caked onto the floor of the car. He rolled the Fakefurter in it until the product had acquired a thick coating of shit and straw. He raised it to his mouth. But as soon as his teeth made contact with the fecal coating, a storm of gagging coughs exploded out from him, and the product again fell to the floor. It was no use. He could still smell the Fakefurter through its protective layer of funky dung.

Maybe he could cook it. This boxcar provided an ample supply of fuel sources. He piled up a nice mound of straw, and then scurried about the car, gathering up the driest dung chips he could find. During this search, he noticed a sixteen-year-old blond-haired boy, drenched and wearing nothing but a white backpack, climbing off the roof and making his way down the outside ladder. Davis thought this kid would show up sooner or later to attempt to reclaim what used to be his. This could work out better anyway, as Davis never did get a chance to look inside that backpack. The rain had come slamming down only seconds after he had removed the kid's clothes.

Now, with great care and deliberation, Baxter edged himself along the side of the boxcar and struggled to stretch his leg into the inside of Davis's car. But the rain kept everything so slippery. Having his shoes on would have made things much easier. How could all of his clothes have simply fallen off of him while he slept? Upon securing himself on the floor of the boxcar, Baxter's eyes met Davis's. The youth swung his backpack around to cloak his private spot.

"Heh, h-hhow do you do, Sir," said Baxter. "I hope you'll, uh, excuse me. You see, I went to sleep up there on the roof, and, and it seems I lost all my clothes." Davis stood there. Davis stared. Baxter continued. "I mean, I don't, sleep, on top of trains, who does that, right?" Davis blinked. "Gosh. That's, uh, that's a nice vest you have on there. And nice trousers," Baxter went on, puzzled as to why the blood-spattered slacks seemed so small on the man. "That tie! It's just like the one I lost. And those shoes look just like mine too. Heyyy, now wait a minute. Is this some kind of joke? Gosh, I hope there's no camera," he said, glancing from side to side. Davis stared.

"You got rain all over my backpack," said Davis.

"Pardon?" said Baxter.

"I said you got my backpack all wet."

"Wh— You mean this backpack? No, you don't understand. You see, I—"

"What? I don't what?"

"I—"

"You calling me stupid?"

"No, I was just—"

"You know how smart I am?"

"Well, I'm sure you're—you're very—"

"You're starting to get on my nerves."

"I'm sorry."

"Sorry nothin', gimme my backpack."

"But it belongs to me."

"Shut up!" Davis shouted. "Now you got about one second before I start getting pissed."

"Mister, please, wait!" Baxter burst out with alarm. He thought it best not to mention the prize check for the Chess Intergalactica inside. The man seemed a little insistent. "Please … It's not that I'm trying to be difficult or anything. If you need the backpack, why I'll be glad to give it to you later. It's just that, right now, well, I don't have anything else to cover up my, you know, my private parts."

Davis shook his head coolly. "*My* private parts."

Baxter's brows crinkled with bewilderment. "Pardon?"

"You don't have any private parts anymore," said Davis. "They're mine now." Baxter had never heard anything so strange. He inhaled several times with the objective of requesting clarification, but he couldn't figure out what question to ask. With the utterance of every initial syllable, he found that the question didn't quite fit. Good thing, though, as it looked like Davis wanted to elaborate, so Baxter stayed the confounded dangling of his jaw and waited.

Davis started circling him. "That neck, that head, and everything on it… Those fingers, those hands and arms… Those toes, feet and legs, and everything in between… they're mine. There is no 'you' in here. Just a little veal chop. Everything that happens with this veal chop happens because I wish it." Then Davis grabbed the freight door and began sliding it toward Baxter. "If my veal chop doesn't release my backpack, I'll crush my veal chop into a pulp with this door." Baxter trembled. The youth stood nowhere near the path of the door but didn't realize that. Davis realized it, but he had every intention of pinning the youth's head to the floor at just the right moment. But Baxter didn't know that either. Still, Davis didn't possess a whole lot more strength than Baxter, but neither of them knew that. Baxter only knew that there were more bullies in the world than he'd ever imagined. Facing the agony of defeat, he tossed the backpack on the floor and cupped his private parts.

"Good," yawned Davis, picking up the backpack. "Did I say my veal chop could cover my genitals?!" Baxter drew a huge breath and forced himself to expose his private parts. His trembling became uncontrollable, and he felt his face turning bright red. "Did I tell my veal chop to tremble or turn red?" Baxter controlled his trembling and stopped blushing. "Good," mumbled Davis, unzipping one pocket, growing bored and discarding the backpack onto the floor. "So, what brought the veal chop into my boxcar?" He asked with a sudden genial vigor.

"Um, well, my bicycle was stolen..." Baxter began.

"Is that right?" Davis mocked.

"Yes, th-that's right. It was after the—" It seemed better to not mention the prize check folded up in his backpack. "I'm just, trying, to get, um, Home."

"Just trying to get home," Davis repeated. "This is home now, veal chop."

"Yes, Sir," said Baxter.

"Yes, Sir," Davis repeated in the midst of a mean little chuckle. "And where did home used to be?"

"Uh, 123456789 North Smiley Meadows Avenue," said Baxter.

"123456789 North Smiley Meadows Avenue," repeated Davis. "And where on God's gray Earth is that?"

"It's, uh, on the north side of Twinkle."

"The north side of Twinkle," Davis repeated, breaking up into a jeering laugh. "This train passed through Twinkle almost eleven days ago."

"It did?!" said Baxter. "Oh, no! Oh, my! Oh, gee! Oh, gosh! Oh, I'm headed in the wrong direction!"

"Be quiet," said Davis.

"Please," he begged. "Please let me go!"

"Hey! Stop assuming your own identity, I won't have it."

"Please give me my things!"

"I told you, you have no things. You don't even have you. And now look! Now you made me refer to you as you, and you know you're not you, you're just a veal chop, so you shut up!"

"Sir, my mom needs my help."

"*Your* mom? *Your* help?! Alright, that's it!" Davis barked. He grabbed Baxter by the ear, hauled him over to the opening of the car, and held him over the threshold. "Long way down, isn't it?" Baxter looked down and felt his heart almost fall out of his throat. They now lumbered along a bridge, over many other sets of thin, rickety, bridges. Most of the tracks were bent, fractured, missing beams, corroded to the point of transparency by the acidic clouds that often clung to them. A few tracks were severed altogether. This seemed to explain all the wrecked trains piled up far below. Thousands and thousands of wrecked cars, planes, satellites, and spacecraft had mixed into this vast lot, which stretched on for miles. A great many of these fluttered with dirty fires, which sent oily, black smoke meandering upward to join the ashy orange mists.

It hadn't always looked so grim and nasty down there at the Seeber Brothers' Giant Junkyard. Old man Seeber had started it up, years ago, after railroad companies had started building lines over his farm and trains had started dropping onto his fields from above. Such surprises made it harder and harder for the old man to plant or harvest his blueberries, so he started selling the scrap metal to factories, and the dead bodies to Arby's. He later passed the family business down to his four sons, who expanded it to include other vehicles.

Most of the vehicles lay there, smashed or gashed open, littering much of the lot with blossoms of sharp, mangled plastic and metal. Baxter wanted to scream, but no sound could find its way out of his gaping mouth. Davis yanked him back into the car. He stared at the impudent youth and tried to throw him onto the floor. But he couldn't gather up the leverage, so Baxter merely stumbled a couple of feet.

"On the floor," he ordered. His impatience mushroomed when Baxter attempted to obey by easing himself down into the filth. "No," he uttered with disgust. "Kneel." Baxter got up and stood on his knees. "Not like thaaat," Davis whined. Baxter knelt on one knee and bowed his head. "There," Davis chirped, "that's the stuff." He turned around and remembered the remaining Fakefurters in their greasy bag. He grabbed one, brought it to Baxter's nose, and said, "Good chop." Instead of taking his reward with gratitude, as Davis had expected, Baxter recoiled. And though the reaction made complete sense to the old professor, he grew furious at the notion of refusal of any reward in his domain. Davis stuck the Fakefurter in Baxter's face, but the youngster continued to back away. This escalated until Davis found himself chasing a naked boy around in a filthy boxcar with a synthetic wiener. It then came to him that this was not how his life was supposed to have turned out.

With a growl, he threw down the Fakefurter, turned around, and grabbed Baxter's backpack. He dangled it over the smoldering junkyard. Baxter yelped and then lost the ability to breathe. He grabbed the Fakefurter and opened his mouth for a bite. His autonomic nervous system intervened and brought his arm to a halt just as the revolting product neared his lips. But, with the faux food wiggling in his trembling hand, and with sweat running down his face, he leaned forward and forced himself to take a big, slow bite. Then he forced himself to chew it. A satisfied smile fanned out onto Davis's face. He set the backpack down. "Lie down," he said. And Baxter lay down, still eating the disgusting frankfurter perversion and weeping.

The roaring downpour outside, which had grown unnoticeable hours ago, fell silent. Spooked by the sudden lack of white noise,

Davis shot looks in all directions, like a hunted animal. Now he could only hear the rattling of the train along the tracks, the squishiness of Fakefurter digestion, and light weeping. And… and that creaking sound from above. Davis fumed at this—this all too familiar sound of another museum worker, wandering about on the roof, looking for food or trying to scout out shelter.

The same sound had drawn Davis up onto the roof earlier, only to find Baxter fast asleep. Well, he'd be damned if he was going up there again. Just let any interlopers try to even set foot on his turf. He listened to the creaking. Sounded like an anthropologist. *Cultural, probably. Sanctimonious assholes.* They all thought of themselves as sooooo crafty, all charismatic and sly with their "I'm one of your tribe" shit.

Then the creaking vanished. As the hair on the back of Davis's neck stood up, he whirled around to discover the eyes of the predator that stared at him from the shadows in the corner. Davis began to ease his way backward. The beast hadn't started growling yet, so the old historian retained some hope. But when the whiteness of the irises came to glow with full intensity, and the face of Cereal Man emerged from the darkness, a frigid rush crackled through Davis's bones. Baxter sat at attention, Fakefurter in mouth. This stranger in black seemed like a nice enough fellow, but also seemed like someone to pay attention to. And he seemed to have more authority than this other, older gentleman, who'd honestly been quite bossy.

The fellow carried a bag of groceries and now searched for a good place to rest it. Upon noticing Davis's nest, he set the bag down. He approached the nest, and the remainder of the greasy Fakefurter container. Davis's eyes, the only parts of his body that could move, followed shakily. With the uttermost tips of his fingers only, Cereal Man lifted the container. The smell was repugnant. Davis gulped.

Baxter sat there, watching. Cereal Man looked over at Davis, a harried, but wise old man, whose many decades on the planet had taught him a thing or two about how to resolve conflict with diplomatic grace.

"HOLY FUCK!" Davis shrieked, stumbled backward, and fell out of the boxcar. He plummeted into the smoldering abyss, so far below.

Cereal Man shifted his gaze to Baxter, who sat there with the Fakefurter hanging from his mouth. The lonesome train moaned far ahead, from an engine smothered in dirty fog. Baxter felt naked with those horrid white eyes bearing down on him. Then he remembered that he actually was naked, which made him feel more naked. His baby-blue eyes fell upon Davis's nest and the tattered rags that constituted the remains of the old man's suit.

Cereal Man, who stood between the rags and the boy, maintained his stare. Then he approached the youth and extended his hand. Baxter paused, lowered his head, and offered the Fakefurter to his new master. With abhorrence, Cereal Man slapped the unnatural product away. Again, he extended his hand. This time Baxter understood and accepted the foreboding stranger's help up from the dirty floor. The man had a strong, but not painful, grip.

"Put your drawers on and get ready for breakfast," he said, clearing some space off one of the empty crates.

"Gosh, Sir, okay," said Baxter, not at all expecting to hear such an order. He tied Davis's shredded old coat around his waist and threw on his backpack. Then he paused. "Did you say breakfast?"

"That's right."

"You … You mean …"

"Breakfast. Also known as the morning meal."

"Well, no, I know what breakfast is—"

"It means to break the nighttime fast."

"Golly, yeah. I've heard that—"

"The most important meal of the day."

"Yes, yes, I know all about—"

"You see, in this world, my friend, there are two kinds of people: those who enjoy a healthy breakfast every day...and those who want to rush to early graves with their hearts full of tears and their shorts full of piss," Cereal Man decreed while sitting and removing a box of Grape Nuts from his grocery bag.

"Y-y-yeahhh..." Baxter muttered, also sitting and attempting to agree with the stranger's ominous words.

"Now this might seem a little strange to you," Cereal Man went on in rebuke while drawing two ceramic bowls from the inside pocket of his duster. "But breakfast doesn't include waffles or doughnuts, or slices of salted sow belly, or gallons of maple flavored syrup." He poured the Grape Nuts. "And it doesn't include gravy or frosting or maraschino cherries, or refried pizza rolls or Jell-O Pudding Pops, or processed cheese-flavored dog shit on a stick." He took two spoons out from his inside pocket and placed them in the bowls. "And it sure as John Harvey Kellogg's shit doesn't include a meat-flavored, plasticky emulsion of synthetic filth sealed up in a polypropylene tube."

The few replies that Baxter could think of evaporated from his tongue the moment he opened his mouth. He had never heard of any of these things. However, he reasoned, since none of these items included tiny nuggets of wheat and barley, the probability of these newly poured and delicious bowls of cereal falling under the domain of that which this scary person seemed to condemn proved exceptionally low. Finally, it looked like all those summers at Probability and Stats Camp had started to pay off, probably. This sure seemed like good news. The youth had maintained a hankering for a wonderful bowl of cereal and milk for so very long. But wait.

"Aww! Darn it," Baxter said, snapping his finger.

Cereal Man paused and squinted at the effrontery. "Say what?" The sight of the kid chewing on a Fakefurter had been offensive enough. But for this brat to complain while in receipt of a real breakfast?

"I feel kinda guilty," the boy continued. "I mean, I usually have a can of powdered milk with me, but..." But Cereal Man had already reached into his grocery bag and pulled out a carton of milk. He poured a splash into each bowl. They both began eating.

"Powdered milk. That's a little strange isn't it?" asked Cereal Man. "Carrying something like that around all the time?"

"Well, it's a darn sight better than dry Rice Crispies, that's for sure," Baxter replied, just finishing a scoop of cereal. The milk was surprisingly cool, considering the amount of heat weighing down the air. "I mean, they're great dry too, but I really go for a good, noisy cereal sometimes. Don't you?"

Cereal Man paused, intrigued. "You have Rice Crispies?"

"Nah, not anymore. Y'see, there was this nice family a while back. Really nice, and, well, they sure looked like they could use them."

"I see. And the only thing you have now is that... abomination you were chewing on?"

"Oh, no Sir, that wasn't mine." Baxter coughed. "I'd sooner eat my own arm than even touch one of those dreadful things. Truth is, that elderly gentleman made me eat it. Honestly, he was kind of mean." The breakfast was renewing his vitality. "But, gee whiz, I dunno. Maybe I'm being a little hard on him. After all, my buddy, HAMN, used to eat things that were just as bad."

"Ham. You have a friend named Ham."

"Oh, sure! HAMN's swell. Helped mount a big trophy on display right after the chess match. Helped me put that huge check in my backp—"

The boy practically swallowed his own tongue. Not wise to mention the prize check, even to a friend. It was for *so* much money! He didn't want to make anyone feel jealous.

"And what did 'Ham' like to eat?" snarled Cereal Man.

"Ugh…" Baxter shook his head. "Candy, soda pop… lots of deep-fried stuff… candy deep fried in soda pop."

"*Candy deep fried in soda pop,*" Cereal Man growled.

"Oh, yes," Baxter said between bites. "Not for me, though. Y'know, I'd really been looking forward to that last little box of Rice Crispies. But . . . I couldn't just leave that family, stuck there in that alley, with no cereal to eat."

Having cleared Junkyard Valley, the train descended back into town. As the light from the fires diminished, grayish-blue hues of the rundown industrial areas pulsed into the boxcar.

"So you carry Rice Crispies around with you?"

"Not all the time. I'd say Wheaties almost as much. It's the breakfast of champions, you know. Mom also likes to pack me up with Chex, Cheerios, Shredded Wheat… And then, of course there's always Corn Flakes, oh they're probably my favorite. Mmm-Mmm!" To Baxter's great alarm, Cereal Man suddenly rose and stood towering over him. "N-not that I don't appreciate this stuff right here," Baxter said, fumbling about. "I love Grape Nuts, too, Sir, aaand-and it sure was nice of you to share your breakfast with me, Sir, yes, really swell. Th-thank you so much. You know, I've been just hankering for a bowl of cereal for I don't know how long, now."

Cereal Man stood there with mist in his eyes and a tremble in his chin. He leaned down, grabbed Baxter's shoulders, and lifted the youth up off the floor until his feet dangled in the air. Baxter closed his eyes and braced himself for whatever the scary man was about to do to him. Cereal Man buried the boy in a tight embrace. This disturbed Baxter less than the shuddering sobs of joy that he felt bursting out from the face buried in his shoulder. And even this disturbed him less than looking to the floor and discovering an image of his own face on the back of Cereal Man's milk carton. Above the image he could read the words, "HAVE YOU SEEN ME?" Below the image he noticed the words, "REWARD," and "CONTACT YOUR LOCAL POLICE."

"What's that?!" he cried. "What's that?! That's me!"

"Yeah," Cereal Man stated, releasing him.

"Well, what am I doing on there?!"

"Filling a lot of eyes with dollar signs, that's what," said Cereal Man, while placing the carton back inside his duster.

"The heck do you mean? Oh, my goodness, how could I already be missing? Maybe I was asleep up there for longer than I thought. What's today? Please, what is today?!"

"Today?"

"Yes, today!"

"It's the first day of the rest of your life with me."

"Mister, that's really nice of you. A-and I really like you too. But didn't you see what that carton said? I need to let people know where I am!"

"No deal. You gotta stay scarce from now on. You know how much you're gonna be worth pretty soon?"

"Ohhh no you don't. You can't put a price on a human being's life."

"Think so, huh? Well, I'll make sure to pass that along to the first fella ties you up and throws you in the trunk of his car."

"I— Wh-why would anyone do that?"

"You're on the run. And you're on the run for life. It won't be long before we start meeting a lot of bounty hunters."

"Life?! We?! Bounty hunters?!"

"Count on it."

"B-b-buh-h-hht, why?! I didn't do anything!"

The piercing, squealing whistle of the Squeezeburgh Squealer tore through the air as the train neared a small, vacant terminal. Cereal Man looked ahead. They had arrived. *Perfect.*

Wait.

The train wasn't slowing down. *Not perfect.*

"Come on," said Cereal Man. "We're ditching this line."

Before Baxter could say anything, Cereal Man enveloped the boy with his duster and launched the two of them out of the boxcar. They bounced and tumbled across the concrete of the platform. As their tumbling slowed, so did the train. They rolled to a full stop right at the platform's edge, just as their boxcar clanked to a full stop right next to them.

Cereal Man heard Baxter hollering objections from inside his duster. He stood up and surveyed the scene. The long platform lay in darkness, but for the pulsing red from the lights on a nearby collection of smokestacks, whose thick issue suppressed the normal orange haze of the sky. Cereal Man had to squint to make out the nearest exit, and the stairs descending into the unknown, below the terminal. By now, Baxter's hollering objections had become more audible and vigorous. Cereal Man opened his duster and the boy tumbled out, dizzy and banged up.

"Wha-hohhh! Ohhh—why did you do that?" he moaned.

"Guess maybe I underestimated the train's brakes."

"Couldn't we have waited for the next stop?"

"Next stop, train gets loaded up with livestock. Next stop after that's the incinerator."

"Incinerator?"

"That's right. You see, the Valhalla Syndicate doesn't much like animals," said Cereal Man, handing Baxter his unfinished and undamaged bowl of Grape Nuts, and then resuming consumption of his own. "Good old cigarette outlet, or Cheez Skwirt plant... turns over a lot more dollars than any farm.

"The Valhalla Syndicate?"

"They're not too fond of locomotives, either. Why haul everything on a train when there's all those cars and trucks just ready to roll?"

"Well, doesn't that jam up the roads?"

"Sure it does. More jams, more gas. More gas, more dollars. But that's not even the best part. Best part's the smog."

"Now, that just doesn't even make any sense at all," Baxter griped. "Who in the world likes smog?"

"Well, we can't have you breathing clean air all day long, can we? Clear up your head, put you in a great mood? Pretty soon you'll start going outside and doing stuff. Pretty soon you'll start thinking about things more than five fucking feet away from your lazy ass. Before you know it, you're not even watching TV anymore. And when that happens, well, then you'll start asking questions, and then... well then you might just lose your taste for Fleshstic... maybe even cigarettes."

"Fleshst— I don't... I don't even know what those things are."

"I know, kid. You're good people," Cereal Man assured him, while gazing off into the chunky sky. "I'm talking about the thirty-three billion other saps infesting this planet. And then all the other suckers, out there, soiling the nest of stars."

"Well, that sounds awfully cynical," Baxter scoffed.

"Oh, is that so," Cereal Man sneered. "Well, let me tell you about a right jolly old elf who refused to cast a cynical eye on the world until it was too late. Know what that fella is up to now?"

"Mister, this is all very nice, and I really, really appreciate the breakfast, but do you know when the next train is coming through in the other direction?"

"What do you got Cheez Skwirt in your ears, kid? Everything's going to the incinerator. Only thing ever coming through here again's maybe a new expressway."

"But I've got to get Home to my mom now."

"No way. First thing any good bounty hunter will do is tail your mom. We gotta keep them guessing."

"Bounty hun— hohhh, no, mister, why are you saying, 'we?'"

"You think you're free now? You think you can gather up every drop of milk that's been spilled and put it back in the pitcher like nothing's happened? You think you're gonna just prance on back now, to your little house in the 'burbs?"

"Well, I—"

"I might as well wrap you up in a pretty package and just hand you over to one of those lowlifes. No way, you're coming Home with me, kid. There's no going back now."

"What lowlifes? You can't be serious with this bounty hunter nonsense. That's just nuts."

"Heyyy," a voice said. "Are you Baxter? Is your name Baxter?"

The voice came from one of the shadows approaching them from the dimness of the platform. In the red light, Baxter made out the forms of five men. The one with the huge, messy scab lining the rim of his scalp looked awful. He seemed to spend a lot of energy breathing. And he had a pistol drawn. None of the others had guns, but they appeared armed. Baxter couldn't tell what kind of weapon the fat, long-haired man in the puffy jacket carried. It looked more like a toy than a real weapon. The guy with the eye patch carried some kind of roundish thing. It looked like a plastic mallet. The guy next to him, with the taped-up glasses, carried a whip. Then Baxter couldn't help but stare at the guy with the torn top hat and banged-up monocle, who looked like a homeless Mr. Peanut. He sported a huge candy cane as a weapon.

"Why, yes," said Baxter. "Do I know you fellas?"

"Same Baxter who was at that chess thing last week?" asked Ike.

"I, well... Yes, that's me," he replied. "Last week?!"

"Chess tournament," said Mike.

"What?" said Ike, peeling back his stupid eye patch so he could hear better.

"It's chess tournament, buttworm," he corrected again. The train began to pull away. Baxter entertained the idea of grabbing hold of it at the last minute, but all the eyes fixed on him, along with his fear of incineration, convinced him that such a stunt may not be his best bet.

"You fellas were at the chess match, huh?" said the nearly naked young lamster. "Well, look... if you're looking for that check, I-I, I already spent it. I gave it to charity. Someone stole it. With my bicycle. Really."

"What check?" asked Heath, biting into a scab flake, freshly picked from his scalp.

"Oh, yeah," hissed Ike. "That bike with the totally gay banana seat?"

"And that pathetic broken bell?" added Heath.

"Yeah, and those faggoty personalized plates?" continued Ike.

"You've seen it?" asked Baxter.

"Yeahhh, I think we have, haven't we, Heath?" growled Ike.

"Yeah," Heath laughed through his teeth. "I seem to remember that last I saw, it was all crushed and cut up along the railroad tracks."

"Oh, no! No, no, no!" moaned Baxter, whose hopes of maybe finding the bicycle and buying it back from the thief were now dashed.

"I told you dudes," grumbled Mike.

"Told us what, you Tellarite turd?" sneered Heath.

"That he'd just find another way home, numb-nuts. That he wouldn't just hang out at the school with his fingers up his ass, waiting for something to happen," Mike bitched, as Heath and Ike tried to mask their discomfort with incompatible mixtures of toughness and indifference.

What a bizarre-looking lot. They seemed mean, yet not all that threatening. Baxter could not decide if he felt fear or just pity. Fear soon won over when the platform lights slammed on and two more meanies joined the complement. Reese came strutting up to the fore, wielding his huge wrench, just aching to clobber somebody. Baxter had seen his kind before at school: tough guys. Tough guys with sunglasses and toothpicks. Zotz, however, presented something new. Baxter had never imagined anyone so scary looking. The way the air seemed to sizzle all around him . . . and those horrifying teeth! He carried some kind of device with lots of switches, lights, and knobs. He turned a knob, then flipped a switch. A blue light came on. The train tracks lit up with electricity. A long moan came from far down the tracks. A crashing sound followed. Baxter looked and saw the train making its way back.

"This the guy?" asked Reese. "This finally the dude?"

"Good god, Sir," snorted Clark. "What a dashing suit you have . . . tied around your nether regions."

"Well, yeah, but I had—hey now, buddy," Baxter chuckled. "That's private."

"Come, come," said Clark, putting his arm around the youth and guiding him away from the philistine discourse of his colleagues. "Join us, will you not? Join us, this band of merry men; us humble travelers, who rove the city seeking only company; company of those such as people like the people such as people like yourself, with . . . er, blond hair, and, wadded up suits, and . . . and . . . stained white backpacks. Let us fill your belly with flesh of a fatted calf, heat your liver with brandy, entertain you with our tales of the road … and adorn you with some decent attire."

"Whllll, shucks!" gushed Baxter. "I can't tell you how tempting that is—"

"He's with me," Cereal Man warned them.

Clark paused. Then he scoffed. Then, he snapped his fingers. Reese scampered over like a small dog and belted out, "Who the fuck is this asshole?"

"You were saying?" said Clark, drawing the youth still further away.

"Oh, well, sounds super fun," said Baxter. "But, of all the rotten luck. I have an urgent situation at hand, I'm afraid."

"Why, dear brother," said Clark, honeying his potion of words. "What could be more riveting than sweet meats, the finest spirits, and sad stories of the death of kings?"

"Well…" Baxter struggled. "I've just got to go, that's all. I've got to go head back. Yes, to Twinkle," said Baxter. "My mom is—"

"You can go to the bathroom too," reassured Ike, from the background, to Clark's puzzlement and irritation.

"Yeah," added Mike. "And play video games."

"My fine, good, dear, fine friend," Clark wheedled on. "Fortune smiles upon us all this fruitful eve. See yon train coming down the track? My friend Zotz has managed to reverse it. For the fair town of Twinkle is our destination as well!"

Baxter's face lit up. "Really?! You're kiddi—"

Baxter was very rudely interrupted. At first he blamed Clark for flailing and screaming at the top of his lungs. But when he observed a hand squeezing and ultimately snapping Clark's clavicle, it became clear that Cereal Man was the one who warranted charges of discourtesy. Reese responded by slamming his wrench onto Cereal

Man's skull, breaking his own hands from the recoil, and collapsing on the ground in agony. Cereal Man grabbed the wrench and bent it around Reese's wrists, binding them together. Baxter's jaw dropped.

Always quick to react, Zotz had been electrocuting Cereal Man for nearly a minute with no effect when the white-eyed menace turned around, took his time removing the taser probes from his chest, and ripped the taser guns out of his assailant's hands. Zotz's quick but very short legs could not deliver his escape from Cereal Man, who caught him after a leisurely stroll. He wrapped the taser wires around Zotz's neck forty-eight or forty-nine times, then used the remaining wire as a slingshot to hurl Zotz straight on down the railroad tracks. His harried little body tumbled and bounced down the tracks until the returning train plowed over it, causing it to burst after only a little flipping and flopping of the limbs. Baxter gasped. Cereal Man returned to Clark and jammed his giant candy cane up his ass. Then he lifted him and drop kicked him far, far away, like the lightest soccer ball. Baxter screamed. Mike, Ike, Heath, and Chuckles, who had all run away as soon as they saw Reese break his hand, would come upon Clark's peppermint-sodomized corpse a few hours later. Cereal Man had forgotten about them anyway. They didn't make much of an impression. Now he turned back to Reese, who lay there, moaning and cursing.

Cereal Man lifted him up, slapped the toothpick out of his mouth, and pinned him up against the wall. Then he drew a Mark VI semiautomatic 52 mm handgun from his duster and pressed the muzzle into Reese's nose.

"You tell your captain the kid is mine," he snarled.

"OW! Who the hell're you?" Reese bitched.

"You tell him anybody wants the kid's gonna have to kill me first."

"But who are you? Who—"

"You tell that little bucket of blubber I can smell his sweet stink coming a mile away. And if he holds any interest in not having his spine ripped out, he'd better stay the hell away from me. Go back and tell him that."

"But—"

Cereal Man blew his brains out. Baxter wet Dr. Davis's suit. Familiar images began to flood his mind with new potency: back Home, those pileups at the intersection of Hypotenuse and Adjacent. Rather ugly stuff, all those people fighting and yelling; all those corpses and heaps of twisted, flaming metal. Now, here lay another corpse— one of innumerable many Baxter had come across in recent days. But this one came with an added feature almost entirely unknown to the boy up until now: cause.

The splattering of blood, brains, and bone fragments all over the shattered concrete wall—the huge, smoldering bullet hole that caved in the lower half of Reese's face; the body that twitched underneath— such things no longer participated as ugly parts of the local scenery. They existed because a yellow umbrella of flame had blasted a pointy piece of lead out from the barrel of that awful gun, and because this big, mean, white-eyed man had decided to make it so by squeezing his finger back, when the toothpick fella had only tried to ask a simple question. For the first time ever, Baxter knew the how. What iced his heart, though, was the degree to which the how amplified the complete absence of the why! Why would Cereal Man have squeezed that trigger? Why was he so angry?

Then the iciness went away. He felt his heart liquify into the heaviest dread he'd ever known when it finally sank in that the fellow with the wrench had now lost his ability to return the anger...forever. He would never do anything ever again. Ever! Cereal Man made sure the toothpick fella, whoever he was, had no claim or stake in anything, at all. He just... no longer applied to this reality.

Horrifying chains and clusters of deep cause and far-reaching effect began to bubble up all around every corpse Baxter had seen. But amidst all the budding fractals of how, he could not detect even the thinnest mist of why. The boy's eyes shifted over to Cereal Man, who stood by, watching him. Then they darted toward the train, which now lumbered past the station again. He looked down the track, baffled by the unimaginable reach of those steel rails, far beyond their vanishing point. And somewhere, far along their way, those rails eventually reached his Home. Home! He felt precious seconds ticking past him. And then, he felt like those white eyes no longer bore down on him. No, they had shifted, down to the tracks, looking at the oncoming train!

Baxter opened his mouth to shout but clammed up at the last second. Doubtless, he could consider any opportunity to get rid of Cereal Man a windfall of fortune. And yet, he just couldn't bring himself to allow a fellow human being to get run over by a locomotive. This created a heart-wrenching conflict within the boy, until one violent shove from Cereal Man sent the train careening down the tracks like a giant toy, off into the burnt orange horizon, bound once again for the incinerator.

And then, with a tingling sting traveling up the back of his neck, Baxter sensed it, almost as if he'd heard it whispering to him. He looked at the wall and set his gaze upon the poster of the mohawked humanoid rat, who seemed now to look right at him from behind that dark visor. A bright stream of fire reflected across the bottom of the impenetrable black lenses. Closer inspection revealed the skeletons of several police vehicles in the background, many overturned, all smoldering, and a few with charred skeletons of humans trapped inside.

Baxter's mind raced with the horror of a hundred and one possible hows, all of which involved the rat, and many of which involved the short cigarette poking out of his mouth. But the whys remained as unattainable as the eyes behind the shades. The gaze of the rat disturbed Baxter. He shuddered and plunged his eyes down into the sea of digits following the dollar sign under the heading, "WANTED DEAD."

"Nickels and dimes," said Cereal Man, standing close behind. Baxter jerked and spun around. Those hard, white irises seemed to press him into the bricks of the wall. "The real dollars'll be for your ass," Cereal Man continued. Baxter stood, trembling in the heavy heat. He clutched a lapel of his piss-soaked crotch suit and edged himself over to an adjacent concrete bench. He sat, not knowing what else to do.

After a moment, Cereal Man sat down on the bench, leaned forward, and gazed off into the dirty horizon. "Tell you a little story, kid. Once upon a time there was a fella—young fella, we'll say about, oh, sixteen or seventeen. Just a kid. Smart kid. He was smart, but he didn't know much. Didn't ask much, either. As long as he minded his own business, he thought, everything was gonna be just fine. So he went about his little life, doing his little things. Never wandered too far from his own hometown, and that was A-okay with him. Small town." Baxter had grown tired of inhaling to almost say things. So he decided against it. "Good place for a nice guy to grow up," Cereal Man added. Baxter felt his muscles starting to relax, just a little, except for the ones in his cheeks. They started to pull the corners of his mouth up, just a little.

"Really nice guy," Cereal Man continued. "Trusting, generous, tender-hearted, unassuming, unknowing, blind, pathetic little pushover. A chump. A fucking sucker among suckers—I mean, this kid'd buy sand with his last canteen from a camel in the Sahara. This worthless little sack of sap—this, this human toilet brush who'd scrub the vilest pebbles of shit out from under the rim of the societal commode just for peer approval... well, he didn't know it, but things were about to change for him. The whole world was about to change."

Well, that sure wasn't pleasant. Baxter started to tense up again.

"People liked to push this kid around a lot—thought it was a lot of laughs," Cereal Man went on. "But he showed 'em. One day, they finally pushed him too far, and he murdered a guy. They didn't think that was funny. 'Course at first, the kid swore up, down, left, right, forward and backward that he never killed anybody and that the guy was already dead when he found him. Then it seemed like no time at all before the kid found another victim like that. Then another, and another."

Baxter stood up, horrified by this callous yank right back into the nightmarish notions and realities he had looked forward to abandoning only moments ago. Cereal Man had become too wrapped up in his story to notice. Baxter noticed him not noticing. So the boy slipped away and dashed off into the dim unknowns.

"Yeah, he swore to just about everyone in the store that he'd had nothing to do with it," Cereal Man rambled on. "Until people stopped asking. Until no one was left. Until every customer and every co-worker in that Safeway was buried under a mountain of old soda cans and beer bottles with their guts ripped out and their heads smashed in. After that, the kid wasn't afraid anymore."

Cereal Man paused to season his words with a dash of dramatic silence. After allowing just the right amount of goosebump time, he went on. "There's people out there'll try to tell you human life's sacred—that it's priceless. Well, they're usually the same sniveling, whining gaggle of slobs who spend every waking hour transforming themselves into giant, quivering bags of garbage. They scatter refuse all over the planet and doom their own putrid offspring to live in more and more filth. That's how they treat the sacred, priceless gift of human life—like a big old heap of stinking trash. Well, guess what. You know what you do with trash, kid? Do you? You throw it away. That's right."

The magnitude of Baxter's silence confirmed to Cereal Man just how much awe his story had inspired within the boy. "Don't like that, huh?" he goaded. "Well, whether it turns your stomach or gives you a hard-on, that's the way this kid started doing business, once upon a time. He threw away the trash. His partners thought this was real smooth for a little while—good investment. Y'see, the kid and two of his buddies had started up a good business in their shabby little studio apartment. Harmless enough at first. But later, when the kid found out they'd been breeding the very trash that he would throw away, well, let's just say it made his mind go snap, crackle, and pop. He went out on his own after that. But those other two sons of bitches kept the business going. Then one day, one of them hired your mother into the business. Then another day, the other one fucked her. She wised up and split before the lowlife scumbag could start in with the standard sperm-donor-turned-daddy bullshit. The guy was a diseased psychopath. He would have found you long ago if he didn't think a clinic flunkie had scraped you out of your mom's womb and poured you down the sink.

"Over time, that company got bigger and bigger—grew faster than a god-damn cancer. And it became the Valhalla Syndicate. They've got eyes all over the universe now. And when you decided to become a big-time chess star, their eyes came down on you. But nobody's ever gonna get you, kid. Not the cops, not the mobs, not the bounty hunters, and not Captain Candyroo or any of his Chocolatiers. Nobody's gonna get you, kid. Not on my watch."

"Kid?"

15. THE CAPTAIN'S MESS

"It was horrible!" said Ike, cornered into a phone booth. "There I was, locked in combat with the black-coat guy, staring with anger into the eyes of those mean, badass white eyes, with my own battle-ax getting closer and closer to my neck, as his great strength started to—started to win. And the guys were all just standing there, not doing anything. Assholes. Anyway, I started to feel the super sharp edge of the blade pressing into my neck. I was completely convinced I was gonna die. But then, all of a sudden, I found a new strength in myself and overcame his strength. Now the tables were on my side. He started begging me for mercy: 'Please, please, I'm really sorry! You can have Baxter! Take him anywhere you want! Just let me go!' Then I lifted up my eyepatch and gave him my hard stare. And I said, 'I'll let you go. Right after I kill you!' You should've seen the look on his face, it was—it was really scared. But then Mike came and screwed it all up. He threw that—that candy powder all over us, and we couldn't see anything. I was like, 'You idiot, what're you doing?' And Mike goes, 'You can't have him, Ike, he's mine. I want all the credit.' And then, by the time my eyes cleared up, both of those guys were gone. Baxter and the mean guy in the black coat were just gone. I'm like, 'You guys!

Goddammit, where the hell did they go?' And they just stood there, 'I dunno, I dunno, I dunno...' So then we came back."

"Yeah?" grunted Skittles. "What about Mr. Peanut?"

"Clark?" said Ike. "We found him on the tracks with a candy cane stuck up his butt. I bet the black-coat guy did that. I bet he did it."

Skittles stepped into the phone booth and closed the door.

"It sucked, dude," said Mike, navigating the narrow, slippery tracks midway across Vanisher's Point Bridge. "Totally blew chunks. He, like, had that candy cane, like, jammed up his ass. I mean it was like, blood-n-shit-city like all over the tracks, and we were all, 'Hoh-h-hhhhly frickin' fuck, I'm gonna' hurl.' And then Ike was like, 'Ohhh! Oh, no! Boo-hoo! No, not Clark! He was the virgin master!' And I'm all, 'Lame-o... any doorknob can be a virgin master. Dad could be a frickin' virgin master,' and he's all, 'Waaah-haaah, booo-hoo, you don't understand, you weren't his bud, you didn't know him as long as I did, waah, waah, waaah!' I mean, I was all sad and everything. I totally get that, y'know, but I was like, 'Dude, we don't have time for this. We gotta get back to the captain and let him know what happened."

"And?" said the Stick.

"Annnd, like, so here we are..."

"What happened? You haven't explained that yet, asshole."

"Whl, I told you: they escaped."

"If I gotta say, 'details' one more time, Combover, your skull's gonna be as bad as your glasses."

"Fine, Adolf! It was like... y'know, the kid wanted to go with us, y'know... But then this, like, dude in a long black coat, he like, totally went psycho on Clark. And we're like, 'Get off our friend, you psycho buttmunch!' And then he was like, 'Make me,' and we like started wailin' on him with our weapons, and then, he bailed.... With the kid! With the kid. Yeah, because he, um, he pointed a gun at his head and said, 'Come with me or I'll blow you to hell.' And then, like, they hopped on another train. A real fast one. And then Reese and Zotz, they like, hopped on too, and chased after them, and that's probably why we haven't heard from them or nothin', 'Cause, I mean, who knows what happened after that.... Talk about balls, dude. I mean, those guys are heroes. Total green berets and shit. I mean, if they show up, I wanna talk to them before anyone. Y'know, have my chance to honor them, y'know, private."

The whistle of a distant train came into the threshold of hearing.

"It was horrible," said Heath, trying not to lean on, or even touch, the flimsy guard rail that encircled most of the rim of the rickety, rusty, old Blustery Bay water tower. "This guy didn't even feel it. And Reese really laid into him good, I mean, you could actually hear it. You could actually hear the wrench go 'CLANGGG' right on this guy's skull, like he was made of solid adamantium or something. But he just turned around and just looked at Reese, like, 'That didn't hurt me, you weakling little stupid... fat, smelly, creepy, perv freakmeister virgin!' Yeah, that's when the other guys ran. 'Cept me. Me and Maggie put five bullets in the guy's chest before he grabbed Baxter and used him as a shield. Coward. I mean, we would've kept going, you know, 'cause Maggie always begs me for more; her appetite is... insatiable, to put it mildly, heh. And, plus, I mean, when you're approaching warp ten, it's almost literally impossible to stop, you know what I mean?" Heath sucked in a bit of slobber as his hyperventilating snicker ebbed. None of this impressed Pops, so the old vet continued inhaling and exhaling through his nose in an unremarkable manner.

"Yeah," Heath continued. "Yeah, so we couldn't even really, well, even begin to govern our passions until a few more bullets had already exploded out of Maggie's hole, you know? But they ended up nailing that poor kid, and by the time we'd, well, curtailed our animal instincts, well, Maggie's hole was just smoking like crazy, and she needed a break. So, we lingered a little bit, you know. I wanted to let her glow with satisfaction for a while before pushing a fresh magazine up inside her and starting up again. Yeah, it's a shame that never happened, because then, um, it hit me, hit me like a mighty Elvish smith of Eregion... we had killed the kid. I'll say it. I'll admit it, and maybe you'll think I'm less of a man now, but I got scared. I got scared and I panicked. And that's when we all took off running. Not us. Not us, like 'us.' Just me and Maggie, I mean those guys, those guys ran off on us way before that, you can ask them. 'Course they'll just lie about it and say I ran off with them.... And I did. We did. You know? But not until now... Like, not now, now... now in the story. Yeah, so we started hauling ass out of there, 'cause, you know, we had to get back and tell the captain that the kid got killed by friendly fire and so there was no reason to look for him anymore, or even try to piece together what had happened, 'cause, well, he was dead now." Pops blinked. "Yeah," Heath continued. "Yeah, but then we found Clark all dead and killed on the tracks. I won't go into details about how his face was all bloody and swollen with bruises, or how his shoulder looked all caved in, or how part of his left arm bone was sticking out of the skin of his forearm and his hand was bent all the way back. And not even one word about how his candy cane had been shoved right through his pants and into his butthole. Yeah." Heath swallowed. "I gotta be honest with you, one man to another... I think the guys killed him. Clark. They never liked him at all."

"Gimme your piece," said Pops.

"Don't call Maggie a piece, pal," Heath warned. "She's a fine—"

"Give it to me," commanded the old vet, yanking Maggie out of Heath's pocket. He released the magazine and showed it to Heath. "It's fully loaded."

Heath coughed.

"It was horrible, man," said Chuckles. "We found him on the tracks about halfway back, just fuckin' totaled—looked like he'd got hit by a train or whatever. How the hell he wound up buttfucked by his own candy cane I'll never know. Ohhh, that was a barrel of laughs. And I dunno how the hell he got there ahead of us, 'cause as soon as Reese pounded that crazy weirdo with his wrench... and it didn't do anything... hoh-hhh, we were so outta there. I mean we were just bookin' down those tracks. I never ran so fast in my life."

Turtle just stared at him with his beak open.

Upon their return to the tracks on the south end of the Stickylips Chunnel, the guys and their assigned inquisitors gawked, somewhat jarred by their leader's ongoing tantrum. Captain Candyroo still stormed back and forth in front of his juju train with all the fury and intensity of a greasy, stump-legged balloon filled with corn syrup. He continued to curse and kick the rails and stub his toes, which led him to curse more and kick the rails harder and break his toes in many places. Diabetic neuropathy, a gift appreciated by so very few, had deadened the nerves in his swollen feet many years ago, so he didn't feel any of this. But blood seeping through the rips in his sneakers always reminded him that he never bothered to buy a pair of badass steel-toed boots back when he could still afford them. Revisiting this reality always added to the loops of huffs and puffs displayed by him now.

His crew had long ago grown accustomed to the long duration of his huffing and puffing and bleeding. But their interrogations had kept them away all day long. This seemed excessive even for the captain. As a habit, he managed to reduce his tantrums to grumblings within the span of just a few Weird Al albums. But having enriched his lifelong distaste for effort, the captain just couldn't help himself. Last night's news of the loss of his crew members left his mind aswirl. And though he had given himself plenty of time to cool off by ordering Pops, Turtle, Skittles, and the Stick to separately interrogate the guys, he still couldn't think straight.

Finally, a particularly awkward kick pulverized his ankle to such an extent that his lower leg disconnected from it and sank into the bloated flesh bag of the foot itself. This caused him to lose his balance, and his gelatinous body enveloped his upper leg as he collapsed. He bounced off the tunnel wall, and then, while uttering grunts and curses anew, rolled down the tracks several meters, like a garbage bag filled with moldy gumdrop soup and dressed in a cheap suit. After watching his semisolid frame slap up against the front of the train and come to a sloshing halt, and after listening to a few minutes of their captain hollering for help, Pops, Skittles, and the Stick all strolled over to pick him up. Turtle stayed behind to make sure the guys didn't interfere by running to him to cry and beg him for candy. So the guys sat down and started crying and begging him for candy.

The captain always proved difficult to lift, as his skeleton had been incomplete for years. His sugary insides had dissolved many of his joints, as well as most of his thoracic vertebrae. His cranium had been reduced to a few scattered islands of soft bone, suspended in the sweet, semi-rubbery membrane of coagulated humors and deposits of artificial preservatives that encased his brain. He tried to avoid scratching the zits and boils on his scalp or combing any of his tiny patches of hair because of this. Not only could the resulting indentations in his head cause great pain, but they could also lead to life-threatening penetration of his cranial membrane. As for his pelvis and rib cage, he could only guess. Layers of blubber, hemorrhages, and fluid buildups had caused him to lose contact with those structures back in his late twenties.

No one could know with any confidence how he remained alive, to say nothing of the enigma of how he managed to move around. But his gang had witnessed, time and time again, that whenever he wound up collapsed into a helpless blob like this, enough structures within him would knit sooner or later, and he would somehow get back on his tiny feet, waddling around and sweating again with just as much vim and vigor as ever. He only needed to have his head propped up, to ensure that he didn't drown in himself.

After a bit of a struggle, the men placed him in a safe position against the side of the train. Pops sat down, out of breath, and whispered his findings into the ear of his captain. Then Skittles and the Stick, also a bit winded, squatted down and participated in this quiet briefing. After a few minutes of conversation that the guys couldn't discern, the captain said, "Take me over there." They looked at the guys for a moment, then looked back down at the captain. Then they paused.

Then Skittles dug his fingers underneath the captain and began rolling him along the tracks toward the guys, with his head and stumpy limbs flapping over and under him. The Stick aided the captain's momentum by prodding him along with the end of his trusty quarterstaff. The captain didn't like this. He attempted to object, but his face rolled into the ground each time he had gathered enough air for yelling. By the time it occurred to him that he should have ordered the guys to come to him, he had completed his trip. After coughing, spitting out dirt, and cursing the guys for snickering at his expense, he screamed, "SHUT YOUR HOLES!" The guys clammed up and began trembling. When he perceived anxiety returning to their eyes, a wide grill of rotten teeth split across his face, like a freshly opened wound.

"So, the Cereal Man has returned," said the captain.

"Who?" said the guys, in unison, which made them all feel like a bunch of total fags.

"You heard me. Long black duster? Nasty looking peepers burning white-hot with rage? Took a wrench to the skull without blinking? Yeah, sounds like you macho men made quite the little bitch out of his punk ass. Especially Ike, turning into the Incredible Hulk and everything, overpowering a guy who once demolished my buddy's car simply by stepping in front of it on the expressway? And Heath, you badass bastard, getting all Charles Bronson on Cereal Man's ass, unloading on him with that hand bazooka of yours… and yet, your last clip is still full. And then pumping Baxter full of lead… Well! Guess I can assume this was before Cereal Man escaped with him… while still fighting off Zotz and Reese on this mystery train that just happened to be speeding by on a line that's out of service. Well, the loss of my engineer and my plumber is a small price to pay when you savage superhero studs were brave enough to jump all over Cereal

Man and pound the shit out of him for ass-raping Clark." The captain paused. His grin dropped.

"I still can't get it out of my head. Clark, our virgin master, dead on the tracks, never to tell another tale. Gone for all time, with his body and possessions left for the sport of crows and the uncaring winds! What I want to know is, where's the candy cane?" He watched the guys squirm for a second before he went on. "Yeah, that's right, you homely horde of hosers. Come on, I'm wait'n. It's time to coat your sugar daddy's stick. The guys stood there, sweating. "Gee, golly, and goody goody gumdrops, where could it be? Hand it over, chumps. No way you wispy-willed weeping wussies came across a perfectly good shaft of barber pole and just left it there, calling your stupid names. Let's see the juju."

The guys shifted around and clenched their legs together. Nobody wanted to be the first chickenshit to wet himself. And yet, that first chickenshit, that craven crybaby, that Grand Sultan of Pussies, that worthless little girl would, in complete ignorance, become a hero, as the wetting of his tighty-whities would free everyone else to soak their own undies without shame. Captain Candyroo waited for the confessions of gluttony due him, and for the blubbering boot-lickery that would appropriately follow.

Then, to the surprise of all, Heath, digging into his pocket, stepped forward. He presented the captain with a chip of candy cane about the size of a mini Peppermint Patty. The other guys gawked at the offering and then grew red with rage at the betrayal. They all had found themselves equally weak, back on the tracks, when the cool, sweet, tantalizing scent of Clark's cane had slinked into their nostrils. They all had rabidly lusted for a fix, to balm the wounds gouged into their souls—to repair the trauma inflicted by witnessing the attack on their revered VM. They all had defecated on him to stake their claim—all vied ruthlessly for his cane once they had removed it from his insides. They all had scratched and sliced one another with sharp fragments of the cane once it had shattered. And they all had found themselves lying next to the tracks a few minutes later in a sugary stupor, with sweetness rushing through their veins, peppermint candy stuck to their teeth, and an unspoken pact branded into their hearts that this greedy frenzy would remain a secret they carried to their graves.

Heath's chin pressed into his double chin with pride. His remaining upper incisors pinned down his worm-like lower lip, and his foolish grin pressed into his cheeks hard enough to loosen some of the scabs on his temples. Everyone knew that the guys should have brought nothing less than the entire cane before the captain. Everyone knew that holding out on him counted as a particularly grave offense—one that they had committed only a few dozen times over the years— one that the captain had declared punishable by death, though never actually punished, due to lack of focus. Yet, Heath somehow believed that salvaging a scrap of the stripy bounty would elevate him above the other guys—those traitors, whose gluttony and selfishness controlled them—those animals, who chose against restraint—who chose against the captain.

With an ongoing and unspoken knowledge of his captain's bidding, the Stick spun around and flashed his trusty quarterstaff across Heath's face. This knocked his remaining teeth into his throat and caused him to start choking. Skittles, equally in touch with the captain's wishes, lifted Heath up over his head and performed a vertical suplex, slamming him onto the tracks and causing his teeth to explode out of his mouth. Skittles propped him up, while Turtle, also possessing a silent understanding of the captain's mind, twisted his spear into Heath's tire-sized gut. Heath doubled over onto the spear. Pops, sharing equally in the captain's collective knowledge, fired a bullet into each of Heath's kneecaps, or rather, cuckolded him by pressing on Maggie's tickle zone and forcing her joyful essence of betrayal into his flesh.

Captain Candyroo, ignorant to any communion whatsoever, helplessly bounced up and down within his own gelatinous frame, screaming, "What the fuck?! Wait a minute! Hold on! YOU MORONS, WHAT THE FUCK ARE YOU DOING?!" The rest of the guys, also ignorant of any communion, but pissed at Heath, joined in the attack. With Heath now helpless on the ground, Ike leaned on his battle-ax lollipop and kicked his old friend's wounded kneecaps. Mike stood behind his little bro and lashed Heath's feet with his licorice whip. Chuckles, dissatisfied with flogging, scalped Heath anew and began to smother him with his own toupee. Turtle stared, while Pops, Skittles, and the Stick stood aside, laughing at the ordeal.

Then, they all fell silent as Heath's muffled screams softened into whimpers. All except the captain, who continued to scream, "STOP IT! STOP IT, I THINK YOU'RE SMOTHERING HIM—"

"Shhhhhhhhhh!" they all hissed. They wanted to hear Heath's last struggles for air. The captain did shut his hole, but only because his skyrocketing frustration had overloaded the speech center in his brain. After a few quiet moments passed, every department of Heath's brain blinked off, and his body went limp. With that, someone's long splutter ushered in a riot of juvenile laughter.

"You..." hissed the captain. "You... You, you puke-sucking, baby-fucking, piss-chugging, pig-raping, mildew-lined sacks of refried rat shit! First the virgin master, then my plumber, then my engineer..."

"N-now wait a minute, Cap," said Pops. "No need to—"

"No need to what, let you keep breathing?!"

"Cap, we're sorry. We're sorry! Come on," Pops pleaded.

"Your mom's hairy balls you're sorry! Chuckles didn't take me seriously. You know what happens to people who don't take me seriously? ... Huh? THEY DIE!"

Pops shot Chuckles in the head. For a brief moment, Chuckles felt the urge to laugh at this unexpected turn, but the loss of his brains and life prevented it.

"NO!" cried the captain. "WHYYYYY?!"

"You wanted someone to get rid of him, didn't ya?" Pops whined.

"You stupid old bedsore," said the Stick.

"Who you calling old, string bean?" Pops snapped back.

"Let's snap this codger's neck, Skittles," said the Stick.

"Oh yeah?" Pops growled, pointing the gun at the Stick's chest. "Well, let's see what you got, man!"

"STOPPP!" the captain hollered with throat-shredding passion.

"Come on, dudes! You guys are like, going totally mental," said Mike, rooting through Heath's pockets for pixie.

"Yeah, totally," said Ike, rooting through Chuckles's pockets for pixie.

The captain broke down into a sobbing fit.

"Aww, you're actin' like a woman," Pops grumbled.

"We had a mission, you assholes! All of us!" bawled the captain. "Life was going to be sweet!" He blew his nose onto his face with no tissue. "Sweet as Mrs. Butterworth's twat. I told all you guys, once we delivered Baxter, we were just gonna lie on the floor and taste tootsie for the rest of our lives."

"Wait a minute, Cap," the Stick began.

"Yeah, wait a minute, Cap," copied Ike.

"What the hell's this mean, we're not doin' it anymore?" the Stick went on. "If you losers have kept me and Skittles from collecting our pixie…"

"What, you'll kill them, too?!" barked the captain. "You thick-skulled Twizzler dicks keep this shit up, I'll be sitting there back at the hub, just tapping the tootsie all by myself. Is that what you want?"

"Whll," huffed Mike. "Then, like, what the hell was that, sending us guys out after the kid while you guys all hang out back here, like, in your like, protective tunnel of protection and hideout place?"

"All I said was haul his ass back here," said the captain. "I didn't know anyone was with him. And if I'd known Cereal Man was with him . . ."

"You guys shoulda come too," groaned Ike.

"And leave the Cap here by himself?" said Pops. "Goddamn. I'd say you're as dumb as you look, but you look so fuckin' dumb…"

"Well, somebody shoulda," Ike said. "Turtle coulda kicked his ass, I betcha."

"You don't know shit, Shirley Temple," said the captain. "We need to find out where these guys went after you sniveling sissies bailed on our friends."

"Wull," said Ike. "He said he had to go to the bathroom really bad."

"What?" said Mike. "Dude, you're makin' that up. He never said that."

"The hell he didn't," said Ike. "He said he had to go and tinkle. And it was urgent."

"Oh, what, so, like, what do we do?" said Mike. "Just, like, go out lookin' for the nearest restroom and hope he's still in there wizzin' away after all these hours, takin', like, the world's longest piss?"

"Or find the nearest puddle and ask it where its owner went?" Pops added with a mocking wheeze.

"Nooo," Ike whined. "He said he had to go to the head and tinkle. You should have seen him. Loser had never pissed on a sidewalk or wet the corner of a building in his life. Pathetic. I mean the guy was holding his crotch. He was looking for a restroom."

"So!" Captain Candyroo whispered as his bones began to knit. "On the edge of the Stickylips Chunnel, our plan is hatched! We hit every rest stop, every gas station, every restaurant, every bar, every grocery store in the area. Somebody would've noticed a guy like Cereal Man traveling around with a kid like Baxter. And that someone can either be rewarded sweetly, or punished sweetly."

16. A RED NOSE FOR
THE GOLDEN SON

O h, the age of competitive television. Though born into it, Baxter never cared for such stuff. He had caught a few advertisements and had overheard students at PHU talk about a few of their favorite programs. He seemed to remember HAMN favored a show called *Top Thumb*, where the teen who typed the most vacuous text message while driving won enough money to circumvent consequences for life. Other popular shows of the like included *Knitting Wars, Jim Beam MD, Cardboard Boxes, Lube of Your Life, Who Wants to Marry a Piece of Shit?, Extreme Gargling, Celebrity Seat Sniffers, Beat Bobby Brady*, and *Flay Bobby McFerrin*. Baxter never became very familiar with any of them. But they didn't seem like the nicest shows to watch, and the last one would not have put a smile on his face.

All of these shows were produced here, at DizneyCramcast Studios, the ventilation system of which Baxter now crawled through with care, wearing only his backpack. Stopping people on the street to hitch a ride Home had not worked out at all. Approaching them in stores or restaurants had also not helped him out. In fact, whenever this filthy young man, with an oily, beaten-up, piss-soaked suit wrapped around his crotch, approached anyone to ask for anything, they would either fly into a rage and try to strangle him to death for being homeless, or they would act like responsible citizens by calling the police and demanding them to strangle him to death for not smelling better and not pulling himself up by his bootstraps.

He had tried reasoning with people, but they found that offensive. He had tried begging people, but that entertained them. He had even tried crying to people, but that made them laugh and demand more. And every time he stopped providing more, the pressing of their thumbs into his windpipe made it impossible to reengage them with any degree of satisfaction.

Hollering to them from afar proved useless too, for nobody could hear his pleas over the sound of their guns firing, or the roaring of their flamethrowers, or the screaming of their engines as they accelerated toward him in first gear. During the most recent and most frightening of these encounters, which involved chemical and biological weapons, he had found his way down into the basement of the studios, not even recognizing the holiness of the premises. But his pursuers had understood the sanctity of these hallowed grounds. After all, this was where television was made. Soon after they had noticed him approaching the grounds, they ceased their attacks. And then they got all caught up in the new episode of *So You Think You Can Belch?* broadcast onto the outside monitors and died horrible deaths in the midst of their own anthrax and mustard gas.

Baxter had remained sharp enough to find his way into the ducts on the main floor, but not mindful enough to keep Davis's suit jacket from slipping off his waist. Unable to turn around, he had little choice but to go forward, hope beyond all hope to slip past any more hateful eyes, and somehow make his way Home. He looked into each room through the grated vents, in hope of spotting something that would cloak him a bit better: a long coat; a broad hat, perhaps—at least some clothes that might fit him.

The garments and costumes in the empty dressing rooms hinted at what kinds of shows the studio was recording at the time. He now passed by rooms likely to host performers on cooking shows. He believed this room right here hosted *Roast Beast* contestants. All the chefs on *Roast Beast* wore traditional garb: white double-breasted jackets, complete with stegosaurus-like plates on the back, scaled trousers with a dragon tail hanging from the back, and of course, white pleated toques with the horns of a ram. None of these would conceal him very well, he thought… unless he could get a hold of the long warthog snout that hung from the front of that tall, golden toque. But he'd heard nobody could get the golden toque unless they came out on top as the beast with the mostest roast, thereby winning the title of *Roast Beast.* Too bad. He was no chef.

The next dressing room hosted performers for *Chapped.* This show smoked and salted a lot of meats. But Baxter found nothing that might help him, except maybe a big cowboy hat made of jerky. Still, he needed something that could cover his face.

The next room looked much more promising, though, as it featured a few Nazi uniforms and lots of surgical garb. He'd seen *Cut Scrote Kitchen* a few times, just in passing, but was never quite sure what kinds of tasty treats the masked chefs had been snipping and frying up for their uniformed patrons. He thought of borrowing one of the surgical masks. But those were for keeping germs at bay. What if the chefs ran short by even one mask, and then someone got sick, all because of his selfishness?

He came across the tastiest looking room of all. It seemed to cheer at him with its bright colors. He spied several canisters of whipped cream and a jar of hot fudge, all next to a giant freezer, decorated with balloons. The freezer said "ICE CREAM" on the front. Oh boy! This looked like the dressing room for a sundae show! And indeed he did spy a trophy shaped like a giant maraschino cherry that said, "Poppo: 11th Annual Split Boss." Oh, how Baxter longed for a scrumptious banana split right now! But this was no time for silly ideas. It was time to spray himself a whipped cream beard and make a stealthy break for it.

He kicked the vent off the wall, slid his naked self onto the floor, and grabbed one of the whipped cream canisters. He tiptoed over to the mirror to compose his beard, but the reflection reminded him of his nakedness. Embarrassed, the youth dashed over to the closet, and to his elated surprise, beheld his ticket Home: an entire clown suit, complete with a crazy wig, a pair of springy satellite shoes, and a makeup kit.

Wasting no time, he smeared the white face paint all over his face. He covered himself up as quickly as possible, lest someone burst in and catch him. He slicked back his hair and pulled the matching white prosthetic scalp over his head. Many multicolored tufts of slick, glittered hair poked out of the top of this scalp. Once he secured it, he noticed how the tufts seemed to bounce with joy, and with great independence, with the slightest movement. The arc of an eyebrow created a different tuft dance than did a smile or a scrunched-up nose. The rest of the face paint looked like a fluorescent magenta. He swabbed some unprofessional-looking magenta circles over his eyelids and smeared an even more unprofessional-looking magenta smile across his mouth.

Then he slipped on the actual clown suit: a loose, silky gown of purple, bursting with numerous cherry shapes of pink and red. Giant red buttons and a white ruffle adorned the gown. He put his white backpack on over the suit, not even realizing how silly it made him look. Then he sat down and strapped on the satellite shoes—nifty things of a shiny, maraschino cherry red with surprisingly powerful springs.

Now he felt like he could simply hop away from his troubles. Finally, he found the clown nose, also bright red, but not ball-shaped, as he had expected. For a queasy moment, its shape, size, and jiggling reminded him of a Fakefurter, but with a color much more vibrant and real than the beige-pink of that revolting product, which he'd happily forgotten until this moment. But upon looking at himself in the full-length mirror, the nausea passed, and he felt the weight of recent days evaporating from his heart.

The fellow looking back at him was a total stranger. He should have thought of this a long time ago. With his chest now swelling with confidence, he hopped out of the dressing room and down the hallway. With the aid of the superb springs, it took no less than a modest twitch of his ankles to leap exhilarating distances.

He soon came upon Ms. Griffith, a small young woman with short hair, wearing a headset and carrying a clipboard. She was busy scribbling something on a piece of paper when he started to leap past her. But at the last second, she nabbed him and said, "Upupupup!" He crashed down onto the hard floor. She grabbed his arm and began to help him up so aggressively that it was scarcely helpful at all. He stumbled and slipped until Ms. Griffith had propped him up into a standing position.

"Chase, what the hell are you doing?" she said. "You bitch and moan through the whole production meeting, you finally get your way, and . . . I'm . . . I've had it. It was jeans and a polo. Your own words, Chase!"

"I'm not . . . but . . . I . . . you . . ." said Baxter, trying to cloak his voice under a whisper.

"Hurry up, get back there," she sighed. "I'll see if I can buy you some time. Go!" Baxter started leaping back toward the dressing room with such vigor that he scuffed his head on the ceiling more than once. "I have got to get out of this place," muttered Ms. Griffith. "If these people had brains, they'd probably play volleyball with them." She watched as Baxter hopped back into the dressing room and slammed the door. "Mike?" she said into her headset. "See if you can get Woody to drag it out a little bit. Chase just came up to me in full costume and makeup, and I think he's drunk."

"You guys talking about me?" asked Chase, just coming out of a nearby vending room with a soda and approaching Ms. Griffith in jeans and a polo.

Fitting himself back into the ventilation duct in full clown garb proved quite a challenge. As Baxter pushed himself through the vent, he smeared some of his face paint and tore the rear of his stolen gown a bit. As he crawled hastily along, he started to wish he had torn the rest of the gown. It was too silky and too smooth, and it picked up almost no traction from the surrounding metal. Half the distance now took him twice as long. The whole ordeal became exhausting, and the long, jiggly prosthetic over his nose made it difficult to breathe. Several times he had to stop and catch a few gulps of air. As he stopped, he listened—no sirens or yelling, or any other audible evidence of an immediate pursuit.

After taking a few turns, he found his way to a shaft, where an elevator was making its way up toward him from the basement floor. If he could just get onto the elevator, he could go downstairs again and escape via the same bowels of the building through which he had entered earlier. The elevator now seemed to be accelerating upward. Baxter tensed. If he waited too long, he might get clobbered, but too long of a drop might break his legs.

The moment came to jump, and down he plummeted, and up the elevator came, and up he sprung when his satellite shoes hit. He'd forgotten about them and found himself surprised to be soaring upward. But then gravity reminded him that it was still the boss, and he began falling again toward the elevator. Again he hit the top of the elevator as it approached, and again it propelled him upward. But this time he rocketed up toward the roof of the building. He felt like Wile E. Coyote, especially when he crashed through the roof, plummeted back down, landed in the top of a small brick chimney, and saw stars circling around his face while a lump grew out of his head.

With only a bit of grunting and whimpering, he managed to wiggle out of the chimney and fall onto the roof. To eliminate the possibility of accidentally hopping off the roof and plummeting to his death, he decided to crawl over to the edge. With great care, he slipped onto the gutter, which groaned and bent under his weight. Before long, the gutter departed from the roof, transported him diagonally downward several floors, and displayed him outside a second-floor window in front of a dance studio full of small children.

The children all wore uniforms, consisting of tank tops and socks of pink, with shorts and shoes of red. They exercised with happy energy at the command of their fun coach, Mr. Strong, who wore a purple jumpsuit with the DizneyCramcast Studios logo on the front. As the gutter creaked and swayed in a manner that forecasted its imminent collapse, Baxter attempted to shift part of his weight onto the windowsill. By this time, the pointing and murmuring of the curious kiddies had drawn Mr. Strong's attention to the spectacle. He opened the window and looked upon Baxter with hyperbolic outrage and shock. Mr. Strong was not just strong. He was wacky and full of comical, youthful energy, which the kids loved.

"Looks like a stranger, boys and girls," he belted out, after whipping his head back with exaggerated shock. His curly brown hair always made the kids laugh when it bounced around on his head. He could have made a good clown himself. "Do we trust strangers?"

"NOOO," they all replied.

"Chase, what is wrong with you?" he whispered to him, while chuckling with scorn. Then he spoke again to the kids. "Looks like Poppo. But I think it's just one of Poppo's helpers." As Baxter shook his head to deny this allegation, Mr. Strong continued, "When do we get to meet Poppo?"

"AFTER ICE CREAM," they replied.

"Yeah, I think this silly imposter has made a big mistake. Should we send him back where he came from?" he asked.

"YEAHHHHH!" they cheered as Baxter shook his head with all his might, and Mr. Strong gave him a good, long shove. All the children laughed as they watched the broken gutter carry Poppo's imposter diagonally out of view with a long, metallic groan. A moment later, they cheered to the sound of a mighty crash on the ground below.

Even though the crash gave him little more than a few scrapes and bruises, Baxter found it more difficult than usual to conjure up gratitude for the gutter that had slowed his otherwise lethal journey to the ground. He sat up, slid off the roof of the car on which he had landed, and bounced up and down with a few ankle repetitions. Then he put his legs into it and began propelling himself down the congested street. What fun it was beating the traffic by leaping over cars! He kept his eyes open for a phone booth but found it difficult to spot one while taking giant leaps into the dirty orange haze of the day, which he found difficult to distinguish from the dirty orange haze of the night. Many blocks down, he managed to slow himself enough to gently hop into a parking lot. He approached a mother escorting her child out of a local Laxall Total Drug.

"How do you do, ma'am," he offered in a cordial tone. The lady stared at him. "How ya doin', buddy?" He winked at the boy, who continued dragging on his Ritalin smoothie. "I... Could you be so kind as to tell me where I might find the nearest phone booth?"

"Stay away!" she barked, cramming her child into their minivan.

"But," he said, as she scurried into the minivan and peeled out of the parking lot. "I just need to find a phone."

Across the street stood Dizney's Magic Karate Kingdom, where everyone is a third-degree blackbelt. Another mom had just exited the place, towing her three children in a little wagon. Baxter couldn't tell if they were boys or girls. Their helmets covered their heads, all of their body padding seemed gender neutral, and he had trouble making out their faces, what with the huge, frozen Adderall Pops plugged into their mouths. As they approached their sports utility vehicle, the mother noticed how Baxter seemed to be studying them.

"Oh my dear God. Don't come any closer," she said.

"Me?" asked Baxter from across the street.

"Poacher, McKensington, Admiral, in the car! Now!"

Before Baxter could ask any more questions, the sports utility vehicle tore out of its parking space and carried the family out onto Family Magic Way. He decided to go somewhere else and try his luck. He noticed a sign on the corner. It pointed to Ignatius Quinnbury University at Smartmouth, but it didn't show the distance. Though he'd never heard of this school, he'd always known schools to be super friendly and helpful.

After leaping several dozen more blocks, he came to another sign, showing the school to be another mile away. He had to stop and rest for a moment. He sat down and removed the spring coils from his shoes. His legs had started to get a little tired. Maybe one of these nearby businesses could help instead. Just a little ways down Snuffy Street, he spotted a dump. He imagined it had dirty phones, though, if any at all. At the corner of Snuffy and Bird, he grimaced at the sight of Oscar's Trash Can Dining by the Dump. That didn't sound like a very nice place. Across the street from that stood Count Von Count's Casino, where thunder and lightning roared over the castle-like building every time the dealer hit twenty-one. Baxter's mom had always told him to avoid lightning, and casinos, whatever they were.

But at the base of the casino, the youth spotted a nice-looking place. The sign for Elmo's Fire featured Elmo's happy, furry red face, and his furry red hand, beckoning with a furry red finger. A furry red eyelid winked at Baxter from under a slick red combover. Baxter marched in, not knowing its reputation as the neighborhood's premier children's strip club because the sign outside didn't identify it as the neighborhood's premier children's strip club.

Once inside the neighborhood's premier children's strip club, Baxter found it very difficult to find a phone, what with having to avert his eyes from every image that came into his view. Bare bottoms everywhere he turned! He didn't understand this at all. It wasn't that hot in here. Yet the children dancing up on the stage in the center of the room must have been sweltering, as they seemed to be trying very hard to air out their no-no places. Many of the infants crawling around on the bar wore really thin diapers, but for some reason, the adults at the bar kept slipping Monopoly money into them.

Greenwood in the Morning populated all the huge TVs in the establishment and seemed to be the only safe place for Baxter to land his eyes. Greenwood's guest, Barney, always provided fun for kids, and even a few fun-loving teens. But the hilarious dinosaur seemed to have some kind of ax to grind right now about the annoying stereotypes continually slapped on him by the general public. "Just beecuhth I'm big and purple duhthn't mean I have a big purple one," he griped to Woody Greenwood, who chuckled it all up. "But it duhth mean I'm engorged," Barney added, as Cathy Lee laughed like a goose with emphysema.

Baxter managed an intense focus on the objectionable show. This blocked out the far more unnerving circumstances surrounding him, which, unbeknownst to him, included Mike and Ike, who stood right behind him, interrogating a portly gentleman with bloodshot eyes and dirty, somewhat olive tan skin. Though his complexion and boozy aroma betrayed a coarse lifestyle, Sully sported a thick, groomed head of salt and pepper hair, which got messier as his exasperation grew.

"Why would I hide anything from you?" he sighed.

"Come on," said Mike. "You're like totally takin' us for a ride, dude. You must've seen, like, a blond kid sometime in the last few days."

"'Course I have," said Sully. "You realize how many great catches the captain lures in here just with those Twizzlers alone?"

"Fuckin' A," Mike exclaimed. "And I'm not sensing a whole lot of gratitude, here."

"What, what gratitude?" Sully defended. What do you want me to say?"

"You're sure you haven't seen him," Mike pressed. "Blond, naked, teenage kid, totally peaches-n-cream … travelin' around with a psycho in a long black coat?"

"Every time someone books an hour in the Crying Room, pal."

"I think he's fulla shit," said Ike, trying to look tough. "I think maybe we're gonna start twizzling kids over to Mr. McFeely's across the street."

"Now, wait a second, just who'na fuck you assholes think you are, anyway?" said Sully, with his nostrils flaring. "I been dealin' with the captain for twenty years, and I never laid eyes on you two little jackoffs ever before in my life."

"Whll," huffed Mike. "Dude, he sent us."

"Yeah," said Ike. "Yeah, I think we're done talking, here. You may have all these young, hairless anuses now, but you'll see soon enough, pallie. Few years, they'll all look just like you and me. And when this place dries out and closes up, you're gonna remember this day."

"Don't you threaten me, you little sonofabitch!" said Sully, jabbing his finger in Ike's soft chest.

"Ow," whimpered Ike. "That bruises."

"Captain's crew," Sully scoffed. "My ass you're the captain's crew, now get your ugly faces outta my place, or I'll snap those fat legs of yours in half."

In an attempt to flee, Ike stumbled onto Mike, and the two of them fell into Baxter. The disguised youth bounced off of a wall, then turned around and tripped over a cop chasing a naked baby around on the floor with his tongue out. Then he got up and almost stepped on another patron's toe. He decided to have a seat on a barstool to gather his bearings, but his handicapped reconnaissance prevented him from realizing that he'd sat right down on a naked six-year-old girl practicing some kind of dance on a man's lap. The man invited him to join in, but Baxter jumped up, covered his eyes, and yelped. The whole establishment fell silent. Then Sully recognized who had come into his place.

"Are you alright, Mr. Budster?" he asked.

Baxter uncovered his eyes and looked across the bar. "Who, me?" said the youth.

"I never thought I'd be lucky enough to see you, hahahh… here! The champion, come into my little place," said the kindly proprietor, brimming with joy.

"Wait. You saw me become champion?" Baxter asked.

"Absolutely I did!" the man replied.

"I ... Sir, I ..."

"Sully. Please, call me Sully," said Sully. "What can I do for you, Mr. Budster?"

"Uh, actually, it's pronounced Baxter," said Baxter.

Mike and Ike gawked at him. Then they gawked at each other. Then they started to move toward him. Then Sully gave them one indignant and threatening look, and they scurried out of the bar.

"How about a few rounds on the house?"

"Oh, no, gee, thank you. I never—"

"A Fleshstic grinder, then."

"Uh, no I really, I just—"

"Anything," said Sully, his eyes twinkling. "You name it, Elmo's Fire is at your disposal. Maybe a couple of freshly oiled preschoolers? Ho-ho, well, I wouldn't presume, ha, ha, ha!"

"I ... I'm just trying to gather a little change for bus fare."

"Sure!" chirped Sully, opening his till and handing Baxter all the cash in the drawer. "Here. Here, take it. Take it all, it's no trouble."

"Well, I," said Baxter. "This is very generous, Sir—"

"Sully."

"Sully. I promise you; I'll pay you back as soon as—"

"No, it's my pleasure! Really. Anything to help out Poppo the Clown. This is the greatest day of my life!"

"Poppo?"

"Sorry. Mr. Budster."

"Uhmmm ... And could I trouble you for one more thing, Sir?"

"Sully."

"Sully."

"Anything. Anything, Mr. Budster."

"Could I use your phone to make a collect call?"

"Can you? Of course, I'd be honored."

"Really?"

"To have your voice ... passing through my phone? I'll have the thing encased in Lucite when you're done with it. Come on in here," said Sully, escorting him over to a small office with a window on the door. "A little privacy, right?"

"Gosh, thanks!"

"Ah, come on, it's the least I can do. And hey, listen, it's on me, I hear any collect calls and I'll kill ya, understand?" Sully winked with a playful chuckle, handing him a landline.

"Are you sure?"

"Am I sure, will ya stop? My pleasure. This room is yours until you say it's not, got it? I'm locking the door behind me."

"Golly, thanks again!"

"You got it. I'll be right out here, so you just come get me if you need anything more."

"Okay," Baxter said with his eyes misting up.

"Alright. No collect calls," Sully reminded him with a warm smile as he shut the office door and locked it. He showed Baxter the key, dropped the key down his throat, and waved as he backed toward the bar. Baxter waved back at him and started dialing numbers.

Back Home, the Spring Break Scrapers had placed Darla in intensive care. This troupe of traveling medical performers, whose signature act was sleight of hand abortions, had hauled her out of the television set, hosed all the vomit and Kryptonian sour mash off her destroyed body, and in no time, had set up a mobile surgical hospital in her house.

Now Darla was receiving the best medical care they could provide, with many thanks to the generous donation of her old employer from across the street, Blackwick Elderly Care.

Well, it wasn't a true donation. Little would have entertained Blackwick residents more than to witness the ruin of their old nurse, whose years of unwavering kindness and commitment to their wellbeing had, in its contrast, called so much attention to how grotesque and disgusting she had become. So, in exchange for the use of Blackwick's equipment, the Scrapers pledged to let residents sit in on the reversal performance. Of course, if by some miracle, Baxter made it Home and forked over that last payment, they would not reverse Mom's oophorectomy, and no performance would occur. Then the Scrapers would compensate for the use of all this equipment.

But the cost concerned them not. They had put their reputation on the line more than their finances. How would it look if they allowed every displayer of fly-infested snatch on the Florida beaches to default on her debts? Granted, Darla never qualified as a beach-combing spring break spooj pocket, but the surgery the troupe had performed on her with such magical grace did not qualify as your average vadge vacuuming either. They needed to make a statement, and she needed to live for them to make it. If she died, she would not experience the consequences of the oophorectomy reversal. Even if the Scrapers had to spend a thousand times the value of the original operation, it would be worth it.

Darla had finished detoxing and had now started to regain her vitality—a frightening thing, since only a few days remained before the default deadline. She knew that when those mutantly fertile ovaries of hers returned, she would resume the runaway spawning of horrid little creatures—perversions of embryos who would themselves impregnate her again and again from within before spilling out of her womb, curdling on the floor, like a tarry scramble, into blobs of semi-formed fetuses, and fouling the air with breath toxic enough to reduce themselves to lifeless, irremovable stains mere days before the next cycle of horrid little creatures came glopping along.

Defiling herself as she had for the past sixteen years had worked well in creating an internal environment so poisonous that it prevented the removed ovaries from growing back. But there existed no degree of defilement that could stop her from pumping out endless broods upon broods of nastiness once the Scrapers plugged those ovaries back in. Dr. M's super pill had seen to that. Last time, the only thing that saved her from literally drowning in a colossal mass of misbegotten filth was the birth of her wonderful mutation: Baxter, who put a hiccup in the cycle of endless reproduction—who simply came out—who brought only smiles to her life—and who she heard on the other end of the line when one of the Scrapers handed her the phone.

"Honey?"

"Mom!" cried Baxter from Sully's office. "I'm so sorry I haven't called until now. Boy, do I have some stories for you..."

Meanwhile, outside the office, the attention of Sully and all the patrons of Elmo's Fire had fixated on Woody Greenwood's next guest.

"With us today is world-renowned professional pedophile and three-time gold-medal-winning Olympic rapist, Chase Budster, also known as Poppo the Clown," said Greenwood. "His new book, *More Than a Funny Face* addresses rapist stereotypes and the hidden degradation of the American sexual assault athlete. Mr. Budster, good morning. And if you'll pardon the expression, boy, that was a mouthful. Now your book, I mean, I'll be honest with you, it's a lot of reading. Could you give us the gist of it real quick?"

"Sure, Woody," said Budster. "It's basically about how society tends to cheapen a serious sport like rape or pedophilia by means of labeling and stereotyping. Y'know, you grow a curly mustache and your friends tell you that you look like a child molester. Or a kid wants to go as a sodomite for Halloween and Mom dresses him in overalls and blacks out half of his teeth."

"Well, ha, Woody Jr. prefers the good old-fashioned clown suit with blood on the front, that's his favorite," said Greenwood. "Last year he went out with his little brother as the victim. It was adorable, he had a chain around his neck, and we painted this hilarious bullseye on his rear end . . . Oh, the neighbors loved it."

Cathy Lee found this amusing, so she honked like a goose.

"See, right there," said Budster. "The bloody clown suit. That's awful."

"Weh-heh-heh-hell, I don't doubt that . . . If you're the victim, that is!" laughed Greenwood. "I mean, nooobody wants to be caught by that clown, right? That's what makes it so amazing when it happens to other people, right?"

"No, I mean it's insulting," said Budster. "You think we're so unskilled, so lacking in nuance and subtlety, that the only way we can lure your child in is with silly tricks? With balloons and candy?"

"Well, don't you always keep sundae supplies on hand?" Greenwood asked.

"As a matter of fact, no," Budster answered. "I keep sundae supplies on crotch. And on anus. Sometimes my own, sometimes the child's. Then, any time the kid hits a Dairy Queen or a Baskin Robbins, it's flashback city. And that . . . That is immortality."

"Wow!" said Greenwood. "I mean, wow! I always thought all that stuff was for bait."

"Please, I stopped using desserts as lures when I was still in high school. You soccer parents are all so busy depicting us as obvious weirdos . . . you wouldn't know a real sexual assault athlete from a

TV set. Any pedophile of even modest skill could snatch your kid out from under you, drill a few permanent memories into his rectum, and have him back at the dinner table with a lifetime of unresolvable issues faster than you could say, 'no one will believe you.' We're not the John Wayne Gacys from the civics group or even the Jerry Sanduskys at school. We're the Michael Boltons of your Christmas parties and the Ann Romneys of your church.

"Well, I dunno, Chase, that's way over my head," yukked Greenwood. "I mean, we all know you as Poppo."

"Right, that's the problem," said Budster. "I mean, that's not me. That's just the clown who won *Split Boss*."

"No, now, you're not just any split boss. Nobody splits those orifices like you! Take the championship match last year, right? That punk? . . . Big fancy athlete? . . . Thought he was gonna just waltz in and steal your title?"

"Tunnel Blaster Tom?"

"Exactly! Got what he deserved, right? You showed him good."

"Well, it wasn't that hard," scoffed Budster. "The idiot used his energy up all at once and destroyed his victim in less time than it took me to force the first shameful orgasm out of mine. I mean, how can you expect to foster hours of begging from victims when you have them hemorrhaging and comatose within the first sixty seconds? Disgusting. I was so angry at that kid, I thought of bending him over and showing him firsthand what it was all about."

"A lot of people said you threatened to kill him."

"I did. Backstage we got into a hell of a fight. It was the heat of the moment. I mean, for god's sake, the guy had pieces of organs running down his pants."

"Yeah," grinned Greenwood. "Yeah, yeah, and a lot of people think you should have just... ended the show with a bullet in his brain. Oh, that would have been amazing!"

"I don't do that," Budster said squarely. "Anybody worth killing is worth killing slowly."

"What about that episode last week? With that stuttering kid? 'P-p-p-please, s-s-s-stop, I j-j-just want my m-m-mom and dad...' I had no idea a seven-year-old's anus could be opened that wide without seeing bone. I tell ya, that was some truly great stuff. Guy like me... I could never split someone like that without the assistance of a team of surgeons or something. Heck, I can't even split my wife in her sleep, right?" Greenwood yukked and reached for a high five.

Cathy Lee thought this was funny, so she brayed like a donkey.

"But see, that's all just fluff," said Budster, ignoring the gesture. "Any clown can force people open—that doesn't take any skill. That angry, sickly little guy on the show last week with the Napoleon complex, looked like a cancer patient?"

"Bartos the Bald," said Greenwood.

"Bartos, right," Budster replied. "Pasty little misogynist split three waitresses, one after another, without even tearing their panties off?"

"Was that amazing or what?"

"Again, just brute force. There was no investment of tenderness; no betrayal... He just stormed in, slapped them around a few times, and drilled them in the ass. The idea is to crush their souls, not just their genitals."

"Hmm," Greenwood said with an amiable and clueless squeak. "Well, all's I know is you are the best. I mean, as far as I'm concerned, I mean, we are talking to the Split Boss right now, right Cathy Lee?" Cathy Lee shrieked in agreement as Greenwood went on. "Yeah, you got a LOT of fans out there, and to us, you'll always be that crazy rapester with the springy shoes and the long, jiggly nose, right?"

"Yeah," said Budster. "And that, Woody, is exactly why I'm here this morning, to announce Poppo's official retirement."

"What?!" gasped Greenwood, as Cathy Lee started fanning her hyperventilating face. "Are you serious, Mr. Budster?"

"I am," he replied. "I've been planning this for quite some time. Last week, after *Split Boss*, I hung up Poppo's suit and his makeup for the last time. You will never catch me in that getup ever again, Woody. Ever. It just makes me feel cheap. Y'know? Dirty."

As Cathy Lee surrendered herself to a grand mal seizure and Greenwood launched into an unfocused ramble about this epic turn of events, the face of every adult in Elmo's Fire turned toward Sully's office and the dastardly imposter who now sat in his chair, bubbling rank, merry words into his phone.

"Sunday? Well, gosh, Mom, don't you worry yourself even a little bit, 'cause I'm coming Home today," said Baxter, oblivious to the cantankerous crowd now forming at the door. "Y'see, I'm hiding out at a daycare center called Elmo's Fire, and nobody knows who I am because, get this... I'm disguised as a clown! Can you believe it?"

"Sweetheart, listen to me," gurgled Darla. "Do not call here again. Do not use the phone for any reason."

"Oh, but I just wanted to let you know I'm on my way Home today, with the prize check!" Baxter reassured her as Sully rapped on the window while baring his teeth and cursing the youth's slimy, lowlife, backstabbing double-crossery. "I was going to take the bus, but this nice man, Sully, lent me enough money to take a taxi... oh, heck, maybe even an airplane!"

"Honey..." Darla pleaded.

"That's it! Of course! Mom," he chirped, as his long nose jiggled, as his colorful hair tufts bounced, as Sully yanked on the door, and as the old barkeep's customers grew enraged at his inability to break into his own office. "I'm getting a taxi to the nearest airport and I'm gonna fly Home to you! I'll be Home before Friday, I bet!"

"No, don't tell me where you are or where you're going!" she shouted as much as her gurgling voice allowed.

"But, Mom, I—

"Baxter! I'm your mother, now listen." Baxter couldn't argue with that. So he clammed up and let his mother continue as the crowd tried to break the window with Sully's head. "Hang up now and do not call again. People are listening."

"Yeah. Yeah, Mom?" said Baxter, unable to hear her over the cacophonous arrival of police sirens, the shattering of the door window, and the clamor of riotous Poppo loyalists flooding into the office. "Yeah, there are people outside who need to use the phone, I'll see you in—"

He wasn't sure how long it would take to get Home, even by plane. But he knew the handcuffs slapped on his wrists would extend any estimate. He imagined the same was true for the ankle cuffs, and the knee cuffs, and the thigh cuffs, the arm cuffs, the waist cuffs, the torso cuffs, and the neck cuffs, to say nothing of the chains, the straitjackets, and the butterfly net now hauling him off toward the armored police vehicle in the parking lot of Elmo's Fire.

"Drat," said Baxter to himself, muffled under a face cuff.

17. HOW THE LAST SUCKER WAS LICKED

"Happy birthday, dear Professor," Amethyst sang with a merry grin. "Happy birthday to you!"

"Your voice is almost as beautiful as your hair," said Gollard, smiling with confidence.

"Oh, shut up," Amethyst razzed back. "I haven't washed it in days, you dork."

"Not that hair," said Gollard, smiling with more confidence. "Or do you shave it? Yeah. You do, I bet."

"Oh, knock it off," Amethyst said with a smirk. "You are such a character. Now blow out your candles. I worked all night on this…. You don't want to hurt my feelings, do you?"

Gollard sat up in his bunk, accepted his pretend cake, and blew out the pretend candles. This just never got old, probably because it made him feel like a man who never got old. None of these rituals marked another trip around the Sun for Gollard. After all, he knew he'd only spent a couple weeks in lock-up, three or four at the most. Maybe five. Or six. He had a hard time telling exactly how long. No windows were visible, and the only TV was downstairs in the chief's office. But Gollard remembered that they'd promised him a trial within eleven days, and it seemed like much more time had passed. Chief Dungswet's childish, three-hour ritual of mockery of every inquiry had reduced Gollard's incentive to mention it. And Amethyst's arrival, probably just over a week ago, had eliminated what remained of even this incentive. She'd sing him songs, surprise him with make-believe cakes, rub his shoulders, and let him kiss her, on the cheek, once. She'd listen to his fascinating stories and sometimes flash him a dizzying smile—one that fueled the cores of every star in the universe. And this ignited Gollard's own core, gifting it with a verve unknowable to any old man, regardless of how many birthdays he'd seen. Now, every day was Gollard's birthday: a day to feel special, and young. Amethyst had seen to that.

Before they had thrown this sweet girl into the cell with him, Gollard had felt ponderous middle age bearing down on his body and soul. Many of his colleagues at Ignatius Quinnbury University, or IQU, even those older than him, had condemned him as old and uptight in response to his outspoken criticism of popular culture. Gollard only recently learned that one could spend time in a jail cell for appearing old and uptight.

Initially, Amethyst's arrival had made him feel worse. Her slim, smooth, twenty-year-old body had called attention to his thin, spongy, thirty-nine-year-old collection of skin-cased limbs and organs. As her breathtaking eyes of aquamarine had looked upon his receding wisps of weak, dishwater hair, his urine-brown eyes cowered behind a tiny set of dark, oval frames, longing for Amethyst's radiant ribbons of platinum hair...on her head. And when Gollard caught the heavenly scent of Amethyst's flawless pale skin, he remembered all those girls back in college who would never sleep with him, which reminded him of all those women back in grad school who also would never sleep with him, which then reminded him of all those female students in his classes who also would never sleep with him, even for a grade.

Amethyst had never taken any of his classes. But Gollard had seen her around campus a few times, sometimes at the coffee shop, sometimes in the library, sometimes in the commons when she kept trying to study, sometimes again at the coffee shop, sometimes at the other coffee shops, sometimes as she returned to her apartment, sometimes as she came out of her apartment the next morning, but mostly when he sat in on all of her classes.

The fact that they both wound up here together came as a rather bittersweet coincidence: sweet for her, of course, as Gollard's sensual service remained a treat yet untasted. Bitter for Gollard, though, as he would have to educate her on this fact. And that would take time. Like all the other women, and all the other girls, Amethyst wouldn't sleep with him either, a fact that he resented with bitter intensity. He had never even bothered asking; he knew the answer. And if one more girl made that little clicking sound from behind the teeth of that pitying smile—if even one more girl gave him that gentle, condescending little pat on the shoulder—she would not even draw enough breath to utter, "Awww, that's so sweeeeet." If this brilliant and potent man had to hear, one more time, about what a great friend he had been or how any other woman in the universe would be the luckiest blah-blah-blahwhatthefuckever, he would not be responsible for his actions.

At least, that's what he'd told himself. Gollard had never gathered up the courage to intimidate girls into submission. He had watched so many members of the tenured faculty add triumphs, such as intimidation, sedation, and hypnosis to their long lists of non-consensually oriented achievement. To harness the flesh they desired, these great men had used the power of their minds. Their game was a noble one—a sweet serenade of trickery—an elegant dance of manipulation—a beautiful abuse of political position, rather than barbarous force, so often employed by the ignorant.

Gollard knew he housed just as much manhood as his senior colleagues. He had never stooped so low as to employ his superior physical power and size to force a woman's affections. The fact that he only rarely possessed these advantages was beside the point. "What hollow victories are pleasures tainted by brutish conquest," he often said to girls when they wondered why he had asked for their phone numbers. He had always graced the universe as a civilized soul. This was further evidenced by the neatness with which he trimmed his goatee. But he was also a man. A man of passions. Passions so forceful and so wild that only the power of his great intellect kept them at bay. The sexiness of his goatee hinted at these passions. It let his middle-aged body project the virile stallion that rutted within.

And yet, when girls thought they had him out of earshot, they still tittered and whispered amongst themselves in the wake of even his smoothest advances. Such a shame. The female species just didn't understand the passion of an intellectual. But Gollard knew, deep down, they yearned for that kind of passion. They needed it. He knew it, even if they didn't.

Amethyst was particularly okay with not knowing it. Having waitressed at a Denny's, she had become quite versed in the art of feigning interest in the tall tales of lonely men, while distracting them from tunneling down into the very depths of their unendingly ugly existences. Usually flashing her soft, pink lips and her pearly white, perfectly imperfect teeth did the trick. But this, of course, would often send the men back into the "ever see a boner?" stage, in which case, she would have to distract them again, either with light flattery or by soliciting additional, though skillfully unrelated, tall tales. Flattery involved a degree of risk, as men would take it as boner fascination, and would often escalate the situation to the "ever see what a boner does?" stage. Still, taking the risk might instead yield gratuities that broke the 11 percent barrier. It proved a tricky situation, ever balancing on the edge of a blade. But it was a living.

This manner of penile puppeteering, however, is what had landed Amethyst here in the campus jail. Longstanding code for family restaurants in many parts of the universe dictated that "Any hot waitress is forbidden from summoning erections with the intent of obtaining monetary or material supplements to income via the psychological influence of said erection, and without voluntary vaginal admittance of said erection within 48 hours of said summoning (72 hours if erections are summoned over interstellar distances) per VSC § 39,135,393.001(XI(9.333.1.3(13i-jj)))."

Of course, most hot waitresses possessed too few years and too much idealism to understand that spreading their legs and waiting would prove an easy solution to all of their problems. Those who accepted this as the only real way to earn a living possessed bodies that age had already ruined for everyone else, via pregnancy, rough life, or any other combination of bad luck. Lawyers had drafted the law with the intention of making the cosmos a great place to live again, rather than a backward universe, where the only open aprons were aprons that cloaked ugly snatch.

Amethyst's judgment remained clouded by youth and idealism. And even though Gollard had to remind himself, more and more, that he would find it less satisfying to force her to embrace the more sublime pleasures offered by an intellectual, his juices had continued to build up, and his patience had started to wear thin. Distractions were few and poor. Thus far, he'd failed to distract himself with his speculations about the possible cosmic significance of the number of bars in the cell. Occupying his mind with music didn't really work either, as his singing sounded idiotic, even to him. He had one concrete wall on which to doodle, write, or perform calculations, but no ink or paint. And he had not grown desperate enough to swab the inside of the rusty toilet bowl with his finger, as previous inmates had done. But he doubted that they had been gifted with a cellmate like Amethyst. Even if Gollard had come into a cell lined with the most intellectually affirming of books, he would have found himself incapable of paying attention to anything other than her. As his fluids continued to bubble and cook, as days and nights became less and less countable, reasons for not acting on base instinct became less and less clear.

But then again, there was always Pick. He was always watching. Lieutenant Pick had always been a real workhorse who used to put in long shifts. But ever since he had hauled Amethyst in here, it seemed like she could never look outside the cell and not see him standing there, wanting to "pump his pee into her," as he would say. Pick was a simple guy. He had great strength and speed, but unlike most other centaurs in law enforcement, he never cultivated much of a gift for paying attention to several things at once. Centaurs proved great for crowd control on college campuses, as they were already mounted, and many of them loved to beat on young people. Pick had found himself mesmerized by all the bouncing boobs, which kept him from meeting his skull-cracking quota.

About a year ago, after three days of frat parties that filled only one hospital to capacity, Chief Dungswet had doled out a nasty reprimand for such negligence. The following weekend, Pick responded by bringing a flame thrower to campus and torching the faces off more than sixty percent of the partying student body. The school voiced its outrage in no uncertain terms. Either the IQU police had to fire Pick, or the officer would have to personally compensate the school for every penny of tuition, rent, book sales, equipment sales, food sales, liquor sales, drug sales, lab fees, media fees, medical fees, administrative fees, education fees, campus fees, faculty fees, staff fees, student fees, tuition fees, rent fees, sale fees, general fees, miscellaneous fees, other fees, and fee fees the school had lost due to his overreaction to kids having fun.

Pick didn't feel like paying, so Dungswet suspended him. He then reassigned Pick to take charge of the jail. This simple job charged him with two cells to maintain. And since other centaur officers remained out there cracking campus skulls with great effectiveness, Pick had to haul kids in here only when other jails ran out of space. This scored a sweet deal for everyone. Pick got a better job, Dungswet avoided paperwork and saved money, and the college got to boast to parents about their zero tolerance policy on burning students alive. Everybody won.

Pick had taken to the job right away. It was easy. He liked easy things. But it had bored him at first, standing around, day in and day out, with Gollard yammering on and on about whatever he would yammer on and on about. Most of the time, Pick would just stand there, looking at the contours of his fingernails. He found it easier than feigning interest.But when Amethyst arrived, the whole place seemed to light up with excitement. She fascinated Pick. And so he watched her every day. And night. The officer didn't know a lot of big words like Gollard did. So he thought he might impress Amethyst by keeping up his appearance. He always kept his hair slicked back, his orangey cop mustache trimmed, his shirt pressed, his badge clipped on straight, and his hooves shined to perfection. Some thought the absence of pants undermined such attention to detail. Pick didn't. Gollard found it annoying, though, especially when Pick became excited and started to swell underneath.

Upon imagining to watch the last pretend candle flutter out, Gollard made yet another wish for Pick to vanish from the universe.

But he knew, just like any other night, Pick would still remain right outside, breathing at Amethyst. But, wait. Just then, Gollard perceived an unusual lull in the jail's general annoyance levels. He looked up and gasped with delight at the sight of a possible miracle. Could it be? A birthday wish come true? It had to be. Pick didn't take restroom breaks, which is not to say that he didn't eliminate waste. The piles of manure annoyed the custodial artists who came through every now and again, but who was about to bitch at a centaur?

"It appears as though our hemi-equine voyeur has galloped on back to his stall," said Gollard, licking his lips.

"Ha," said Amethyst. "You are so funny! Hey, tell me all that stuff about the mythological roots of centaurs and everything!"

"Oh, yeah," Gollard said smoothly. "All came from when Greeks first saw nomads riding on horseback for the first time. Speaking of riding…"

"Wow," Amethyst whispered, flashing one of her core-fueling smiles. "I swear, you are so smart. You should totally teach me how to play tic tac toe again."

"Ooo-hooo, I'd love to tickle attack your toes again," said Gollard, grabbing her foot and wiggling his tongue in between her toes.

"GLLLAHAHAAAAAAHA, STOP!" she protested.

"My, my, listen to that laugh. I knew you'd like it," he groaned, working his way up her calf.

"No, please, PLEASE, WAIT!" she yelped. "Please, honey. Please, let's just talk, okay? Can we just talk for a minute?"

"Come on, we'll love this," he said, grabbing her knees and trying to force her legs open. He couldn't. He tried again, but the gates to paradise continued to seal him out. Upon realization that she had exerted only a small effort to keep them closed, a snicker bubbled out of the gatekeeper's nose. The keymaster did not find this funny. He felt his passions boiling up. And with explosive fury, he backhanded her like a bitch. Here, he had shown Amethyst something new. Nobody had ever backhanded her on the shoulder before. It felt like a child had punched her. She shoved Gollard aside and walked over to the other end of the cell, so she could giggle in peace.

In this unexpected moment of repose, Gollard found himself delivered from the province of the drooling savage back to the universe of the thinking man. He curled up in his bunk and covered his face. He had crossed that line. He could never uncross it. He was weak. Shame flooded his little soul. It was not like he'd never watched anyone force a girl's legs open. How hard could it be? All those campus parties at which he thought he'd been welcome should have taught him something. So he meditated on this for a moment. Perhaps, it was more of a martial art: less an application of physical force and more a discipline in focus and quiet energy. Fuck that. It was force. He just needed to apply the force intelligently.

This called for rape trig. Let theta equal the optimum angle subtended between thigh L and thigh R. The maximum amount of force, F, exerted by both the gracilis muscles with adrenaline surge, M, minus the cosine of lateral resistance created by the quadriceps femoris... And divide by the square root of torque, T, caused by general thrashing... Yes, he had found the answer. So now, he simply needed to wait around for her to drift off to dreamland. Why ruin a sublime experience by allowing the recipient consciousness, anyway? He could pounce on her when she entered REM sleep. By the time she gathered her senses, he would have her legs pinned to the bed and would already be pistoning away inside of her. And only moments later, she would find her objections melting away, as her sexual savior's skin flute fluttered the music of ecstasy into her body. Then she would finally underst—GODDAMMIT! Gollard fumed with frustration at the sound of Pick clippety-clopping back to the cell while carrying on his back a strange pile of metal and cloth.

"Great," Gollard began, as he slid out of his bunk. "Gee. Fucking hi, Pick."

"Hi," replied Pick, pleasantly enough.

"Perfect timing as always."

"Thanks. For what?"

"Can't you take a hint?"

"Sure. What's the hint?"

"Oh, for God's sake. How can you mythological freaks have your ugly mugs so far in front of your tails and still keep your heads so far up your ass?"

"Ho-ho, I get it, I love these! Kay, gimme a sec."

"Wh-what the fu—"

"D'ah, I give up. Okay, gimme another one."

"Another one what?!"

"Another riddle."

"I never—You don't—Pick... don't you have a family, or a home to go to, or any friends to spend time with?"

"Nah," Pick replied with an innocent smile. "You?"

Gollard's narrow shoulders dropped. Pick waited a moment to find out if he had solved the new riddle but then forgot all about the conversation. He found himself wondering why he was just standing there, watching Gollard look down at his own feet. This was dumb. He'd much rather look at Amethyst. He hadn't told anyone this, but girls turned him on. And Amethyst beat everyone in the whole place, as far as prettiness. He never got to know Deb, the lady across the hallway. Ever since Deb had started to decompose, she had really let herself go.

"Hey there, Pick," flirted Amethyst. She would never have welcomed his staring until now. Gollard turned around and glared at her in a manner that made it difficult for her to not resume her giggling spree. Pick, however, almost tipped over, having never received one of her core-fueling smiles until now.

"Hi," he said, beginning to swell underneath.

"Who's that on your back?" she asked, wide-eyed, while trying to keep the swelling down.

"New prisoner," Pick boasted.

"Really?!" she said. "Oh my god, that is sooo amazing! Can I see?"

Pick unlocked Deb's cell and trotted inside. He yanked the prisoner off his back and removed the straitjackets and the chains. Then he removed the handcuffs, ankle cuffs, knee cuffs, thigh cuffs, arm cuffs, waist cuffs, torso cuffs, neck cuffs, and then, the face cuff.

"Hey there?" Gollard mocked. Thoughts of kicking Amethyst in the vagina formed in his head, and then, the thoughts evaporated with the distraction of who Pick had just left in the other cell with Dead Deb. Gollard pressed himself up against the bars. Never in his life had he dreamt he would ever have the honor of occupying the same room as this giant among giants, to say nothing of sharing jail time with the guy.

"Mr. Budster?" Gollard squeezed out of his throat. "Poppo, if I may be so bold? Sir, I would venture that scarcely a day goes by for you without being mobbed by hordes of gushing fans, all with their platitudinous claims of idolatry and their groveling squeals for your autograph. But Mr. Budster, Sir, at the risk of joining the packed ranks of such tiresome sycophants, I daresay only a handful of us have been fortunate enough to have been truly touched by you, in the dawn of our lives, when we were but golden children. I say this because during the three short seasons in which *Poppo's Playplace* blessed the airwaves, only a few dozen children were lucky enough to win the Vertical Smile Contest. Most of us committed suicide as teenagers, and so, tragically, never did grow to understand the gift that you gave us: the gift of entertaining America by overwhelming us kids with feelings we were not yet designed to understand—feelings that no child could ever have provided. I know, chances are, there's hardly a version of this rant you've not heard. But in this drab world, Mr. Budster… Poppo . . . I hope you have room for the gratitude of a five-year-old boy, whose special glands had still not descended until you pushed them out from behind. You made me a man, Poppo."

Amethyst stood in a corner, trying very hard to think about sports, or recent movies, or tasty baked goods, or current trends in popular music, or. . . something. Pick watched her. Gollard wiped the tears from his eyes and expelled a lungful of air. Baxter maintained a dim gaze upon the floor, then he sat down with his back against the bars. He didn't want to see anyone or deal with anything. His colored tufts of hair bounced a bit, then hung there.

"Poppo?" said Gollard. "POPPO!"

"Hey," said Pick, annoyed by the distraction. "What's the big idea?"

"Big idea?" Gollard bitched. "A salt lick is a big idea for you, you ugly ungulate half-man halfwit. Do you realize who you just dumped in there like so much jail fodder?"

"A clown?" guessed Pick.

"A clown?!" Gollard mocked back. "Fuck you, Pick. A clown. Sorry, Mr. Budster. Centaurs these days, I tell you."

"Hey, cut it out," said Pick. "You're being loud. I'm trying to look at the girl's soft place."

Amethyst turned around. She sat down in the lotus position and leaned over, blocking off the portions of her that were the most interesting to Pick.

"See?" Pick whined. "Now look what you did."

"I didn't do shit, shit-for-brains!" Gollard snapped back. "She went all bashful beav on us because of your stupid mouth."

"Did not," Pick argued.

"Did too," Gollard countered, with his eyes fixed on his hero. "And what's more, you empowered her with a sense of rebellion when you should have been gradually eroding her will by projecting subtle but continuous streams of degradation and objectification, like I've been doing."

"What?"

"She's turned her back on us, Pick. You let her do that and you're nothing but a squeaky little mouse. Right, Mr. Budster?" Baxter turned around, compelled to inform this nice man that he wasn't Chase Budster, or Poppo, or even a clown at all. But what then? He dared not tell anyone his real identity. Best to just sit here and not say anything. He had gotten himself into enough trouble. He turned back around and left Gollard standing there, pining. "Mr. Budster? Sir?" Gollard added.

"Not even one word?" Waves of dread flowed into him. This hurt him even more than when the college faculty shunned him. "Am I so low, so unworthy, as to not even merit a simple nod of support?" he said now with rage. "Nothing? MISERLY SWINE! I'M ONLY A FAILURE BECAUSE OF PEOPLE LIKE YOU! THINK YOU CAN JUST HOARD ALL THE TALENT AND LEAVE NOTHING FOR THE REST OF US?! YEAH, I GUESS YOU'RE NOT REALLY THE BEST UNTIL ALL MEDIOCRITIES ARE DEMOTED TO COMPLETE FUCKING LOSERS! Well, I'm no loser. I'm not. You don't believe me, do you? Come on, Pick, come in here and help me."

"Help you what?" Pick asked.

"You wanna 'pump your pee' into this thing, don't you?" Gollard replied. "Well, get in here, we got a peach to split."

"Aw, I can't do that," Pick whined, as he started to swell. "The chief will yell at me."

"Oh, chief shmief," Gollard replied. "You can always say it was me."

"Honest?"

"Cross my penis and hope to die."

Amethyst leapt up when the cell door opened and she heard Pick trotting in. He shut the door behind him. Then he stood there, swelling to an alarming degree. Baxter started paying attention when Amethyst gasped with fright. His weary eyes of sky blue fell upon her gentle eyes of aquamarine, then her warm ribbons of platinum hair. And something flashed inside of him. That smile! That heartwarming smile, with those sweet, pink lips and those perfectly imperfect teeth. Somehow, he could see them gleaming down to him with adoration. But had that smile ever been so young? So untouched?

"Ow, dammit," Gollard whimpered after tackling her and hurting his pinky. "You know, that whole cliché of your attacker loving it when you put up a fight is a total myth," he said, struggling to keep her underneath him. "Man, these kids. Too much TV. Come on, get over here." The centaur loped over while Gollard distracted his victim by fumbling an Indian burn and then giving her a wet willy. Then he tried to open her legs again, to no avail.

"No! What are you doing?!" cried Baxter. "Indian burns aren't nice, and you should never stick anything smaller than your elbow in your ear. . . . Or anyone else's!"

"Oh my god," Amethyst said to Gollard. "You are so disgusting."

"Here—" Gollard grunted. "Come on—Here—Here, Pick, get her leg down, right here." Pick pinned her left knee down onto the floor with his hoof. This freed Gollard to pry her thighs open with both of his hands. With a struggle, he worked himself in between her thighs and leaned in. "Alright, now. Just lie still. Just lie there and let your professor educate you."

"Oh, you ugly pervert," Amethyst sighed, realizing she wouldn't feel much. "Let's just get this over with."

"Oh, nice reverse psychology there," Gollard scoffed.

"Just do it, goat face!" she shouted.

He paused. That one hurt. He knew he looked kind of like a goat and everything, but she didn't have to just say it like that. Besides, he preferred to think of himself as more of a ram.

"Professor," he insisted.

"Prof— HA! Wait. You mean you think you actually are a professor? You're just an adjunct!" she said, laughing at him. "Let me know when you're finished, 'Professor,'" she managed to add before the enraged adjunct pushed all of his body weight onto the inner side of her right knee, opening her legs. He fumbled around and got Pick to pin her left knee with his hoof. Gollard peered back to make sure he had sustained his hero's interest. Then, as he struggled with his own zipper, his ass backed into the dripping centaur penis that pulsed behind him.

"Will you get that thing out of the way," he griped.

"I can't help it," said Pick. "She's got a . . . a really soft, soft place."

"Yeah, well, you're distracting me," Gollard said, embarrassed.

"Well, you're not going!" the centaur objected.

"The hell I'm not," Gollard replied.

"I'm doing all the work," said Pick. "You can have her afterward."

A glance back confirmed the undivided attention of the clown, whose eyes looked on with horror. Gollard cracked a shiny half-smile and turned back to his business. "Pick," he said. "I don't have time to explain every little thing or go through every little detail about the way this works. Just control yourself. I'll be done in a minute."

"But I want it now," Pick whined.

"Be quiet."

"But I want it really bad."

"Just a fucking second! You're ruining shit!"

"But I'm really turned on."

"Rape is not about sexual arousal, it's about power, you unenlightened motherfucker!"

"Don't call me that," Pick protested. "She's not my mother."

"You're not putting that thing in her, Pick." Gollard insisted. "Not until I've had my squirt."

"Nnnngh!" Pick groaned. "I can't wait anymore." Then he wiped the frustration off his face with a grave scowl. "If you don't move, I'm gonna ram my pee right on through you until it gets into her."

"Fuck you," said Gollard, turning around with a savage growl. "I'm rammin' her first, and I'm rammin' her hard!"

"NO!" Baxter screamed. "NO, YOU CAN'T!" He white-knuckled the bars and passed into a liminal state, somehow looking straight inward on himself while his eyes pointed straight outward at Gollard. "You will not do this. You cannot do this. You will not do this. You cannot do this," he chanted in a loud whisper. "This will not happen."

This wounded Gollard. But upon a moment's thought, he realized Poppo had every reason to not believe in him. After all, the clown had seen nothing but talk—nothing but bickering. No action. Well, that time had ended.

"Do what you will, freak," Gollard said. As he struggled again to open his fly, Pick mounted him and started pumping away. Amethyst began objecting anew as Gollard became sandwiched between her and an equine penis longer than his back.

"NO! Wait, just a minute," Baxter hollered, tearing off his wig, his jiggly nose, and his clown suit. He knew this would get him killed, perhaps, but anything to stop this savagery. "I AM NOT POPPO!" he announced. "I AM NOT MR. BUDSTER, I'M AN IMPOSTER! I BROKE INTO THE SPLIT BOSS'S DRESSING ROOM AND STOLE THIS COSTUME FROM HIM!"

"Wait," Gollard said as Pick kept thrusting into him. "Wait, wait, wai-wai-wai-wai-wai-wait, WAIT A MINUTE! WAIT A MINUTE, WILL YOU STOP THAT?!" He managed to kick Pick in the dick, and with a groan, the amorous centaur stumbled off of him. He removed himself from Amethyst, who rolled over and crawled away. Gollard took a good gander at the declowned bamboozlist in the other cell. He looked like... just some kid!

"That's right," said Baxter. "I'm no clown. I'm, um, Baxter."

"What?" whined Gollard.

"I'm Baxter. I... I disguised myself as the Split Boss."

"You..." growled Gollard. "You are vile, Sir. What demented scheme, hatched in your twisted little mind, prompted you to defile the icon of Poppo the Clown?"

"Yeah!" said Pick. "Wait, what?"

"Drop dead, you sicko," said Gollard. "Come on, Pick. Let's get back to raping Amethyst."

"Yeah, let's get back to raping her," Pick agreed.

Just as Baxter started to object again, the floor rumbled. Then the concrete underneath Amethyst exploded, sending pieces of her flying all over the cell. As the smoke cleared, a large, humanoid turtle poked his head up through the newly formed hole and stared at everyone with his beak open.

"Thanks a lot," Gollard snarled. "THANKS A LOT, WHOEVER OR WHATEVER THE FUCK YOU ARE! I've been trying to make sweet, succulent love to that woman ever since she got here. Now look at her."

Baxter gasped at the sight of Amethyst scattered all over the place. Then he used all the extra air to moan in horror at the sight of Pick finding her head and using those sweet, pink lips and perfectly imperfect teeth to give himself full service.

Turtle's head sank back down.

"Come on, Pops," said Captain Candyroo from downstairs. "He can't get through. Get another charge up there while you still can."

"The hell's the rush?" griped Pops. "They're not goin' anywhere."

"How do you know we didn't blow up the kid?" said the Stick.

"Relax, man, I done this a thousand times," said Pops. "Only kids I ever blown up was a mess of little yellow gooklings what shouldna been goin' to the bathroom there in the first place."

"Pick," said Gollard, as Pick continued doing himself with Amethyst's head. "Pick!" Gollard repeated. "PICK!" he yelled, finally catching the centaur's attention. "What's wrong with you? You got terrorists down there."

"Yeah, but this feels real good," Pick countered.

"Think it'll feel good when the chief visits, and he sees this hole in the floor?" asked Gollard.

"No," Pick grumbled.

"How do you think he'll react?"

"He'll yell at me. He always yells at me."

"Well, get down there. They're gonna blow up the whole place unless you stop them!"

"Yeah."

"You'll teach them to blow up your jail."

"Yeah!"

"If anyone's gonna blow it all up, it's gonna be you!"

"Yeah!"

"And think about how much you'll impress Amethyst."

"Yeah."

"Now get down there and fight for your turf, and then BLOW IT UP YOURSELF!"

"CHARRRRRGE!" Pick opened the cell door and galloped down the hall, toward the stairway, with Amethyst's dead face still wrapped around the tip of his bouncing centaur dick.

With the gullible sentry now off to distract the marauding nasties downstairs, Gollard found himself free to plot his escape. Sure enough, a huge ruckus soon broke out below, featuring smacks, whacks, cracks, biffs, and pows, as well as shattering, tinkling, clanking, and other sounds of bodily injury and furniture destruction. He crept over to examine the escape possibilities of the new hole in the floor and stopped dead in his tracks when Pick's head came flying through it. The head bounced off the ceiling and fell at Gollard's feet. Jets of centaur blood shot up and stained his leg. By the time the jets ebbed, he could hear the argument resume downstairs.

"Any more fuckin' surprises, Turtle?" Pops bitched. "'Cause if a dragon or a fuckin' cyclops is comin' down here next, you may wanna fuckin' speak up, man!"

"Hey, cool your jets, hoser," said the captain. "Turtles don't talk."

"Then why the fuck'd you fuckin' send him up there?" snapped Pops. "Send a guy on recon what can't even report nothin'?"

"Yeah, but," said Mike. "Like, he's the only one that can, like, reach the ceiling and pull himself up there."

"Yeah," said Ike.

"Bullshit, man," Pops argued. "The Stick can jump up there easy."

"Oh, thanks for volunteering me, you old crust," said the Stick.

"Would you just blow the rest and stop pissing and whining?" whined the captain. "Christ almighty, it's like I'm sittin' here kidnapping a kid with my brother's kids or somethin'!"

As Pops told everyone to get under a table, Gollard scrambled around in a panic. He tried climbing up onto the bars, but only slid right back down to the floor. As Pops told Ike not to touch the equipment and to "stand over there," Gollard clenched his fists together and tiptoed in one place. Then he remembered the bunk bed attached to the wall. As Pops told Mike to get his fat ass away from him and stop breathing on him, Gollard scrambled up into the top bunk and hid under the blanket. As Pops told Mike and Ike that he didn't give a sow's stinky snatch if they had to go to the bathroom, and screamed at everyone again to get their stupid asses under a table, Gollard curled up into the fetal position. Baxter's daze of shock prevented him from doing the same. He continued to just stand there, staring straight ahead. He sniffled. Then, a new explosion blew away most of the floor inside the cell. Many of the concrete slabs were too large to make it past the bars. Many bounced off the walls or the ceiling. Only one hit Gollard's bunk, but it hit with enough force to unhinge an end of it and send his blanketed body sliding down into the pit of accumulating debris below.

A silence fell. Baxter peered out through the cell across from him, Most of the floor had fallen down into the chief's office, below, where the youth could see the dust beginning to settle. Turtle, unharmed, crawled out from the rubble first. He picked up the captain, who he had covered up for protection, and set him upright on top of a pile of debris. Skittles lay on his back, struggling to push a piano-sized slab of concrete off his chest. The Stick dropped down from somewhere far above and tried in vain to assist his old friend.

"I told you guys to get under a table," chided Pops, still crowded under the only table by himself.

"Shut your hole and help him, Pops," ordered the captain.

Shaking his head and enjoying a smug chuckle, the old vet crawled out and joined them. "Okay, on three," said Pops. "One, two, three." They all lifted, but to no avail—that is, until Turtle walked over and lifted the slab by himself. Skittles hopped up and brushed himself off. Gollard, still balled up in his blanket, poked his head out just in time to observe the last second of his own life, as Turtle discarded the concrete slab onto his head.

"Mike?" hollered the captain, scanning the rubble. "Ike? Where are you guys? We'll dig you out."

Ike came in through the door labeled, "UPSTAIRS." "What?" he asked.

"Where's Mike?" asked the captain.

"Dude, look," Mike called out from what remained of the floor in front of Baxter's cell. "The kid's up here, in this one!" Before Ike fully processed this information, the stampede for the stairway was already in full force, headed by Pops, who shoved him aside, then Skittles and the Stick, who both went out of their way to trample him. Then, after picking up the captain, Turtle jogged up too, stepping on Ike's hand along the way. When Ike had finally huffed and puffed his way up the stairs to join the guys, they all had their backs to him, and all stood clustered up next to Baxter's cell. With Ike's loud mouth-breathing defeating the purpose of his chickenshit tiptoeing, he came upon the sight of what had given pause to his comrades.

"So, we meet again, at last," said Captain Candyroo.

"Yeah," Cereal Man replied. "And I see you started a new little club for yourself."

"At least I have friends, unlike some losers I know," countered the captain.

"Well, I'm all broken up over my stunted social life," said Cereal Man. "And when I get Home I'll be sure to cry into my pillow until I fall asleep all alone in the cobwebs. Now if you'll excuse me, me and the kid have other places to be."

"He's not going anywhere, chum," the captain declared. "Right guys?" The guys all grunted in agreement, except for Turtle, who maintained a menacing, open-beaked stare at Cereal Man.

Cereal Man scanned them, then focused on the captain. "Why don't you all go back home and share some more pipe dreams with one another before you feel the kind of pain you've only seen on TV." As the captain's smile dropped, Cereal Man stepped over to Baxter's cell and began bending the bars.

"Not so fast, Cereal Man!" commanded the captain. Though Cereal Man ignored him, the guys glared at him with disdain.

"Not so fast, Cereal Man?" Pops mocked.

"Fuck you, hosers," the captain's voice cracked. "Get him!"

As Cereal Man continued bending bars upward and out of the floor, Skittles grabbed hold of him, turned him upside down, and prepared to pile drive his head into the floor. But the pain just from holding Cereal Man swiftly became unbearable. Skittles collapsed to the floor with bruises all over his inner arms and hands as the Stick launched a combination of strikes and kicks that accomplished nothing other than the bloodying of his own feet and the decimation of his trusty quarterstaff. Mike and Ike's cheers of support had just started to leave their lungs when this defeat reduced their vocalizations to awkward fizzles. Though Turtle had his speargun aimed at Cereal Man's heart, he couldn't fire because Pops kept stepping in the way. The old vet grew annoyed at how difficult he found it to plant a plastic explosive on the back of Cereal Man's head. If only the guy'd stop bending those bars and hold the fuck still for half a second...

Cereal Man made it into the cell and started dragging Baxter out. With that, Turtle threw down his speargun and rushed him, knocking

Baxter and Pops on their asses. Then the captain watched with glee as his most lethal assassin dug a set of horrible reptilian claws into the chest of his sworn enemy. Then the captain looked on in horror as his most lethal assassin ripped those claws right out of his own hands by attempting in vain to rake his sworn enemy's chest open like a balloon full of gummy worm stew. As Turtle backed off and gawked at his bleeding hands, Cereal Man noticed a grin growing back onto the captain's face.

"Just as tough as ever," the captain said. "But we both know the score, don't we, buddy boy? You're just a tiny little island, and the tide is still rising. Yeah, pretty soon, the waters over you will be just as deep and flat as everywhere else. And every stupid-ass thing you ever tried to stand for will have drowned in the sea of progress. We both know it, don't we, old friend."

Cereal Man drew his Mark VI semiautomatic 52 mm handgun from his duster and pointed it at him. "You got some nerve calling me that," he said.

"You're the one who split, not me, pallie."

"If it's a choice between solitude and friends like you... you and your band of wasteoid slaves... I'll walk Home by myself forever," Cereal Man declared. "You think he's your friend?" he said to the guys, while still staring at the captain with disgust. "Look at him. He's nobody's friend. He's nothing. Without you, he's less than nothing. He's been conned, big time. And so have all of you. You're all a bunch of suckers, and you've been duped by the biggest sucker of all... this worthless bag of filth right here."

"Shut up and lose the piece, pal," the captain ordered.

"I'm not your pal," said Cereal Man. "I'm not your pal, or your pallie, or your chum, or your buddy boy." He cocked the gun. "And I'm not your old friend."

"Uh, chump?" said the captain. "You might wanna rethink that."

Cereal Man turned to discover that the rest of the guys had gathered up behind him. Skittles had sat down on Baxter's chest. The Stick had the youth's head twisted back as far as it would go without making a horrible crunching sound. This caused Baxter to whimper in pain, which caused Skittles to guffaw.

"One wrong move," said Skittles, "and Sticky twists tinker toy boy's neck around until the weak little bones inside it crumble into itty-bitty pieces. Ain't that so, Sticky?"

"You said it, Skittles," said the Stick.

"Now who's the sucker?" jeered the captain.

"Still you," said Cereal Man. "Remember when you could walk and run and feel your fingers and toes? Remember when you were a person, with hopes and goals? 'Cause I do."

"Lose the heater... old friend," the captain insisted.

"Friends like this guy," said Cereal Man to the guys. "Who needs a noose?" He uncocked the gun, set it down, and slid it toward the captain, who waddled over with satisfaction and picked it up. He found it too heavy for one hand, but with a struggle, his arms could stretch far enough across his gelatinous front to hold it with two. But he managed the task, and now pointed the pistol right at its owner.

"There are two kinds of friends, my friend," professed the captain. "Those who keep the pixie comin'..." He tossed a handful of Nerds out on the floor, for which the guys scrambled around, whimpering, grunting, and squealing. "And sanctimonious, wandering assholes like you."

As the captain struggled in vain to cock the gun, Cereal Man reached into his duster in hope of finding another weapon and ending this annoying little game. He found another handgun... Then there was the sniping rifle with laser sighting... Annnd... a couple of old-

326

school scatterguns...Then the elephant rifle...Ah. Finally, his Mark B-89 automatic assault rifle. *Perfect.* He drew it out, turned around, and began blasting Turtle's chest full of bullets.

"WHAT THE FUCK! WAIT A SEC!" cried the captain, as Cereal Man shifted his fire over to Pops, then Skittles, then the Stick. "HOLD ON, WE CAN DISCUSS THIS, YOU BATSHIT MANIAC FUCKING COCKSUCKER BASTARD PIECE OF SHIT MOTHERFUCKER SON OF A BITCH!" he screamed as Cereal Man finished spraying down Mike and Ike. The firing ceased, and as the room fell silent, Baxter cowered on the floor, blubbering and drooling. "Shut your goddamn taffy hole," the captain sobbed, incensed by this display. They weren't the kid's friends; they were his friends! His oldest and truest!

Rivers of salty despair flowed down Captain Candyroo's face as he looked upon the last members of his gang, who now lay twitching in a pile on the floor, their mouths frozen agape, and their mutilated bodies gushing fountains of blood. The loss was unbearable. A perfectly good screw-over had now been flushed down the toilet. If not for Cereal Man's monstrous act, those mouths would have instead gaped from the hilarious betrayal of the captain breaking his promise of endless candy for life. And that blood would have instead flowed as a result of the quarrels and fights that would have erupted amongst them once he had laid the side-splitting news of this betrayal on their laps like a long, oily turd. Alas, now his dear friends were gone forever, and he wouldn't get to do his joke.

Cereal Man put away his assault rifle, picked Baxter up, and swung him over his shoulder. He strolled over to the captain, reclaimed his pistol, and put it away too. He left Captain Candyroo alone, sobbing, with no friends to screw over, and no bounty to present to his boss.

18. OUTLAND

There was the taxi.

Friday's dawn slightly reddened and more slightly brightened the pukey night, and Baxter could no longer shake off the sweat of anxiety. If he didn't pay off the Spring Break Scrapers by high noon on Sunday, he would doom Mom to a short life of suffering. This guy, Cereal Man, sure didn't offer any help, that was for darn sure. And even though Baxter had repeated his plight with piss-pantsingly urgent emphasis, Cereal Man just didn't seem to get it. He had promised they would head Home, but this looked like the wrong direction. So far Cereal Man had handled this crisis with all the urgency of a glop of warm vanilla pudding. He had not even allowed them to seek alternate modes of transportation until, after sitting in gridlock for three days, their taxi ran out of gas. Back at the intersection of Telegraph Road and West End Boulevard, Baxter had chuckled off what he'd mistaken as hyperbole from the cab driver, who had complained about having to sit through the longest red light in the universe. Cereal Man had neglected to point out that it truly and literally did rank as the universe's longest until after abandoning the ride. Not only that, but he didn't even volunteer to pitch in for cab fare. Good thing Sully had lent out his till, or they would have been in big trouble. Alas, the exorbitant and fruitless holiday in the taxi had left Baxter again penniless, except for the prize check in his backpack, of course, which he protected with his life. But how could he get Home now? Cereal Man didn't even care. Baxter had never met anyone like him before. The youth had sure met some disagreeable people during recent days. All those strange people at the jail, all those folks at Elmo's Fire, and that mean guy on the train. But Cereal Man seemed different altogether. He seemed worse than mean. He was just... heartless. It hurt for Baxter to regard someone with such ill feelings. But he had to accept it as reality. And he knew he could never convince this heartless murderer to go away.

Oddly enough, though, his presence provided Baxter with a little taste of life back Home in Twinkle. For sixteen years, open arms, opened doors, and cheerful smiles had blanketed the boy. It was a warm, cozy blanket—a blanket that the universe had recently ripped off of him, filled with gears and bolts, then folded up into a sling and used to flog him without mercy. But now, people started to smile again, albeit with abject fear. Doors opened, carpets rolled out, and everyone paid deference, especially when he and Cereal Man stopped to get a new set of clothes. Not only did the sales staff at Dickie Featherfield remain silent about a young customer who entered their store wearing nothing but a backpack and a face full of smeared clown makeup; not only did they say nothing about the grim-faced transient who prodded him into the store, but they also turned a blind eye to this odd pair walking out of the store without paying for the yellow Culture Club half shirt, the matching short shorts, the tasseled white knee-high socks, and the tutti frutti–colored Converse. And yet, getting stuff for free somehow failed to instill confidence in the lad.

Then there was the flight.

Everyone else needed a plane ticket. But a simple look from Cereal Man constituted his boarding pass, as well as Baxter's. The youth spent most of the flight darting all over the plane, peppering strangers with propeller-mouthed accounts of Mom's dire situation, then drenching the same strangers with braying pleas to help him ditch his ominous captor. The long, nonstop flight provided plenty of time for him to deal out these fruitless bombardments. Baxter had no idea how he had managed to get so far away from Home. And even though he possessed no flight experience with which to compare anything, three days somehow seemed excessive. Maybe they had boarded an exceptionally slow plane. He couldn't tell. The flight staff never answered any questions. They remained far too busy shuffling around the plane in a panic, keeping every passenger stocked with mini boxes of cereal, whether they felt hungry or not. Looking outside proved pointless too. A ubiquitous haze of dark smog smothered everything outside the oily windows, making it hard to tell just how far they had gone. Such a shame. He may as well have stayed back in the ventilation ducts at the DizneyCramcast Studios.

Then there was the subway.

What a smelly place. And what smelly people! Baxter felt uncomfortable with all the strangers looking at him, sniffing him, slobbering on him, licking him, belching on him, belching *in* him, singing to him, grinding themselves on him, babbling nonsensically to him, and begging him for things he didn't want to surrender. He didn't know what to say to the old lady with the empty cup, who grilled him more than the others about his charitable capacities. True, Baxter had plenty of pee to spare, but the donation she demanded would not have yielded as much privacy as he preferred. The lady's impatience seemed rather unwarranted. But in her defense, she had guzzled down her own urine so many times that it had started to become too thick for her to swallow. Being a woman of honor, she made sure to show him the evidence too. After much wincing and squirming, Baxter's selfishness finally won out. He politely, but firmly, refused to pee in her cup. Being a woman of understanding and flexibility, she offered her salt-crusted mouth as a receptacle, which made Baxter gag. Being a woman of dignity, this offended her, and she hollered out, with her nasty breath of infected piss concentrate, to summon the compassion of every excretion-swilling loyalist in the car. Before long, she had dozens of crusty mouths shouting a cocktail of foul vapors into the boy's face.

Though Baxter could not decipher any of it, Cereal Man was no stranger to the frustrated cries of the desperate—the sorrowful pleas of the hungry. His benevolent offer of a hearty bowl of Grape Nuts to every empty belly in the car shocked everyone into a profound silence, which they extinguished with riotous outbursts even more indignant than before. Though many complained that they had little hope of eating Grape Nuts with no teeth, many others found it more important to make their distaste for such lowlife hog slop solidly known. It took little time at all for someone to cross a line. Then Cereal Man heard that phrase—that ungrateful, insidious term of such moral outrage. He only needed to hear it once. The blast from his shotgun silenced and froze everyone. He began pacing the aisle.

"Who's the fella said, 'dirt food' in here?" he coolly demanded. He approached a short guy dressed in a black garbage bag. "You, bag man. Speak up," he said, pointing the shotgun at the man's gut.

Baxter couldn't tell, at that point, whether his covert scurry out of the subway car was motivated more by the acute drive to avoid

331

additional scenes of mass murder, or more by the noble opportunity, afforded by this distraction, to escape and save Mom. He jettisoned such luxurious contemplation when he reached the space between the cars. The subterranean part of the city screamed by at breakneck speeds, and each city block produced a low pulsing sound as it flashed by, like a mad helicopter blade. Gawking down at the rickety tracks, Baxter realized that fleeing the scene might have brought him into an even more perilous position. And to be sure, it had not occurred to him that even Hercules himself would have broken down sobbing in frustration after trying to push open the impossible door to the next car. Then, after pulling, the door swung open and revealed a dark, eerie car, lit only by the lights that pulsed in and out from the city whizzing by on the outside.

The strobing light revealed a vacant car, except for some guy, who sat at the other end. He wore a long coat, much like Cereal Man's, but tattered, wrinkled, and not quite black—just a dark olive green. He had a tangled, shiny mess of black hair. But this mess looked like the combed mane of the finest racing horse compared to the wiry black train wreck that constituted his beard. Inside this nasty nest gaped a huge mouth, ever locked into an open frown and lined with an array of gravelly teeth. He had a thin and bony nose, with one nostril larger and higher than the other. Under two unevenly bushy eyebrows, what remained of his eyes languished in a reptilian state of consciousness. One had shriveled up to the size of a yellowish bead, which darted around inside its deep socket to follow swiftly moving objects. The other eye had burst from him pinching it in frustration, and now hung down within his other socket, reduced to blackening flaps of leaky flesh. The functioning eye detected Baxter, and he stood up, with his head touching the ceiling of the car. Baxter felt unsettled about the way the guy moved, almost like a marionette, especially as he swung his arm up and pointed at Baxter with his filthy fingernails. His mouth moved with a puppet-like lifelessness as he gurgled out some kind of incomprehensible threat to Baxter.

The youth slammed the door shut and flew back through the previous car. The terrifying guy followed closely behind him, moving nothing on his body, save his long legs, which were spread out to the sides, flailing up and down as he ran, like a frilled lizard. The cars grew more and more crowded as Baxter continued his way toward the back of the train. This slowed him down, but his thin, spooky pursuer slipped through the crowds with no effort and continued to gain on him. The boy squeezed his way into the very back of the rear car. When he reached the door and beheld the tracks vanishing behind him, he wheeled around, ready to beg for his life, and noticed the guy had vanished. Baxter crept a little closer back to the front of the car and observed that his pursuer had not yet caught up because he had distracted himself by disconnecting the car from the rest of the train.

A wave of anxiety washed over Baxter, but it was soon drowned out by a tsunami of panic created by the crazed, furry creature whose toothless, black mouth chomped its way through the back door from outside the car. The monster looked all too much like a familiar friend Baxter had watched on Sesame Street all his life, except this fella looked just terrible. Googly, bloodshot eyeballs darted around on top of his head, which had sporadically patched tufts of dark blue fur all over. The bare spots were streaked with black scabs and yellowing bruises from fingernails and combs that had groomed him far too well. While the pupil of one eyeball had contracted to a mere black dot, the dilated pupil of the other took up most of a hemisphere. This monster, cranked up from snorting several lines of snickerdoodle, and higher than a kite from an extra lid of gingersnap, presently perceived the whole world as a giant macaroon to devour. And yet, despite the googliness of his eyes, his focus terrified Baxter.

With an assortment of ferocious vocal eating sounds, the monster gobbled his way into the car. The horrid, skinny man entered the other side of the car, pulled a machine gun out of his long coat, and began firing. The recoil kept his light frame off balance, which kept the bullets flying in many directions. After gunning down dozens of onlookers within a few seconds, he began reloading. By this time, the monster had countered with two machine guns of his own. While clutching them in his arms, and holding three Uzis with his big, furry hands, he had somehow managed to begin firing all five weapons at once. The monster had so tweaked his brain, however, that hitting any target smaller than an aircraft carrier proved difficult. But that didn't stop him from scattering manic squalls of bullets far and wide, in an amped-up hope of making the kill. Baxter could do little more than cower in the middle of both assailants' crossfire.

After a few reloads on both ends, the car had come to a stop, and the two assailants had reduced most of the passengers to hamburger. The ceiling of the car now existed as a mere technicality. Baxter, however, remained unscathed. He opened his eyes to discover that the blue-furred terror had just become the last muppet standing. The googly-eyed monster stood, riddled with bullets, but didn't seem to mind. None of them had punctured his head, and he knew a few injections of oatmeal raisin would have him sailing, in about a half hour, when the snickerdoodle and the gingersnap wore off, and the pain would hit him like a cluster of wrecking balls. The barely existent body of the unknown skinny guy had managed to catch a few of the innumerable bullets that had ripped his long coat to shreds. He collapsed, bleeding and twitching on top of all the other bleeding and twitching people. The monster's adrenaline had ebbed, placing him well on his way to a crash. During this swift plummet, he continued to fire his guns sporadically. His strength began to fade. The whole ordeal left him with such a case of the munchies that he even attempted to eat one of his Uzis. Normally, this would have given him acute indigestion. But since he still had the Uzi spraying out bullets when he tried to cram it down his mouth, it gave him acute death instead.

Baxter stood up straight and surveyed the mounds of carnage surrounding him. The piles of greasy, gritty skin and filth-saturated clothes had started to ripen with added notes of diseased blood and flies that had already begun to fuck inside the open wounds. The roar of other subways rattled the wispy webs of metal that now constituted what one could dubiously call the roof of the car. Looking across the tracks, Baxter could see the public bustling along the avenues of the lower city, going about their business, vending, buying, stealing, arguing, fighting, killing, excreting, mating... He turned around to exit the car and bumped into Cereal Man, who stood between him and the closed doors.

"How–?! How long have you been standing here?" he asked.

"A little while," Cereal Man replied. He walked into the aisle, stepped over a few bodies, and began looting the monster's corpse.

"What are you doing?"

"Souvenirs."

Baxter hated to be rude. "I hate to be rude, but you were just standing there the whole time while these two maniacs were trying to kill me? I've got to get Home, and... and without you. Yes. I have to insist, okay? I mean, you're a swell fella and all, I, I just... bad things are happening, y'see, and, and I can't have it. I have to put my foot down. So, goodbye."

"Yeah? Well, before you go prancing on out there all by your lonesome, maybe you ought to take this with you," said Cereal Man, handing Baxter a photo that the monster had been carrying. "Dear old Mom will like it. One of the last pictures of her baby boy."

"Wh?! Ohhhhhh, what happened to this world? Why do people want me dead?!"

"Nobody wants you dead."

"Are you crazy?" he asked the mass-murdering cereal fanatic. "They're after me! Both him and that weird man over there, they were chasing after me and firing automatic weapons like a couple of lunatics! And you're going to stand there and tell me nobody's out to kill me?"

"They were firing at each other, not you. They've got to haul you in with that delicate heart of yours still pumping, or they won't get their money."

"Haul me in where?"

"The Valhalla Syndicate," said Cereal Man, now looting the assailant with the horrible black beard. "Your old man will never forget your face, now that he's set his eyes on it."

"Oh, mister, are you still going on with this bounty hunter stuff?" Baxter whined. "And just what is there in this world that would make me think you're right about all this nonsense?"

"Souvenirs," Cereal Man replied. "You see, in this world, there are two kinds of people: those who keep watching the tube, and those who come after you." With that, Cereal Man showed Baxter the creepy bearded guy's ID card for the Bounty Hunter's Guild:

NAME: Unknown.
MEMBERSHIP#: 1-2MEDDL
KNOWN ALIASES: Unknown.
ORIGIN: Nonoxynol 9
SPECIES: Unknown (possible human/muppet hybrid).
RACE: Unknown.

SEX: Male.

HEIGHT: 6' 11"

EARTH WEIGHT: 111 lbs.

AGE: Unknown.

KNOWN LANGUAGES: Unknown.

MENTAL LEVEL: Reptilian.

RATES: Three live chickens, a large pepperoni pizza, and a glass of beer.

KNOWN HAUNTS: Cockfights, penis fights, stadium parking garages, gas stations, behind vending machines, most subway systems.

KNOWN CONTACTS: Unknown.

KNOWN EMPLOYERS: Valhalla Syndicate.

"Unk … Un …" Baxter read with growing frustration at all the things not known about this assassin. "You made this all up! Who's going to hire some man with no name to go out and kidnap someone?" The absolute magnitude of his own skepticism made his stomach turn. To question someone's accuracy felt troublesome enough, but to not trust another human being? A full audit of his conduct now became a top priority when his mouth blurted, "This card's a fake."

Cereal Man showed him the monster's card. "That fake too?" said Cereal Man. "Cookie Monster's name is written on it."

No. Baxter had thought the crazed creature to be some junkie who looked like Cookie Monster. *No.* Well, he also sounded a lot like Cookie Monster. *No. No.* A beloved cast member of one of his favorite shows, and he'd wasted himself away to this? *No. No way.* It was a tragedy. *No. It couldn't be. No. No. Just, no.* But there it was on the card:

NAME: Cookie Monster.

MEMBERSHIP#: CS4COOKIE

KNOWN ALIASES: Wheel Stealer, Arnold, Munching Monster, Sid, Cookie, Alistair Cookie, El Monstro, Googlicious, C-Dawg.

ORIGIN: Sesame Street

SPECIES: Muppet.

RACE: Monster.

SEX: Male.

HEIGHT: Arm length.

EARTH WEIGHT: Varies with amount of materials consumed.

AGE: 51.

KNOWN LANGUAGES: Rudimentary English.

MENTAL LEVEL: Human toddler.

RATES: A box of cookies, please.

KNOWN HAUNTS: Sesame Street, Keebler Tree, Pepperidge Farm.

KNOWN CONTACTS: Mrs. Fields, Kermit the Frog, Grover, Big Bird, Mr. Snuffleupagus, Bert, Ernie, Oscar the Grouch, Maria, Bob, Susan, Gordon, David, Linda, Luis, Mr. Hooper.

KNOWN EMPLOYERS: Jim Henson, Frank Oz, Valhalla Syndicate.

"These guys are nothing," said Cereal Man. "They're just a little taste of what's coming." He looked around and then opened the roofless subway car doors. "Let's go Home, kid."

Baxter squirmed. "No," he muttered.

"It's too cramped down here—too easy to be trapped," Cereal Man said.

"No," Baxter managed again.

Cereal Man grabbed Baxter by the arm and led him over to the nearest elevator, despite the youth's scuffling protests. He pressed the button to go up. The doors opened. Cereal Man shoved Baxter inside and pressed the button for the ground floor, 3,311 levels above.

Then there was the gondola.

It lumbered along, but it remained one of the cheaper means of ferrying down the misty banks of the River PepsiCo. The awkward gondolier tried hard to earn a tip by serenading his two passengers while pushing their way through the thick stream of blackened water and garbage. At first, no coherent song came to mind. But then, he remembered, "Who Will You Run To." Luckily, the gondola's motor, which put forth just as much effort as he, drowned out most of his awful falsetto. When the guy's oar broke, the motor struggled on its own and managed to gurgle and wheeze for a few more boat lengths before bursting into flames. Cereal Man and Baxter hopped out and skipped across the larger islands of refuse, which included the remains of other abandoned gondolas. They made their way to shore just as the fire engulfed both the gondola and the gondolier, whose criminally inept endeavor to emulate Ann Wilson's powerful voice transitioned with smooth ease into the screams of a burning human being.

Then there was the carriage ride.

Clippety-clop down the north end of Crustcock Avenue did the fine, healthy young mare strut. Her first day on the job of piloting young lovers through the heart of her fair city had proven rewarding indeed. Randy, the kindly driver, shared his old girl's sentiments as he conducted his tour as best he could amidst the deafening orgy of honking vehicles and yelling drivers that surrounded him.

"Now behind this bank of smog, folks, is Smogworks, the city's newest smog recycling factory, which converts a total of thirty-three thousand cubic miles of carbon dioxide into eleven thousand cubic miles of the same carbon dioxide every day! Now, what do they do with all that CO_2, you may ask? Just throw it away? No Sir, that's what its predecessor, Smogstacks, used to do, back in the day. But Smogworks takes all that newly compacted smog and releases it right back into the atmosphere where it belongs. Yessir, with the new environmental movement, everyone, more and more, is "going gray." In fact, Smogworks was just rated the third grayest company in this part of town. And now, with new and improved safety regulation regulations, Smogworks boasts its healthiest, most job-creating mortality rate to date. Yessir, here in this part of town, smog works," he concluded with a little chuckle that escalated into a riptide of hacking, wheezing coughs that doubled him over in his seat for a couple of blocks. "Now if you kids'll fancy a glance over to your left," he continued. "You can smell Salty Slot's Saloon... and next to that, Windy Wanda's Weaverium. Across the street from them is Auntie Alanna's Anti-Irish Pub. 'Course you can't see them right now on account of the smog.... Annnd, directly across the street from them is Ma Loan's Title Loan and Pawn, also behind the smog.... Over there's the ATM Palace, can't see that either just—"

Neither Cereal Man nor Baxter paid any attention to their guide until the sound of a gunshot cut his words short. After that, the words were drowned out by a painful gurgling sound. Baxter thought the man might have simply taken a cool, refreshing sip of water. Cereal Man, however, noticed the blood jetting out of the bullet hole in the man's throat. He tried to grab Baxter's shoulder, but someone had already scooped the boy up into a burlap bag marked, "BAXTER," and tossed him over the shoulder of a burly old Appalachian woman running into the smog. Cereal Man leapt down, tackled her, and concealed Baxter under his long coat. Remembering the injurious launch out of the Squeezeburg Squealer, Baxter objected with vigor, and in vain, while Cereal Man jumped back up to commandeer the carriage.

As he grabbed hold of the reins, the old Appalachian woman's skinny husband jumped out of the smog with their teenage son. With long rifles, they both shot the horse in the head. Then, with the help of the old lady, they tossed ropes around the carriage and overturned it. Cereal Man drew a bouquet of firearms, and the family of assailants disappeared into the smog. By the time Cereal Man had neutralized the attackers by spraying the beige haze with lead, Baxter had emerged from the bag and coat only to find a bullet-riddled horse and driver twitching in the street, and his captor holding no less than three smoking guns. Swell. Another massacre. More carnage. And maybe murdering everyone in sight, for whatever unimaginable reason, no longer felt like enough. Now this guy, this Cereal Man, had taken to killing innocent animals too? What did that nice horse ever do to him, anyway?

Then there was the bus.

"What is this place?" Baxter moaned with unease, as Cereal Man dragged him onto a city bus. If the boy had been anyone else, he might have had the ability to ask, "Why are those buildings so tall?" But this question was beyond his comprehension. Buildings, as he knew them, had at least one entrance, which led you into one or more rooms, many with windows. And, on a few occasions, some buildings might even feature an additional layer of rooms on top of the entrance rooms. This way, the floor of the additional layer of rooms was simultaneously the ceiling of the entrance rooms! He called these, "buildings with an upper and lower level."

Here, as the bus barreled down Screaming Little Richard Drive and took the ramp onto the expressway, poor Baxter strained the back of his neck. The boy had so seldom looked up in his life and had not developed his tender little occipital muscles. They grew sore from all the craning and gawking at these monstrous shafts of brick, black glass, plastic, and steel—these thousands and thousands and thousands of windows lighting up the tentacles of smog, which caressed different areas of each shaft with all the misguided seediness of a desperate old whore trying to score enough change for her vaginal cancer operation, one handie at a time. The shining glass stacked upward without relent, into and beyond the vanishing point above. These were buildings but not buildings—scary looking structures, flashing with jarring cacophonies of neon and piled with innumerable upper levels, which seemed to hiss with dread as they stretched off into a dimension Baxter had scarcely even known about. He wasn't a dope, though. He knew what up was. He had just never thought about the fact that up kept going.

After a while, these towering spires of urban terror loomed in the background, dwarfing the ocean of skyscrapers, transmission towers, chemical plants, smokestacks, and flare stacks that led up to them, which themselves bruised Baxter's mind with their size and ugliness. And intermixed all along the way, buzzing tangles and loops of expressways and rail lines became indistinguishable, after a distance, from the endless combinations and crosshatchings of power lines and tram cables. Likewise, the islands of mini-cities, like Gasolineville, Stratopornopolis, Abortionton, and many others that levitated over the suburbs, often looked similar to the sickly clouds of radioactive soot hanging in the air.

Baxter noticed that these awful sights had started leaning to one side. At first, he thought he had become dizzy. But then he felt himself getting much heavier. By the time the city outside had come close to rotating upside down, he understood that centrifugal force now kept the bus on the road. Like many of the other large bypasses, this segment of the Broken Will Rogers Expressway soared, in a sickening banked arc, over the city and below the smog line, such that one could survey everything for hundreds of miles, bearing witness to the vast planes of suburbia and dozens of other iron groves, along the way to the ashy fuzz that smothered all horizons. Baxter felt sicker than when the Spinning Spaghetti Spider had flailed him about without mercy at the Twinkle Town Fair. "I don't even know where I am, and … and I…"

"What's your problem?" said Cereal Man.

"Everything's so tall, here," he replied with queasiness reverberating up his gullet, now watching the top of a cluster of skyscrapers pass between him and the ground. "How could they put so many floors on top of each other—it doesn't make any… oh my goodness, this is nothing like Home, I thought we were going Home!"

"Home? Yeah. Only, it's going to be a while. A long while. If I were you, I'd cancel my next chess tournament."

"Wha? Wait a minute? How far is it? HOW FAR AWAY?!"

"More than a couple of songs, I can tell you that."

"But how far? What's the distance? How many miles?"

Cereal Man paused, then got up from his seat and walked up the aisle of the empty bus. Baxter sat there, with his face twitching and his hands rubbing his lap, as the view outside rotated back to an upright position and the expressway descended into the city again. Having not extended the boy even the mildest courtesy of an explanation, Cereal Man approached the front of the bus with nary a thought in his head about the optics of looming over the driver while she concentrated on the road ahead.

"Where we going?" asked Cereal Man.

"Where?" said the wilty-haired, saggy-titted driver, tossing an irritated smirk his way. A skinny cigarette wagged on her leathery lips as she continued. "Where I'm going, buddy. Down that way..."

Cereal Man looked far ahead and calculated that they were headed toward the Looselips Chunnel, one of the tunnels that burrowed under Sicktrout Bay, a lair of aquatic mutants who bred with homeless humans too dysfunctional to make a name for themselves in the alleys and underpasses of the world.

"No deal," said Cereal Man.

"No deal?" she mocked, with her sandpaper voice.

"Too bottlenecked. Too many degenerates and creepy crawlies," he said. "Take us out to Cornholeus Pass."

"Who'na fuck do you think—" she said as her top dentures fell onto her tongue. She spit them out and continued. "This ain't no cab, dummy. I got a circuit to make, and the next stop's down there in Slut Hole Junction. We're the only bus left in this part of the city. All the rest got scrapped. So in a few minutes, it's gonna be wall to wall in here with Valsalvalhallaville's nastiest. You can smell their yeasty uglies the second they step onto the bus. So you and your little mail-order virgin better find a good place to stand, 'cause, believe me, you do not wanna be sitting down when they're all standing right in front of your face."

"Pull over," Cereal Man said. "We're getting off here."

"Right here, on the expressway?" she coughed. "Fuck you, you can get off at the stop like a normal person."

"Pull over, I said."

"And 'fuck you,' I said. Why don't you go back there to your nervous friend and jerk him off while you wait. Maybe you can get him to calm down."

Cereal Man noticed her Froot Loops T-shirt.

"The toucan flies at dawn," he said.

"What?"

"You heard me."

"Yeah … Yeah, I heard you. So, who's Don, and why's he got a couple of cans flying at him?"

"You think I don't know the scene?" he said, teasing a box of Froot Loops out from his grocery bag. "You think I don't see your need? Now, how about you just pull us over here? Me and the kid will get out, and you can just … follow your nose." She stared at him. She got it. And he knew he had her.

"'The fuck're you talking about?" she said.

"I'm talking about you," he said. "I'm talking about you, a bowl, a bottle of milk, and this whole box, with no one else around to bother you."

"You're trying to bribe me with fuckin' Froot Loops?!"

Cereal Man paused. "Thought you were a fan."

"What, because of this stupid shirt?" She snorted. "I've had this old thing since I was nine. Last Froot Loop I ever ate was probably during rotary dial phones."

"Some Trix."

"Come again?"

"Frankenberry."

"F-Franken … Are you out of your—"

"Apple Jacks, then, what do you want?"

"How'bout some Philly Slims."

"What?"

"Philly Slims."

"Never heard of that cereal."

"They're not cereal, you moron. They're smokes. All I got's this last one."

345

Cereal Man twitched. "You're choosing ... . cigarettes over a box of cereal?"

Baxter watched from his seat as Cereal Man, who had been standing in front, talking about heaven knows what, clutched the bus driver's head with his arm, shoved her burning cigarette into her mouth, and clamped her jaw shut with his hands. Baxter watched as the world outside the windows began to rock and spin. He watched as his quadrant of the bus knocked smaller cars, trucks, bikes, and trikes off the edges of the expressway and down into the city below. And he watched as Cereal Man held on to the driver's jaw, yelling, "PULL OVER!"

She pulled the bus over to the left shoulder, and Cereal Man released her. She hacked out a smoky cloud of sparks and collapsed into the aisle, overtaken by coughs that sounded like a handsaw running through a knotted plank.

"How's that cigarette taste now?" Cereal Man asked. "Still feel like a Philly Slim instead of a wholesome breakfast?"

She rolled over and managed to force her way through coughing to inquire, "Why, you got one?"

Cereal Man grabbed the driver by her thin, oily hair, opened the bus door, and launched her out into the expressway. Her yelp of distress was cut off in a fraction of a second by the tires of hundreds of speeding vehicles mangling her into a messy hash and scattering that hash into a long streak on the pavement in less time than it took for Cereal Man to peer back at Baxter and say, "Come on, kid. Let's go Home."

Baxter glared ahead in a daze. Then he got up and obeyed. Approaching the front of the bus, he grumbled, "Swell. Yeah, let's go Home. What's Home for you, anyway? Another murder? Another fifty murders? Another million? What's the magic number? When do you come to journey's end?"

"You think I like killing these scumbags?" he replied as they stepped off the bus and into traffic. "That's not Home, kid. Home is where you belong," he said with honking cars zipping by or swerving away from him as they crossed the expressway. "It's where you're safe, and where things make sense. Any of this shit make sense to you?" he asked as an SUV swerved to avoid him, ran over an old couple on a tandem, and crashed into a fire truck, which swung around and knocked an ambulance into two oncoming police vehicles. "Not everyone has a Home, kid. Sure, they might have a place to hang their hat or a place they keep going to because the idea of doing something else never even enters their Cheez Skwirt brains," he asserted as a minivan slammed into him, killing a family of nine. "But I promise you, we are going Home. Problem is, we gotta find a way out of all this city, if there even is one anymore," he said as they stepped out of traffic, and onto the right shoulder. "Yeah, what a dirty, rotten trick of fate that's left us without a driver."

"Why can't you drive the bus yourself?"

"I don't have a license."

Then there was the little ass.

It was a tired, old, bony little ass. But it came dirt cheap, and it eased their burden across this... barren sand heap. As the sage population dwindled, and the ailing burro panted more and more from the strain of carrying both Baxter and Cereal Man, the swift, silent wind replenished deposits of fine, stinging dust into the deepening cracks on the once-smooth lips that Baxter now incessantly licked. The boy's eyes had become strained from scanning the horizon for so long, and with such intense effort. The plains looked the same everywhere, in every direction. Never before had Baxter's eyes stretched so far with nothing in between them and the horizon, so very many miles away. He remembered, hours ago, when this modest pass itself formed the horizon. Now taxing his eyes with the rolling mounds ahead, the boy came upon the dreadful suspicion that when they rode over the next horizon, yet another equally empty expanse would then surround them. The burro's sides heaved, and his legs wobbled, until finally, he stopped and stood wheezing in the wind. It had now become quite clear that Cereal Man had guided them to a place that made no sense at all—a dreadful, oppressive monotony of emptiness that went on forever, and lay far beyond the most desperate reaches of anything related to Home.

Cereal Man did not know this place. He found it even harsher and dryer than the basin through which he used to trek to get to the old Safeway, which now lay in absolute degeneracy under one of the newer parts of the city. He remembered how the spires of steel and concrete had followed him before covering the defunct supermarket. Escaping urbania grew into a greater struggle every year. And wherever new iron forests sprung up, seas of parking lots, strip malls, and McMansions spilled out all around them, chasing down and coating every square foot of what the stupid planet had offered of itself for the last four billion years or whatever. But right now, Cereal Man could look back and find no spires. No towers. No malls or houses, or even roads. Just sand and sage, rolling back, and back, and then a bright, gray, overcast sky.

He reached into his grocery bag and pulled out the last of the Cheerios. Then he glanced back into the bag as a second thought. He had to choose between the last of the Cheerios or the last of the Wheaties. The Plutonium Sugar Bombs had far too much value to consume in quantities beyond starvation rations. With all of his sack-stuffing talents utilized to the fullest, he could bag enough cereal to last himself a full three years before heading back to the old Safeway. But it wasn't the Cheerios or the Wheaties, or even the Total that sustained him for that long. Any one box of these cereals could last a week or so. But a modest handful of PSBs, a dose so overwhelmingly rich in energy that it would kill most other humans on the spot, kept up his immense strength for months. But common times had ended. The cereal with a half-life was no more. He had become the custodian of the last box. It had to last him the rest of his life.

He broke a Cheerio in two and offered one half to Baxter, who shoved it away. Then the youth paused, took a breath, and remembered his manners. Then he ignored them.

"Come on, we gotta keep up our strength," said Cereal Man.

"You said we were going Home," grumbled Baxter.

"I said it was a long way," he reminded the boy.

"Oh, horsefeathers!" the boy objected, climbing down off the wheezing burro and pacing around in the sand. "You're never letting me go; I know it. What kind of awful place is this?" He kicked sand into the air. "No buildings..." He kicked more sand. "No houses..." More sand. "No bikes or trikes or cars..." More sand. "Not even any roads." Then he started picking up handfuls of sand and throwing it everywhere. "Just all this nothingness in every direction. I have to get Home!" His behavior spooked the burro and caused his wheezing to accelerate.

"We're headed Home, I told you."

"No! You've got to stop saying that. Every time you say that, we get further away from my house! Please stop saying that!"

"Not your house. Home: where everything falls into place—where you can rest your head without feeling like you'll drown in a raging torrent of bloody, flaming shit. I've been looking for it for thirty years, kid. And I know we can get there."

"What in heaven's name are you talking about?"

"Your old man. He keeps that river of shit raging, all the time. You and me, we can beat him. And we can turn this world around."

"My mom is about to have her surgery reversed! If that happens... I-I don't know how to explain it to you..."

"The monsters will return."

"What?"

"She'll create broods of horrible little monsters."

"How did you know?"

"I know it all, kid. I was there when it began. But there's nothing you can do to save her."

"Like heck there isn't," said Baxter. "You know what's in this backpack? A check. That's right. Three thousand dollars, friend— exactly the amount I need to finish paying for Mom's surgery. All I need to do is head on down to Orville's."

"Orville's."

"Why, sure. Orville's Friendly Family Market, in Twinkle. They were a major sponsor of the Chess Intergalactica. They'll cash this thing lickety-split."

The burro collapsed and lay motionless, with sand blowing into his open mouth and bare eyes. Baxter and Cereal Man stood there for several minutes, assaulted in cycles by the mocking reality that their ride had died. Each assault was interluded by a fleeting hope that perhaps the little ass had merely decided to rest its old bones. By the time sand had covered half of its unmoving body, this hope ceased to revisit them.

"Guess we should have watered him before we started crossing," said Cereal Man.

As wisps and streams of sand continued to cover the burro, Baxter started to feel an intense warmth on his backside. He readied himself to blame Cereal Man, bringer of nonsensical phenomena, for this strange, irritating, inexplicable sensation. But Cereal Man stood right next to him, so his role in this experience seemed unclear. He did look weird, though. His face looked bright, and all the shadows on his face seemed sharper and darker than before. It seemed almost as if, behind them, some kind of super bright light had turned on. But that made no sense. This wasteland had no electricity. The sky constituted a light source. But, as everyone knows, the sky lights things in every direction. Baxter turned around to determine what on Earth could be causing this. But it was nothing on Earth.

The terrifying answer stared down at him from 93 million miles away. High above the horizon, the normal, textured grayness of the sky had seemed to part, revealing a dimensionless dimension of intense blue. The world had broken, and outside the shattering sky lay the void, beyond. But the worst part was the yellow ball in the middle of the void, so staggeringly bright that it, too, looked flat and unnatural. It was at once a hole inside the hole in the sky and also something else entirely. How could a hole shine? How could it be bright?

"Whah—whah—what's that? WHAT'S THAT?!" huffed Baxter, stumbling to the ground and hyperventilating.

"What?" Cereal Man said, squinting at the plains.

"What's happening to the sky, what's that horrible thing?!"

Cereal Man was dumbfounded. "Horrible thing?"

"That horrible, horrible bright thing, up there! Right THERE!"

"What, the Sun?"

"No, where the sky is all split apart and blue, and that awful round thing—looks like it's burning a hole into everything?! You don't see it?"

Cereal Man was torn between disgust and pity. It came to him: Baxter thought the Sun and the sky were the same thing. The boy had grown up in an overcast world—a suburb ever shrouded from the heavens by a blanket of smog. To him, night was when the Sun faded out and all the lights in town came on. A daytime sky looked bright and fuzzy—some variation of gray or orange, but never a cartoon-like, uniform chasm of unnatural blue! And a nighttime sky didn't look black or blue, as Cereal Man had once known them, or even gray or orange.... It just didn't exist. Night was when the sky went away—when it faded into the glare of all the lights in town.

There seemed no way to explain the true sky, or the blinding interloper it hosted while the boy broke down into this level of panic. It had taken hours to explain the towers of the iron forests to him after leaving the city. And those let him off easy with a queasy anxiety. But the broken sky, with its orb of terror, showed no such kindness. Baxter would pass out if Cereal Man didn't do something quickly. So he removed one of the paper grocery bags from his double-bagged supply of cereal and placed it over Baxter's head.

"Take it easy there, kid," said Cereal Man, rolling his eyes. "It's nothing. Sometimes a fella gets too hot and he just sees stuff, that's all."

After a moment, the hyperventilating faded away. "You mean like, like hallucinations?" Baxter asked.

"That's right," said Cereal Man. "Now you just keep this bag over your head for a little while. It'll cool you down, and you'll be alright." After dark would be better. Then he could explain everything without the Sun ass-raping the boy's mind with the fiery dildo of confusion. So they embarked on a long march across the many miles of beautiful Sun-baked sand. After some hours, the thinning clouds phased into a sapphire sky, ruled by the sinking orange Sun.

Then there was Nightfall.

Now Baxter found the inside of the grocery bag as dark as the inside of his room at bedtime. Cereal Man had come to set his weary gaze upon a line of lights on the flat horizon. No iron groves visible anywhere, at least not yet. He grabbed a handful of Cheerios and munched on them with abandon, knowing the city outskirts ahead would have grocery stores that would replenish the cereal supply. They still had a long way to go, but not so far that he would need to tap into the PSBs. It seemed the two travelers had eluded the noses of any enemies, for now. It would have made no sense for a bounty hunter to follow them all the way into this wasteland and wait for so long to attack. This seemed like a good time to debag the boy's head.

"See those lights up there, kid?" Cereal Man said, removing the bag. "That's a new part of town." Baxter gasped at the jarring darkness. How could outside be this dark? "We can hole up there for a while, then split before the bounty hunters pick up our trail," Cereal Man continued. Baxter took a deep breath. It was okay. Even this made more sense than that terrible ball of light eating the sky. "Who knows, maybe you can even cash that check of yours and mail the money to your mom," said Cereal Man. Baxter tried to ease his breath out of his chest. The lights ahead actually soothed him a bit. They reminded him of Christmas lights. But when he looked up from the horizon, just above those lights, the sight shredded his mind. His brain had a hard enough time accepting a black sky, but now his eyes showed him a black sky that housed little white lights of its own, as though the city lights had floated off into it. But these were not like the city lights. There were thousands. Millions! Millions of infinitesimal points and specks of light, spattered everywhere. And a dense streak of them squirted like Mother Earth's milk across the heavens.

"Ghhhhnnnnn! Ghhnnnn!" Baxter moaned between heaving breaths. "Ghnhnnnnhnnn, this is impossible! Nohhhhh, thiz iz impozzible!" he brayed, as he snagged the grocery bag of cereal from Cereal Man and began throwing handfuls of Cheerios out onto the ground. Before Cereal Man had delivered himself past his own shock, the youth had chucked the empty box away too.

"Hey! Hold on a minute, we're kinda stretched right now. We need these," said Cereal Man, recovering the box. He started salvaging Cheerios, but Baxter interrupted by throwing an open box of Wheaties into the side of his head. By the time he turned toward Baxter, the boy had already gone for the Plutonium Sugar Bombs. The youth now meandered around aimlessly, screaming and slinging glowing Plutonium cereal nuggets far and wide.

By the time Cereal Man caught him, the youth had flung the lead-lined box far out into the night. "GHHLLLGNNNHHHH-I HADE YOU," Baxter screeched and sniveled. "I HADE YOU AD EVERYTHIG YOU'RE ABOUD! YOU BROGUE EVERYTHIG! YOU BROGUE EVERYTHIG-GHAAAAAAHHHHHH!"

Baxter tore away toward the city lights as Cereal Man scrambled around with frantic haste in the sand to recover every Plutonium cereal nugget.

19. THE DESERT

The havens of grey had returned. They now obscured the wheel of fire, whose hellish intensity marked but a slightly brighter smudge on the celestial canvas. But the damage was done. Feeling microjolts of hard energy still buzzing through his body from the uncountable white specks that scrutinized his soul all through his first true night, different parts of him shook in different ways as he wandered into town. Tendrils of hair bounced from his head as it wobbled, much in the same way a line of drool danced from under his top incisors, which lightly pinned the left half of his lower lip. His red corneas accentuated the toilety blue of his irises, which now seemed a bit frayed at the edges. His skin had hardened, his throat had dried, and his mind had fried.

He surveyed the long commercial strip as he wandered down its edge. Though quite familiar to him, the white noise of moderate traffic seemed loud for the first time—a world apart from the black silence of the wilderness he had just left behind. But the sound of his growling stomach seemed louder to him than the traffic. Recalling his complete lack of funds, he hoped that maybe one of the restaurants might be nice enough to spot him just enough to get him through the day, so he could do ... whatever the heck he needed to do. What had he been doing, anyway? Whatever. He had no time for extensive research and thinking, he needed to take action. So, instead of putting any thought into his optimum choice, Baxter walked into the closest place—an annoyingly close place, right next to him, almost like it needed him. *Stupid, needy place.*

This dim place had cream-colored walls and coffee-colored tables and chairs, none of which hosted a single soul. Kind of pathetic, but whatever. It looked like some customers stood at the counter. They sure did seem annoying. He got in line behind the two annoying, professional, thirty-something women, and tried to not roll his eyes at the pickiness of the first one and how she refused to make up her dumb old mind, which probably took up about as much space as a walnut. A bean, even. Then, after they all stood in line for what seemed like most of the morning, she reached an unamended decision. Baxter wondered what this bean-brained lady could have ordered.

When he observed her shelling out enough cash to make his jaw drop, he concluded that she must have ordered enough to feed her entire family—probably a stupid family, with loud, rude children, and a husband who also couldn't make decisions. Then, upon watching her leave with just a paper cup, presumably filled with liquid, his face crinkled with puzzlement. This puzzlement soon devolved into unfocused irritation. In hope of shedding light on what seemed like a purchase of unjustifiable expense, Baxter listened to the next lady as she placed her order. This didn't help one bit, as the youth had never heard of a short, tall, half non-decaf, low fat, full soy, undecuple semi-white, gluten-free, vegan, dry cap, super nutty dingleberry ristretto mocha latte macchiato non-breve, extra lukewarm, with triple light whip and saccharine sprinkles.

"Okee, awesome," said Rhyan, as he turned to prepare her drink. "Be a few minnits." Rhyan, a young barista with white, sheeny skin, sported dusty dreadlocks, clever-looking glasses with no lenses, a thin, studded, brown leather choker, and an offering of facial hair, which he groomed and trimmed each day to maintain its unkempt patchiness. His many facial piercings aided in this endeavor, particularly the studs and rings, which made their way into the beard itself, whether by means of deliberate installment, or by happy coincidence afforded by his habit of crashing on the couches of friends who seldom brushed off their furniture. Baxter watched this tie-dye-and-jeans-wearing dope as he pumped some kind of nasty black liquid out of a loud machine into a boring white paper cup, dumped a dumb assortment of other cruddy looking liquids in on top of that, used the loud machine again to froth the stupid concoction into a gross foam, put a lame plastic lid on top, placed the boring paper cup into an additional boring paper cup, and then strolled back over to the ugly counter like a dunce and start ringing it all up in his own hypo-urgent, hyper-casual way.

"Hey, you," Baxter insisted.

"Hey, mahn, how's it going?" he said. "Thanks for choosing Yuppiccino. Be with you in just a—"

"Yeah," Baxter dismissed. "Just what in the name of Madam Curie is this ridiculous magic potion you just concocted?"

"That is my morning coffee, Sir," objected the lady, who clearly preferred to channel most of her shrill voice through her nail-shaped nose.

"What's that supposed to tell me?" Baxter complained. "Isn't coffee that stuff that, it's all bitter and, what, it's related to drugs or something? Like caffeine?"

"Oh, no, no, it's like, a bean?" Rhyan tried to explain. "Y'know, it's real dark brown, and it grows in . . . in, um—"

"Wait a minute! Grows?!" the lady objected again. "You mean your coffee is dirt food? You want me to drink something that came out of the ground? What do you think I am?"

"Oh, nonono," Rhyan replied. "It's destroyed dirt food, ma'am. Believe me, you will NOT taste the coffee in this. It's our guarantee."

"Um, look," she bitched. "I got a ninety-nine in Organic Chemistry," she said, remembering the sixty-six she saw when her Consumer Health instructor had handed her final exam to her upside down at the end of her freshman year. "You may as well make me eat cleaned poop. If you put enough bleach on it, I won't taste it, right? How insulting! I am NEVER coming back!"

As she stormed out, displaying her well-rehearsed huff, Rhyan shrugged off the protest, looked at the cup, and sighed. "You want this one?" he asked.

"No, why would I want that?" Baxter replied. "Doesn't caffeine stop you from being able to go to sleep?"

"Oh, not this stuff," he replied. "All the sweeteners we put into this, you'll be lucky not to slip into a coma."

"Well, then, isn't it just a cup of liquid candy?"

"Oh, no, this is specialty gourmet coffee." Then, feeling an electric jolt from his choker, he added, "We have a passion for it."

"Excuse me," bitched another thirty-something professional woman, standing behind Baxter. "I'm in a hurry, so if he doesn't want it, could you please place it in an extra cup and give it to me?"

Rhyan accepted a roll of large bills from her, placed the drink in an extra cup, and again began ringing it up.

"You actually drink these things?" said Baxter.

"Yeah," she boasted, thinking of all the worthless losers in the world who couldn't afford to advertise their status in this manner. "Three, maybe four or five a day, if I'm stressed."

"What's the point of combining all this coffee and sweeteners if they nullify each other?"

"Whll," she scoffed in the absence of a clue. Then she remembered what she'd heard other professional thirty-something women say so many times of their drinks: "It's just a little indulgence."

"A little indulgence? You just said you consume three to five of these per day."

"I deserve it."

Baxter picked up the drink and poured it over her head. He walked out to the sound of the lady screaming and telling Rhyan that she would NEVER be coming back, and to the sound of Rhyan shrugging off the protest.

Back out on the street, he resumed his quest for a restaurant that might help him out with some actual food. Something down to Earth. Something less fancy.

Greasalon's sign, which read, "Satterday Speshel: Boddumless Fry's" tipped him off as the least fancy place. He shuffled himself inside. It looked like a restroom, with its dirty tile walls and floors and the moldy grout peeling out of the corners. He crinkled his nose at the cracked nylon counter of zit-core yellow, littered with crumbs of food, with a long brown stain stretched over to the cash register. He approached this register. The gum-chewing cashier, named Squizelda, burned with annoyance at him for interrupting her texting orgy.

"Good morning," he mumbled. "Do y— Do you have a—"

"Have a what?" she scowled.

"Do you have a breakfast menu?"

"Whatchyou think this is?" Squizelda said, pointing at the menu display behind her.

"No, look, I can read, dang it!" Baxter snapped. "But 'Skwirt Smoothy?' 'Fleshsticciato?' 'Syrup Curls?' 'Pink Stax?' 'Ramen Stix?' 'Puff Log?' 'Row House Roll?' I don't even know what those things are. They sound disgusting. Are those even food?"

"The nutritional information's online, you want to look it up," she sighed, getting back to her text.

"And look at those prices," he said. "How am I supposed to afford that?"

"I don't set the prices, 'Sir.'"

"Listen, I just want a piece of bread, okay? Could you just spare a piece of bread?"

"The MSG Twists got bread in 'em."

"Ugh! Do you have any soup?"

"The smoothies is like soup you want to heat 'em up."

"What about a salad?"

"The fuck is a salad?"

Baxter looked back into the kitchen and spied another worker, named Skid, standing in front of a cauldron of boiling oil. Skid had started to lift a fry basket out of the oil but distracted himself by picking his nose until it bled. Then he distracted himself from that with a plastic bag full of frozen, lumpy things, marked "Sacchro Tots," which he had forgotten about earlier. Skid emptied the contents into another frying basket, submerged the basket into a cauldron of still, dark-brown oil, and walked away. Then he came back, turned the heat on under the oil, and walked away again.

Baxter looked at Squizelda, the bubble-blowing, stupid little trout-mouthed, fat-face frog lady in front of him, as she continued texting her life away. He took the phone out of her hand and threw it into the cauldron of boiling oil. As the gum-snapping stupid little pig-nosed, dirty-face hog bitch scurried into the back and began shrieking from the pain of reaching into a deep fryer for her phone, Baxter walked out the door.

Scanning the strip again, he observed lots of burger places, like Shiny Patties, Chez Burger, and Pinchloaf. He had no idea who Pattie was, or what made her shiny, and he wasn't sure what a pinchloaf was. He recognized Chez Burger only in the sense that it made him think of the word "Cheeseburger." He assumed the word had been misspelled by a restaurant owner who was stupid. He started to go inside when an employee named Monsieur Cliff came out with a large container of wrapped hamburgers. Long, blondish hair draped Monsieur Cliff's youngish face, which featured tannish skin and grayish eyes that ignored the world from behind a dingy pair of roundish metal-rimmed glasses. He wore the standard Chez uniform, complete with a red beret, a prosthetic black mustachio with a cigarette, and a black-and-white striped shirt. Baxter watched the faux Frenchman walk past him, over to the large trash receptacle, where he lifted the lid. Baxter ran up to him and grabbed him by the arm.

"Hey, you," said Baxter. "What the heck are you doing?"

"Who are you?" said Monsieur Cliff.

"I'm a hungry guy who's watching you throw away perfectly good food, that's who," Baxter said, poking his finger in his chest.

"The rules says it's not perfectly good anymore. Lookie here," Monsieur Cliff said, pointing at different burgers. "That one gots ketchup on it, s'not supposed to ... that one gots too much ketchup ... them's got not enough ketchup ... these is supposed to have ketchup and don't ... Then there's all of these ones here ... They's all got the ketchup on the wrong buns. Then these, they got no ketchup and no nothin', just some buns, but nobody never put nothin in 'em, not even hamburgers. And this last one's not even a hamburger at all, it's a chicken samwich that someone put in a hamburger wrapper." Then Monsieur Cliff leaned over and confessed, "Actually, I did that one. I wasn't really lookin' real good. Don't tell Madame Peg." Then Monsieur Cliff dumped everything into the trash, on top of a huge pile of other hamburgers. He chuckled at himself. "Oh, yeah, and all them's the burgers we accidentally made a while ago. We forgot that we was supposed to be serving breakfast until eleven, not burgers. No big deal. Happens every day, right?" With another chuckle at himself, Monsieur Cliff closed the lid. He started back inside, whistling his butchered version of "We Are The World." Baxter grabbed his arm again.

"What the triple-heck is wrong with you?" he insisted. "I just told you I'm hungry and you threw all that food away, right in front of me!"

"Whoa, whoa, whoa," said Monsieur Cliff. "You don't wanna eat those, they're garbage."

"They weren't garbage until you put them in the garbage, you idiot!"

"Listen, those isn't all the food we got. We still got plenty of real burgers left. And when we don't, we'll get more. There's always more."

"Just shut up!" Baxter yelled, pushing him. "Just get back into your stupid restaurant, you stupid dumbface!"

Monsieur Cliff stood there, incensed. This heat really brought out the worst in people, he knew. But to yell and scream at someone for throwing away garbage? This kid clearly had some issues to work out. As Monsieur Cliff continued to shake his head in pity, Baxter huffed and stormed over to the trash. He threw open the lid, jumped into the receptacle, and started gathering up the freshest burgers. With his jaw dropping open, Monsieur Cliff turned around and hurried inside the restaurant.

Baxter stepped outside of the receptacle and started to make off with his arms full of burgers, when he felt a painful tightness gripping his ankles. He found his feet yanked out from under him and his arms crashing onto the pavement. This squashed many of the burgers and sent the others flying everywhere. Then the tightness went away. He looked back at the restaurant. At the entrance to the Chez Burger stood Madame Peg, the manager, as signified by her black beret, longer cigarette, and curlier prosthetic mustachio, which she twirled as she drew back the long snake whip that had felled the youngster. She was a sour woman in her late seventies, with powdery skin and a set of headlights for glasses. The beret on her small head topped a fluff of curly hair, which she dyed an iridescent black. She spit at Baxter and readied herself for a strike.

"Beat it," she said.

"What?!" said Baxter.

"Get your thieving butt out of here before you tick me off," she said. He whimpered, got up to a crawling position, and started to brush the pebbles of asphalt out of the scrapes on his elbows. Then he made a desperate grab for a squished burger and sprung up to run but was knocked flat on his ass by the shock wave from the tip of the whip, which cracked centimeters from his face. He rolled over on the pavement and groaned. "Get up," ordered Madame Peg. With a grunt of frustration, he obeyed. "Good. Now, you're going to step back. Then you're going to watch Monsieur Cliff pick these up and toss them back in the trash, where they belong."

"What the—? What the HELL IS YOUR PROBLEM?!" Baxter screamed as he obeyed. "You protect what you're throwing away? WHY?!"

"Why is right," she said. "Why pay your way when you can just wait around until we take out the garbage? Why not save yourself a step? Why don't you just come on in and take some money out of my till? Or bring your sorry self over to my place and take food right off of my grandchildren's plates. Hell, why not just pry their mouths open and scoop their dinner right out of their mouths while they're trying to chew it? In fact, why don't you just hang them upside down, slit their throats, and sell their blood? Might as well. Why not?"

"I'm not stealing from you! You already surrendered this food."

"I'll never surrender to a bum. If I let every starving, lowlife, piece of shit eat out of my trash, pretty soon it's swarming with parasites just like you, every day. Now... you're going to scoot your scheming little rip-off butt off these premises, and you're going to stay no less than three hundred yards from here for good. Or I'll feed you, alright. I'll feed you a mouthful of leather. Do I make myself clear?"

"Besides, these ain't breakfast," said Monsieur Cliff, discarding the burgers again and heading back inside. "We made them by accident, and now we're cookin' some real breakfast to make up for it, 'cause we forgot it's not eleven yet."

"What're you talking about?" said Madame Peg, following after him. "It's almost one in the afternoon."

"Uh oh," said Monsieur Cliff as the door closed behind them.

Memory rushed over Baxter like a chilling shower of needles. He now had less than twenty-four hours to pay off the Spring Break Scrapers! Panic blasted him out into the street, where a car stopped just in time to knock him into a puddle of assorted liquids. As he sat up, coughing, the driver of the car quacked out a gurgly snicker and drove away. Behind followed a police vehicle, with a cop inside who witnessed the hit and run. She also quacked and gurgled, then drove into the edge of the puddle, sloshing the assorted liquids onto Baxter anew. Her snickering mushroomed into laughter, and she drove off. Drivers of cars that followed started to emulate her pioneering of this hilarious paradigm, but Baxter undermined it all by getting up. As he ran away, drivers honked at him, cursing him as a discriminatory rat-bastard for denying their right to entertainment.

He rested himself on the street corner, battling the urge to bawl in despair. Then, he noticed the street sign hanging over the intersection, that read, "FAR NE SPINE STREET." He knew this street! His eyes darted around the intersection, looking for more information. He spotted a mileage sign that read:

NAGG 3

ODORTON 51

UPPER SHIT CREEK 99

SHAZAM INTERCLUSTERAL SPACEPORT 6,780

He'd never heard of those places. He spun around and looked down the street in the opposite direction. The mileage sign read:

NELL 3

ZAX BYPASS BYPASS 11

WHOVILLE 31

LOWER SHIT CREEK 333

TWINKLE 1,331

SHAZAM INTERCLUSTERAL SPACEPORT 18,080

All feelings of despair evaporated from his heart at the sight of a direct path Home. One second later, all of that despair, and a drop extra, rained back down on his mind when it grasped the vast distance involved. He scanned the area, hoping some kind of transportation option would present itself. Perhaps a trolley headed toward Twinkle… Or, with a little luck, a hot air balloon… Or a stray bicycle.

Or maybe…

Or maybe, he realized, this had all gone far enough. Maybe the time had come for this young small-towner to know when he had been beaten, and to finally understand that this big, bad, mean old world was stronger than him—that his very best just wasn't good enough. Maybe the time had come to admit defeat, rather than continue humiliating himself by languishing in the mires of futility. The boy who left Home on his bicycle was gone now. Now there was only a man. And the time had now come for this man to surrender his dignity and abandon everything his mother had ever taught him. And worst of all, the time had come to finally let her down, for the first time ever. It was time to hitchhike.

He cringed and stuck out his thumb. Instantly, a kindly young woman pulled up to him in a beat-up old '69 Plymouth Hellion.

"Need a lift, sweetie face?" said the driver between heavy breaths. If one took a close look, one could discern in Jenny's heartwarming smile a youthful verve still trying to break free from under her gentle, rodentian eyes of cloud blue. Baxter found himself unapologetically put off by how many of her imperfectly imperfect teeth no longer contributed to her smile. He found himself scowling at her pink but flakey lips and her pale, blemished skin. The beige scarf wrapped around her head smothered the flair of vitality carried by her long ribbons of straw-blonde hair. It went well with her red tank top and her pale, pink, summery calf-length skirt. Her plump frame had grown plumper in the last eight months, due to the twins, who had overstayed their welcome in her womb.

"I ... I just have to get ..." Baxter growled to himself. How was he going to explain this? "It ... It's really far ..."

"Awww, just get in," she said, blowing out a cloud of used smoke. "Me and Wheeler love road trips, don't we, Wheeler?"

"Wode twipp," said the unharnessed, slobbery-skinned toddler in the back, who used a cheeseburger wrapper as a washcloth and his overloaded diaper as a booster seat. Baxter didn't know what to do, so he got in.

"What's your name, baby?" she asked with sweet geniality.

"Baxter," he said.

"Ah, that's a cute name," she chuckled with a genuine smile, while flicking her cigarette out the window. "I'm Jenny. So, where we going?"

"Twinkle," said the youth. He watched her reach to her dashboard and open up a new carton of Philly Slims. She unwrapped a fresh pack.

There they were again, those little white tubes that people put in their mouths so they could light them on fire and drink the smoke out of them. He had noticed the bus driver drinking one, back in the city, before Cereal Man murdered her. And they must taste good because he remembered Mom could never seem to drink them fast enough, out on the porch, after she thought her little boy had fallen fast asleep for the night. Now he watched this lady light one up and take a puff. Then he watched her take another puff. And then another. "Twinkle," he repeated. "And it's extremely urgent."

"Twinkle? Hot damn, that is a long way," she laughed, pulling onto the road and punching into high gear. "We're gonna have to gas up a lot. This old boat is a fast one, but you would not believe how much it guzzles."

"I don't have any money right now," Baxter shouted with haste over the gargling engine as the car roared down the road toward Twinkle. "But I'll pay you back, I swear! I'll pay you back triple! I just gotta get Home. And fast!"

"Oh, I understand," she shouted back. "Home's where the heart is, as the saying goes. But Wheeler and me, we're always home, as long as we got the Hellion. We're adventurers, right, honey?"

"Aventoowuhs," Wheeler confirmed.

"What? You mean you just drive around all the time?"

"Well, we do stop for food and gas, dopey. And sometimes sleep. It's all you can do, you know? Hell knows, it's a lot cheaper than the rent our last landlord charged, right, Wheeler?"

"Mean Daddy," snarled the child.

They pulled up to pump thirty-three at a Sky-B-Gone Supermart, where you stop in for sky-high octane and be gone before you know it. Jenny opened the car door and struggled to a standing position. She waddled over to the pump, selected Super Leaded, nearly dropped her cigarette out of her hand as she fumbled about with the nozzle, then squeezed and jammed the spraying nozzle into her gas tank. As the fueling commenced, she leaned back against the pump, huffing and puffing, but not before taking a long, refreshing drag off her ciggie.

"Momma, I'm hungwee," said Wheeler.

"I'll get you something inside, honey-love," she said. "You just wait here with Uncle Baxter while the car fills up." Baxter watched her make her way across the parking lot, toward the convenience store. She climbed up onto the sidewalk, then leaned on the handle of the entrance door for a moment. Then she swung her huge, tight belly around to aid the rest of her body in turning toward the restrooms. Baxter watched as she made her way into the ladies' room and closed the door.

An hour or so passed. Wheeler had fallen asleep. Baxter opened the car door, just about to run to the restroom door and demand an update. Just then, Jenny came out and headed toward the store entrance. She had a little more spring in her step, and her belly looked much smaller and looser. Baxter watched her enter the store and approach the counter. He watched the cashier scan her credit card and present her with several long streams of multicolored tickets, which she proceeded to scratch with a coin. Every so often, she would hand the cashier a ticket that she had finished scratching off, and the cashier would exchange it for additional tickets, sometimes five, sometimes ten, but almost always one. This seemed like a very inefficient way to pay for gas.

After a while, the streetlamps started to come on. Baxter jostled around in his seat, tearing out tufts of his hair. He wanted to go in there, scream at her, and call her a stupid, dumb piece of garbage for taking so long. But what good would that do? She couldn't leave without paying. Baxter did not need police officers on their trail. The gas nozzle outside clicked. Baxter watched as the cashier pointed toward the pump. Jenny poked her head out the door and waved to the youth.

"Baxter, honey, could you hang up the nozzle, please?" Baxter stepped out, stormed around the car, and pulled the nozzle out of the tank. That seemed simple enough. But he couldn't figure out how to hang it up. It didn't seem to fit anywhere. "Pull the lever down," said Jenny. Baxter kept looking. What lever? He could make out this weird thing that looked like . . . well, not a lever. "Pull the lever down, sweetie." Baxter kept looking. Then he looked at her. Then he looked back and started pressing buttons. "No, not..." she started. "No, babe, the lever. The lever." Jenny came waddling toward the car. Then she stopped short and gasped. "Oh, no, not again!" At about half the speed most others walked, she sprinted to the car, reached inside, and turned off the ignition. "Ohhh my god, this is gonna cost me." She pulled the lever down and hung up the nozzle. The amount charged came to $E99999. "Ohhh, Jenny, when will you ever learn?"

"What is the problem?" said Baxter.

"I can't put that much on my card," she sighed with dread. "I can barely scrape up enough to make the minimum payments now!" She got into the car and fumbled around shakily for a smoke.

"Momma, I'm stiw hungwee," whined Wheeler.

"Just hang in there, baby love," she replied. "Momma's got to have some more medicine right away, so she can think." Baxter watched her come back out with a Slim in her mouth, which she lit and puffed. "Okay, think," she said, as she began pacing. "Think, think, think... Okay, I could probably leave the Hellion here as collateral for a few days, and... I'll get Bowles down here, I'll just be like, 'How many times did I bail your ass out,' I'll say that, and he'll just, he's got to come through for me. I mean, that Boston Terrier of his has gotta be worth maybe a hundred down at Los Perros Hermanos. Annnd... and

I could always call up Drakie, offer him a little jelly roll... 'Course, my luck I'll end up preggo again. Maybe Kristin'd be better... 'Course then she always wants you to stay and do a bowl with her after, and then you're there for like two or three more days..."

Baxter's heart began knocking against his chest at this forecast of further delays. He watched as she tossed away her cigarette butt, then took out another Slim and lit it. She leaned against the car and sucked down a lungful of "Philly's phinest phumes." Baxter snapped it out of her mouth and threw it into a puddle next to one of the leaky pumps. "Hey!" she yelped. "What the hell was that?"

"I HAVE TO GET HOME!" Baxter screamed. "This is a matter of life or death!"

"So are these," she objected, drawing another cigarette out of its pack. "I mean you don't make it home, you don't make it home. But I don't get my smokes and I'm sick in bed for days, dangling over the grave by a thread."

"Momma's medicine," said Wheeler.

"You said it, sweetie love," she said, smiling back at her son while lighting up. "Momma'd be a wreck if it weren't for—"

"NNNO!" yelled Baxter, tearing her medicine out of her mouth and throwing it in another puddle. "NO, HOW CAN YOU JUST STAND HERE?! YOU CAN DRINK YOUR MEDICINE ON MY WAY HOME!"

"Well, you'll excuse me if I'm having second thoughts, now, bucko!" said Jenny, half hurt, while drawing yet another ciggie. As she raised her lighter, Baxter snagged it. Then he tried to grab the pack, but she pulled her hand away. He dove into her and secured his hands around the pack, initiating a nasty struggle. "What're you— You bastard, get your hands off my—Stop it!" she said as Baxter yanked the pack out of her hands and sent her sliding into the pavement.

As Wheeler hollered out for his momma, Baxter scrambled inside the car and made off with the cigarette carton. Jenny saw this and struggled to her feet. Baxter got out on the other side of the car and watched her come after him, grunting out whiny objections. He let her come within a foot of him before dashing around to the other side of the car. She continued the chase. This time Baxter let her get even closer before dashing away. "Please! PLEASE!" she begged, as she continued after him again. He noticed she had begun bleeding from between her legs and had started to leave a rather gruesome trail around the car. He stepped away from it. This time, when Jenny approached, Baxter tossed the carton over her head and ran to catch it. Then she chased after him again, and he tossed it to himself again. Then again. And again. By now every spectator at the station was having a good yuk at the ordeal, except for Wheeler, who began to cry. He didn't understand these goings-on. He just knew they were bad.

Jenny collapsed onto the side of the car, shuddering from the force of her desperate gasps for air. Her eyes never left the carton, which Baxter continued to hold hostage at a safe distance. She reached out for her cigarettes, and when she found enough air to resume begging, she found she could only blubber in despair.

"Now, you listen to me," Baxter commanded. "You're going to get in there and pay for the gas. Then you're going to take me Home."

"But I can't afford it," she bawled. "They'll take the Hellion! They'll put a lien on Wheeler and sell him to Monsanto!"

Baxter took out a cigarette, lit it, and sucked a pocket of smoke into his mouth. It tasted awful! Like a mouthful of burning dirt! And yet, the youth did allow for the probability that this simply indicated strong, great-quality medicine, which adhered to the old folk wisdom, "If it tastes bad, it must be good for you." The carton did, after all, feature an image of middle-aged friends enjoying their smokes and cooling off in a dumpster filled with water. That seemed disgusting, but these people weren't retching with disgust. They were having a great time. Any medicine that could ward off the filth of a dumpster party must be potent stuff, despite its flavor. And the carton did also say, "Welcome to Phlavorville!" At least that made them seem like they could have a pleasant flavor. But regardless, Baxter understood the primary importance of appearing to enjoy them. So he blew the smoke back out and recalled how Mom's eyes used to roll back upon the first exhale, as if her smoke tube loved her and massaged every aching bone she had.

"Ahhhhh," he groaned, attempting to emulate whatever manner of pleasure he had witnessed. "That sure makes me feel better. A lot better, that's for sure! I'll bet you wish you felt this good, huh?"

"Please," she whimpered. "It's my last carton. I've got nothing. What am I going to do, ohhh, what am I going to do?"

"The faster you get me Home, the sooner you get these back."

As Jenny "ran" into the store to finish paying for the gas, Baxter got into the back seat of the Hellion, stretched out next to Wheeler, and continued puffing away.

"That's not yew medicine," the teary-faced toddler whimpered with his lips curling into a heartbroken pout, which gave rise to a shout of despair. "That's Momma's medicine!"

"Be quiet," Baxter ordered. "Or I'll drink all of her medicine, and she'll get sick, forever. And you'll never see her, ever again. Ever." Wheeler's face crinkled up with hurt. As the little boy brought forth a storm of terrified braying and sobbing, Baxter wondered what kind of medicine companies put in these things. Then he realized the magnitude of what he had just said to Wheeler. Would this lady get sick, or even die, if he withheld them for too long? Or did he just make an ignorant and empty threat? No matter. This filthy kid didn't know any better. Baxter had convinced him, and nothing else mattered ... even though the noise level had now actually increased. Oh well. Let the kid cry. Maybe that'd give Miss Snaily McSlowpot even more reason to get her bottom in gear.

And yet, no matter how calculating and detached Baxter tried to become, he couldn't help but worry about the very real possibility that his actions could yield permanent, irreversible, and tragic consequences. What if keeping these tubes from her proved dangerous? What if she went blind, or became paralyzed, or passed into a coma? Or what if she keeled over, dead, and crashed the car before they got to Twinkle? Rolling her body out of the way might be possible, but driving a car? Well, he'd have to figure out how, and that's it. No other options.

Jenny made her way back to the car and dumped herself into the driver's seat. Her son tried to get her attention, but she ignored him. She punched the ignition and threw the engine into gear. And with a gurgling roar of power, the Hellion tore out of the parking lot like a bat out of hell's third asshole. And even though Baxter knew they had many hours before arriving in Twinkle, he could not keep himself from scanning for familiar sights.

Hundreds of miles and dozens of additional fill-ups later, he grew weary of the continued sight of chain restaurants and stores lining the median of the highway, their glitzy signs of red and yellow flashing by with soul-numbing regularity. No Meatball Time! No Shucky Darn's Frankfurter Barn. Just an endless river of places foreign to his hometown. Lots of hot dog places, like Stankfurter, Puffdoodle's Poodledogs, Willy DeVein's Wurst, and Chez Hot Dog. And in addition to countless replicas of the burger joints he'd encountered hours earlier, he also beheld innumerable drive-throughs for Pet Burger, Jack in Your Box, and Seth T. Dickrot's STDelicious Loose Meat Sandwiches, much like Arby's, but classier. But a few pizza places also made themselves known: Chez Pizza, Mama Scabbi's, and Piebot's Pizza Planetarium. And chicken places abounded, like Cluck'n Whack, Combstompers, Beak-Fil-A, Chez Bird, and Lieutenant Colonel KG's Chicken-Stuffed Chicken, where your bird is naturally stuffed, and stuffed fresh, while still in its cage. Many Mexican places also populated the sides of the highway, like El Burrito, El Taco, and Chez El Taco.

But even with this diverse selection, the redundancy became staggering. The Hellion continued to pass most cars like they were standing still, and at any one time, some grouping of these places filled Baxter's eyes. Often the grouping included chain supermarkets and discount outlets, as well. He kept searching for Orville's, but for hours he only saw gargantuan outlets like Grab-N-Go, Cheap-Mart, Count Von Discount, Theftway, Get-Co, Coupon Castle, Coupon Castle City, Stuff 4 Less, and Carb-Rite. Each of these housed a few express versions of the aforementioned fast food holes, and at least one Billy the Kid's Child Beatery, which allowed frustrated moms to finally shop and text in peace. Superstores also housed a Cap'n Hook's Abortionarium Express, which allowed imminent moms to finally shop and text in peace. What a sickening display! No feeling of down-home goodness here. They hadn't even come close to Home yet.

Dawn began to brighten the dim, orange sky, and everything slowed to a crawl as they hit the morning commuter traffic. Many times, Baxter yelled at Jenny to go faster, but that only made her bawl and squeal and beg for "just one smoke" or "just a little, tiny drag" to get her through it all. But when they passed a mileage sign that showed Twinkle still remained 810 miles away, Baxter began screaming with abandon, drowning out her cries and her pleas for him to act like a reasonable hijacker. Finally, she stopped in the middle of the road and froze. She rocked back and forth in her seat, screaming at him. Then, Baxter performed a quick calculation and replied, "Oh yeah? Well, you just might want to accommodate this shit-for-brains, lunatic, psycho, asshole son of a bitch, because if you don't, it's bye-bye, smokes for you, lady!"

"What do you mean?" she quivered, snapping back into the world of the focused.

"What do I mean?" he mocked, lighting up a Slim. "I mean this is the way it's going to be: Every couple of minutes that I'm not Home, another one of these things goes up in smoke!"

"WHAT?!"

"Thaaaat's right," he goaded. "So the slower you move, the fewer of these delicious dealies you'll get."

"NO! YOU CAN'T!" she screamed, reaching toward the back, grasping in vain for the cigarettes. Baxter only needed to lean back in comfort to remain out of reach. To accentuate his image of cavalier and carefree luxury, he put his arm around Wheeler, whose moaning and bitching had long ago become white noise.

"Ohhhhh, yeah," he said, sucking in smoke and blowing it in Wheeler's face. "That makes me feel great! Yeah, you don't know what you're miss—"

Baxter had thought he was leaning all the way back until Jenny pinned him to his seat by gunning it onto the narrow shoulder of the highway. After about a minute, Baxter managed to sit forward again and behold the terrifying view of careening through a shallow and narrow canyon of lights: a canyon populated with blurring strata of red brake lights to the right and choppy avalanches of fast food filth to the left. Despite the terror, he could also feel the satisfaction of making damn good time. He sat back again and continued to advertise each and every coveted Slim that Jenny's needless delays had cost her.

Before he knew it, he had started inhaling some of the smoke. At first, each drag launched him into a coughing tempest so hellacious that he nearly blacked out. But it only took about eleven practice smokes for him to adapt. He soon found that inhaling enabled him to go through each cigarette faster. Before long, he could suck them down like a pro. After a while, however, Jenny's fear of the tiniest error started to get the better of her.

"Hey!" Baxter belted out. "I sure am feeling your foot hit that brake pedal an awful lot."

"NO!" she cried at the sight of him lighting up yet another cigarette. "No, no, please, it was just a couple of times. PLEASE!"

"Nah, I don't think you're taking this seriously," he said, puffing away. "And look at how much you've slowed down. A hundred and eighty-one, are you kidding me? That speedometer needle should be on the floor!" She gunned it again and ended up back on the road, weaving between cars. "Nooooo," he groaned. "This isn't solving anything. All this zigging and zagging and showing off may look impressive, but you know as well as I that it's not getting me Home any faster."

"Listen," she offered with as much kindness as she could scrape up.

"Oh, there it is," Baxter grumbled in his dried out, shredded voice. "The pathetic sob story of the lady who drove too slowly. What's the matter? Need one of your smoke tubes?"

"Look, we've been driving for hours, my head is killing me, and I can't think straight."

"Ohhh, having a rough time, are we?" he coughed.

"I'm serious," she moaned, white-knuckling the wheel and blinking her eyes with enough force to mint a coin. "I feel like I'm going to crash soon! I really think I could drive a lot better if you just give me a smoke."

"Boy, you sure are gonna be sick after a while," he said, hacking up a glob of crud. "Suuure will be nice to have allll these smokes to yourself when you get me Home. 'Course, that's assuming there are any left."

She pulled over to the shoulder and jammed on the breaks. "Alright, look," she hissed at him with her teeth grinding. "Just shut the fuck up and fork over a fucking smoke, or so help me God, I will drive this fucking car onto the other side of the road and flatten us all, and you'll go home in a fucking plastic bag. Do you understand me, you disgusting little fucking brat?"

Baxter gawked at her. Then he drew out two cigarettes. He put one in his mouth and lit it. "One for me," he said. Then he touched the tip of it to the other cigarette until orange embers crackled, then held it up. Then he said, "And one for me," and took a spiteful drag on both. Now Jenny gawked back at him. Baxter blew the smoke in her face. "And one for Wheeler too," he said, lighting up a third cigarette and handing it to the little boy. "Yeah, one for you too, Wheeler, buddy." Then Baxter looked at Jenny. "Just none for you."

"Hewe, Momma," said Wheeler, offering the cigarette to her, and having it intercepted by Baxter, who took a drag off all three.

"Boy," he said, exhaling. "These sure are vanishing fast, huh? Any other threats you want to make?"

The Hellion barreled out into the highway with more abandon than ever. They found more speed on the shoulder, and through the parking lots in the median than on the highway. Only on special occasions did they have to tap pedestrians, bump other cars off the road, create accidents in the opposing lane, pass beneath some of the higher semitrucks, or drive-through shopping centers to circumvent congestion. In time, Baxter watched the highway turn from FAR NE SPINE STREET to NE SPINE STREET, then, much later, to

SPINE STREET. As the clock on the dashboard struck 11:01 a.m., the Hellion pulled into the parking lot of Orville's Friendly Family Market.

20. BEING INFALLIBLE

With many breaks for coughing, hacking, and gagging blood and poisons out of his ruthlessly abused respiratory system, Baxter ran as fast as he could through the parking lot, leaping over piles of greasy paper and broken glass, toward the main entrance of Orville's. Of course, if dumb, stupid, selfish Jenny had cooperated from the start, Baxter wouldn't have had to administer these brutal throat lashings to himself. Running had made them so much worse. And he wouldn't have had to run at all if Jenny hadn't driven the Hellion like such a stupid old idiot face. She didn't understand that if she had driven faster through the parking lot, she would have already passed the stupid old lady backing out of that handicapped parking spot, and the collision would never have occurred.

Instead, the Hellion T-boned the old lady's car, thereby flattening the old lady herself, catapulting Wheeler through the front windshield, smashing Jenny's face straight into the top of the steering wheel, and popping her remaining twin baby out onto the filthy car floor under the gas pedal. Baxter did feel a little guilty about fleeing an auto accident where so many people needed help, but not enough to not flee an auto accident where so many people needed help.

The clock on the store had hit 11:11 when he reached that old, familiar front entrance. He felt like his adventures had kept him away for years. And there it waited for him: the poster of the humanoid rat, under which he had parked his bicycle so many days, or weeks, or... so long ago. Wait, no. The familiar old poster, that crude drawing that had loafed around in his mind all his life was now gone. A full body shot had replaced it. Baxter found himself startled by the extraordinary resolution of the image. And despite the urgency of the matter at hand, it drew him in. He felt as though he could step into the photo.

Baxter could discern the texture of every thread, every scuff, scratch, rough patch, and imperfection on the rat's open black trench coat. Under the coat, the rat wore a black T-shirt with that strange "R" symbol and a pair of dark blue jeans, the ends of which bunched up behind the tongues of a pair of loosely strung, steel-reinforced combat boots of black leather. He stood in front of a greasy, grimy wall of chipped concrete, clutching some kind of shiny, black cord, which he had wrapped around some unfortunate person's neck. He held the unfortunate person up in the air the way a fisherman used to display his catch.

Looking closer, Baxter observed that the victim's face, nay, the victim's entire head, had been destroyed. The rat had squeezed his brain from his skull down into his mouth, and the brain now bulged out the front, splitting his upper row of teeth in the middle. This made his incisors and his black mustache point outward in kind of a funny way. But Baxter didn't find it quite as comical as the way in which that tuft of curly, blackish hair topped the victim's skull, the upper half of which resembled a thick stem, and the lower half of which looked like a melon that the rat had wrung clean of all its inner flesh.

Then Baxter noticed that the rat's other hand held an enormous pistol, and had it pointed right at the viewer. Right at him. The youth scoffed at this. Was this supposed to look like a threat? Baxter stood there for a moment, amusing himself by making faces at the rat, daring him to shoot. Then this became boring, and his eyes wandered down to the reward offered for this rat's death. Finally, someone had decided to use scientific notation! But still, had anyone even come up with a name for a number this big? It made the stupid reward check in his backpack seem like a pitiful afterthought. $3,000? That's all he got for proving himself the smartest kid in the universe? He knew he deserved more. All his life, he'd tried to acknowledge gratitude for everything he had. Now he came to realize, he'd never get those years back. Well, no more! He and Mom had lived like frightened little shadows of shadows for too long. The time had come at last to save her. But he wouldn't just save her life. He'd bring her new life. He'd bring them both out into the real world, and he'd go to any length to take what they deserved.

With the fullest vigor, Baxter swung off his battered backpack—his treasure's protective shield for so long—which had endured hot rain, sand, the razor wind of the dusty plains, and the stare of that blazing eye that had opened the sky. His poor backpack had gone through hell with him. The outer zipper, weathered, kinked, and fused in some places, presented a major battle. At first, he could only sit on the ground, tugging in vain, and whimpering with frustration. Passersby scowled with contempt at the annoying sight of a struggling human being that wasn't them and then waltzed into the store with newly born intentions to buy, not only more groceries than they had originally planned, but more groceries than they could afford, all in an act of decadent spite, aimed at their unarticulated and unknowing source of annoyance.

Baxter picked up a shard of the same glass that he had observed on the pavement the last time he had visited this store. He jabbed it into the canvas and ripped the bag apart. Then the inner zipper slid open like a breeze. The prize check, which HAMN had helped to fold with his or her great android strength, sprung out from behind the zipper, knocking Baxter over. Passersby chuckled at the amusing sight of a possibly injured human being that wasn't them, and then they sambaed into the store with newly born intentions to buy, not only more groceries than they could afford, but more groceries than they could use, to celebrate how someone else's misfortune had entertained them.

Baxter threw glass at some of them, curmudgeonly ruining part of their ass-shaking fun. His satisfaction from this victory was brushed aside in favor of the greater satisfaction of setting his gaze upon the $3,000 prize check that he had been too tired to read upon being awarded it. But he felt this greater satisfaction blasted out of existence when he discovered what the check actually said. Baxter heard his insides scream, and his heart sank into despair.

It was worth $3,000, alright. But it didn't quite qualify as a check after all. He blinked his eyes in disbelief, but nothing changed what the document said:

"Pay to the order of: <u>BAXTER</u> exactly three thousand and 00/100 dollars, upon completion of in-store purchases totaling exactly eleven thousand and 00/100 dollars in goods or services sold at Orville's Friendly Family Market."

Baxter had not heard the automatic doors slide open behind him, nor the soft rumble of the wheels of green bow-tie roller skates, nor had he perceived the much more audible squeaking sound made by the corners of a mouth wiping against pearly whites as the owner of the mouth promoted his already present smile from "disturbingly genuine" to "violatingly euphoric."

"Well, goody, goody gumdrops of a morning to ya, Sir!" squealed Joilio, as he skated up to Baxter. "Heyyy, I remember you, Sir! You bought that great 'Hometown Proud!' pencil from us, didn't ya, Sir?! Wow, so great to see ya again, Sir!" he added, kicking in a 360-degree twirl upon his skates. "How's this beautiful day treatin' ya today, Sir?! Sayyy, that sure is a honeydew of a rebate you got coming to you, Sir!"

Never in all his life had any experience made Baxter feel more like he needed to take a shower. "Oh," he groaned. "Swell," he snorted. "It's you again."

Joilio stopped talking and demoted his smile back down to "disturbingly genuine." Then he started talking again, "Yeah, I'll betchya—"

"Listen up, Oilio…"

"Joilio, Sir!" he chuckled.

"Oilio, I say."

"Certainly, Sir!" After all, the customer is—"

"Be quiet and listen," Baxter insisted. "Where are the most expensive items in the store?"

"Oh, so it's top quality you're after today, huh, Sir? How about a couple of filet skwirtignons, over in the gourmet section, Sir? They're a real—"

"Are they the most expensive?"

"Oh, no, Sir! But they sure are the best, that's for positive, Sir! You know, they have over a thousand different preserva—"

"What's the most expensive, dammit?"

"Well, Orville's has a tremendous bounty of high-end items for our more poverty challenged guests, Sir! You want the top ninety-nine, Sir?!"

"Just tell me what's the aisle that the fewest people visit."

"Oh, that'd be Wholesome Foods, all the way down on the other side of the store, Sir! Just hold on tight and we'll be there in the twinkling of an eye, Sir!"

Oilio moved in to sweep Baxter up off his feet, but the youth resisted. "No, don't touch me."

"But, Sir," said Oilio, continuing to grab and touch. "Providing you with a level of customer service far above and beyond the value of my wages is of paramount—"

"No, get off me, I said!"

"But you don't want to walk all the way down there yourself, do you, Sir?"

"You're right," Baxter said after a beat. "You go! Fast as you can! Grab a shopping cart, fill it up with the most expensive junk you have, and meet me at the checkout in ten minutes."

Oilio stepped back with shock, "You want... a... a... cart full of . . . of... dirt food, Sir?"

"MOVE!" Baxter screamed.

"Yes, Sir!" said Oilio. And with that, he began a sprint for the shopping carts. Only one step into the sprint, however, Baxter stuck his foot out and tripped him. Puzzled, but not losing a single picometer of his disturbingly genuine smile for even an instant, Oilio looked up at his honored customer. Baxter shrugged with indifference. True, the stakes were higher than ever before in his life, but this delay was still worth it. "Heh, Sir . . ." Oilio shot him a playful chuckle, then hopped up, grabbed a cart, pumped his skates a few times on the smooth floor, and leaned into a glide. With just a couple more pumps, he zipped out of sight.

Baxter rolled up the check and crammed it into his shorts, so that one end protruded up from his crotch and the other protruded up from his ass. He grabbed a cart of his own and sprinted off too. He rushed past Narcissus Duckbill's Selfie Studio, then through Dr. Bitch's Tanning Salon and Maternity Ward, through the nail salon inside of it, through the Starbucks inside of that, then out to the nearest aisle,

Hard Candy and Noisy Snacks. Many of the items were minuscule. He would have to move like the Tasmanian Devil to fill the cart. But at least now he could go full speed ahead with his shopping spree without having to fend off the boot-lapping efforts of that overanimated vessel of human slime.

"HHHWOW! JUST HOW ARE YA TUDDAY, SIR?! ANYTHING I CAN HELP YA WITH TUDDAY ON THIS SUPER-DUPER TERRIFIC DUCKY DAY FOR YA TUDDAY, SIR?!" trumpeted a voice from behind him. He ignored it and continued crushing bags of chips to decrease their volume. Alas, he could not ignore the owner of the voice popping her head in front of him as he turned around to dump a load of chips and candy into the cart.

Suzzanne's psychotically enthusiastic smile gave him such a jolt that the candy and chips exploded out of his arms, and into the far reaches of the aisle. Contrasting with the bright green of her bow tie and pressed apron, her hair formed a wild tornado of red, secured with hundreds of protruding bobby pins, on top of her quivering head. A pair of flaring nostrils pressed into her pencil-thin, pencil-sharp nose. The upper part of this olfactory collector of terrificness seemed pinched in between the two massive, white orbs of her visual collectors of terrificness. She had two folds of skin, which science loosely referred to as eyelids, tucked into her eye sockets, thereby leaving at least a hemisphere of each orb unblinkingly exposed to all twenty-two waking hours of each and every super terrific day. She had no eyebrows. She had replaced them, in soaring arcs, with the same eleven-alarm red lipstick that defined the thin border between her thin, freckle-spattered face and her brigade of gleaming white teeth. Even under the corners of her wide smile, her teeth seemed not to recede or relent in any way. Baxter was not the first to wonder how far they continued. He wondered if they wrapped all the way around her skull, such that one might expect to find them if one removed the skin from the back of her head.

Due to the terrific excitement of everything in general, Suzzanne breathed through her nose and mouth simultaneously, and therefore always had access to plenty of oxygen. This became evident to Baxter when he tried to inhale to tell her to go away, but found the required air sucked out of his mouth, and a breeze whistling through his hair, en route to supply the empty laugh that Suzzanne, by personal policy, employed to fill the void created by conversations she'd ruined. The laugh sent the very same air, now infused with the scent of cinnamon gum, whistling back through Baxter's hair.

"You stupid, million-toothed, crazy lady!" he belted back at her as he scurried about, trying to recover all the items she'd blown out of his arms with her nuclear blast of friendliness, "Look what you made me do!"

"OH, GEE, WELL, SUFFERIN' CINNABONS, SIR!" she lamented while losing not a trace of her psychotically enthusiastic smile. "I SURE AM SO VERY SORRY ABOUT THAT FOR YA TUDDAY, SIR! HERE, I'LL BE ONLY TOO ECSTATICALLY HAPPY TO HELP YA WITH THAT TUDDAY, SIR!" With a stroke of each skate, she flashed over to scramble around on the floor with him, but only got in his way. Baxter abandoned the recovery efforts and went back to throwing wads of candy and snacks from the aisle shelves into the cart. As soon as Suzzanne identified this as the goal, she flashed over to him again and tried to help by wrestling the wads out of his arms and slamming them into the cart for him. "HERE, JUST LEMMY GET THAT FOR YA TUDDAY, SIR! MY PLEASURE TO HELP YA TUDDAY, SIR. THAT SURE IS FOR SURE FOR YA TUDDAY, SIR!"

Baxter tried to grab another armful of items before Suzzanne had finished dumping the armful she had just ripped away from him. But he just couldn't make it work. Suzzanne would glom onto every armful of items he picked up. "What the blazes are you doing?" he cried.

"PROVIDING YOU WITH A LEVEL OF SERVICE FAR ABOVE AND BEYOND THE VALUE OF MY WAGES IS OF PARAMOUNT IMPORTANCE TO ME, SIR!" she announced, slobbering this celebration of her lot in life.

Then it dawned on Baxter that she moved much faster than him, and that the struggle between them was eating up precious seconds. So he stopped to allow her to fill up the cart unfettered. To Suzzanne, this signified that the goal had changed. So she stopped as well.

"SO HOW THE HOWDY DOODY HUNKY DORY HAS THIS TERRIFIC DAY BEEN TREATIN' YA TUDDAY, SIR?!" she asked. Baxter stopped breathing. "HOW'RE THE WIFE AND KIDS FOR YA TUDDAY, SIR?!" she pressed.

Baxter turned and sprinted off in the other direction. He had almost made it out of the aisle when he found his legs swept out from under him with no reduction in speed. "WHERE WE HEADED NEXT FOR YA TUDDAY, SIR?!" asked Suzzanne who now carried him with ease and skated fast enough to blur the aisles as she whistled past them.

"Nowhere," said Baxter, as he pulled her wild tornado of red hair over her face and stuffed it into her huge mouth. What with her intimate knowledge of every cubic micrometer of the store, Suzzanne was unaffected by the blindness. But inhaling a cluster of bobby pins did slow her down enough for Baxter to jump off and tumble several hundred feet behind her.

But she still managed to ask, "IZV VTHERE AMMY FING MORE I CAM BOO FO YOU PUBBAY, FIR?!"

"Just stay away from me!" Baxter commanded, as he rounded the corner and entered the nearest aisle, Canned Brown Foodish Items. He heard her in the distance, hollering, "YES, SIR, ANYTHING YOU SAY, SIR! THE CUSTOMER IS ALWAYS..." But then he heard another voice.

"Suzzanne's a pistol, isn't she, Sir!" said Codge, peering with genial expectance from behind a massive, partially constructed tower of cans of Pappy O' Ploppy's Hot-Pumped Stew Creations. The kindly old clerk had finished most of the tower. And even though it already stood as tall as him, he still had a full shopping cart full of cans left to add to the stack. Baxter ignored him and focused on the part of the aisle most distant from the tower. He began removing cans of owl soup, moose bisque, and elk gumbo from the shelves that featured Machine Gun Sherman's Shaved Earth Selections. "Yeah, she sure is a spark, that Suzzanne, huh, Sir?!" Codge repeated, coming down from his stepladder.

His tan, leathery wattle swung left and right between the frills of his green bow tie as he shook his chunky head left and right with endearing admiration for yet another gal that he saw as incorrigible and colorful. Since Codge looked at all folks this way, whether he knew them or not; just about every thought cooked up inside his smooth brain made him shake his head this way. And doubtless, the energy needed for so much head shaking accounted for why his head seemed just a little oversized, while the rest of him seemed just a little undersized.

Baxter didn't notice these attributes, because he did everything he could to avoid eye contact with the old man. Instead, he continued to pile cans of soup into his arms, in spite of how unsustainable his endeavor proved. Codge chuckled with affection at the futility of it. Seeing everyone as "a card" sure did make life fun all the time. And from the moment old Codge had laid his soil-tinted eyes on Baxter, why he just knew he'd spotted a young buck what held more stories under his belt than most kids his age. Codge couldn't wait to hear them! He approached Baxter with the glee of a skip, and yet, with the casual ease of an old-fashioned mosey. He had discarded his skates to climb up the ladder, so a mosey proved easier than usual. Codge preferred the mosey, anyway. Easier and more becoming than the stroll or the cruise.

Out of the corner of his eye, the youngster could observe his own reflection in the old timer's IMAX-sized dentures, which he kept fixed to his upper gums with a gray layer of medicated Fleshstic, and which he exposed nonstop, due to the nonstop joy inherent in each and every day. "Well, just how do you do there today, Sir, sure is a great day out there for ya today, Sir, isn't it, Sir?! Name's Henry, but everybody just calls me Codge, Sir," he said, touching up his short waves of gray hair and brushing off his green apron, which somehow looked hardier, rougher, and more denim-like than the aprons of his co-workers.

"Codge," Baxter dismissed.

"Yeah, that's just what they call me, Sir," Codge said, finishing the thought. "Y'know."

"Right," Baxter further dismissed.

"Just a nickname they got for me, Sir," added Codge. "Y'know."

"Fine," Baxter dismissed with as much disinterest as he could without diverting precious time and energy toward a full-fledged rejection.

"Well, lookie there, Sir," said Codge, tapping one of his thick, labored fingers on the end of the rolled-up rebate check that looked more like a paper tail than a paper penis. The youth paused, trying to think of a way to get him to go away without shoving him onto the floor and jumping up and down on his oversized head until he lost consciousness. Doing so would mean dropping the cans he'd already gathered up, which would put him even further behind. Codge took no notice of how scarlet the youth's face had grown and just kept right on talkin'. "Whatchya got here for ya today, Sir? School art project, Sir?" He winked his wrinkly eye at Baxter. Art was cute, as long as kids grew out of it before the time came to buckle down and get a job.

At a complete loss for ideas, Baxter resumed collecting cans with a nasty huff. Soon he amazed himself with just how many he could hold. Equally impressed, Codge gave him a friendly clap on the shoulder, almost causing the youth to drop his bounty all over the floor. "You know, if it's a lot of canned stuff that'll do ya for today, Sir, I gotchya a humdinger of a deal over here for ya today, Sir!" Codge pointed to the tower. "Them cans are starting to bulge, so we're putting 'em on special, Sir! Ninety percent off, and I'll tell you what, that's an exceptional bargain for ya today, Sir!" Then he lowered his voice a bit. "And I'll tell ya what else, Sir ... I wanted to let you in on the deal before I put the sign up, y'know, Sir."

Baxter paused again. "So, just what makes me so special?" he asked.

"Why you're our guest, Sir! Ain't nothin's' more special than that!" he laughed to celebrate this universal truth.

"In that case, get me all the cans from the bottom row of the tallest side," said Baxter.

"The bottom row, Sir?"

"Yes, make it snappy. I'm in a hurry."

"Did you say the bottom row, Sir?"

"I sure did."

"Are you sure you don't mean the top row, Sir? 'Cause you said the bottom row, Sir."

"You think I don't know the difference between top and bottom?"

"Oh, no, no, no, Sir! No, the customer is always—"

"Where's your manager?"

"Oh, no really, Sir, tha-that's not what I meant at all, Sir! It's just that . . . well, it's just that there must be twenty somethin' rows already stacked up on top of the cans you want, Sir, so—"

"Any stupid buttface can have a can from the top! Listen, 'Codge.' You think you can obtain the most beautiful jewels by just lollygagging around and pivoting your dumb arm half a meter away to grab me one of your silly, sorry old cans from anywhere, like some afterthought? The most precious gems are buried deep! It takes blood, sweat, and tears to get them! Do I deserve just any old can, or do I deserve a treasure?!"

"Sure, sure ya do, Sir! Absolutely you do! 'Just that it's gonna take me a little while to take all them others back down, y'see... Sir."

"I don't have time to wait around here all day because of a problem you created! Just get me the cans, or should I take my business elsewhere?"

"Oh, no siree, Sir! I'm right on it for ya today, Sir!" As Codge rambled himself over to the tower, Baxter zipped ahead of him. He approached Codge's shopping cart and dumped his armload of soup cans inside, on top of the stew creations yet to be stocked. Then he noticed Codge's roller skates sitting next to the stepladder. By the time the youth had managed to put the skates on and turn the heavy cart around, Codge had managed to lay himself on the floor and even get one of the bottom cans moving. "Hot dog! I got one for ya, Sir!" he cheered, waving at Baxter, who ignored him. He started tugging, then came up to a crawling position to get more leverage. Then he started tugging harder. "Now just... ngh... just lemmy see if I can—"

As the tower toppled down and buried him, Baxter pumped the skates and cruised off toward the checkout lane with a full shopping cart. He could still discern Codge, muffled under the pile, but carrying on with his folksy small talk. "Boy oh, boy, lookie here at that, sure is get'n dark early these days, isn't it, Sir! Guess that means winter's just around the corner, huh, Sir?"

After only a second or two of racing with all haste toward the front of the store with the heavy cart, Baxter realized Codge had filled it with products cheaper than dirt's own dirt, even before heavy discounts. The realization came not a moment too soon. He made his decision to release the cart just as another wide-smiling clerk named D'Squeeziius rounded the corner. The speeding cart mercifully cut short D'Squeeziius's mirthful salutations by slamming the wind out of his big belly. The cart then bounced off to the side and tipped over onto a small child. At that point, the child's mother appointed herself Grizzly Mom. She liked that term, and she used it to describe herself in conversations she held at the store while her child ran around doing whatever. Grizzly Mom finished her text, took a drag off her soda, and stormed over to the scene of the accident to issue forth a diatribe of the most self-righteous variety, as D'Squeeziius gasped for air and the child moaned in pain from under the tipped cart.

Baxter had long since skated off in the opposite direction, and he now entered Overpackaged Lunch Kits. Here, another neglectful mom yapped on her phone, while behind her Pepsi-toned rump, her kid sat in an empty cart, tearing open a fun-sized packet of Fleshstic cookie icing and decorating his hair with the hot pink contents. As the mom continued to yap, she dropped a couple of the cheaper lunch kits into the cart, she thought. But because Baxter had raced past her and made off with her shopping cart, those lunch kits counted as the first of several items to land on the floor under the baroque bouquet of dimples that constituted her ass.

As Baxter stopped to lift the disgusting toddler out of the cart, a new clerk appeared, inhaling to greet him with rapture. So the youth threw the kid at the clerk and rocketed away with his cart into TV Dinners - Frozen. But another clerk appeared, also happy as heck to see him! He skidded to a halt, scrambled away, and rolled down into TV Dinners - Refrigerated. Two clerks in that aisle! Then TV Dinners. Another clerk. Finally, he came across the first empty aisle: Foods of Other Race. He began raking boxes and cans into his cart at full speed. And even though each item came into his field of vision for only a flash, he marveled at their exoticism. These constituted forms of otherworldly fare he had never even heard of before, like "Chinese Food." Next to that he found "Mexican Food," which came in cans, jars, and tubes, rather than boxes. Then he started to grab "Italian Food," which only came in round disks, and then "Irish Food," which only came in bottles. He had just noticed a bucket of "Black Food" when a high-pitched voice came up behind him.

"I am you help, Sir?" said the voice.

At this point, Baxter could afford to help nobody but himself. But the voice sounded weak and insecure enough to make him feel like he could make it go away by yelling at it. So he took a breath, selected just the right words for yelling, cleared his throat, and then turned around to be confounded by the sight of a thin, barely pubescent Asian girl of the naked variety. The sharp worry lines between her eyebrows betrayed a lifetime of suppressing a need to beg. She blinked more than most, especially when spoken to, and every smile she could muster strained her face. According to the name tag pinned into her left nipple, her name was Toy. Someone might have given her this name during the days before the agency had shipped her, but continuous stress had never allowed her brain to form even the germ of curiosity that would lead her to inquire about what might have been her "self." Toy's long, black hair was fastened at the top of her head with a tiny version of that green bow tie for which Orville's claimed to be so very famous. This adornment echoed the larger, glassy bow tie on the front of a metal collar clamped around her neck. The theme concluded below her navel, with a design of that famous icon branded into her skin and tattooed with green ink. And tattooed just below that, in an elegant yet playful font, the "Hometown Proud!" slogan crowned Toy's most popular customer service region. Her roller skates were topped with thick metal anklets, similar to the collar around her neck, but with a short chain connecting them. Seeing this harried girl riddled with all these oppressive adornments prompted Baxter to stop, slow down, and rethink the way he had perceived her. He asked himself, his true self, *Is she really naked? No. Not really.*

"I am ah-you help, Sir?" she asked again, with a mild, nervous smile. "Uh, no. I mean, I am help you. I am help you, Sir?"

"What is this game?!" he snapped. "First a babbling fool who, I swear, was about to start humping my leg... Then some maniac with picket-fence teeth and grabby hands set me back another five minutes... Then some doddering old fossil wanted to talk my ears off... Then all you other stupid, crazy imbeciles... What is the object of all this lunacy? Some kind of plot? Are you poppycock-noggined kooks trying to rob my mom of her life? Well, allow me to let you in on an itty-bitty secret, Little Miss Crackpot: Everything I have, I owe to her, and I'll be gosh-darn hot damned if..." He looked at his filthy self, in his half shirt, with a giant rebate voucher stuffed down his shorts and chaffing his taint. "She brought me into this world," he huffed, recalling the sights, sounds, smells, tastes, and feelings of the world he'd recently toured.

After several failed attempts to process this rant, Toy struggled to maintain her dubious smile, and said, "Oh, uh, is nice weather we have today, huh, right, Sir?"

"It's sweltering, now get your bare butt and your butthole-stupid questions out of my face! I only have a couple minutes left!" he yelled, trying to rake in more items.

"Oh, you want I say what is on ah-super sale today, Sir?"

"NNNO, YOU NEARLY NAKED WEIRDO!" he screamed and threw a can at her. She let it hit her in the eye, while making sure to tread that thin line of expressing pain without objecting to it. Toy had already barreled well down the dangerous road to failing in her duties. Avoiding the can, or downplaying the intended damage, would have defied her honored customer's wishes.

"Uhhh..." she whimpered as her smile dropped. "I uhhh, how are kids and wife, Sir?"

"SHUT UP!" he screamed again.

The glassy bow tie on her neck began to glow green, and a look of horror came over her as she looked beyond Baxter's face, toward the ceiling. He turned to look but found nobody behind him. But he did notice that, inside the larger of the nearby dome cameras, a little green light was flashing. Toy began to hyperventilate. "Hand job, Sir?"

"WHAT?!"

"I give ah-best hand job, Sir."

"GIVE YOUR HAND WHATEVER JOB YOU WANT, JUST SCRAM!"

"Or you beat me! You give uh me beating, Sir, and you get big and hard!" Then she beheld the camera's black glass bubble starting to expand out from the ceiling, and she began screaming. Baxter tried to leave, but she grabbed him and started begging him for something in Korean. The black camera bubble had now grown very large. It looked like a giant black egg passing through the ceiling. As Toy stood, frozen with horror, the giant egg dropped to the floor, and upon impact, cracked up to its apex. Shards of the shiny black shell broke off to reveal someone inside, folded up in some kind of disturbing parody of a fetal position. A slim old man, with white hair encircling his balding head, began to move. He unfolded his body and began to stand upright. His green apron and bow tie were spotless, flawless, and pressed to razor sharpness, as was his white, short-sleeved shirt. His face, however, looked less professional, with all of its peeling layers and hanging patches of skin.

But what could Orville Jr. have done? He had no real skills. True, he did have a knack for taking up space and for telling people what to do. But he took up relatively little space, and his orders, though always barked out with unshakeable confidence, bred sniggers aplenty in every aisle to which he ever found himself adjacent. Junior thought his installation of the surveillance system would eliminate this impudence, especially after he had upgraded it with death rays. But the magnitude of his unpopularity exploited the limitations of the system, and whispers of stifled laughter at his expense still managed to seep out of every unmonitored crevice of the store. He never inspired the same level of fear and/or respect as did his daddy.

So, when Orville Sr. had met his demise in the dunk tank during the company picnic, Junior spared no expense to ensure the continuation of the store's owner and CEO. Junior had his father's watery corpse hauled to the back of the store to be "saved by the very best doctors." The doctors he recruited were Dave, the local auto mechanic, Gary, who took a computer class in college, and his friend's brother in law, Gus, who worked at RadioShack. The technical know-how and lucky guesses of these three provided the operational cybernetic endoskeleton for the ROT-1000, while Orville Sr.'s ever stiffening corpse provided the flesh grafts and Orville Jr. provided the name. Apparently, a lifetime's exposure to very little outside the store never let Junior's imagination get off to a rocketing good start.

He had convinced himself that Robot Orville Terminator was a pretty darned awesome handle for his dad's cybernetic reincarnation, even though both of his friends kept mocking him by abbreviating it to ROT and insisting that the full name sounded like a robot designed for terminating Orville, rather than a terminator named Robot Orville.

Junior had put an end to the mockery and misunderstanding right away by firing them. Nothing held more importance than standing behind the new and improved form of the store's great founder, a point emphasized by Junior, in lengthy diatribes, to troupes of grieving workers; employees loyal to the founder, but who felt no allegiance to some clinking, clanking, clattering collection of cybernetic junk. To Junior, no conflict existed. To him, this was Dad. New Dad. Dad, the founder, to whom all must pledge their lives. The irony came during the most impassioned of Junior's lengthy diatribes, when the ROT-1000's circuits became overloaded by the excitement of it all, at which point, the shoddy cyborg had wrapped his unhinged mouth around Orville Jr. and consumed him like a python—a terrifying spectacle, which proved effective at convincing the employees to pledge their loyalty, while simultaneously inviting Junior to doubt his own. Since that day, the ROT-1000 had ruled with even greater fear than his organic incarnation, especially over imported employees, like Toy, who had now demonstrated the need for some corrective counseling.

The young girl's ignorance made her valuable to an increasingly escapist population. These qualities, coupled with the eroticism of her ribby, half-starved body, remained the only things that had so far saved her from a lethal death ray zap from above. Policy dictated that pleasure clerks like her, who freight workers had only recently released from the crate, would receive her counseling from one of the managers. But Toy had racked up major violations so fast that the ROT-1000 calculated the necessity of immediate intervention in order to protect the store's investment in her. She had failed to "Keep That Smile." She had also failed to "Make the Customer Feel Special." Her failure to accomplish these goals had contributed to her probable failure to "Exceed Customer Expectations." Taking the necessary action had become critical. If the honored customer left the store at this point, all would be lost.

Baxter found himself unable to even leave the aisle, transfixed as he had become with the sight and sound of this bizarre humanoid thing. He cringed at the whirring of the ROT-1000's gears and belts as the cyborg lumbered toward Toy with his heavy feet, and his legs of slightly different strengths, and even more slightly different lengths. Locomotion proved an awkward process, but it had improved since the removal of the roller skates, which had secured a reputation for costly accidents within seconds. His patchy face always wore the same huge, almond-eyed, heart-freezing smile that used to fan across Orville's Sr.'s face whenever he sat down on the toilet after leaving the plunger in the bowl with a ribbed condom on the handle. He looked dead as a skull and alive as a cranked-up clown when he placed his poorly grafted right hand on Baxter's shoulder.

"Well, bless my bow tie," said the tinny voice of the ROT-1000, with his bow tie twirling whimsically. "Baxter himself!" he continued, accessing all files on venues that the store had sponsored, even stupid ones, and employing the optimal algorithms for "Making a Customer Feel Special." "Say, son, I hope you realize that this is your store, and that our friendly family is here for you. The Chess Champion of the Universe has the run of the place!"

"I've had it," said Baxter. "Just let me pay for this loot and skedaddle out of this nut bin." Suddenly perceiving only a 3 percent probability of repeat business and a 68 percent probability of bad publicity, the

ROT-1000 tightened his grip on Baxter's shoulder, causing him to yelp, "HEY!"

"Wait, my friend!" said ROT, punctuating this invitation with an electronicky clicking sound from the depths of his speech circuit. "This pretty young thing has something to say to you!" Baxter winced from the painful grip. ROT shifted over to Toy and extended his telescopic left arm. His arm remained bare and robotic because Orville Jr. had so mismanaged his inventory of skin grafts. "Don't you, Toy?"

"Uh-hullo, Sir," she struggled into a smile. "Welcome to Orville."

"Annnd…" ROT prodded.

"WHAT IN THIS FORSAKEN WORLD IS WRONG WITH YOU PEOPLE?!" Baxter grunted, squirming to release himself.

"I-I'm sorry, Sir," she whimpered.

"Make the customer feel special," ROT reminded her, while squeezing her ass with his metallic hand.

Toy's smile vanished, not from the considerable pain of the squeeze, but from the fear of the metallic hand making the same inward journey as the time when she had sneezed without asking permission. "You like uh the blow job, Sir?"

"Keep that smile," ROT reminded her, with his hand edging further inward to explore her intestines.

"Yeah," she said, forcing a huge smile. "I give uh you best one. What uh you think, Sir?!"

"I THINK YOU BOTH WANT MY MOM TO DIE!"

"No, no, Sir!" she corrected. "You wrong, Sir, we no—"

The ROT-1000's eyes rolled back, and intense beams of red light shot out of the sockets. His bow tie jutted out from his neck and began spinning at a ferocious speed. From his speech circuit emanated a piercing siren. He released Baxter and clutched Toy's shoulders with both hands. Baxter watched as the telescopic arms of the smiling cyborg pulled his terrified employee inward. She managed to scream for her life until the spinning bow tie had bored all the way through the upper half of her face, and out the back of her head. As ROT withdrew the bow tie and released Toy's twitching corpse to the floor, Baxter made a break for it, but not before the ROT-1000 had cheerfully proclaimed the store's core maxim, which Toy had failed to observe: "The Customer is Always Right."

Baxter skated as fast as he could, in an effort to put several aisles between him and the ROT-1000, who he could still hear, lumbering along and searching for him. "Wait, my friend," the cyborg continued to call out like a cheerful broken record. Baxter rounded a corner and began tearing ass down the bottled water aisle, not stopping, not slowing, only accelerating. So much for the shopping spree. He could only hope that Oilio had amassed enough items on his own to get to $3,000. Recalling the clerk's overwhelming zeal, Baxter's confidence grew. *Yes, Sir, good old Oilio will come through—that mindless, shiny-faced, trumpeter of super-concentrated nonsense!* He zoomed past several other clerks, each one of them eager to strike up a conversation. But Baxter proved too fast for all of them. They skated after him, all shooting out as many compliments and mundanities as possible, like a tribe of annoying hunters trying to bring down a mighty beast with platitudes. Just when they started to fall back out of audible range, another clerk, with downy blond hair, named Billiam, seemed to appear from out of nowhere.

"Well, I'll be a shiny red balloon, just about to burst with joy!" he screeched. Baxter zoomed on by, but the energetic young clerk caught up with little effort. Soon Baxter again looked with dread upon Billiam, skating right along with him and blathering, "Gorgeous day today, huh, Sir?! Anything I can do for ya today, Sir?! My pleasure, Sir! Providing you with a level of service far above and beyo—"

Baxter screeched to a halt. "Give me your uniform," he said.

"My... Give you my—"

"Give it to me!"

"Why, yes Sir, Sir," Billiam said, taking off his apron. "After all—"

"INSTANTLY!"

In slightly less than an instant, Billiam had handed over his black slacks, his bright white shirt, his clean green apron, and his snazzy bow tie. Baxter turned down the roller skates, the name tag, and the bow-tie-patterned boxer briefs. Within seconds, he had dressed himself as one of the crew. And not a moment too soon. Down the aisle barreled the tribe of clerks, so ready to please their customer. Baxter skated off with confidence. Behind him, the tribe bore down on Billiam, who they had identified as their new customer. Then he heard the poor lad start to scream, like an ostrich defecating a small gas engine, as a cyclone of relentlessly vacuous small talk numbed his mind so profoundly that it oozed out of his ears.

Soon Baxter was racing past the checkout lanes. Customers to his right, who had intended on entering a lane, found themselves having to dive out of his way in a panic. Numbered signs flashed past him on the left as he scanned each checkout lane for the familiar, smiling face of the young man in whom all hope now rested. Customers continued to dive out of the way. The checkout lanes continued to flash by. Off in the distance, at the threshold of perception, he heard the ROT-1000, still calling for him, "Wait, my friend."

By the time the lane numbers had passed the low seventies, Baxter began to despair. The last of the checkout lanes now approached, and nowhere had he spotted that familiar smile. Maybe the time had come to find an intercom and attempt to find the one clerk who had, in the last eleven minutes, become a keystone to Mom's salvation: Oilio. That stupid, worthless, butt-smooching peddler of sycophantic gas! More lanes flashed by on his left. More customers dove out of his way on his right, until someone's foot tripped him and sent him careening into the impulse rack of lane ninety-nine. Then, face down on the floor, he felt the wheels of a loaded shopping cart run over his back and head, followed by the wheels of a pair of skates. Groaning from the pain, he stood up to find Oilio, standing next to a cart full of groceries and frowning at him. The young clerk slapped him in the genitals, and then slapped him in the mouth.

"You self-centered son of a bitch," said Oilio. "That customer back there in Synthetic Cooking Oils asked you for assistance, and you skated right past her without so much as a smile. I'm telling on you, you lowlife piece of cockroach shit!"

"Oilio, it's me!" said Baxter in a screaming whisper, while digging under his pants and pulling the folded check out from inside his shorts. "Remember, the fella with the rebate check? The one who sent you to Wholesome Foods? The one you're meeting with right here?"

With the smoothest and most instantaneous transition, Oilio turned his frown upside down. "Well, hey there, Sir!" he beamed. "Gettin' ready for Halloween, are ya, Sir?! Ha, that's just crazy, Sir! Well, here you go, Sir! If this cart doesn't suit your needs, you just let me know, okie dokie, Sir?!"

Baxter stuffed the check back into his crotch. Then he grabbed the cart and rammed it into a raggedy little girl at the checkout who had just paid for a box of Ensign Crunch—a rare luxury, as her destitute family could not afford crunches of higher rank. Baxter threw her money at her, scattering coins all across the front of the store. The scraggly waif got up and limped away, weeping. Then he pulled the cart back out and gave it to Ojectica, the same sexy cashier who'd rung up his pencil during his last visit. Oilio rushed around to begin triple bagging the items he'd just gathered up.

Baxter shifted about as Ojectica scanned a gross of bottled crabgrass root water. She read one of the labels. "Ooh, 'the original neohippie aphrodisiac.'"

"Who cares," he said, as she moved on to a case of peeled and individually wrapped organic bananas.

"Mmm-mmm," she said. "Wanna break one of these off in me, baby?"

"Shut up and move!" he said.

Then she picked up a large plastic bag filled with sunflower nuts, individually wrapped for your convenience. She shot an amorous look at Baxter and began to lick the sack of nuts when he yelled, "HURRY UP!"

After scanning each nut, she rang up eleven finely sanded oaken crocks of Mac of Gaia elbow macaroni, made from 100 percent organically grown, humanely planted whole flaxseed, fermented, sprouted, and massaged to the music of Dhraijizrajj Yogi and immersed in a rich, vitamin K–fortified cheese sauce made from cave ripened, celestially aligned, cannabis-infused human breast milk. She issued another seductive gaze and began running her fingers over her nipples.

"COME ON!" Baxter growled.

"That's eleven thousand dollars and one cent, baby," she sighed.

"What?!" said Baxter. He went over to Oilio and kicked him in the shin. "Look what you've done, you greasy dirtbag!"

"Thank you, Sir!" said the young clerk, wincing from the pain with a cheery smile.

"Shut up and let me think," Baxter snapped. "You there!" he said to an old lady shuffling through checkout line ninety-eight with a handful of coupons. "Hand those over."

"Reachy, grabby lot of bow-tied bandits," she said, struggling with him as he grabbed hold of the coupons. "You corporate misers have glommed enough from us."

"Wrinkly, useless coven of coffin scratchers," he struggled. "Why don't you leave the world for the living."

"Why don't you leave the world for the deserving. Greedy swine!"

"Fossilized stain!"

"Bloodsucker!"

"Fart in a hurricane!"

With that, Baxter yanked the coupons away, sending her to meet the hard floor, which would have shattered her elbow, had her brittle hip not intervened. The youth started back to his checkout lane, but a blue bolt of electricity zapped him and sent him also to the floor, right next to the old lady, who passed out from the pain. He looked up to find the ROT-1000 hovering over him. He tried to get up, but ROT zapped him again with a bolt from an electrode now protruding from his metallic index finger.

"Return those coupons," ROT commanded, pointing to the old lady, who had slipped into a coma. "Then smile, and apologize to your customer," he continued, as her heart stopped. "Then you're fired."

"I'm trying to save my mom's life, you sick, cybernetic psychopath! Do you even have a mom? Imagine if she... or it... needed you."

"When you wear the Orville's green bow tie, the customer is your mom."

"Ah, but I'm a customer too. Saying yes to this stupid, dead old lady is saying no to me."

"Wrong! You're never a customer. You wear the green uniform. That makes you part of the Orville's Family. Now, smile, apologize, turn in your uniform, and hit the bricks."

"Ohhh, well, I am sorry," Baxter smiled, removing the green apron. "I'm sorry you don't understand the errors you've made."

"Errors? The boss? Wrong! You're fired! Fired after you apologize to this dead customer."

"No, you see..." Baxter shook his head with cool confidence. "You are not my boss. I am your boss."

"Wrong!" declared the ROT-1000. "Orville's pays you and you obey."

"Check your records. You've never paid me a penny, and I've never worked for you," said Baxter, removing his dress shirt to reveal his gross-looking half shirt. "I bought a pencil from this place on the day of the Chess Intergalactica. That babbling strumpet sold it to me, and that smarmy leg-humper paid for it," he continued, removing his pants to reveal his short shorts. "Then I won the Chess Intergalactica, and I was awarded this prize check," he said, pulling the damp check out from his crotch, unwadding it, and waving it for all to see. The ROT-1000 began to jerk and twitch, as the buzzing of overloaded circuits became audible. "Then, just minutes ago, you tried to help me... as your customer. I am Baxter! Winner of the Orville's-sponsored Chess Intergalactica, and your customer!" He removed the bow tie and threw it at the jerking cyborg. "I, your customer, whose needs you personally dismissed—I, your customer, whom you personally have restrained with force, whom you personally have delayed, whom you personally have twice electrocuted—I, your customer, identified by you as an infallible being, yet whom you personally have condemned as ...wrong."

"Wrong............. Wrong........ ...... Wrong........ ..." blared the smoldering ROT-1000, with his tinny voice climbing in pitch. "Wrong... Must satisfy... saaatisssfyyy cusssstommmer." His voice soared higher and higher as he began eating all the skin grafts and clothes off of his metallic frame, which grew soft and misshapen. "Smile... Smile... .... Must keep that smile. Keep that smile... .. .... Wronnnnng.. ...... Wrrrrrronnng........... Smmmiiiiiile... .." The cyborg melted into a semisolid glob of metal, topped with the upper half of his gaping smile, which issued not another word, only sluggish twitches inside the upper half of his silvery skull.

The staff stood there, frozen with shock. But Baxter had no use for such nonsense. He thumbed through the coupons: One third off of all Fizzlewink's AAAAAAAAA sized batteries . . . Three dollars off a great gross of Bubble Numb, Novocain-filled chewing gum, recommended by four out of five snickering dentists . . . Buy two Etch A Sketch cell phones and get the third for twice the price . . . All he could use was an in-store coupon for 0.1 percent off of all purchases.

He shoved it in Ojectica's face, and she rang it up without delay. Her solicitous manner had vanished. To he who melted the great founder, only swift obedience was to be solicited.

"You've saved eleven dollars and a thousandth of a cent, Sir," she said, as Baxter watched the total come to ten thousand nine hundred eighty-nine dollars and nine hundred ninety-nine hundred-thousandths of a cent."

"Fine," said Baxter. "Now, it's nine hundred three dollars you charge, right? Per hour, right?"

"I—Only for the best time, sweetie," she said, surprised by the question.

"Right, right, for a pencil sharpening, right?"

"I could whet your wood real good."

"No, I don't have a pencil. Oilio! Pencil!"

"Beg your pardon, Sir?" Oilio squeezed confusion into his disturbingly genuine smile.

"She's going to sharpen your pencil."

"M-my pencil, Sir?" squeaked Oilio, having never dreamed a customer would ever toss such a bone to him.

"Yes, yours, you living puddle of poop! I used up all the lead in mine to impress a bacterium, so it seems pretty obvious that my mom's life now depends on *your* pencil."

"I-I ..." he stammered.

"Oilio," Baxter said, grinding his teeth. "You better not be telling me you don't have a pencil! You better not be telling me that, 'cause if you are—"

"That's okay, baby," said Ojectica, pointing a scanning gun at a bar code on her tongue, and, upon hearing a friendly beeping sound, ducking her head underneath Oilio's apron. "I can find your pencil." The sound of a happily opening zipper whizzed into the air, and sure enough, she found it. As the front of Oilio's apron began thrusting back and forth, Baxter monitored the ever-increasing numbers on the cash register screen with meticulous care.

After eleven seconds, Oilio's jaw dropped, his teeth twinkled, and his eyes started to roll back. Baxter kept his eyes fixed on the screen. He didn't hear any sharpening and wondered how two people with anything more than dirt for brains could take so long to find a pencil. *Oh well.* As long as the meter was running, he didn't care. After twenty-two seconds, Oilio began grunting and hyperventilating. *Why is this such an effort?* Sheer exasperation fueled Baxter's temptation to belittle them by finding a pencil on his own. But he didn't dare take his eyes off the register screen. After thirty-three seconds, Oilio's shuddering got out of control. Though Baxter found it very distracting, he managed to ignore it. Forty-one seconds, and Oilio was gasping and crying out with joy, as visions of assisting customer after customer after customer flooded his mind. Forty-two seconds, and his hands gripped the counter like a vise, as his body braced itself for the mind-shattering unknown. Then, as the forty-third second passed, all of his teeth began twinkling with mounting bliss, and he found himself about to rocket through the portal to infinity, and Baxter ordered Ojectica to stop the transaction, and she stopped it. The register read "BJ 43.85386046511634 sec = \$11.00001."

"YES! YES! GREAT MOTHER OF ALL MOMS, YES!" screamed Baxter, as Ojectica rang up his grand total for exactly \$11,000.00. Oilio could not move. Every muscle had cramped up with frustration.

"Hey! Rise and shine, Pencil Man!" snapped Baxter, kicking Oilio in the shins until the young clerk unknotted enough of his flesh to move again.

"Gee, Sir," he whimpered. "Sure do appreciate it, Sir! No pain, no gain, right, Sir?"

"Shut up. Just take care of this. I'm in a hurry."

"Sorry, Sir?"

"Don't play dumb with me, dummy. Last time I was here, you said you gladly pay for all your customers' merchandise. Were you lying then?"

After a few seconds of digesting the entire situation, Oilio uttered, "Ohh-ho, uh... Uh, no, Sir! Certainly not, Sir!"

After sliding his debit card and all three of his credit cards, and maxing out all of them, Oilio forked over all the bills in his wallet, and all but eleven cents of the change he had in his pockets. He then triple-bagged all the groceries, which, as Baxter had taunted, were about to simply be left behind. Having the order paid, Baxter then presented the rebate check to Ojectica with the first smile he'd worn on his weathered face for quite a long while. Oilio's facial muscles now worked overtime, however, in a supreme effort to keep the corners of his mouth from plummeting down to his nipples, as he watched Ojectica hand Baxter three one thousand dollar bills.

"Now, now, Oilio. Let's see that smile." As he glanced up to watch Oilio muster a strained smile, Baxter's own smile melted at the sight of the ominous white eyes that stared at him as they approached the glass doors behind the young clerk. As the doors slid open and Cereal Man entered, Baxter grabbed the box of Ensign Crunch. "You know what?" he said. "I'll need a treat after choking down all this repulsive dirt food."

"Gosh, the Ensign's a super treat, Sir!" said Oilio.

"Are you kidding me? All the money I just spent in this dump, and the richest indulgence you toilet-drinkers can throw my way is this box of glorified rat pellets?"

"I'd be glad to grab you a couple boxes of Lieutenant Commander Crunch from aisle one forty-four, Sir! Got a real bargain goin' on those, Sir!"

"No, no, I don't want cereal. Cereal's disgusting. Don't you think so?"

"Oh, absolutely, Sir! The customer is always right! Yeah, I can't stand cereal either, Sir!"

"Do you sell any kind of grease candy?"

"Why, the sweetest and the greasiest, Sir!"

"Then off with you," he commanded. "Get this disgusting cereal out of my sight, and select for me your very shiniest and stickiest treats directly. On the double, now! I'm in a hurry!"

"Yes, Sir!" Oilio dashed off in a glide that accelerated into a breakneck ass-tear while Baxter stood there, whistling, and waiting for Cereal Man. Ojectica also stood there, now rather apprehensive toward Baxter, and unnerved by the foreboding stranger approaching from behind.

In the middle of a tune Baxter was struggling to create, Cereal Man arrived at the counter and stood next to him. He stared at the youth only for a second before coolly commanding, "Let's go."

"Hey, good morning," he replied with cheer. "I was just getting some cereal."

"Here you are, Sir!" said Oilio, flying back from the aisles and screeching to a halt at the checkout line. "You're going to flip over these, Sir!"

"What happened to that box of Ensign Crunch I had here?"

"Oh, I took that yucky box of crud back for ya, Sir! I got a mega-canister of Glucoclots just for you, Sir!"

"I never ordered those!"

"Wait'll you try them, Sir! My late uncle lost a foot to these babies, but y'know, they are worth it, Sir!"

"Just a second," said Cereal Man, blocking Baxter off. "What's in these things?"

Oilio erupted into a mischievous, slobbering chuckle. "Oh, heck if I know, Sir! Why it'd take me a whole shift just to sound out the name of the first item in the ingredients booklet, Sir!"

"Booklet?!"

"Oh, sure, Sir! I mean you'd have to pay a few processing fees, and it'd take a while for the whole thing to arrive, but we could special order it from the plant, and you could pick up the first few volumes in just a few months, Sir!"

"Why aren't they on the package?"

Oilio gurgled his way up to a big laugh at the strange, scary customer's joke. "That's a good one, Sir! Y'know I hear they used to actually do that?" Then with a chuckle, he added, ". . . Put ingredients on the package itself?"

Cereal Man, only now realizing he'd not seen the ingredients listed on anything for perhaps three decades, flared his nostrils and hissed, "And you want him to put these things in his body?"

"Well, everybody deserves a treat now and again, right, Sir?!" And then, winking at Baxter, he added. "And anything's better than cereal, eh, Sir?!"

Baxter, maintaining an icy smirk, did not have to listen to much more of Oilio's yuk-riddled attempt at bonding, as Cereal Man's arm soon occupied the whole of the young clerk's gullet. Soon Oilio found his love of Glucoclots waning. But to be fair, he had never had this many all at once. He tried to politely ask Cereal Man to stop force-feeding him, but whenever he tried to inhale, another fistful of wrapped candies was already scraping down his throat. Not until Cereal Man felt Oilio's esophagus stretch to the point of disconnection from his throat did he look up and realize that Baxter was gone.

21. BEATING THE WILD MAN

A h, the strength! The ferocity! The sheer force of life that shook the forests with every thunderous, celebratory roar! It felt great to snort, growl, and roar, then drink half the river and devour a god's bellyful of fish. This kept the inner furnace hot enough for the Wild Man to snort, growl, and roar even louder, then rip a tree out by its roots and thrash it about, just to get the other creatures going, and spread chaos throughout the forests. And so it would be until the dawn of counting.

Times had changed. The frosts had dropped ever lower with each winter. His people had stopped coming to his cave. Now, with the Golden Father lowest in the sky, the beast neared his people's frontier.

When out from the town there emerged a small band
Of well-seasoned hunters, all grim-faced and tanned
With the usual weapons of spears, clubs, and priest.
But the short swords of bronze were new to the beast.
He growled and he smiled, and he scratched up the sod
As the brave, hardy outfit surrounded their god.
Three mighty huffs did the beast belt with force.
And the men all did brace to stay their full course.
Now trap him! Now grab him! Now stab him and hit him!

Then block him! Then dupe him! Hornswoggle and trick him!
Bludgeon and batter and hammer and maul!
Now bash away, gash away, thrash away all!
He roared with great joy as he stumbled and bled,
And the men sang him praise when he finally fell dead.
Into the cart, he was thrown with a huff.
The cart was the priest's. He had such nice stuff.
They hauled in the beast on those newfangled wheels.
And the people bid welcome with sing-songy peals.
Upon a great altar, the priest raised his arms
As he drew out the Life to give to the farms.
Then placing his hand on the creature with care,
He felt a great spirit. 'Twas that of a bear.
The Wild Man then gasped and woke with a start
But felt a strange warmth that melted his heart
From the gaze of a harlot so foreignly fair
That his wildness boiled off and left but a stare.
She climbed on his big, hairy frame with a smile,
Then slid up and down on his flesh for a while.
And she heard him exclaim as he lapsed into bliss
Hohhh! HOHHH! HOHHHHHHHHH!

22. BAX END

Once upon a time in the universe, there lived a little planet called Earth. She was a good planet, kind-hearted, generous, and bursting with life. And classy! She had never made a name for herself as one to go crazy with her tectonics in some sad attempt to look younger than she really was. No, she entered her middle age with grace, understanding the fine art of gradual and subtle continental drift. She was a real looker, who seemed to glow with particular verve when her most precocious children had finally taken their first upright steps upon the grassy plains of her cradle continent. It pleased her when they grew fruitful and scattered abroad to the continents of her nursery, and even to the two playgrounds that divided the great ocean surrounding these continents.

It did not please her, however, when the children's increasing lust for tear-thirsty laughs emptied the cradle and nursery and converted the playgrounds to a frat house. And it certainly did not please her when children from all over the universe began to crash the kegger that already showed no end in sight. But it did please the Valhalla Syndicate. So the kegger raged on. But there were some who got lost in all the wacky fun and games—some whom the kegger had left in the shadows.

In the heart of Earth's capital, Valsalvalhallaville, there was the urban forest of Valhallaville. And next to the urban forest of Valhallaville was the nice little town of Twinkle, whose main road was Silverhorn Highway. But also running through Twinkle was Stankumm-Twinkle Road, a narrow, neglected backroad that ran underneath the Silverhorn Highway on its way to the unfocused hamlet of Stankumm, which the third-largest hatchery in the Kuenzi Family Sushi Bar and Sewage Recycling Facility had flooded some years back.

About ninety-nine feet south of the underpass, along the northbound side of Stankumm-Twinkle Road, wearing a dark blue suit, lay a young man whose ancestry traced directly back to the cradle continent. He lay motionless, face down in a shallow ditch with eleven bullets in his back. He also had a bullet in the back of his right leg. And also one in the back of his left leg. And his elbow. And his other elbow. Also one in the back of his skull. Actually, it was two. Actually, three. Also one in his ass. Well, two. Well, three. Well, make that nine.

"Stop resisting!" ordered the fair-haired, fair-eyed, fair police officer of the fair complexion, while blasting three more assholes into the ass of the man in the ditch. Then his gun began clicking, and he extended his hand. "Gimme another one."

"That was my last one," replied the handsome, brown-skinned officer behind him.

"Are you serious?"

"I mean, I got this one here, but there's only one bullet left in it."

"Hand it over."

"Hey, come on, partner, I think he's had enough."

"Has he? Or is it you who's had enough?"

"Look, the guy must've had at least half a dozen bullets in his back when we got here. But apparently, that wasn't enough for you!"

"He was comin' at me."

"Hey, you looted his pockets, jerked off to the photos of his wife ... I mean, the guy never moved, even when you texted the dick pics to his kids. I mean, Jon ... buddy ... He wasn't comin' at anybody, man."

He knew Ponch was right, and that was hard to take. For the past forty years or so, Jon had always commanded the good old-fashioned voice of White reason that could steer Ponch away from the wilder, more savage tendencies wired into his DNA, or La DNA, or El DNA, or whatever stuff a Mexican had in him that made him do the stuff he did. And now, to be restrained and mellowed out by him? This subordinate, who, even eleven years after Jon's promotion to corporal minor, still referred to him as "partner?" Jon found this even more embarrassing than that time when Ponch had corrected his grammar in front of a busty blonde they had pulled over to hit on. Still, Jon had always found enough tolerant grace to laugh off the egalitarian streak so espoused by his "naive, piñata-whacking little pal." But not now. This time, Jon threw his gun at Ponch as hard as he could, just to keep himself from pistol-whipping him in the crotch. The sight of the lead-filled dead guy gnawed ever more at them both. How could they ever have let this come to pass? This never would have happened on their old beat, way back, all those decades ago. "Good Old Days" was an understatement.

Back in the '70s and '80s, Jon could cast an accomplished grin over practically every perforated corpse of color that ballooned up inside any lootable car on the shoulders of the Southern California highway system. Back then, the Sun always kept the skies sunny, and no road led you astray. But all along, cloaked by the satisfying scent of fast bikes and easily impressed women, the stink of betrayal soured in wait. By the turn of the millennium, the highway system had become too convoluted and dangerous for the aging cops to comprehend. So the California Highway Patrol turned them over to Cop Drop, an employment agency for those too slow-witted to remain effective, but too good-looking to retire. That's how their old precinct put them both out to pasture on the Stankumm-Twinkle Underpass Beat.

Now, no longer CHP officers, the duo had been reduced to patrolling this run-down strip of shame. The beat that ran underneath Silverhorn Highway constituted a domain of pretty meager space, so they spent most of their shift just riding around in circles. That demeaned them enough. But to find an unarmed Black man next to their beat, gunned down by someone other than them, well, that could fuck with a man's pride. True, their beat technically extended only to the space underneath the overpass. But no way would the boys back at the station see it that way.

"Look, I know what you're thinking," Ponch added. "But don't beat yourself up. Sarge don't want to assign a night watch... Man, that's on him." As usual, this "tortilla-slapping simpleton" had no idea what went on in a man's head. No, far more advanced worries plagued the corporal minor. More and more, and more, the wounding possibility filled his mind that this might have happened during their shift, right under their noses—a notion unthinkable back in the old days. How many dirty, rotten, no-good highway pirates had they foiled back then? How many bank robbers who happened to be students of Evel Knievel had they put behind bars? Back then, how many wayward skateboard punks had been lessoned? How many runaway vehicles neutralized? How many escaped zoo animals punished? And how many unlicensed moving casinos had these honorable enforcers discovered and shut down for good?

But now, those golden days had also been shut down for good. And after spending their twilight years circling the parameters of this underpass and having to fill out a stupid status report for each trip around, Ponch and Jon's wits had become about as sharp as their soft, puffy asses. At least, the report for this circling would prove a little more interesting than highlights of the last seventeen years, like "hitchhiker ticketed," or "hitchhiker escaped," or the far more frequent, "litter showered from above."

Ponch climbed back onto his cycle, which grumbled and burbled with ennui. He revved up the engine, to ready himself, just in case any hitchhikers came into view as Jon filled out their 203,995th report. That's when Ponch noticed the enormous Ra Sewage tanker truck rambling along the right eastbound lane of the overpass, en route to return a lifetime collection of liquid and solid Ka Ka to some pharaoh in preparation for the afterlife.

"Hey, partner," he said.

"Corporal," Jon corrected.

"Last time I looked, the law says only gas-powered vehicles on Silverhorn Highway."

"So?"

"So unless that kid's roller skates got little engines on them, I'd say we're looking at a Class Three Super Felony." Jon looked up, with a scoff, and whitely resisted the urge to inform his "tequila-brained buddy" that there was no such thing as a Super Felony, only to drop his jaw at the sight of the godly chariot of shit speeding down the highway and towing a blond-haired teenage boy in roller skates. It was like a blast from the past! Some wayward punk, thinking himself clever, had snatched a free ride on the business end of a moving biohazard. Fate had presented them with a sight too good to be true.

But their beat only extended so far. Sarge didn't want them poking their noses into highway matters anymore. Only the young played that game. They had pushed their luck already just by investigating what could very well qualify as another precinct's Black shooting.

They couldn't just abandon their post to chase down some stupid kid who had decided to put the economy to sleep by using a mode of transportation that required no gas. They'd seen it before. Petulant, bitchy moms, convinced that their "good kid" had made a harmless mistake, would just snivel and bitch at Sarge until they annoyed him enough to drop the charges. It wouldn't take long. And yet, this wasn't just some two-bit punk doing his own thing, nor some roadside slob, sticking his thumb out to panhandle a ride. This was not just a beggar. Not just a moocher. No, Ponch had spotted a true criminal, who had stolen transportation—in essence, stolen gas from the oil companies.

Their moment was passing with every breath. If they didn't act now, their opportunity to become heroes, or at the very least, their opportunity for a few final minutes of real action, would vanish, perhaps forever. Jon looked at Ponch and knew that look in his eye—that excited, dangerous look from the old days. It made Jon's penis move a little. He tossed the report into the ditch and sprinted toward his grumbling cycle, which gurgled out a hopeful sentiment as he hopped on. He revved the engine as though ramming his dick into the exhaust pipe. The cycle responded with a burbly grunt of equally lecherous force. Then the duo tore away. Just two STUB cops, blazing onto the entrance ramp of Silverhorn Highway.

As they picked up speed, Jon checked his ride's highway-worthiness. Front wheel, check. Headlight, check. Tail light, check. Siren, check. Then the duo realized that, in their haste, they had started off in the wrong direction, and did an immediate about-face. As they cruised into the left lane and began passing all the cars on the highway, Ponch checked his cycle too. Headlight, check. CB, check. Turn signal, check. Red flashers, check. Front wheel, check. Everything looked good. Good, except they realized they had originally taken the correct direction after all and did another immediate about-face.

Now everything felt great. The two old buddies zoomed down the highway just as they once had. Jon cruised along, basking in his own pleasant smile and feeling the warmth of meaning once again shining down onto his White soul. He took care not to look at Ponch, in the same way that he took care not to look at a dog when that dog would most likely wag its tail and mistake eye contact as an invitation to come on over. He adjusted his shades, then looked down with adoration at his ID medal, then his badge. Then he squeezed the brake to avoid slamming into the car in front of him. Ponch cruised alongside, wearing the exuberant smile of someone who mattered again. And he couldn't help but direct that smile to his right, toward his partner. But Jon's failure to return the smile wouldn't get Ponch down. Thinking about his own sexy smile just made him smile even more. His badge looked impressive too. And his ID medal looked damn sharp. Even his Stankumm-Twinkle Underpass Beat shoulder patch looked snazzy as hell. He had arrived, back on the scene, and now blazed forth, ready for anything! He squeezed the brake to prevent rear-ending the car in front of him. Then he smiled again as they began to gain on the sewage truck now entering the outer limits of Twinkle.

The whine of sirens pinched Baxter's brain as he, with accelerating desperation, clutched the huge faucet on the back of the speeding tanker truck. Sweat sizzled between the faucet and his hands, while the steely gleam of the truck conspired with scalding exhaust fumes to magnify the already sweltering air blowing in his face. He managed to turn his head far enough around to catch a glance of two asinine smiles topping two obsolete pairs of red flashing lights, as they weaved closer to him. Before he knew it, they had come alongside, Ponch on his left, Jon on his right. Their smiles had disappeared.

"You're under arrest," Jon shouted. "Get on the ground and put your hands on your head."

Baxter stared at him. "Are you out of your mind?"

"Slowly," warned Ponch, trying to look all tough.

"Do it," Jon ordered.

"No!" said Baxter.

"What'd you say?" Jon barked. "Put up your hands, and I mean now!" Baxter shook his head and held on tighter. "Now, I said!" Baxter shook his head again and continued to cling to the faucet.

Ponch reached over and jerked on his left arm. "You heard him, punk! Let go!"

Then Jon yanked on his right arm, "I told you, you're under arrest!"

"Yeah, now you got three seconds before you make me mad, pal. One..."

"Don't make this harder, buddy."

"Two..."

"We're not fooling."

All the while they yanked and jerked on his arms, and all the while Baxter shook his head with more and more vigor as he drew himself closer and closer to the faucet. By the time Ponch had inhaled to say "three," Baxter had curled up around the faucet, with his legs folded over the pipe, his arms wrapped around the cross handle, his head just under the mouth of the faucet, and his back mere inches above the hot pavement that continued to scream past him.

"Hey, get off of there!" Jon ordered.

"Alright, now you made me mad," said Ponch, whipping out his pistol and aiming it at the youth as best he could while still watching the road. "I'm gonna count to three again..."

"Wait a minute, you can't just shoot him," Jon hollered.

"What?"

"Put the gun away."

"I can't hear ya, partner."

Jon got on the CB. "You can't just shoot him. We gotta think of something else," he said.

Ponch picked up his CB. "What do you mean I can't? He's not coming down," he said, trying harder than ever to keep his aim with his other hand.

"Yeah, but you can't shoot him."

"Why? Because he's White?"

After a three-second pause, Jon said, "You only got one bullet left, remember? What if you need it for something?"

"I can get more at the store, on the way back."

"Goddammit, we are not stopping at the store, Ponch!"

"Hey, there's a cute Asian girl I like there."

Jon paused again, "Rong Shi?"

"No, no, on the contrary, Shi Right... Fo Mai Dong!"

As the two septuagenarian flatbutts shared a juvenile laugh while manning their motorcycles with a collective total of one hand, Baxter worked his way up to a squatting position on top of the huge faucet. He managed to hold himself steady by gripping the cross handle that controlled the valve. Ponch and Jon noticed this just as a small dump truck came zooming up from behind, honking and blinking its headlights. By the time it came within arm's reach of the faucet, the Ra Sewage driver, with a strong sense of etiquette, shifted into the right lane, to allow this rude dump truck driver to pass. The tanker veered to the right, causing Baxter to swing around counterclockwise on the cross handle on the faucet. Then, like a frog wearing roller skates, the boy launched himself from the top of the faucet toward the dump truck. As the truck passed, he caught its right side mirror and found his skates roaring along the pavement again. The door to the truck had a decal that read, "Red's Herring Hookup."

422

As Ponch and Jon began to catch up, Baxter grabbed the handle of the door and made his way down the side of the speeding truck. Ponch caught up with him first and commanded him to get on the ground. Baxter shook his head and continued to claw his way toward the back. Just as Ponch took out his handcuffs, the wheels on Baxter's right skate gave out. The metal under the shoe hit the pavement, showering sparks all over Ponch. The old officer fell back, allowing the sparks to fly onto the leaky gasoline tanker that the dump truck was now passing. Baxter climbed up the outside of the truck and jumped straight down into the dumping bed, which could hold up to three tons of herring on a lucky day.

It was empty. Not that Baxter would have recognized a herring, even if he had landed in a truckload of them. Herring had swum past the extinction line years ago, around the turn of the millennium, like most aquatic life. Red didn't mind driving around aimlessly in an empty truck, though. To not do so would undermine and betray the job creators, a heresy as un-American as going to school for non-profiteering purposes. This was the same as letting the terrorists win, whatever terrorists were.

A gunshot cracked the air. The truck collapsed to the right and began grinding along the highway. Ponch had used his last bullet to blow the right front tire, much to his corporal's annoyance. Baxter, feeling the rapid deceleration of the vehicle, climbed over the left side of the bed and jumped onto the top of the next passing car—specifically, onto the red and blue lights of a patrol car for the Twinkle Constabulary. Recognizing his stroke of bad luck, he tumbled down the back of it, grabbed the rear bumper, and landed his remaining skate on the highway. Jon caught this acrobatic stunt and buzzed ahead in hot pursuit. Ponch soon followed, after issuing Red a traffic impediment citation and abandoning him in the middle of the highway.

Constable Trent had just finished stirring some artificial sweetener into an ice cream soda from Shucky Darn's Frankfurter Barn for Constable Brent when they both jolted from a huge slamming sound on the roof of their squad car. After a long silence between the two of them, Trent handed him the beverage and asked, "Did we just go under an overpass or something?"

"Nah, man," said Brent, tapping the brakes. "Sounded like some kid wearing roller skates just fell from an empty fish truck or something." He rolled down the power windows.

"Jeezis, what're you doing," said Trent.

"Take a look and see if you can see anything."

"It took all morning to cool it down in here," Trent bitched.

"Hey, come on," Brent smiled. "These are the sacrifices of service, right?"

Trent climbed out, sat in the opened window, discovered the crushed red and blue lights, and traced a line of bloody smears to the rear of the car, where Baxter shot him a look of dread.

"It is a kid! On one roller skate," he yelled, leaning down into the window. "He's hooked onto the bumper. We gotta get off the road, now!" As Brent started slowing and merging toward the shoulder, Trent hollered to Baxter, "Hold on, kid! We're pulling over right now! Don't you let go, you hear me, buddy? Stay with us!" Trent climbed back in. "Okay," he sighed as Brent continued to merge right. "Okay," he repeated. "Okay, dude, can you shut the windows, now"

"How much cool-off time you think you got anyway," said Brent, rolling them up. "Like thirty seconds?"

"Oh, dude, don't even."

"What, we pull over, and then what? We just sit here with the engine running until he lets go, and then we just, what, take off and go about the rest of our day? No questions, no nothin'?"

424

"Questions, my huge hard honker! What're we gonna ask this guy? 'Good morning, kid. How about those Twinkies? Man alive, do they have a team this year or what?'"

"Dude, this poor guy might have some serious problems. We can't just drop him off and go."

"Are you fuckin' serious?"

"And you gotta put your shirt back on."

"What the fuck?! What about you?!"

"I'll put mine on too."

"If I had known when we got in this fuckin' car this morning..."

"Hey-hey," Brent chirped.

"Yeah, yeah," Trent grumbled. "Sacrifices of service. Tell me this, then: If we were just going to go around wearing shirts all the time like a couple of assholes, why the hell did we waste all that money on these badge tattoos?"

Before they could get all the way over to the shoulder, the STUB officers came upon them, with Ponch on the left, ordering Brent to pull over, and Jon on the right, ordering Trent to order Brent to pull over.

"'The hell?" said Trent. "What do these guys want?"

"Only one way to find out," said Brent, with his finger moving toward the power window switch.

"Du-uude," Trent whined.

"Oh, fine," Brent sighed. "Can't live without your AC for five fuckin' seconds? What do we do, then? These clowns want something."

"Holy shit," said Trent upon closer inspection. "Dude, they're fuckin' STUBs!"

"Are you sure?"

"Ch-ch-yeah, dude," he belted out with horse-like cackles. "Dude, they're like a hundred and eleven years old, and they wanna race!"

"Hoh-hoh-hoh-hoh-hohhh…" Brent laughed dangerously while handing Trent the ice cream soda. Trent rolled down his window and threw the entire cup right at Jon, beaming the old dipshit in the face and splashing the pink, sugary, jizzy-looking dessert drink down on his pressed uniform. Trent blasted out a wild, childish laugh as Brent stomped on the gas. With a squeal of smoking rubber, they tore ass down the highway, running the bright red light at Choo Choo Train Lane. Ponch drew his pistol, aimed at their rear tire, and pulled the trigger multiple times before gawking in astonishment at the magically impervious squad car of the Twinkle Constabulary, as it escaped undamaged.

Brent and Trent blazed on ahead, celebrating with merry laughs and inarticulate cheers as they zigged and zagged between all manner of trucks, and cars, and other things that go. They passed a Pontiac Laneswiper, a Yugo Putster, a Dodge Dirtster, a Jeep Shitster, a Ford Viagro, a tractor converted into a stretch limo, a Buick Rapscallion, a fleet of Harley-Davidson Dicktreats, Sasquatcholas, Vadgewreckers and Roadswines, a terrified child strapped with duct tape into a Big Wheel with a small but effective rocket mounted on its aft, a 747 that had wandered off its runway, a Volkswagen Frankenfucker, a Suzuki Myagi-go, a Geo Clerk, a Nissan Etcetera, a Plymouth Afterthought, and another teenager on roller skates clinging to the bumper of a slower police vehicle.

Ponch and Jon had almost caught up with Brent and Trent as they barreled past Sultan Scott's—rebuilt, upgraded, and shinier than ever. Beholding this dazzling petrol palace only worsened the sinking feeling in Baxter's stomach. The familiar sight of Tarbutts, Cyclie's, and Shucky Darn's, which he'd absorbed only minutes ago, and which he had craved with such obsession during his high-speed adventure with Jenny and Wheeler, had met him with an unaccountable emptiness.

They all looked exactly the same as he had remembered, yet they made him feel rather swindled. But this new Sultan Scott's seemed worse. It made him feel almost... violated.

Just then, Baxter noticed another dump truck ahead, sputtering along in the adjacent lane, transporting a load of old people down the highway. The youth could not behold this sight without experiencing a pang of sentimentality. He craned far over enough to spy the familiar Blackwick Geria-truck design on the vehicle. No doubt about it, he knew this truck. But then he told the sentimentality to go fuck itself with a cast iron pan. This homecoming held nothing in store for him. How could anyone kiss the soils of an island that bobbed atop such a stinking sea of manure? Though he'd gladly hang himself from the ceiling fan of his bedroom to avoid braving the eddies of that sea again, what would he do here in Twinkle? Sure, he'd save Mom. Goody. Mom, who'd brought him into this world. Out of all the worlds in the universe, she brought him into this one. So, he'd save her, and then what? Nothing, that's what. He'd do nothing, and then he'd die.

The truck now slowed for its turn onto Sparkling Creek Drive. If he didn't catch it now, he would lose his chance to save her forever. Might as well. What else did he have going? Nothing, that's what. But what if he just let go and allowed himself to be smeared all over the highway and washed off the pavement into the sewer drains like any other insignificant, less cleverly disguised road vermin? What if? But then his recent adventure would prove an even bigger waste of time.

With a sneer, he released himself from the squad car and propelled himself toward the truck, just as it turned. The pile of old folks all watched the youth teeter and sway on his remaining skate before he managed to latch onto the edge of the open dumping bed. He tried to pull himself forward and climb on board, but many of the old fogies scoffed and attempted to shame him with wandering tales of how, back in their day, kids used to hitch dump truck rides while wearing ice skates. This became so annoying that Baxter found himself happier to hang back and contemplate how long a streak he would create on the highway if he just opened up his hands.

By the time the truck crossed Winking Sun Lane, some of the more focused boastings had degenerated into inter-codgerly exchanges of one-upmanship, which gave rise to assorted knots of grunting and struggling, known to them as fighting. Soon after, they began to pass the Big Bright Lakes Drive-Thru Mall and Super Cigarette Outlet. He hated that place. He wished someone would burn it to the ground. But what difference did it make? He would still be here. He chuckled with scorn, then realized how useless it was to do so, which caused him to chuckle with even more scorn at the previous scornful chuckle. A lot of good that did. He chuckled with still more scorn. By the time his chuckles reached their thirty-third degree of scorn depth, he passed the Merry Weather Service Station. As always, Lewis shot him a hearty smile and an encouraging thumbs-up. But, seeing Baxter return his support with a gaze so foreign, so divorced from warmth and familiarity, caused the friendly and busy attendant to just sit down in a puddle and reevaluate his world.

Baxter felt someone slap a handcuff onto his left wrist. He turned around to find Ponch riding along next to him, and punctuating this maneuver with a toothy, staccato laugh. The youth looked down at the pair of handcuffs dangling from his wrist. Unable to perform a calculation that explained Ponch's perception of victory, he looked back to the officer, searching for clues in his stupid-looking face. Then, he felt someone slap another cuff on his right wrist. He turned around to find Jon riding alongside, wearing a grin whose depth of satisfaction could accommodate only the most supreme administration of justice.

Baxter looked down at the pairs of unconnected handcuffs dangling from his wrists, then watched the two cops lean over on their bikes and attempt to finish their cuffing jobs. Jon succeeded, but Ponch's ability was undermined by his collision with the corner of the truck as it slowed down to turn. Jon bumped into the other corner immediately afterward. Then Baxter watched them wobble along behind him for a moment before they lost control and crashed into the street sign posted at the corner of Sparkling Creek Drive and Smiley Meadows Avenue.

A savory aroma wafted into the boy's nostrils, which, in a magical instant, regenerated a bit of morale. He took in the succulent olfactory issue from Meatball Time!, just down the street. And there stood the big old sign that now boasted "Over 311 Served," and that great big giant meatball clock on top, which indicated that, no matter what time of day, it was always "Meatball Time!" The clock struck 11:55. Thank heavens! He still had time!

As the truck rambled past the restaurant, Baxter's chest swelled at how much more he had become. He no longer considered himself a mere child of his hometown. He was more than just a Twinkling. He had become an Earthling. As the young Earthling gulped in a nose full of deliciousness, he warmed to the appetizing, comforting aroma of Home. But hunger soon turned into nausea, and comfort soon became anxiety. The aroma had become tainted by the ubiquitous, though previously cloaked, void that lay in wait as the shadow of every small pleasure and every joyous occasion. It had always been here, he knew now.

But now the veil was gone, and the void lay there, naked, spread out, grinning flirtatiously as it fanned its rotting genitals at him. And yet, something remained beyond all of this; something about Mom and her unconditional love that seemed to place Baxter back in the moment, where time seemed to vanish. With Mom, no past or future existed, and thus, no regrets or worries—nothing outside. This was Home.

Well, almost. This was the nursing home. Emerging from his battle between hope and hopelessness, Baxter now found himself submerged in a heap of writhing, whimpering old people, freshly dumped with him onto a tile floor. Despite his bound hands, he clawed his way out from under the pile to get a look around. He recognized it as the main lobby at Blackwick! That dirty, rotten place! If they hadn't fired Mom for looking so ugly, she could have finished paying for the operation reversal herself, just as she had done for years, and he would never have needed to embark on such a terrible adventure. This place had ruined his life, and he'd be damned if he would ever set foot in it again.

He hopped up on his feet, slipped upon his roller skate, slammed his ass down on the tile floor, crawled over to the nearest door, grabbed the handle, clawed his way up the door, stabilized himself on his skate, then opened the door and propelled himself outside, into the loading zone. At the main entrance, he noticed a new obnoxious flashing sign, which showcased this month's main events for active seniors:

Hospice for Dummies: Tuesdays, 8:00 a.m. – 8:30 a.m.

Name That Relative: Thursdays, 8:00 a.m. – 8:15 a.m.

Open Mic Night: Mondays, 10:15 a.m. – 11:00 a.m.

Casino Night! BINGO and all-night Pill Poker: this Sunday, 9:00 a.m. – 11:00 a.m.

Baxter ignored the rest and skated away. He had no time to indulge himself in how disgusted he was with this place for developing such a high-profile entertainment scene. The giant meatball clock read 11:57 a.m.! He skated himself across the street to the pleasant-looking yellow suburban house in which he had grown up. In his haste through the living room into Mom's bedroom, everything seemed just as he remembered it. The immaculate carpet of sparkling white, the soft lemony hue of the walls, and the softer pink of the plush sofa and easy chairs, which faced the huge, old-timey TV set. He failed to notice that someone had smashed it in and flooded it with a stomach's bounty of rejected Kryptonian sour mash.

"Mom, I made it! I have the—"

Where was Mom? Where was everybody?! Where was anybody?! Nobody in the bedroom. Nobody in his room. Nobody in the kitchen. Nobody in the bathroom. Nobody was Home! Baxter skated out to the front door. Maybe someone left a note. No note! No note! He danced around on his one leg with his eyes darting every direction at once. Then he noticed the obnoxious sign across the street again. The bottom of it read, "TONIGHT ONLY! The Magic of the Spring Break Scrapers: 11:30 a.m - Noon."

Across the street, past the lobby, in the dining hall, the clock struck 11:58 a.m. Hungry Blackwick residents fingered through their saucers of Fleshstic mush. Most of them normally ate with utensils, but they couldn't see their lunches with the lights dimmed like this, and they had no time to argue. Only another hour until dinner, and then, off to bed. In the meantime, the Great Dr. Dice continued to draw their awe with his whirling satin cape of black and scarlet, but mostly with the gallon-sized sandwich bag that he held on sweeping display in his white-gloved hand. His crew held the spotlights on the bag with such precision that even the more cataract-stricken spectators could confirm its emptiness.

In the stirrups behind the great magician lay Amber, a nineteen-year-old sociology major who had drunk far too much during the last spring break to know or remember any of her seed donors, but not enough to poison the figure-wrecking parasite inside of her that had chased away new donors for the last six or seven months. Dr. Dice's lovely assistants, Ms. Lisa and Ms. Leslie, spun the wheeled stirrups around and around on the stage, as the drum rolled and rolled, and the audience oohed and ahhed. Dr. Dice whirled his cape, then flashed his other white-gloved hand over his patient's swollen abdomen. Then the crescendo ended with a magnificent clash of cymbals as Dr. Dice flapped the bag in the air. His stunned onlookers were delighted to behold a bloody fetus sealed in that same plastic bag that had been, just an instant ago, empty.

As his crowd applauded as loudly as they could without fracturing or rupturing anything, Dr. Dice bowed with majesty and removed his famed black top hat from his head, showing its empty interior for all to see. Then, just as the fetus began to untangle one of its legs from a cluster of blood vessels, Dr. Dice dropped it into the hat. When he flipped the hat downward, nothing fell back out. Cymbals clashed! As the crowd cheered, he placed the hat back on his head, and his crew played a celebratory tune. This distracting cacophony always marked the part when he would secretly press the little puree button on the rim of the hat. Then, Lovely Ms. Leslie took his cape and his hat to the dressing room. As she hung the cape and poured the gloppy contents of the hat down the toilet, Lovely Ms. Lisa introduced the hat and cape for his final act.

By the time Dr. Dice donned this outfit of black and purple, the crew had moved Darla onstage. She also lay in a hospital bed with stirrups, so doped up that her screams and pleas for mercy only came out as moans and groans of incoherence. As the lovely assistants rotated her around and around onstage, and the drums began to roll once again, Dr. Dice drew from his cape a small glass jar. Suspended in a solution of Crystal Fleshstic Jelly, a pink pair of ovaries quivered with anticipation and started to grow little cilia that began reaching for their original host. As the drum roll built, and Darla's moaning and groaning intensified into actual screams, little black bubbles formed on the cilia. As the clock struck 11:59 a.m., Baxter burst into the room.

"I HAVE YOUR GODDAMN MONEY, YOU SHIT FACES! THREE THOUSAND DOLLARS! I HAVE IT HERE!" he bellowed toward the stage.

The music stopped, the audience gasped, and Dr. Dice darted his head toward the youth. Baxter pumped his way toward the stage on his skate, amid the confused murmurs of the audience. Dr. Dice did nothing to help, not even motion for his crew to assist the youth. Instead, he stood there, twirling his mustachio with one hand, while stretching his other hand out for payment. Supremely annoyed, Baxter rolled himself up onto the stage. With a lump of mutilated metal beneath one foot, a set of wobbly wheels beneath the other, and his hands still bound, the youth found it impossible to prop himself up. Dr. Dice didn't want anyone to help, but he could perceive his audience grumbling with boredom. So he had Lovely Ms. Leslie help the boy up. But then, Baxter found digging into his pockets for the payment almost as difficult. The audience found this funny, so Dr. Dice allowed it to go on. The boy had to tear the pocket open to even get his hands inside. but then he couldn't move his hands around at all. He jerked and twisted and tore his shorts open. They fell down to his ankles, and the audience laughed at his bare ass. Ignoring them, he bent down and reached inside the pocket.

The money was gone. Baxter checked again. The money was gone. After all that! His mind raced. The money was gone. The money was gone. It must have fallen out! Fallen out of his pocket. At any time on the road. Luckily, he found it in his other pocket and he stood up to fork it all over—one thousand, two thousand, three thousand—as the clock struck high noon. Dr. Dice pocketed the money and tipped his top hat in a most gentlemanly fashion. Then a drum roll began. In another sweeping gesture, he again presented the jar of lustful ovaries to his spectators. Baxter detected police sirens outside—really stupid sounding police sirens. With finality, Dr. Dice dumped the contents of the jar into his top hat. Then he flipped the hat over. Nothing came out, and the cymbals clashed!

As the crowd cheered, he placed the hat back on his head. His crew joined him on stage, along with the band, who played a final celebratory tune for the merriment of all. Dr. Dice smiled and shot a big old wink at Baxter, who tittered in response. Then the magician pressed the puree button and made sure Baxter could hear the blender inside his hat, destroying those awful bringers of awful life that had once plagued his mother. The Great Dr. Dice wrapped his arm around the youth's shoulder, then wrapped his other arm around Lovely Ms. Lisa's shoulder. Then they all faced the audience with grateful smiles.

Then Dr. Dice's head exploded. Then the top hat dropped onto his shoulders and the rest of him collapsed. Lovely Ms. Lisa's head also blew up, then the Lovely Ms. Leslie's too, causing Baxter to fall to the floor right along with her. Then Katie, the little drummer girl's head was blown off; well, most of it. Then Cybil the cymbalist's, then Trudy the trumpeter's. By the time Baxter watched most of Suzy the sousaphonist's head leave her shoulders, he realized these heads hadn't actually exploded. The huge hole in the sousaphone bell revealed that everyone's heads were being shot off by someone from the back of the room. The bullets simply did so much damage that not much more than a jaw was left on the top of each neck. Crew members scurried around, trying to do their duties and clean up the mess, but they found their heads blown off as soon as they got close to Baxter. Then the gun went silent, perhaps to reload.

Baxter sat up and found that everyone surrounding him had been shot. There he sat, alone in the spotlights, an open target. Luckily, dozens of residents had bottlenecked at the nearest exit. He rolled off the stage and pumped his way over there in a desperate hope to lose himself in the crowd, at least long enough to remove his skates. He dove into the middle of the crowd, knocking over a few oldsters, but also securing himself a sheltered spot on the floor. Then, one by one, the unknown assailant began shooting the members of the crowd. By the time the assailant had blown the heads off half of the residents shielding Baxter from view, the skates had come off.

As fortune would have it, the entire crowd kept filing through only one side of the double doors at the nearest exit in the dining hall, leaving each side of the double doors at the other ten exits free. Baxter bolted for the next nearest exit. But just as he touched the handle to the door, he heard another shot fired, and Mom screamed worse than that time when she had dropped her last cigarette into the garbage disposal. Baxter turned around to find a bloody crater in her chest. He flew from the door, up onto the stage, then tripped and crashed onto the bed, bowling himself and Mom onto the floor. He turned his head and his face met hers. Her look of profound puzzlement morphed into horror.

"Hang in there, Mom!" he said, scrambling into a sitting position and grabbing hold of her.

"Get away," she said.

"What?!" he squeaked with outrage. "After all I've—"

"GO!" she screamed. "STAY AWAY FROM ME!"

"Now just a minute!" he demanded, with a struggle. Never in his life had he ever talked back to Mom. But how could she say that to him? "You can't just leave me alone in this, this—"

"Look what you've done," she said.

He surveyed the room full of corpses, then turned his head back to his mother's opened chest and watched her heart stop beating. The clamor of the escaping crowd seemed to fade into the sound of police sirens. His face dropped into catatonia.

A gloved hand came up just behind him and nabbed him.

He was gone by the time Ponch and Jon walked in. They were pretty banged up, but no worse than their adventures had banged them up, each and every week, back in the old days. It made them feel young and tough. Jon glanced over at Ponch's sunglasses, trying to sneak another look at the reflection of his own toughness, but grew annoyed instantly.

"Would you put that thing away?" he criticized. We're out of bullets, for god's sake."

"Hey, relax, partner," Ponch said, putting his gun away. "You can never be too careful, you know?"

"What the hell happened in here, anyway?" said Jon, now putting his own empty gun away.

"Why don't we ask one of them," said Ponch, indicating the remaining handful of residents still trying to make their way out of the exit.

"I don't feel like it. Last thing I need is a bunch of old folks talking my ear off with their tall tales of old times."

"Hey, that reminds me of that one time, back in seventy-six! 'Member? The bicentennial parade on the ten, with all those World War One vets who just wouldn't stop talking? And then there was that earthquake? With the tsunamis? And we cleared that freeway up, man, and saved every one of those vets?! Maaan, the girls were hot for us that night, huh? WHOO!"

"Hey, cool it, alright? Let's just see if we can find that punk."

"What if he's one of these stiffs?"

"Well then I'd say our work is finished, wouldn't you?"

"No, I mean ID. Everyone's head is blown to bits."

"Then look for tufts of blond hair. I'll look for the faggoty half shirt and shorts."

"What about skates?" asked a menacing voice from behind them. They both wheeled around to find a rather disturbed-looking stranger walking in from the lobby: jet-black hair, long black coat, white eyes, like David Banner used to get in the *Incredible Hulk* TV series. Jon had seen those eyes before, long ago. He took a step back, trying not to shudder. Hulk-like eyes were nothing to take lightly.

"Hey, what do you know about it, pal?!" said Jon's former foolish partner and current naive subordinate in his most well-rehearsed macho posture. This blockhead had no clue how angry someone had to get in order to have white eyes like this. But it served him right for having spent all of his off-duty hours back in the '70s with all those hot girls, instead of making a single appearance at Jon's Friday night Hulk parties.

"Yeah, what do you know about it, bub?!" Jon blurted out for reasons beyond his own calculation.

"The kid was on a pair of roller skates, right?" said Cereal Man. "Little green bow ties on them?"

"Yeah, so what?" said Ponch.

"Just what do a couple of glorified meter maids like you want with a kid like that?"

"Hey, watch it, buddy," Ponch replied. "For your information, we're hauling his butt in. For moving violations."

"Moving violations," Cereal Man repeated.

"That's right," said Ponch, pointing to the surrounding carnage. "But we were thinking he might be here in this room. You know, dead."

Then Cereal Man noticed Darla, lying dead on the stage. He rushed over to her. The STUBs followed. Regret poured into his chest as he knelt and embraced his ruined friend of old. "Whoever

437

did this didn't kill the kid," he said. "The kid's out there somewhere. Somebody's got him."

"Damn it!" said Jon. "You mean another precinct?"

"Aw, Sarge'll really have our hides now," moaned Ponch.

"No, I don't mean another fucking precinct," Cereal Man growled.

"Man! Now I wish he *was* dead—all mangled up and blown wide open like this elephant lady here," Ponch complained, indicating Darla's corpse.

"Yeah, no need to haul him in then," Jon chuckled. "I think he'd have learned his lesson."

"Yeahhah-hah-hah-hah," Ponch cackled. "Good one, partner!"

"Corporal," Jon corrected.

"Yeah, I guess we'd just have to drop him off at Grossie's place," Ponch added. "Satisfy that kinky fetish he's got for stiffs."

"At least it wouldn't be a moving violation," quipped Jon as the two of them spluttered into a raucous storm of back-slapping guffaws. Then time seemed to freeze for Jon as Cereal Man slit his throat. Then it resumed as Ponch's laughter melted into the very beginnings of realization of the bloody deed. Then time seemed to freeze for Ponch, right after Cereal Man had run the same blade across his throat. Then it resumed as Cereal Man walked past the residents, still trying to make their way out of the exit nearest the stage. Then it seemed to freeze again as Ponch and Jon writhed around on the floor, trying in vain to stop bleeding. Then it resumed as Cereal Man made his way toward another exit. Then it froze again as Jon began strangling Ponch for calling him "partner." Then it resumed as Cereal Man walked out the door.

From space, the Earthling watched as the horizon of diseased clouds curved, then formed a sphere. And for the first time, Earth was a place. Not a flat, ill-defined experience that faded away when you weren't looking: one place, which was there whether you knew it or not—and had been there. Just one place. He tried to shed a tear for Mom as he watched Earth get smaller and smaller. Then he stopped trying.

It's a shame she didn't live. But then again, who cares?

The infected urine hue of the streetlight cast Cereal Man's long, blue-black shadow in front of him as he roamed along the narrow shoulder of NE Knopfler Street. Even though night had fallen, the heat had become unreal. The overcast sky glowed from the city it smothered. Talons of ashy mist clawed the wet pavement and laid such a tarry stench on what remained of the air that Cereal Man could hardly breathe without getting sick. He turned into an alley where dumpsters overflowed with trash, the pavement glittered with litter, the residents burst with bile, and the red brick walls flapped with posters old and new. All of it cooked under the pink neon sign for Lady Buckley's Tarot Card Casino and the green neon sign for The Vomiting Bear.

Cereal Man now added a light of his own upon drawing a small Plutonium Sugar Bomb from his grocery bag. As he munched on the green chunk of raw power, he noticed an odor worse than the nearby hills of trash—worse than the slick pavement, from which filthy fluids evaporated in the heat, leaving rankness of ever higher concentrations. It wafted along as a sordid, sweet scent. One that he knew all too well. Sure enough, right next to him, sweating worse than the pavement, stood Captain Candyroo, who had waddled into the alley after him.

"Hey, hoser," he said, grinning with satisfaction. "Well, jerk my jellybean. Looks like you're all alone, again. Sucky business back at Blackwick. Guess nobody can really go back Home, huh?"

Cereal Man grabbed the front of his filthy brown suit and began wringing it. As the suit got tighter and tighter, thick, dark humors began to burst out of the captain, who, despite the pain, grew more and more amused.

"Putrid fucking vomit slug! You think this is a fucking hoot, is that it? Darla's lying dead back there with a hole in her chest the size of a cereal bowl!" growled Cereal Man.

"Bummer," said Captain Candyroo, struggling to squeeze the word out between gurgling laughs.

"WHERE'S THE KID?! Where is he? Or maybe you think you'll still be laughing after I pop your fucking insides out all over these walls."

"AGHHH!" yelped the captain, as the intensity of the pain began to win out. "I don't know where the fuck he is. What, do you think *I* fucking did this?!"

"Then what're you here for? Waddling your sweet-stinking frame in here after me just to get cute?"

"Whll, yeah," said the captain, knowing full well that his old friend would remember the beauty of the antagonistic friendship they once enjoyed.

"Say hello to your crew for me," said Cereal Man, reminding his old friend that he never saw any beauty in it and that such antagonism had only been enjoyed by him, the eternal instigator, and only during the brief moments that preceded terrifyingly huge doses of pain, like this one...

"AGGHCK-CK-CK! WAIT! I swear. I swear I didn't do it—it wasn't me! But I know who it was!"

"Bullshit," said Cereal Man, wringing him again.

"Listen to me!" begged the captain. "He's still alive. On his way to see the boss. We still got plenty of time."

Cereal Man reduced the pressure. "Time for what?"

"To catch him. It's a long-ass trip. To the other side of the universe."

"You and me," said Cereal Man. "What the fuck makes you dumb enough to think I'd even go halfsies on a carton of chocolate milk with you?"

"Listen, hose... You and I intercept the kid. I turn his ass in and get my just desserts. Then we break him out and he's yours. I was supposed to turn that kid in. Me! Me and my crew, and now this other goon has him. This nobody!"

"What nobody?"

"You think I'm telling you, you baggy-eyed, five-star fucking hose-a-thon?"

Cereal Man released him, absorbing the full magnitude of the proposal: A direct path to Baxter! He never could have dreamed of such fortune twice in his life. But once in the custody of his father, Baxter would remain heavily guarded, and inside the strongest fortress in the universe, wherever it was. But the opportunity made his nostrils flare and his heart race. Captain Candyroo's buddies were Cereal Man's as well.

The time had come to administer justice far beyond the rescue of a downy-haired young man. At long last, the time had come to crash this nightmarish orgy—to pop in on the two founders of the corporate monster from which this endless megalopolis took its name. Time to cripple that which had long ago absorbed comparatively puny entities like Exxon/Pepsi, Vulveeta/Trojan, Monsanto/Tyson, and Lego/Hormel, and which had merged everything else—that which owned essentially *everything*. Checkmate was coming. This would not please the Valhalla Syndicate.

As the pair of them looked outside the alley, their gazes rose from the wet, black pavement, to the image of the headlights of cars, which rippled and distorted from the radiation of the street. Then they looked up toward the billowing overcast sky, lit goldenrod by the city. Their mind's eyes scanned past the blanket of smog, to the stars they knew waited out there. Their bounty also waited, somewhere out there among those stars. Then, down from the ceiling of smog, flakes of snow, some the size of dimes, others the size of silver dollars, began plummeting down to the pavement.

"Times have changed," said Cereal Man.

"Sure as sugary shits they have," agreed Captain Candyroo. "No matter. It's fuckin' hot out. No way this shit's gonna stick."

The two of them stepped out into the streets, avoiding further dialogue and eye contact in the interest of preserving this barely tolerable alliance, at least for now. Behind them, the posters and flyers on the alley walls fluttered from a hot, snowy gust. The poster that had hung behind Cereal Man was a large one, which showed the humanoid rat in full color and infinite resolution, this time only from the chest up. An obnoxious sign towered over him from behind. Most of it remained out of the shot, but the bottom of it read, "TONIGHT ONLY! The Magic of the Spring Break Scrapers: 11:30 a.m – Noon."

A deeper look into the poster showed the reflection in his visor to include a terrified security guard with a cheap shield badge on his chest that said, "Blackwick Elderly Care." The guard's hand held a camera pointed at the rat. In the guard's mouth was the muzzle of a handgun, pointed at his own brain. Pulling back the hammer on the gun was the rat's gloved right hand. Still deeper inspection of the reflection from the rat's visor revealed another sign, back in the distance, just to the right of the guard's head. The sign said, "Meatball Time!," and, "Over 311 served." The meatball clock read "11:54 a.m."

Above the image of this rat, the poster read, "WANTED." Below the image, the poster read, "ANY PRICE."

TO BE CONTINUED